# IRRESISTIBLY BOUND

## THE COMPLETE SERIES

ANNA STONE

D1260984

ISBN: 9781922685025

# CONTENTS

# BEING HERS

# CHAPTER ONE

Smooth, bass-heavy pop music pulsed through the room. The patrons drank, danced, and lounged on plush chairs under glittering lights. Gorgeous women adorned in diamonds and designer dresses flirted with rich businessmen in Italian suits. B-list celebrities flaunted their wealth, throwing away wads of cash on two thousand-dollar bottles of champagne.

Mel walked over to a table occupied by a young woman and a man who looked old enough to be her grandfather. She cleared the empty glasses from the table. "Can I get you anything else?"

"Another bourbon on the rocks," the man said, not bothering to look up at her. "And another of those fruity things for her."

"Coming right up." Luckily for him, Mel remembered what cocktail that 'fruity thing' was.

Mel returned to the bar and relayed the drink order to the bartender. She plucked a soggy napkin from the bottom of her shoe. Just another night at The Lounge. Part high-end bar, part nightclub, it was one of the city's most exclusive night spots. Or so she was told. When she wasn't working, Mel spent most of her nights at home or at the library, writing papers and combing through law textbooks.

Mel delivered the drinks to the couple on a silver tray, then took another order. She went back and forth, serving drinks and wiping down tables until her feet ached and her muscles burned. Mercifully, by that time her shift was almost over.

"Hey, Mel?" James, her manager, beckoned her over to the bar.

"What's up, James?" Mel leaned down on the bar, grateful for a moment to catch her breath. She'd spent the whole day in classes and had been on her feet all night.

"Here." James handed her a large envelope. "It's your new contract."

"Does this mean I'm off probation?" Mel flicked through the pages. Everyone who worked at The Lounge started on a probationary period due to the clientele's high standards. The patrons expected nothing short of the royal treatment, and they did not tolerate mistakes. Mel had never worked at a club before starting at The Lounge, but she was a fast learner.

"Yep. I recommended you for a permanent position weeks ago, but I've been waiting for the owner's approval. He likes to have the final say in everything."

Mel found that surprising. The identity of The Lounge's owner was a complete mystery. No one seemed to know who he was, and none of the staff had ever met him. As the manager, James was the exception, but all he would tell anyone was that the owner was an extremely private person.

Mel signed the contract and handed it back to James.

"Congratulations, you're one of us now," he said.

"Thanks." Mel breathed a sigh of relief. A little job security was a huge weight off her shoulders.

"By the way, a few of us are going out for drinks after we close. Want to come?"

"Thanks, but I have a paper to finish." It was one of her standard answers. A paper to finish, an exam to prepare for, some supplemental reading to do.

"Come on, Mel. You're always here or at law school. Do you ever do anything fun?"

"I go running sometimes."

"That doesn't count."

"I have a social life. Really." Mel didn't mention that her 'social life' mostly involved going to law school networking events.

"Okay. But you're missing out. If you think the crowd at The Lounge is wild, you should see us after a few drinks."

"Maybe next time," Mel said.

James grinned. He wasn't a bad guy. For a manager, he was extremely laid-back. James was in his late twenties, and he treated his staff like friends. This included Mel, despite her constantly knocking back his invitations to come out for drinks. She hoped he didn't have an ulterior motive. It wouldn't be the first time a guy didn't realize that he was barking up the wrong tree.

James pushed a tray toward her. It held a single glass of whiskey. "Can you take this to table six?"

"Sure." Mel grabbed the tray and edged past the crowd. Table six was at the far corner of the room. As the crowd thinned in front of her, Mel's heart skipped a beat.

It was her.

She sat alone, upright in her chair as if it were a throne. She wore an ivory silk dress that clung to her slender curves. Her jet black hair cascaded down her shoulders in loose, perfect waves, and her blue eyes were framed by long, dark lashes.

The woman was a regular at The Lounge, coming in around once a week. She always came alone and sat at that table by herself, watching the crowd but never speaking to anyone. Unlike all the other regulars, none of the staff knew anything about her. Not her name, not her job, not how she made her riches. And she had to be rich to afford to come to a place like The Lounge. All that Mel knew about her was that she always drank the same brand of top-shelf whiskey.

As Mel walked toward the woman's table, she was cut off by a sharply dressed man in a suit. He'd had more than a few drinks. He leaned down toward the woman and flashed her a pearl-white smile, then said something to her that Mel couldn't make out.

The woman gestured for the man to lean down closer. She whispered something into his ear. Slowly, his face turned redder and redder. Then without another word, he stood up and scurried off.

Mel watched the man depart. What did the woman say to him? When Mel turned back to her table, the woman was staring straight at her.

"Enjoy the show?" the woman asked.

"I..." Mel trailed off, flustered. She had never spoken to the woman before, beyond taking her orders and serving her drinks. "What did you say to him?"

"He tried to impress me with his name and his job. And he had some rather vulgar words for me. I told him my name, and that he should pray that we never cross paths out in the corporate world, because after speaking to me like that, I would make sure that no one does business with him again."

Who was this woman that she could intimidate a man with nothing more than her name and some harsh words? Mel remembered the tray in her hands. "Your drink." She placed the glass of whiskey on the table.

"Thank you." The woman's velvet voice sent a shiver careening down the back of Mel's neck.

"Can I get you anything else?"

The woman didn't answer immediately. She picked up her drink, swirled it around and took a sip, leaving a red lip print on the rim of the glass. She placed it down on the table before her. "No. Thank you."

Mel lingered at the table. She was intrigued by this woman. It wasn't just that Mel found her irresistibly attractive. There was something different about her. On the surface, she undeniably belonged to the elite. From her stylish clothing down to her short, manicured fingernails, everything about her pointed to someone accustomed to a life of luxury. But she made no effort to flaunt her wealth and showed none of the entitlement of the other customers.

"Is there something else?" the woman asked.

Mel paused. She felt compelled to ask the woman something, anything. "Why do you come here?" The words tumbled out of

Mel's mouth. "It's just that... you're always by yourself, and you don't seem to want to talk to anyone."

The woman leaned back in her chair and studied Mel's face. "You've been watching me."

Mel's face grew hot. She tucked a stray lock of her brown hair behind her ear.

"I like to watch people too," the woman said. "That's why I come here. And to enjoy the fine selection of whiskey that The Lounge has on offer." Her eyes never leaving Mel's, she picked up her glass and took another long sip.

Mel stood there, held captive by the woman's gaze. Her heart raced. There was something in her eyes that Mel couldn't quite decipher. Flirtation? An invitation?

A command?

A raucous shout from somewhere behind her broke Mel out of her trance. "I should go. Let me know if you need anything else."

The woman nodded, her expression inscrutable. As Mel walked away, she swore that she could feel the woman's eyes on her back.

Mel pulled herself together and made her way back to the bar. She was probably imagining things. Mel doubted that the woman even remembered her, considering how many servers worked at The Lounge.

"Mel, can you take these to the VIP section?" James handed Mel a tray holding two bottles of top-shelf champagne and half a dozen crystal flutes.

"Sure." Mel gritted her teeth. There were two ways that a customer could get into the VIP section. One was fame. That got them in for free. The second was money. So much money that even the regular patrons couldn't afford it. Serving in the VIP section meant big tips; however, VIPs tended to be far more demanding. Mel had quickly learned how to deal with difficult customers, but that made it no less stressful.

Mel made her way through the crowd, balancing the tray carefully in her hands. The contents were worth more than her entire bank account. She couldn't help but feel nervous about toting a small fortune in fragile glass in a crowded room.

She climbed the steps up to the VIP area. A group of men were seated around the table. As Mel approached them, one of them let out a drunken cheer. *Great, frat bros in suits.* As she reached the table, another man stood up and swiveled toward her. His arm hit the tray in Mel's hands and it fell to the floor with a loud crash, leaving Mel standing in a puddle of champagne and broken glass. She cursed under her breath.

"What the fuck?" The hulking man leapt back.

"I'm sorry, sir," Mel said as politely as she could manage. He was the one who had knocked everything out of her hands. But she wasn't about to argue with him. She grabbed the dish towel from her apron and tried in vain to contain the spill.

"Look. Look at my shoes!" The man waved his foot in front of Mel's face. There was a tiny spot on his suede shoe. It could have been anything. "Do you have any idea how much these cost?" His face was bright red.

Mel stood up. "I'm sorry. Let me go get-"

He grabbed her arm and pulled her toward him. "Sorry isn't good enough."

Mel froze. His clammy hand felt like a vice around her arm. She could smell the cigarettes and alcohol on his breath. Before she could react, a voice rang out from behind the man.

"Take your hands off her. Now."

The man released Mel. She looked over his shoulder. It was the woman in the ivory dress from earlier. She had her hand on the man's shoulder and a look on her face that sent a chill down Mel's spine.

"Get out," the woman said, her voice cold and clear. "And take your friends with you."

The man looked her up and down. "Who the hell are you?"

"I'm the owner of this establishment."

Mel's eyes widened. *She* was the owner of The Lounge?

The man scoffed and looked over at his friends. They averted their eyes and shifted in their seats. He looked back at the woman. "You own this place?"

"That's right. Get out of my club. Now."

The woman stared at the man, her face set like stone. He stared back at her, eyes narrowed. He was easily twice her size, but she held his stare.

Finally, the man looked away. "Like I'd want to stay in a place like this anyway," he mumbled. He turned to his friends. "Let's get out of here."

He grabbed his jacket and walked off toward the door. The others filed out after him, looking sheepish and apologetic. The woman watched them leave, a dark look on her face. As soon as they were out the door, she turned back to Mel.

"Come with me."

# CHAPTER TWO

*T*he woman placed her hand on Mel's arm and guided her toward the back of the club. Mel's head was spinning. All this time, the woman had never given any indication that she was anything but another customer. And Mel wasn't sure how to feel about being 'rescued.' She wasn't some helpless damsel. Mel could have dealt with the customer herself, yet she couldn't deny how this woman's hand on her arm sent her pulse racing.

The woman led Mel into a dark corridor tucked away in the corner. As far as Mel knew, all that was down there was a fire exit. To her surprise, there was another door to the right of them that was barely visible in the dim light. The woman opened the door. Mel followed her up a flight of stairs to another door. The woman typed a code into a keypad and the lock on the door clicked open.

Mel followed her into the room. It resembled a generously-sized hotel room, with a large bed at one end and some seating arranged around a coffee table in the center. With minimalist décor and the clean, sharp angles of the furniture, the space both looked and felt immaculate.

"Sit." The woman gestured toward a leather couch.

Mel sat down. The woman's tone made her wonder if she was in trouble. "Is this about the broken bottles? It was an accident, he-"

"I didn't bring you in here to reprimand you. The loss of a couple of bottles of champagne won't make the slightest dent in the club's profits."

"Oh." That didn't make Mel feel any less restless. "Then why did you bring me back here?"

"I want to make sure you're all right."

"I'm fine," Mel said. "I could have handled it myself," she added.

"I'm sure you could have. Show me your arm."

Mel held her arm out. The woman took Mel's wrist and pulled it closer to the light. The brush of her fingertips against the inside of Mel's wrist made the hairs stand up on her skin.

"Does anything hurt?" The woman inspected Mel's arm.

"No. He didn't grab me very hard."

She released Mel's wrist, apparently satisfied. Her face clouded over. "That man. I'm going to make sure he and his friends never set foot in here again." The woman clenched her fists. "I should have had him arrested for manhandling you like that."

"It wasn't as bad as it looked." Mel wondered if the woman had seen the entire incident, or just Mel standing in a pile of alcohol and glass with a large, angry man's hand around her arm. "He knocked my tray out of my hands by accident and got mad. That's all. I'm used to dealing with difficult customers." Mel was supposed to be serving said customers right now. Had anyone cleaned up all that broken glass? She stood up. "I should get back to work."

"You're not going anywhere until I'm sure you're okay, Melanie."

"I'm *fine.*"

"Indulge me then." It was clear that there was no point arguing with her.

Mel sat back down. As she looked around the room, she spotted a few personal items. A silk robe hanging from a hook on the wall. A fluffy white towel on the back of the door to the bathroom. A bottle of whiskey and some glasses on the counter. It was the same whiskey that the woman always ordered downstairs. The space didn't look lived in enough to be more than an occasional hideout, but it was clearly hers.

Mel's eyes wandered over to the bed. As she admired the black satin sheets, something caught her eye.

Hanging from the bedpost was a black leather riding crop with a crimson handle.

Heat rose up Mel's body. For a fleeting moment, an image of the woman wielding the whip played in her mind. She tore her eyes away and pushed the thought out of her head. But she was suddenly hyperaware that she was alone in the room of a domineering woman who she felt an undeniable attraction toward. One who owned a whip.

And that woman was looking straight at Mel.

Mel looked intently down at the hem of her skirt. Had the woman noticed her staring at what was on the bedpost? Mel peeked up at her. Her face gave nothing away.

The woman stood up. "Let me get you a drink." Without waiting for a response, she walked over to the counter and poured two glasses of whiskey. "Here."

Mel took the proffered glass and drank, wincing as it burned her throat. But the taste wasn't bad.

The woman sat down in an armchair across from Mel. "I take it you're not a whiskey drinker?"

"Nope." The only whiskey Mel had ever tried was cheap stuff that tasted like a campfire.

"Would you like something else?"

"No, this is fine." Mel took another sip. "It actually tastes pretty good."

"It should. This is arguably one of the best whiskeys to come out of Scotland in the last decade or two. It's well worth the price tag."

Mel recalled how much even a single glass of this particular whiskey cost downstairs. For the second time that night, she held a small fortune in her hands, so she figured she may as well enjoy it. Mel sank into the soft couch, her tension clearing. There was a faint floral scent in the air. Rose, and something both sweet and spicy that Mel didn't recognize. She could hear the faint thrum of the music from the club below. It was far softer than it should have been. The room must have been soundproof.

Mel sneaked a glance in the woman's direction. The soft light of the room highlighted her elegant beauty. High cheekbones. Full red lips. Porcelain skin. Her hands had felt so soft on Mel's arm.

Mel suddenly realized that she didn't even know the woman's name. As she opened her mouth to ask, another thought occurred to her. "You called me Melanie earlier. I haven't told you my name."

"There isn't a single person who works here whose name I don't know. And I know more than your name. Melanie Greene, twenty-three years old. Raised by a single mother in a small town in Ohio. Got into college on a full ride scholarship and graduated with honors. Currently studying law. And not even a parking ticket to your name."

"How do you know so much about me?" Mel asked.

"I assure you it's nothing sinister. I require thorough back-ground checks on everyone who works at my establishments before I hire them. I have an excellent memory." She leaned forward and placed her drink on the table. "And you're very hard to forget."

Mel took another sip of her drink. Her glass was emptying quickly.

"You stood out to me, Melanie. It's clear that you have a lot of drive and aren't afraid of hard work. Those are desirable traits to any employer."

Mel remembered her other question. "What's your name?"

"How rude of me. It's Vanessa. Vanessa Harper."

*Vanessa.* Even her name sounded elegant.

"So, tell me. Why do you want to become a lawyer? You don't seem the type who aspires to work at a big corporate law firm."

Mel would have been bothered by Vanessa's presumption if it hadn't been true. "I want to help those who really need it. For some people, legal services are a luxury they can't afford. Without it, they face poverty, or homelessness, or even prison." Mel knew this well from her own childhood. She grew up in a world that was the complete opposite of the one that Vanessa and the patrons of The

Lounge inhabited. "I want to give people like that a chance at a better life."

"How benevolent of you." It was hard to tell whether or not Vanessa was being patronizing. "But you're at one of the top law schools in the country. Simply doing pro-bono work seems like wasted potential."

"I want to do far more than that," Mel replied. "I want to make a difference on a bigger scale. I don't know how exactly yet. But I do know that change comes from the top. And that's why I have to get there."

Vanessa smiled. "You're very passionate. You remind me of myself when I was younger. Big ambitions. Fighting your way up in a world where everything is stacked against you. I can tell you from experience that it isn't easy being a woman in a male-dominated profession. Not to mention a gay woman. Which I'm sure you know already."

Mel almost choked on her drink. "How do you know I'm a lesbian?" She was the kind of woman who flew under most people's gaydar.

"Reading people is one of my talents. I'm an executive. And in the corporate world, it's a valuable skill. Learn someone's tells, and you know when they're lying, or stalling, or when you have them right where you want them. And once you know how to read people, you can learn all sorts of things about someone by simply watching them for five minutes. I've watched you in the club, Melanie. I've watched you interact with people. It's obvious that you're not interested in men, but you are interested in women." Vanessa leaned forward, her eyes locked on Mel's. "And I've seen the way you look at me."

Mel's heart stopped in her chest. The heat of Vanessa's gaze made Mel's skin burn.

She glanced away. Her eyes landed on a clock on the wall. Her shift had ended ten minutes ago.

"I've kept you here long enough," Vanessa said. "You can go." She reached out and took Mel's empty glass from her hand. Their fingers touched, and Vanessa's hand seemed to linger on Mel's. Then Vanessa placed the glass down next to her own and stood up.

Mel got up from the couch, feeling a mixture of relief and disappointment. As she followed Vanessa to the door, her eyes flicked over to the riding crop hanging from the bedpost.

A hint of a smile formed on Vanessa's lips. "Goodbye, Melanie."

# CHAPTER THREE

Mel jogged down the busy sidewalk, upbeat music blasting through her earbuds. As she narrowly dodged a woman on a bicycle, she wished she could afford a gym membership and avoid the crowded city streets. But for now, she had to make do. Running was her only outlet. She loved the feeling of pushing her body to its limit. The burning muscles. The aching lungs. The high. It was satisfying in a raw, visceral way.

In truth, she preferred the freedom of running outdoors. The heat of the sun on her skin and the wind in her face added to the rush she felt.

Her apartment building came into view. Mel slowed her pace and checked her watch. She didn't have long until she had to leave for work. She'd barely been able to squeeze in a run at all. Wiping the sweat from her brow, Mel jogged the last half mile to her building and made her way up to her apartment. Calling it an 'apartment' was generous. The one-room studio had room for a bed, a table, and little else. But it was the only place that Mel could afford by herself.

She stripped off her sweaty clothes and threw them into the hamper. She'd tried as hard as she could to make her apartment look inviting, adding some color and personal touches. A few throw pillows in a bright, cheerful blue. Posters to cover the marks on the walls. A bookshelf salvaged from the curb that Mel had filled with books she didn't have time to read. It did little to improve the ambiance of the space. But Mel liked it. It was more of a home to her than any other place she had lived in.

Mel made her way to the bathroom and stepped into the shower. She tipped back her head and let the warm water trickle down her body, washing the sweat from her skin and revitalizing her tired muscles. She wished that she had a bathtub. It had been a long day. Six hours of classes, followed by a quick run, and now a shift at The Lounge. She wouldn't get home until well after midnight.

Mel let out a long breath. She was used to it. The long hours. The late nights. The never-ending pile of school work. She'd been working hard since high school: first to get into college and escape her middle of nowhere hometown, and then to get into law school, all while working to support herself.

But as she scrubbed the dirt of the day off her body, Mel felt the weight of it all creep back onto her shoulders. Running provided a brief escape. It didn't last.

She sighed and tried to push it all aside. For what felt like the hundredth time this week, her thoughts drifted back to the other night at The Lounge. To Vanessa. When Mel closed her eyes, she could see Vanessa's smoldering eyes staring back at her. She could feel Vanessa's fingers wrapped around her wrist. She could hear Vanessa's voice, somehow gentle and commanding at the same time.

*I've seen the way you look at me.*

Mel stepped out of the shower. How had Vanessa managed to get inside her head so easily? It didn't matter. Even if Vanessa was interested in her, which seemed crazy, Mel didn't want to go down that road. Not with Vanessa, or with anyone.

As she toweled herself off, an image of the riding crop hanging from Vanessa's bedpost flashed across Mel's mind. And then, Vanessa holding the crimson handle...

*No.* Mel refused to let her imagination go there. She left the bathroom and started to get dressed for work.

As soon as Mel arrived at work, James pulled her aside.

"Hey, Mel." His usually cheerful expression had been replaced by one of concern. "How are you doing?"

"I'm fine. What's going on?"

"Vanessa told me about what happened the other night."

Vanessa had told James that she had taken Mel up to her room?

"You know, with that asshole in the VIP area."

Of course. She'd forgotten all about that part of her night. "Right."

"Just so you know, that guy will never set foot in here again. No matter how rich or famous a customer thinks they are, lay a hand on my staff and you're banned for life. He's on Vanessa's blacklist now, which means he's banned from a long list of venues," James said.

"Okay. Thanks, James." Mel paused. "So, you've known about Vanessa all this time?"

"Yep. But I'm not supposed to tell anyone. She has her reasons for keeping her identity private." He held up his hands apologetically. "Don't worry. She doesn't come in here to monitor anyone. She just likes to check up on the place every now and then."

That wasn't particularly reassuring. Would Mel have treated Vanessa any differently all this time if she'd known? It was probably a good thing. Mel didn't need another reason to be intimidated by her.

It turned out to be a quiet night. For what seemed like the twentieth time since her shift started, Mel wiped down an already clean table and rearranged the chairs around it. She ran her fingers through her hair and looked around for something else to do.

"Mel?" James waved her over to the bar. "Want to practice your bartending skills while things are quiet?"

"Sure," Mel replied. James had been training her as a bartender so she could help out when things got busy.

"If you need any help, I'll be right here unpacking these." He pointed to a stack of boxes behind him.

Mel slid behind the bar and began making drinks. She knew most of the cocktail recipes by now, so it was mostly a matter of honing her technique. In between customers, James gave Mel the latest of many informal lessons on bartending. Today, it was about different wines. Mel listened carefully and filed it all away in her mind.

A few minutes before the end of Mel's shift, James pulled a bottle of amber spirits out of a box. The label was written in Japanese. "This must be one of Vanessa's special orders," he said. "Now that you're in on her secret, you can give this to her for me. Here." He held the bottle out to Mel. "She's upstairs looking over some paperwork."

Mel's heart jumped. "Sure thing."

"You might as well head off early. It's dead tonight. Just take it up to her on your way out."

Mel took the bottle from James and grabbed her bag and coat. She said a quick goodbye to her coworkers, then made her way across the club to the corridor that led to Vanessa's room. Her stomach filled with butterflies, she climbed the stairs and knocked on the door.

"It's unlocked," Vanessa called from inside.

Mel entered the room. Vanessa was sitting at the table, her back toward Mel, looking down at some papers spread out before her.

"I need a minute, James-" Vanessa turned her head. She seemed entirely unfazed to see Mel standing in her doorway. "Hello, Melanie."

Usually, Mel didn't like it when people called her by her full name. But it didn't bother her when Vanessa did. "Hi."

"Come in. Sit. I'll be with you in a moment." Vanessa turned back to her work.

Mel sat down on the couch, bottle in hand. She couldn't help but glance over at Vanessa's bed. *Yep.* It was still there. The crimson-handled riding crop.

Vanessa's chair scraped across the floorboards. She gathered her papers and placed them to the side neatly, then walked over to Mel. "What can I do for you?"

"Here." Mel held the bottle out to her. "James asked me to give you this."

Vanessa took the bottle from Mel and held it up in front of her eyes. "I've been waiting for this. Single malt Japanese whiskey. Aged for thirty years, cask finished. Very difficult to find."

To Mel's surprise, she knew what all of those terms meant. James's lessons had stuck with her. Mel got up to leave.

"Stay. Drink this with me." Vanessa's eyes fell to the coat and purse slung over Mel's arm. "Unless you have somewhere to be?"

Mel hesitated. She did have a lot of work to do. But she wanted to stay. One drink wouldn't hurt. "No, I don't," she said, sitting back down.

Vanessa walked over to the counter. She took two glasses and poured the amber liquid into them, then brought them over to the couch and handed one to Mel. Vanessa took a seat in the chair across from Mel. She swirled the whiskey around in her glass and held it up to her nose. She took a sip. "Not bad," Vanessa declared.

Mel followed Vanessa's lead. She couldn't taste any difference between this whiskey and the one she'd tried the other night.

"So." Vanessa placed her glass down on the table carefully. "Last time you were in here, I ambushed you with questions. Now that I know so much about you, it's only fair that I give you a chance to get to know me. Is there anything you'd like to ask me?"

Mel's mind went blank. There was so much she wanted to know about Vanessa that she didn't know where to start. "*You're* the mystery owner of The Lounge?" It was the only thing she could think of.

"I've heard that I'm quite the mystery to you all. Yes, I own The Lounge. It's one of quite a few bars and clubs that I own. I moved on to bigger things long ago. But I have a soft spot for this place. It was my first investment." She leaned back in her chair. "You seem surprised."

"A little," Mel said. "Everyone thinks you're some rich old man."

"I assure you I'm not a man, and I'm only thirty-four" Vanessa said. "I haven't done anything to discourage those rumors. I may have even dropped a few hints to throw people off my trail."

"But why the secrecy?" Mel asked.

"A few reasons. I run my own investment firm now. Most of the firm's clients are extremely conservative. And some of the clubs and venues that I own privately could be considered unsavory to some. Not all of them are as respectable as The Lounge. So I don't want them associated with my name and my firm."

What kind of place was less respectable than The Lounge? It wasn't uncommon for Mel to find little white powder smudges on the restroom countertops.

"And quite simply, I'm a very private person. I don't want anyone digging through my life. There are certain things about me that would scandalize people if they knew." Vanessa said. "Is there anything else you want to know?"

"What's this room for?" Mel asked. "Is it yours?"

"Yes. It was empty when I acquired the premises. I later decided to repurpose it to be something of a second apartment. For when I have company. I don't like to take women back to my home, so I bring them here instead," Vanessa said casually. She seemed determined to get under Mel's skin.

And it was sure working.

"That can't be all you want to ask me, Melanie," Vanessa said.

Mel kept her mouth shut. She had a lot of questions on her mind. But there was no way she was going to ask them.

"All right then. I have a question for you." Vanessa leaned back and crossed her legs, her eyes fixed on Mel's. "Both of the times you've been in here, you haven't been able to stop staring at my riding crop."

Mel's face flushed. She'd hoped Vanessa hadn't noticed. No, that was a lie.

"Does it make you uncomfortable?" Vanessa asked.

"No," Mel said softly.

"Does it scare you?"

"No."

Vanessa examined Mel's face silently. "Could it be that you're curious?"

Mel's heart sped up. "Maybe a little..." She couldn't help herself.

There was something about Vanessa that made Mel feel compelled to answer her truthfully.

"Would you like to take a closer look?" Vanessa asked, her voice a low purr. Without waiting for a response, Vanessa walked over to the bed and picked up the riding crop. She sat down on the coffee table in front of Mel and held the whip up before her chest. "It's a lovely piece of workmanship. Custom made. Leather. Narrow tip. The thinner the tip, the greater the bite." With a flick of her wrist, Vanessa slapped it against her palm.

A soft gasp escaped Mel's lips. The sound of the impact surprised her. And it set off a spark somewhere deep inside of her.

Vanessa's lips curved up almost imperceptibly. "Here." She held the whip out toward Mel, balancing it on her palms. "Hold it."

Mel turned the riding crop over in her hands. She traced the weave of the handle with her fingertips then ran them up to the supple leather tip.

"What do you think?"

"It's beautiful." Mel couldn't help but wonder what it would feel like against her skin, somewhere fleshy and tender.

"Have you ever used one?" Vanessa asked. "Or had one used on you?"

"No," Mel murmured.

"Have you ever wanted to?"

Mel hesitated. "I've thought about it. Once or twice." Another lie.

Vanessa reached out and took the crop from Mel's hands. "And when you think about it, do you see yourself as the one holding the whip? Or at the other end?"

"I don't know." The crop didn't feel at home in Mel's hands. But there was a niggling feeling at the back of her mind that prevented her from admitting the truth.

"Another way of looking at it is this," Vanessa said. "Which do you prefer? Being in control? Or giving it to someone else?" She began to tap the whip against her palm. "Being in control means having all the power. But it also means responsibility. Giving up control means you get to let go completely. But it requires you to place yourself in someone else's hands. To trust them. It can be terrifying." She stilled the crop in her hands. "And it can be exhilarating."

Mel didn't respond. The sound of her own breath seemed deafening in the silence.

"I've said before that I'm good at reading people. And I think I know the role you'd like to play. I know your type, Melanie. Ambitious. Driven. Always striving for perfection. Never allowing the slightest lapse in self-control. It must be exhausting." Vanessa ran her fingers along the shaft of the crop. "Don't you ever want to just let go of all your problems and let someone else take the reins?"

"Sometimes…" Mel had never even admitted that to herself, let alone to someone else.

"This here? This is one way to do that. To escape it all, if only for a moment. To lose yourself so completely that everything falls away and all that is left is pure ecstasy. To surrender." Vanessa leaned forward, her face barely an inch from Mel's. "Does that tempt you?"

"Yes," Mel whispered.

Vanessa brought her lips to Mel's ear. "It's more freeing than you could possibly imagine."

A shiver went through Mel's body. Vanessa's eyes seemed to strip away all her defenses. And Vanessa's face was so close to hers. Vanessa's lips were so close…

*What am I thinking?* Mel dropped her empty glass to the table and stood up. "I should go." Within seconds, she was out the door.

# CHAPTER FOUR

*M*el sat in the lecture hall, waiting for her professor to arrive. Class didn't start for another five minutes. Leaning back in her chair, she closed her eyes and tried to clear her head of all the thoughts swirling around inside it. Inevitably, her mind went back to the same thing: Vanessa.

Since that night in Vanessa's room, Vanessa had come into The Lounge a few times while Mel was working. Mel didn't go out of her way to speak to Vanessa. But somehow their paths kept crossing. And with every word that Vanessa spoke to her, with every glance they exchanged, the pull of Mel's desire grew stronger.

Vanessa was all that Mel could think about. Vanessa's hips, swaying in her tight, silky dress. Her voice, like velvet, in Mel's ear. Her eyes, that seemed to see into the depths of Mel's being, while revealing nothing of what lay behind Vanessa's own.

And Vanessa's words. *Surrender.* It wasn't hard to figure out what she meant. Her dominant personality. The riding crop. Her talk of giving up control. It all pointed to one thing.

"Looks like you could use this."

Mel opened her eyes. Her friend Jess stood beside her, holding a coffee in each hand.

She handed one to Mel and sat down. "Finish all the readings?"

"Yep." Mel had stayed up 'til 3:00 a.m. to get them done.

"How are you always so on top of everything? I barely got halfway through them before I fell asleep." Jess groaned. "If I'm on call, I'm going to look like an idiot."

Cold calling. Those two words filled every first-year law student with dread. During class, their professors would call upon a student and ask them probing questions about the cases being discussed. Preparation was essential. Professor Carr liked to assign a few random students to be 'on call' at the start of each lecture, so no one knew if they would be on call until class started. Because law school wasn't stressful enough already.

"Here." Mel passed her notes to Jess. "I've already memorized everything."

"Thanks, Mel! What would I do without you?"

As Jess flipped through the notes, Mel closed her eyes again. Her mind picked up where it left off. She couldn't deny how the idea of submitting to another woman made her hot all over. These desires weren't new. No, they had always been there. But Mel had never allowed herself to even consider letting them play out. They went against everything she believed about herself. So she'd buried them deep inside her where they remained a half-forgotten fantasy. Until Vanessa had reawakened them.

"Mel? Hello?" Jess waved her hand in front of Mel's face.

"Huh?"

"I said, do you want to come over and study tonight? You know, for the quiz tomorrow?"

"Right. Sorry, I can't," Mel replied. "I have work."

"What's the matter with you?" Jess asked. "You've been spacing out all day. Something on your mind?"

"No, I'm fine," Mel replied.

Jess narrowed her eyes and studied Mel's face. "Or could it be… some*one*?" A smile broke out on her face. "I knew it!"

Mel sighed. Jess knew her too well. They'd been friends since freshman year of college when they ended up in most of the same pre-law classes together. Jess wanted to become a criminal defense attorney. But for now, she had to settle for interrogating her friends.

"C'mon, spill," Jess said. "I want every detail."

"There's nothing to tell," Mel said. "It's just a stupid crush. Nothing's happened."

"Do you mean, nothing's happened *yet?*"

"No. Nothing is ever going to happen."

"Why not?"

"Because I don't have the time or energy for a relationship of any kind." It wasn't a complete lie. "Why are you so interested in my love life anyway?"

Jess sighed. "Because mine is non-existent."

"What happened to Brandon?"

"You mean Brendon?"

"Yeah, him." Mel found it hard to keep up with Jess's ever-changing list of boyfriends. "I thought things were going well between you two."

Jess shrugged. "We broke up. He was kind of boring."

Mel shook her head. A week ago, Jess had been sure that Brendon was the one.

Professor Carr strode into the room. "Okay everyone, settle down."

The class fell silent. Even though Professor Carr was five foot two and old enough to be Mel's grandmother, she commanded the respect of everyone around her. She was Mel's favorite professor. She had a long and impressive career behind her. Fighting civil rights violations. Taking on corporate giants. Representing thousands in large-scale class action suits. Now she spent her days running a nationwide legal non-profit organization. She was everything that Mel aspired to be.

"Before we get started, I have a small announcement to make," Professor Carr said. "By now, you should all be thinking about summer internships."

Murmurs went through the class. Summer internships were the first opportunity that Mel and her peers would have to get hands-on law experience, and finding an interesting internship as a first-year was almost impossible.

Professor Carr continued. "I've decided to take on a first-year student as an intern this summer. You'll be working for me personally at The Legal Services Project. For those of you who haven't heard of it, The LSP is a non-profit that provides free legal help. It connects lawyers who are willing to do pro-bono work with the clients who need it the most. And it provides individual lawyers and law firms with incentives for providing legal aid. We're making waves in the legal world. And I'm giving one of you the opportunity to be a part of it."

Mel's ears pricked up. She had to have that internship. An opportunity to work under Professor Carr was too good to pass up. Not to mention that a number of influential people, lawyers and otherwise, were involved in the project. The connections a law student would make working there would be invaluable. So would the experience.

But Mel's interest in The LSP was far more personal. Projects like this were the reason she decided to go to law school. When she was young, her father walked out on Mel and her mother, leaving them destitute. Mel's mother spiraled into debt, depression, and alcoholism, leaving the two of them always on the verge of home-lessness. It was a rough time for both of them.

It was only through legal aid services that Mel's mother was able to pursue her ex-husband for child support and get her debt under control. The lawyer assigned to her mother was a kindly old woman who did far more than her job required to help them get their lives back on track. Mel would never forget how much of a difference the woman had made in her life. She wanted to do the same for others someday.

"I know that a lot of you will be interested," Professor Carr said. "So I'm going to make my choice based on merit. And I don't mean whoever gets the highest grades. Out in the real world, it doesn't matter what grade you got on your final. To make it as a lawyer, you need to be willing to put in the hard work. You need to have a deep understanding of the law. You need to be able to use that knowledge as a weapon. So if you want this internship, show me that you have what it takes. Come to class prepared. Pay attention to my lectures. Prove that your understanding of the law goes beyond what's written in your textbooks. Impress me, and the internship is yours."

The class broke out into loud whispers. Mel wasn't the only one excited about the internship. She would have some tough competition.

"Settle down, everyone. Let's get started." As the conversation faded, Professor Carr put on her glasses and picked up a sheet of paper. "The students on call today are-"

The class collectively held its breath as Professor Carr rattled off a list of names.

"-and Melanie Greene."

Mel downed the rest of her coffee in one gulp. She was prepared. She had this.

---

Mel made it through the hour without any problems. Not everyone was that lucky. One of her classmates had slowly broken down over the course of the lecture. She was almost in tears by the end of the class. Most law students, especially those at her prestigious school, were highly competitive. Many of them didn't handle failure well.

"That internship," Jess said. "You're going to go for it, right?"

"Definitely." Mel gathered her things, and they joined the stream of students heading out of the lecture hall. "How about you?"

"No way. I'm not crazy enough to want to compete with you and all the others who want it. Besides, I already have an internship in mind. I'll be spending my summer at the District Attorney's office."

"Melanie," Professor Carr called out. "A moment, please."

Mel told Jess she'd catch up with her later and walked over to the professor's desk.

"You did well today," Professor Carr said. "Handled my questions like a pro."

"It was an interesting case. I did lots of research."

"I expected nothing less. So, about The LSP internship. Are you interested?"

"Definitely! Working at a place like that would be a dream come true."

"I'm not going to lie. I'm rooting for you, Mel. The others? They only want the internship because it will look good on their resumes. But I know that you care about this kind of project. I was the one who reviewed your law school application. And your personal statement showed that you're doing this for all the right reasons."

Mel shifted from one foot to the other. Her personal statement had touched upon her experience with that lawyer who had helped her mother, and how it had affected her life. Of course, she didn't mention the parts of her childhood that had really shaped her. Those weren't the kind of things she could put in a law school entry essay. But her essay had revealed more of herself than she usually gave to people, even those closest to her.

"You're a talented student, Melanie. I want to see you succeed." Professor Carr crossed her arms. "But I'm not going to hand you that internship. It wouldn't be fair to anyone, you included. Earn it. Don't disappoint me."

Mel nodded.

"I'll let you go now."

"Thanks, Professor Carr." As Mel left the lecture hall, she knew it was time to put Vanessa out of her mind. There was no time for games, not now. She had to stay focused.

———

"Coming to drinks tonight, Mel?" James asked.

Mel gave him an apologetic smile. "Sorry, James, I have a quiz tomorrow. I'll be up all night studying."

"You're off the hook this time. But one of these days, I'll get through to you." James wandered off back to the bar.

Mel shook her head. It was an hour into her shift and the night was beginning to ramp up. There would be no chatting behind the bar tonight. She went over to a recently vacated table and began to clean up. As Mel placed a half-finished bottle of very expensive wine on her tray, something caught her eye. Someone.

*Vanessa.* The crowd seemed to part before her as she walked through it with long, purposeful strides and a regal air. She looked more stunning than ever. She wore a blue silk cocktail dress that flowed down her hips like water. Her long dark hair hung loose around her shoulders. Her pearlescent skin seemed to shimmer under the sparkling lights.

Vanessa strode closer. She wasn't heading for her usual seat. She was heading for the corridor that lead to her room upstairs. And it was right behind Mel. Mel stood frozen in place, unable to tear her eyes off the woman who had taken over her thoughts since that night.

As Vanessa passed Mel, she said nothing, but simply shot Mel a look. The same look she had given Mel in her room that night. The look that made Mel want to come apart.

Vanessa slipped around the corner. Mel inched toward the corridor, as if drawn by a magnet, and peered around the corner. The door at the bottom of the stairs was ajar, a thin beam of light shining through the tiny crack. Mel crept closer, pulled the door open, and looked up the stairs.

Before Mel knew what she was doing, she followed Vanessa up to her room and knocked on the door.

# CHAPTER FIVE

"Come in," Vanessa called from inside the room.

Mel opened the door. In the dim light, she could make out Vanessa's figure reclining in an armchair. Something long and thin lay across her lap. The riding crop.

Mel had stumbled right into Vanessa's trap.

Vanessa stood up, whip in hand, and walked toward Mel. She reached around Mel's body and closed the door. It clicked shut, locking them in. The music from downstairs faded to a soft hum.

"Why did you follow me in here, Melanie?" Vanessa asked.

"I want to know," Mel said, her voice barely a whisper. "I want to know what you meant about giving up control. Surrender."

Vanessa pressed the tip of the crop into the base of Mel's neck and drew it down the center of her chest. "You know exactly what I mean."

Mel's lips parted slightly. Vanessa was so close that she could feel the heat radiating from Vanessa's skin and Vanessa's breath on her neck.

"We both know what you want. We both know what you're longing for. I can give it to you." Vanessa took Mel's chin in her hands and tilted Mel's face up toward her. "All you have to do is let go."

Mel's heart pounded. She stared back at Vanessa, her mind swimming in conflict and doubt. Then she closed her eyes and let her body take over. At once, Vanessa's lips were on hers, a soft, light kiss that lingered even after they parted.

Mel exhaled slowly. She didn't know who had kissed the other first. All she knew was that it had charged the room with an energy that desperately needed to be dispelled.

Vanessa dropped the riding crop to the floor with a clatter. She grabbed Mel's wrists, pinning them above her head, and kissed her again. This time the kiss was deep, hungry, insistent. Mel responded in kind.

Vanessa pressed her body against Mel's, trapping Mel against the wall with her hips. "I can tell how much you want me." Vanessa pushed her thigh firmly between Mel's legs, stoking the fire deep inside her. "I've wanted you since the first night I saw you in my club. And I always get what I want."

Her words sent a ripple of heat through Mel's body. Vanessa released Mel's wrists and began to tear at her clothes. She ripped Mel's blouse from the waistband of her skirt and up over her head, then unclasped Mel's bra and pulled it from her shoulders. She swept her hands up Mel's chest, teasing her pebbled nipples with her fingertips.

Everything was happening so fast. One moment, Vanessa's hands were grasping at Mel's breasts. The next, they were down at the hem of her skirt, pushing it up around her waist. Then Vanessa's fingers were between Mel's thighs, pressing her wet panties into her lips.

A silent moan formed in Mel's mouth. Vanessa trailed her lips down Mel's neck, all the way to her chest, and took Mel's nipple into her mouth, sucking, licking, and flicking.

Mel gasped and writhed against the wall. Vanessa's skin. Vanessa's mouth. Vanessa's sweet, floral scent. Every part of her was intoxicating.

Vanessa slipped her hand inside Mel's panties and ran a finger up and down her folds. Mel's head rolled back, and she grabbed the wall behind her to steady herself as darts of pleasure shot through her. Vanessa's fingers and lips seemed to zero in on places where Mel had never been touched before.

Vanessa slid her finger further down and drew slow, teasing circles. "Do you want me? Do you want me inside you?"

"Yes," Mel said between breaths.

"I want to hear you say it. I want to hear you beg."

"Please, Vanessa... I want you so badly!" Mel meant every word she said. "I need you inside of me. Please!"

Satisfied, Vanessa slid a finger inside her, then another. Mel let out a strangled sigh as Vanessa found that sensitive spot inside her. Her thumb worked its way up to Mel's stiff bud, rubbing against it with every thrust of her fingers.

Wedged between Vanessa's body and the wall, Mel could do little more than cling to the other woman, her hands slipping on the smooth silk of Vanessa's dress. It didn't take long before Mel felt control slipping away.

"Come for me," Vanessa said. "I want to hear you scream."

It was as if Mel's body had been waiting for Vanessa's permission. She came hard and fast, a wordless cry on her lips.

Mel leaned against the wall behind her, her arms still around Vanessa's shoulders. Vanessa's satin dress was cool against her skin.

Vanessa brought her hand up to Mel's face, drew Mel's bottom lip down, and gently pushed her fingers into the other woman's mouth. Mel sucked on them lazily. She could taste herself on Vanessa's skin.

"So eager," Vanessa said. "So obedient. Do you like following my orders? Do you like pleasing me?"

"Yes," Mel said softly.

"Then show me."

Vanessa spun them both around until her back was against the wall. Mel's breath caught in her chest. She desperately wanted to touch Vanessa, to taste her. Instead, she stood and waited, gazing up at Vanessa with a silent plea in her eyes.

Vanessa answered it with a single word. "Kneel."

Mel's knees crumbled beneath her.

A faint smile crossed Vanessa's lips. "Go on."

Mel slid her hands up the sides of Vanessa's legs and under her dress until her fingers reached the soft black lace of Vanessa's panties. She drew them down Vanessa's hips, all the way to the floor, and pushed her slippery silk dress up to her stomach. Vanessa's scent was dizzying. Anchoring herself on Vanessa's hips, she traced her tongue up the soft skin of Vanessa's inner thighs. Vanessa was as wet as Mel had been, and Mel had barely even touched her.

Mel kissed the peak where Vanessa's lips met, then slid her tongue between them. She ran it up and down in long, languid strokes, savoring Vanessa's taste. Mel probed with the tip of her tongue until she found Vanessa's tiny, hidden peak. She stroked and sucked it thirstily.

"Don't stop." Vanessa threaded her fingers through Mel's hair and pulled Mel harder into her, bucking and rolling her hips against Mel's mouth.

Mel redoubled her efforts, relishing the satisfaction she was giving Vanessa. Vanessa didn't make a single sound, but Mel could feel Vanessa's thighs quiver around her. Mel ignored the ache in her knees from the hard floor.

Vanessa gripped tighter at Mel's hair and her movements became more and more frantic. At last, Vanessa's entire body shuddered, and her mouth opened in silent ecstasy. Mel lapped away, drawing every last drop of pleasure out of her. When Vanessa's body stilled, Mel released her hips and let her silky dress slide back down her legs.

Vanessa let out a deep breath. She reached down toward Mel and cupped Mel's face in her hands, drawing her up onto her feet. Vanessa tucked a stray lock of Mel's hair behind her ear and whispered into it. "I believe you have a shift to finish."

Instantly, the spell was broken. Mel cursed. How long had she been in here? Their frenzied encounter had both felt like it had stretched out into eternity and had been over in a heartbeat.

Mel gathered her clothes and began to pull them on. The club would be getting busy now. Had James and the others noticed Mel's absence?

"Here." Vanessa handed Mel's skirt to her, a hint of amusement in her eyes.

Mel finished dressing, then smoothed down her hair in a nearby mirror. As she turned to leave, Vanessa pulled Mel back to her in a ravenous kiss. Mel had to tear her body away when she felt herself sinking into Vanessa again.

Mel dashed from the room. She stopped at the bottom of the stairs to catch her breath.

*What the hell just happened?*

# CHAPTER SIX

*A*nother night at The Lounge. Another night, and no sign of Vanessa. Their late-night tryst in Vanessa's room had left Mel more confused than ever. She had no idea what it meant. Was it a one-time moment of passion? Or the start of something more? Did Vanessa even want to see her again? Mel had no way to contact her. All she could do was wait for Vanessa to turn up again.

Mel sighed. This all seemed so unreal. Mel didn't normally have sex with women she barely knew, let alone women like Vanessa. She was far too disciplined to allow herself to be controlled by lust. Yet she couldn't stop thinking about how Vanessa's lips made her melt, or how Vanessa's touch made her quiver. How when Vanessa had ordered Mel to get on her knees, her body had obeyed before her conscious mind even registered the command. This simple act of submission had felt completely natural to her. But there was still a part of her that resisted it all.

"Everything okay?" James asked. "You look distracted."

"Just thinking about school," Mel lied.

"I should have guessed. So, Mel, how confident are you working behind the bar? Ben had to leave early and I need someone to take his place."

"Sure, I can do it."

"Great. I'll be in the back. Come find me if you have any problems. It's pretty quiet tonight. I'm sure you'll be fine."

Mel nodded and slid behind the bar. Soon, she had a steady flow of customers. She had no trouble keeping up. James had taught her well. Eventually, she got into a rhythm, working on muscle memory alone, allowing her thoughts to wander. How well did James know Vanessa? Mel wanted to ask him about her. Would it be suspicious if she did?

The stream of customers gradually died down. Mel took the time to tidy up the bar. She was returning a few bottles of tequila to their place on the shelf behind her when she heard a familiar voice.

"Hello, Melanie."

Mel turned. "Vanessa?"

Vanessa stood before her in a sleek red dress. A thin gold necklace with a sapphire pendant hung around her neck. Mel's eyes fell to Vanessa's lips. They were the same deep red color as her dress. Mel couldn't help but recall how those lips had felt on her lips. And on her nipples. And for a brief moment, she imagined how they would feel on certain other parts of her body.

"Make me a drink," Vanessa said. "Your choice."

"Sure." Mel chose one of the club's signature cocktails, a variation of a whiskey sour. She could practically make it with her eyes closed now. She placed it before Vanessa on the bar.

Vanessa sampled the drink. "Not bad."

Mel couldn't contain herself any longer. "I've been waiting for you to come back."

"Have you?" Vanessa leaned down on the bar. "Why?"

"Because the other night was incredible. Because falling to my knees before you made me feel freer than I've felt in years. Because it made me realize that there's this whole side of me that craves this..." Mel trailed off, suddenly self-conscious.

"What exactly is it that you crave, Melanie?" Vanessa asked. "I want to hear it from you."

Mel looked straight into Vanessa's eyes. "Submission."

Vanessa beckoned Mel closer. "If you let me, I can show you

what it really means to submit. I can make your darkest desires reality. I can grant you your wildest fantasies. Do you want that?" She slid her hand up Mel's arm.

"Yes." Vanessa's touch sent a shiver along Mel's skin. "More than anything."

The door to the back room swung open and James emerged. Mel snapped back upright. Vanessa seemed unfazed.

"Vanessa." James's voice was subdued. "Do you have a minute?"

Vanessa nodded. She took another sip of her drink and pushed it toward Mel. "Hold on to this for me. Our conversation isn't over."

James looked from Vanessa to Mel and back again, scratching his beard. Mel busied herself behind the bar, hoping that her expression hadn't given anything away.

Vanessa and James walked off to the side. Mel focused her attention on cleaning up the bar. But her curiosity won out. Vanessa and James were too far away for Mel to hear them. Instead, she watched the conversation out of the corner of her eye. She couldn't tell what they were talking about. After a while, James placed a hand on Vanessa's arm and spoke into her ear.

Vanessa transformed in an instant. Her expression darkened and her body tensed. Then the two of them started arguing. Vanessa was clearly angry about something, although her anger didn't seem to be directed at James. As the conversation died down, James placed a hand on Vanessa's shoulder as if to try to calm her. Mel was surprised by the intimateness of the gesture. She didn't know that they were that close. Before Mel could finish her thought, Vanessa turned and stormed off toward the corridor that led to her room.

*What was that about?*

James returned to the bar, his face scrunched up with concern.

"Is everything okay?" Mel asked.

"Yep. Just business stuff." He looked at Mel curiously. "What were you and Vanessa talking about before I interrupted you?"

"She was just saying hi," Mel said quickly.

"Right."

Mel couldn't tell if James was convinced or not. She took Vanessa's drink and placed it behind the bar. As the night went on, the drink sat there, the ice slowly melting. By the time Mel's shift ended, Vanessa hadn't emerged from her room. Mel wasn't bothered by the fact that Vanessa hadn't returned to finish their conversation. It was clear that Vanessa had more important things on her mind.

Mel made her way home. As she walked through her apartment door, her phone buzzed. It was a text message from an unknown number. As soon as Mel read the message, she knew who it was from. It contained no greeting, no explanation. Just a single sentence.

*I'll be in touch.*

---

Mel sat at her table, her laptop open in front of her, half a dozen textbooks stacked up beside it. Her eyes glazed over as she scanned the screen. She took off her headphones in defeat. She should have gone to the library instead of staying in. It was hard to get anything done in her tiny apartment.

She would take a small break and then get back to it. Mel had to work much harder than her classmates to stay on top of everything. Most of them didn't have to work while they were at law school. They were trust fund kids, or at the very least had parents who helped support them. But Mel didn't have that luxury.

And for Mel, simply doing well enough to pass wasn't an option. If she wanted a good job when she graduated, she had to maintain a competitive GPA. She had to remain disciplined. It was what got her this far, and it was the only way she knew how to be.

Ever since Mel was a kid, she'd had no one else in her life to provide her with structure and direction. Her father had left when Mel was young, and her alcoholic mother had never been a reliable parent. She resented Mel for being a constant reminder of the man who had broken her heart and left her with nothing. So she did the bare minimum, keeping Mel fed, clothed, and sheltered from the cold. But otherwise, Mel was on her own.

So Mel took control of her life, to the point where it became an obsession. Eventually, she decided to focus all her energy on making a better life for herself. College was her ticket out of her hometown, and she'd thrown everything into her studies to escape.

Mel stretched out her arms and looked around the room. Her hard work had paid off. She'd left her old life far behind her. But after years and years of fighting her way through the world, she wanted to just give in to temptation and let go of it all.

Mel shut her laptop. She needed to go for a run.

There was a knock on her door. Mel jumped. No one ever came to her apartment unannounced, and she wasn't expecting a delivery.

Mel opened the door. A woman stood before her, dressed in a crisp black suit and a matching overcoat. Her short, dark hair was parted at the side, and her shoes were immaculate. She looked to be around forty. Did she have the wrong apartment number? Or was she lost?

"Melanie?" the woman asked. She had a thick accent that Mel couldn't place.

Mel nodded.

The woman pulled a package out from under her arm. It was a black box with a silk ribbon tied around it. "A gift for you. From Ms. Harper."

"Ms. Harper?"

"Yes. Ms. Vanessa Harper."

"Oh." Mel took the package from the woman. "Thanks."

With a nod, the woman walked off down the hall.

Mel shut the door, her head filled with questions. Vanessa was sending her gifts? And having them hand-delivered to her apartment? She placed the package on the table, eyeing it warily. Mel had always felt uncomfortable receiving gifts. Her mother always saw them as 'charity.' She'd said that if Mel accepted handouts, people would think they were poor. If only she'd cared as much about Mel as she cared about what other people thought of her.

Mel's phone buzzed. It was a message from the same unknown number as the other night after her shift. Mel hadn't saved the number, but the digits were imprinted on her mind. She opened the text.

*Tomorrow. 9 pm. Same place. Wear my gift.*

*Wear her gift?* Immediately, Mel's reservations about the package were replaced by excitement. She grabbed the box from the table and untied the ribbon. She lifted the lid and was met with layer after layer of black tissue paper, until finally, Mel reached her prize. It was a set of lacy lingerie in a shade of purple so deep that it was almost black. She held the bra up to the light. The thin, delicate lace was almost entirely transparent. There was a clasp at the front between the two cups. The panties were made of the same sheer fabric, and tied up at the sides with little bows. Both pieces left little to the imagination.

Mel ran her fingers over the soft lace. She had never owned anything so luxurious. How much did this cost?

It didn't matter. If Vanessa wanted to Mel to come to her dressed in pretty things, who was Mel to deny her?

Mel put the bra and panties back in the box and threw herself down onto the bed. She read the text again carefully. She had no idea what Vanessa was planning. But she knew that if she went to Vanessa's room tomorrow night, there would be no going back.

# CHAPTER SEVEN

*M*el walked into The Lounge the next night with Vanessa's gift on under her clothes. She gave the bar a narrow berth, hoping to slip by unnoticed by her coworkers, and made her way up to Vanessa's room. The door at the top of the stairs loomed before her. She took a deep breath and knocked.

"Come in, Melanie."

Mel stepped into the room and shut the door behind her. Vanessa sat in her armchair, a glass of whiskey in her hand. Her raven hair was gathered over one shoulder, and she wore a black satin robe, belted at the waist. Mel couldn't help but wonder if she was wearing anything underneath it.

"Come here," Vanessa said.

Mel walked over and stood before her.

"Are you wearing my gift?"

"Yes, Vanessa."

"Show me."

Mel slid off her coat and let it fall to the floor. She did the same with her dress, leaving her standing before Vanessa in nothing but the lingerie gifted to her by the other woman. Vanessa stood up and walked around Mel in a slow circle, inspecting her slight figure from every angle. Under Vanessa's unwavering gaze, Mel felt even more naked than she was.

"You look divine," Vanessa said.

Mel's breath quickened. The hungry look on Vanessa's face made Mel feel like her prey.

"If I'm going to give you what you crave, you will have to give me something in return," Vanessa said. "Complete and utter surrender. You will submit to me. You will obey me. You will belong to me in every sense of the word. Do you understand?"

"Yes, Vanessa."

A slight smile played on Vanessa's lips. "You're going to need a safe word. Do you know what that is?"

Mel nodded.

"What will yours be?"

Mel closed her eyes and searched her mind. "Velvet," she said. Like Vanessa's smooth, low voice.

"Velvet it is." Vanessa sat back on the arm of the chair. "Go sit on the bed."

Mel walked over to the bed. Up close, she saw that each of the four bedposts had a black silk scarf tied to it. Anticipation and anxiety warred in Mel's mind. She sat down. The mattress was firm and springy.

"There's a blindfold on the pillow next to you," Vanessa continued. "Put it on and lie down."

Mel picked up the blindfold and tied it around her eyes. Darkness flooded her vision. She lay down on the bed and rested her head on the pillow. The silky bedsheets felt cool against her skin. Vanessa's bare feet padded against the floorboards as she approached Mel on the bed.

"Raise your arms up to the corners of the bed." With a practiced hand, Vanessa secured Mel's wrists to the bedposts, then repeated the process on her ankles.

Mel's heart pounded. She lay spread-eagled on the bed in nothing but the sheerest of lingerie. She tugged at her bonds to test their strength. In the same moment, Mel realized that she could no longer hear or feel Vanessa's presence. "Vanessa?"

"I'm right here." Vanessa's voice came from somewhere beside Mel. She traced her fingers along Mel's stomach all the way up to her cheek. "Stop thinking. Stop worrying. Just feel." Vanessa kissed her gently.

Mel cleared her mind and relaxed her body. She stopped straining to hear, and feel, and see. She surrendered to the darkness and focused her mind on what she could sense. The hammering of her heart, the whoosh of her breath. The scent of Vanessa's perfume, jasmine and rose. The touch of Vanessa's fingertips on her skin. It was like she and Vanessa were the only two people in the world.

The bed swayed underneath Mel as Vanessa climbed onto it. Her long, silky hair brushed against Mel's skin. Vanessa ran her hands over Mel's body, touching every inch of her skin. Silence hung in the air. Mel didn't dare speak, fearing that a single word would break the spell.

Vanessa slid her hands up to the clasp at the front of Mel's bra. With one deft motion, it was undone. Mel's breasts spilled out of the cups as it fell away. Vanessa caressed them with her hands, her fingertips sweeping over Mel's nipples.

"How does it feel to be at my mercy?" Vanessa asked.

"Good. So good..." A ripple of delight went through Mel's body. With her senses dampened, Vanessa's touch was electric.

Vanessa shifted down the bed and straddled Mel. Her weight was heavy on Mel's small, bound frame. As Vanessa's body pressed against hers, she realized that Vanessa was naked. She yearned to break free and tear off the blindfold, and touch and kiss Vanessa's soft skin. But bound as she was, she could do nothing but lay there. Bound as she was, she was powerless to stop Vanessa. But stopping Vanessa was the last thing she wanted.

Vanessa drew a line of kisses down Mel's stomach. Mel trembled. Slowly and gingerly, Vanessa untied the ribbons at the sides of Mel's panties. Mel lifted her hips as Vanessa pulled them out from under her. She felt like a gift that Vanessa was unwrapping. Vanessa slid her hands all the way up the insides of Mel's legs and dipped her head between Mel's thighs. Vanessa's hot breath on Mel's mound sent a wave of warmth through her. Vanessa kissed the soft, sensitive skin of Mel's inner thighs. Her kisses turned into nibbles, then gentle bites. Mel groaned and arched herself up toward Vanessa.

"So impatient," Vanessa said. "You're not trying to take charge, are you?"

Mel bit her lip. "No, Vanessa."

"The only sounds I want to hear from you are cries of pleasure."

Vanessa dragged her fingernails down Mel's sides and grabbed the other woman's ass cheeks, pulling Mel harder into her. Finally, she slid her tongue between Mel's lips and drew it up Mel's folds, eliciting soft gasps.

Mel twitched on the bed as Vanessa devoured her. Every sweep of Vanessa's tongue, every brush of her lips sent a tremor through Mel's body and murmurs spilling from her mouth. Vanessa had complete control over Mel's pleasure, and she was determined to show it. Vanessa teased and toyed with Mel until she was close to peaking, then she held Mel there, at the precipice, never quite letting her tip over the edge.

Mel twisted and tugged, fighting her restraints. She wanted to scream. She wanted to plead with Vanessa for release. But she understood the rules of this game. She had to take whatever Vanessa gave her with nothing less than gratitude. And eventually, her submission would be rewarded.

Once again, Vanessa brought Mel to the edge. But this time, she kept going. Mel let out a cry, bucking and thrashing as her orgasm rolled through her. Vanessa's mouth was unrelenting, licking and sucking away until Mel fell back down to the bed and her body calmed.

Vanessa kissed Mel, stealing the last of her breath. She could taste herself on the other woman's lips. Vanessa pulled the blindfold from Mel's eyes and untied her wrists and ankles. Mel blinked rapidly, her eyes readjusting to the light.

Vanessa lay down on her side next to Mel. As Mel recovered, she ran her eyes up Vanessa's body, drinking her in. This was the first time she had seen Vanessa naked. Her curves seemed more pronounced, and her dark hair, both on her head and the small patch between her legs, stood out against her milky skin. Her areolas were a rosy pink on her pale breasts.

Vanessa watched Mel watch her. For whatever reason, it made Mel blush. Vanessa smiled and pulled Mel into an embrace. After being restrained, her senses muffled, having Vanessa's arms around her felt heavenly.

"Did you mean what you said earlier? About belonging to me?" Vanessa asked.

"Yes, Vanessa."

"Then we'll have to talk about exactly what that means. But it can wait."

They lay in silence. As Mel came down from her post-orgasm daze, familiar doubts crept into her thoughts.

"What's the matter?" Vanessa asked.

"It's nothing," Mel mumbled.

"Tell me." Vanessa's usually inscrutable face wore a look of concern.

Mel's resolve wavered, and she finally gave voice to the thing that had been bothering her since the first time she walked into Vanessa's room. "It's just that, I want this. I want to explore this side of me so much that it makes me ache. But I'm not a submissive person. I'm not passive, or helpless. But I can't help but wonder. Does this mean I'm weak? For wanting to be submissive? For wanting an escape?"

"No, Melanie. You're not weak at all."

"Then why do I want this? Why do I crave this?"

"Being submissive in bed has nothing to do with who you are out in the world. And submission does not equal weakness. In fact, it takes a great deal of strength to do this."

"It doesn't feel like it takes strength. It's easy for me. Effortless."

"I'm sure it is. But it takes strength to embrace that side of you. And to act on it. I've tried it myself, you know. Only a few times. I wanted to get a better understanding of what it feels like to be on the other side. It was terrifying. I could never do it again."

Mel was surprised. She couldn't imagine Vanessa being

subservient or vulnerable. She always seemed so fearless. Who was Vanessa behind her impenetrably cool façade?

"It does take strength to do this, Melanie. Putting yourself in someone else's hands. Making yourself vulnerable to them. Trusting them with your everything. You are anything but weak." Vanessa kissed Mel gently on the lips. "And you should never, ever be ashamed of your desires."

"Yes, Vanessa." Mel snuggled in closer to her.

"Now, about these desires of yours." Vanessa reached out and ran her hands along Mel's side, following the contours of her body. "I want to know more. All your secret fantasies? I want to hear about them. Tell me everything."

# CHAPTER EIGHT

*M*el sat in class, eyelids drooping at her professor's low monotone. She looked over at Jess. Her friend was having a hard time paying attention too. She was doodling in the margin of her notebook, a vacant look in her eyes.

Mel's bag vibrated on the floor beneath her. Trying to be discreet, she pulled her phone out and peeked at the screen. She grinned.

"A message from your lover?" Jess asked.

A student sitting in front of them turned to glare at them. Mel shushed Jess.

"Is that a yes?" Jess asked, quieter this time.

"Maybe." Mel unlocked her phone and read the message.

*What time do you get out of class? V.*

*5 pm*, Mel sent. She thought for a moment and typed. *Why?* Her finger hovered over the send button. She erased the message.

"So are you going to tell me who she is?" Jess asked.

"Just someone from work."

"A coworker?"

Mel hesitated. "She's a customer." It wasn't a lie. Although she trusted Jess, Mel didn't feel right giving away Vanessa's 'secret.'

"Wow. Isn't everyone who goes there a millionaire?" Jess asked. "I'm totally jealous. What's it like dating someone like that?"

"We're not dating." At least, Mel didn't think they were.

"Then what is it? Are you her sugar baby?"

"Definitely not. It's purely physical." Mel fiddled with her pen. "I doubt she's interested in anything more."

"Why not?"

By now they had both given up on the lecture. Luckily, their eighty-year-old professor had poor hearing.

"I can't imagine someone like Vanessa being interested in someone like me," Mel said. "She's from a completely different world than me. She drinks whiskey that costs more than my month's rent. And she's so successful, and sophisticated, and elegant."

"All of those things are superficial, Mel. Do you think she cares you don't have money? When it comes to love, none of that stuff matters."

"Love? Love isn't even a possibility. I'm not interested in her that way. I'm not even looking for a relationship."

"Come on, Mel. It's been ages since everything with Kim. Are you going to spend the rest of your life alone because of one bad relationship?"

'Bad' was an understatement. Mel sighed. "I don't know. It doesn't matter. I don't need any distractions right now."

"You can't shut everyone out forever, Mel. Life is so much better when you have people to share it with."

Mel shrugged. "I have plenty of people in my life. And I like my life the way it is."

"If you say so." Jess stretched out in her chair. "So, her name is Vanessa?"

"Yeah."

"What's she like?"

"She's amazing. Gorgeous. A little older. And she's so confident and magnetic. She turns heads when she walks into a room."

"Look at you, all dreamy-eyed. The sex must be something else if she's making you act like this."

Mel rolled her eyes. She looked down at her phone. Still nothing from Vanessa. Jess was right. She was obsessing. Even though Mel definitely didn't have feelings for Vanessa, she would have to keep her guard up. The temptation was there.

Five o'clock rolled around and Mel and Jess made their way across campus.

"Finally," Jess said. "I thought this day would never end."

"Me too. I can't wait to go home and go for a run."

"Seriously? That's what you want to do at the end of a long day? I will never understand you."

They reached the main entrance. As they walked past the parking lot, Mel froze on the spot. "Vanessa?"

Vanessa stood in the parking lot leaning against the side of a sleek, black convertible. The top was down, showing off the white leather interior.

Vanessa took off her sunglasses and gave Mel a brief wave.

Jess's eyes widened. "Is that her? Vanessa?"

Mel nodded. Her mind went back to high school when girls would get picked up by their older boyfriends in banged up wrecks that to their teenage eyes were luxury cars. Of course, Mel was never one of those girls. She'd known she was gay since she was five, and dating girls was not an option at her conservative high school.

"Wow, she's gorgeous." Jess stared at Vanessa, wide-eyed. "If I was into women, I'd be all over her too."

Mel had to agree that Vanessa looked stunning. She was dressed a long tan coat that went down to her knees, and glossy black heels. Her dark, wavy hair was blowing in the wind, and she wore her signature red lipstick.

"Sorry, Jess, I gotta go. See you tomorrow." Mel hurried over to Vanessa, leaving Jess to gawk from the sidewalk. Mel was torn between shrinking with embarrassment and running up to Vanessa and throwing her arms around her.

"Hello, Melanie." Vanessa pulled Mel into an embrace and kissed her on the cheek.

"What are you doing here?"

"What do you think? Picking you up."

Mel looked over her shoulder. There were a handful of students standing around waiting for rides. And they were all looking Mel's way. Expensive sports cars weren't uncommon at Mel's prestigious school, but women like Vanessa were rare everywhere.

"Where are we going?" Mel asked.

"I thought I'd take you somewhere nice so we can talk." Vanessa opened the passenger side door. "Hop in."

Mel got into the car and buckled her seatbelt. She looked around. The interior was as luxurious as the outside of the car.

"Do you like it?" Vanessa got into the driver's seat.

"It's nice. But I don't know much about cars."

"My father was a mechanic," Vanessa said. "He was always working on something in the garage. As soon as I was old enough to hold a wrench, I was his little helper." Vanessa saw the look of surprise on Mel's face. "What, did you think I was born with a silver spoon in my mouth?"

"I hadn't really thought about it..." Mel found it hard to see the elegant, glamorous Vanessa as anything other than who she was now.

"I wasn't born into this life. I grew up as an only child in a normal working-class family. I had to fight to get to where I am. Everything I have, I've earned through hard work." Vanessa put her sunglasses on and turned the key in the ignition. The engine burst into life. "I've missed this sound. I don't often get the chance to take my Maserati for a spin. It's far more exciting than being chauffeured around everywhere."

As soon as they left the parking lot, Vanessa slammed her heeled foot on the pedal, sending them flying down the road. Mel clutched the side of the seat as the wind whipped around them.

Vanessa glanced at Mel, a hint of amusement on her face. "You should see what it's like on the track. It's the most incredible feeling. It's almost like flying."

As they sped off from a red light, Mel began to relax. Although the sheer power and acceleration made Mel feel like she was on a roller coaster, Vanessa wasn't driving recklessly. She was in complete control the entire time.

Still, Mel was relieved when Vanessa parked the car and announced that they had arrived.

---

A few minutes and an elevator ride later, Mel and Vanessa walked onto the roof of a small cocktail bar. There were only a handful of other people around. They took their seats at a long bar that ran around the edges of the rooftop. The glass walls allowed for a view of the city below.

"Wow." Mel leaned forward and looked through the glass. The sun was setting, and the sky was a haze of orange, pink, and blue.

"This is one of my favorite spots in the entire city," Vanessa said. "Especially at this time of the evening. I love catching that moment when the sun disappears behind the skyscrapers and the city comes alive with light. It's spectacular."

A waiter brought out their drinks. Whiskey for Vanessa, and a cocktail recommended by the bartender for Mel. They chatted about nothing of consequence as they watched the sun sink below the horizon.

"So, Melanie." Vanessa ran her fingers through her hair. Not a curl was out of place, despite the windy drive. "It's time we had a little talk."

"What do you want to talk about?" Mel asked.

"About this. About what we're doing."

Mel pushed the ice around her drink with a straw, recalling the conversation she'd had with Jess earlier. Did Vanessa want their physical affair to be something more?

"I'm making you nervous?" Vanessa said. "Why?"

"I have been wondering. What exactly is it that you want? It's just, I'm not looking for anything serious. Like a relationship. Not right now."

Vanessa raised an eyebrow. "Last time we got together, I tied you to a bed. Do you really think I'm interested in romance?"

Relief flooded Mel's body. "I guess not."

"I assure you, I'm not looking for a relationship either. Well, not in the conventional sense. I want nothing more than what I've already told you. I want to show you all about the pleasures of submission. Do you still want that?"

"Yes. I do."

"Are you sure? No more reservations?"

"I'm sure." That voice at the back of Mel's head telling her that her submissive desires made her weak? It had faded to nothing after that conversation with Vanessa.

"That's what I want to talk about. It's very clear from what you've told me that you want more than being tied to a bed. Am I right?"

"Yes." Mel flushed. She had been far more open with Vanessa that night than she had intended. Vanessa seemed to have that effect on her.

"If we're going to do this, there are quite a few things we need to discuss," Vanessa said. "We need to be responsible. I'm not going to just tie you up and flog you without any prior discussion."

Vanessa's words planted a very sexy image in Mel's mind. She couldn't help but grin.

"Really, Melanie?" Vanessa shook her head with a smile. "You just can't help yourself, can you?"

Mel shrugged sheepishly. She found it hard enough to keep her imagination in check even without Vanessa feeding it suggestions.

"In all seriousness, you need to know what we're getting into. BDSM can be risky. Physically, mentally, emotionally. So it's essential that we communicate. About boundaries, consent, limits, and a whole host of other things. You already have a safe word. That's a start. But do you know what your hard limits are? The things that you won't do under any circumstances?"

"I haven't really thought about it," Mel said. "But there are definitely things I never want to try."

"You don't have to tell me them now. I'll give you some time to think about everything. And this is an ongoing conversation, not a one-time discussion. But what I need you to understand is that this kind of relationship is all about communication."

"Okay." Mel tried to ignore Vanessa's use of the word 'relationship.'

Vanessa's phone rang. "I should check this. It could be work." She took her phone out of her bag and looked at it, an almost imperceptible frown on her face.

"Is everything okay?" Mel asked.

"Yes. It's nothing important." Vanessa silenced the phone and slid it back into her bag. "Now, where were we? Is there anything you'd like to ask me?"

Mel thought for a moment. "What do you get out of this? Out of having someone submit to you?"

Vanessa looked out through the glass. "I've said it before. We're alike, you and I. Hard working, ambitious, obsessed with control and self-discipline. It can be consuming. We both want a temporary escape from all of that. It simply manifests in us in different ways." Vanessa looked back at Mel. "You want to give up control, to lose yourself in a way that you would never allow yourself to out in the real world. Me? I want control in its purest, most absolute form. What I do gives me complete power over another person in the most intimate of ways. I become her Master, her whole world. Her everything."

Mel felt a chill wash over her.

"There's an immense satisfaction that comes from having the power to make someone fall apart with nothing more than a word. Or, a touch." Without breaking her gaze, Vanessa placed her hand on Mel's knee under the bar and slid it up the inside of Mel's thigh.

Mel's body stiffened as Vanessa's hand crept higher. Mel looked around. Could anyone see them?

"All those fantasies you told me about? I'm going to grant them, and so much more. I'll show you how good it feels to relinquish control. I'll take you to heights of pleasure that you've only dreamed of. I'll show you the sweet oblivion that comes with total submission."

Vanessa's fingertips brushed against Mel's panties. Heat rippled through her.

"And in exchange? You'll be mine, body and mind." Vanessa slid her fingers up and down, pushing Mel's panties between her lips.

Mel stifled a gasp. Was Vanessa going to do this here? As Vanessa's fingers stroked faster under the bar, she found that she didn't care.

"That's right. You belong to me now. And I don't like to share. Which means no one but me is allowed to touch you. Not even yourself. The only release that you're going to get is at my hands. Do you understand?"

Mel nodded, fearing that if she opened her mouth, she wouldn't be able to control what came out.

"Good." Vanessa leaned over and kissed Mel, her lips soft and tinged with whiskey. Then she drew her hand back down Mel's leg, sat back in her chair, and picked up her glass.

Mel blinked. She didn't want Vanessa to stop. She was practically throbbing.

"Unfortunately, I have to go. I have a business trip tomorrow and need to prepare." Vanessa drained the last of her drink. "Which means we won't get to see each other for a little while."

It took a moment for Mel to realize that Vanessa had gotten her all worked up and left her hanging on purpose. And now Vanessa was going to disappear on her?

"Don't look so distraught," Vanessa said. "I promise you, when I get back, the fun will really begin."

"When will you get back?" Mel asked.

"Oh, I don't know. I have a lot to do. It could be a few days. A week. Maybe even longer. And don't forget what I said. No one is to touch you." Vanessa shot Mel a stern look. "I'll know if you break my rules. And I don't want to have to punish you."

*Punish me?* Mel immediately pictured that crimson-handled riding crop in Vanessa's room. She was sure that whatever punishment Vanessa had in mind would be sweet torture. But Mel wasn't going to defy Vanessa. There was an intrinsic part of her being that needed to obey. And Vanessa knew it.

# CHAPTER NINE

*M*el flopped down onto her bed, unconcerned that she was still wearing her sweaty running gear. Since Vanessa had gone away, she and Mel had been texting nonstop.

Mel pulled out her phone. Sure enough, there was a message from Vanessa.

*How was your run? Did you work off all that pent-up frustration?*

*Yes, Vanessa.* Mel let out an exasperated sigh. She had been in a state of fevered arousal all week. Vanessa's constant reminders were not helping. In the past, Mel could go for weeks, even months without masturbating. But somehow, Vanessa forbidding Mel from touching herself made her want to do so even more. And Vanessa kept sending Mel vague but suggestive hints about what she had planned when she came back. It was maddening.

Mel's phone vibrated in her hand.

*Good. Now, where were we? How about hair pulling?*

That was an easy one. *Yes.*

*Okay. Nipple clamps?*

Mel paused and thought for a minute, then replied. *Maybe. And I've thought of another limit.*

*Yes?*

*Fisting.* Mel finally wrote.

*Which kind?*

*All kinds! Hard limit!*

*Okay. Fisting is a hard limit.* Another message. *How about whips? Floggers? Paddles? Crops?*

*Yes, yes, yes. And definitely yes.*

*So my suspicions were correct.*

Mel smiled. So Vanessa knew how much that riding crop had occupied her mind.

*Strap-ons?* Vanessa didn't bother to add which end of the strap-on she expected Mel to be on.

*Yes. But I've never used one before,* she admitted. She'd never done any of this before. Kim, her only ex-girlfriend, had been disgusted by the idea of using even the most vanilla of sex toys. Mel had had other casual partners since then, but she'd never felt comfortable enough with them to ask for what she really wanted.

*Noted. I have to go prepare for a meeting. But you've earned a reward for your obedience. You'll receive it shortly. V.*

What did that mean? Was Vanessa finally back? Mel wanted to ask, but she knew better. The first time she had asked, Vanessa had told her to be patient. The second time, Vanessa had threatened to punish her if she asked again. Mel wasn't sure whether or not she was joking.

Mel put down her phone and walked into the bathroom. She stripped off her clothes and turned on the shower. Cold water only. As she washed the sweat from her skin, she wondered: did Vanessa expect her to crack? Should Mel want to disobey her to see what Vanessa would do? She was torn between her growing need and her strong compulsion to obey Vanessa.

As Mel was drying herself off, there was a knock on the door. Mel's heart leapt. It had to be Vanessa's 'reward.' She wrapped her towel around herself and hurried to the door.

"Hello, Melanie." The well-dressed woman from the other week stood in her doorway.

"Hi." Mel's eyes were drawn to the package in the woman's hand.

"From Ms. Harper." The woman handed her the box.

"Thanks."

Did this woman know what was going on between Mel and Vanessa? Did she know what was in these packages? She constantly maintained a professional demeanor, so it was hard to tell. She and Vanessa had that in common.

The woman nodded and turned to leave.

"Wait," Mel said.

"Yes?"

"Is Vanessa back from her business trip?" Mel didn't even know who this woman was in relation to Vanessa, but there was a chance that she knew.

"Not yet." The woman said, a hint of a smile in her eyes.

"Oh." Mel considered asking if she knew when Vanessa would be back, but thought better of it. "Thanks."

The woman gave Mel a cordial nod and walked off down the hallway.

Mel raced back into her apartment and sat down on her bed, the black box on her lap. She still felt slightly uncomfortable receiving expensive gifts. But if the last gift was any indication, this one would be as much for Vanessa's benefit as Mel's.

Mel untied the ribbon and lifted the lid. The scent of leather rose from the box. She ripped back the tissue paper. Unsurprisingly, the box contained another set of lingerie. But sitting on top of it were two thick leather cuffs. Mel picked them up. They were black with red lining, and each cuff had a metal ring attached to it. They were the perfect size for Mel's wrists.

Mel's phone buzzed. *Did you receive your reward?*

*Yes*, Mel wrote back. The timing of the text suggested that Vanessa already knew the answer to her question. Had the woman informed Vanessa that she had made the delivery?

Another message came through. *Try them on. The cuffs too.*

Mel had forgotten all about the lingerie. She pulled the matching bra and panties out of the box. They were made of black lace, so delicate that Mel feared that they would tear at the slightest touch. Both the bra and panties had several thin straps attached at various points around the top and sides. Mel removed her towel and put the lingerie on. It wasn't easy with all the straps. She buckled the cuffs around her wrists snugly.

Mel turned to the mirror. She was surprised by what she saw. Her long dark hair, still damp from the shower, was tied up in a messy bun, leaving her shoulders and chest bare. The straps on the bra crisscrossed across the tops of her breasts. The Brazilian panties covered only the tops of her ass cheeks.

Mel liked the way the lingerie looked on her. She liked the way it made her feel. Sexy. Powerfully so. Would Vanessa find her irresistible in it? There was something exciting about the idea that she could drive Vanessa wild in her own way.

Another text arrived. *Send me a picture.*

Mel smiled. She snapped a photo in the mirror with her phone and sent it to Vanessa. She waited. A minute passed, then two, then five. Her impatience got the best of her. *Did you get it?*

*Yes. You look ravishing. I'm going to enjoy making you come apart. V.*

Mel sprawled out on her bed. What naughty things did Vanessa have planned for her? If she closed her eyes, she could almost feel Vanessa's fingertips running along her curves. She could almost smell her perfume and taste her soft lips.

*No.* The last thing Mel needed was another cold shower. She glanced at her phone. Nothing more from Vanessa. Mel wasn't surprised. That "V." at the end of Vanessa's texts always meant one thing: *this conversation is over.*

---

The message came the following Sunday morning. Mel had slept in after a late-night shift at The Lounge. She rolled over in a daze and picked her phone up from the nightstand.

*Tomorrow night. 8 pm. I'll pick you up. Wear my gifts. And only my gifts.*

Mel's heart jumped. *Finally!* Her stomach dropped as she read it again. *Only* her gifts? Did Vanessa expect Mel to leave the house in nothing but lingerie? And *that* lingerie? It barely counted as underwear.

Another text followed a minute later.

*You may wear a coat. And shoes. But nothing else.*

Mel rolled onto her back, a smile on her face. Finally, her torment would end. Vanessa's mind games were far more potent than any whip.

At least, that was what Mel thought.

# CHAPTER TEN

*M*el left her apartment at 7:55 p.m. the next day, keenly aware of how naked she was under her long coat. The leather cuffs peeked out from her sleeves. The day had passed with excruciating slowness. She'd barely been able to concentrate in class.

She stepped out onto the sidewalk. A large black Mercedes Benz was parked out in front of her apartment building. Standing next to it was the sharply dressed dark-haired woman who had delivered Vanessa's gifts. So she was Vanessa's driver. Something told Mel that hand-delivering gifts to her boss's lover in a dodgy part of town wasn't part of the job description. Perhaps Vanessa's expectation that everyone cater to her whims went beyond her sex life.

The driver opened the back door.

"Hello, Melanie." Vanessa sat in the back seat, her legs crossed in front of her. She wore a long, dark coat, and black stockings and heels.

"Hi." Mel hopped into the back seat next to her.

"Thank you, Elena," Vanessa said to the driver.

Elena nodded and shut the door. Shortly afterward, the car

pulled out and joined the slow stream of traffic. It was a much smoother ride than Vanessa's convertible.

"Where are you taking me?" Mel asked Vanessa.

"I'm going to show you one of the other clubs I own," Vanessa said.

They were going somewhere public? Mel barely had a thread of clothing on her.

Vanessa read her mind. "Don't worry, it's closed. We'll have the place to ourselves."

Mel sat back. Why would Vanessa be taking her to an empty club? She remembered something that Vanessa had said in her room all those nights ago, that not all of her clubs were as 'respectable' as The Lounge. Was Vanessa taking her to one of those?

Mel looked out through the tinted windows, vainly trying to see where they were going. The privacy screen between the front and back seats blocked her view of the windshield. She sat back in defeat.

"So, Melanie," Vanessa said. "Have you been following my rule?"

"Yes, Vanessa." Mel didn't know when she had started to answer to Vanessa like an obedient schoolgirl. But it seemed to please Vanessa.

"Really? You didn't slip up? Not even once?"

"No, Vanessa." Mel couldn't tell whether Vanessa was pleased or disappointed.

"But did you want to?"

"God, yes."

"That must have been agonizing." Vanessa slid a hand underneath Mel's coat and up the inside of her thigh.

The ache deep inside Mel grew. She closed her eyes.

"Did you think about me while I was gone?" Vanessa brushed her fingertips all the way up between Mel's legs. The thin panties were no barrier to Vanessa's probing fingers. "Did you imagine all the things I'm going to do to you?"

"Yes, Vanessa. Every single day."

"It will be worth the wait. I promise."

Mel bit back a moan. She didn't want to test whether the privacy barrier was soundproof. But Vanessa was doing everything she could to derail her efforts.

"Now I know that you're telling the truth about not touching yourself." Vanessa pressed her finger into the wet spot on Mel's panties. "This is far too easy."

Mel whimpered. If Vanessa wanted to, she could make Mel come in seconds.

The car glided to a stop.

"We're here." Vanessa withdrew her hand and sat back.

Mel flattened out her coat and slowed her breaths. She was beginning to realize that Vanessa torturing her like this was not going to be a one-time occurrence. Elena opened Mel's door. Mel thanked her and stepped out onto the sidewalk. At some point during their drive, they had crossed into a nicer part of town. Mel scanned the shop fronts before her. She wasn't sure what she was looking for.

"Here we are," Vanessa said.

Mel followed the path of Vanessa's eyes. Nestled between two boutiques was a small, black door. There was a sign above the door with a name written on it in red cursive script: *Lilith's Den.*

"It's closed on Mondays. But I have a key." Vanessa pulled a key out of her purse and unlocked the door. They walked inside. "This is it. Lilith's Den."

Mel looked around in awe. The large space looked like any other nightclub, but in addition to the tables and barstools, there were some unconventional furnishings scattered around the room. A seven-foot-tall wooden cross with small metal rings at each of the ends. A bench that resembled a horse with leather cuffs attached to it. A long, wide table with padding on the top and rings all along the sides which Mel assumed were tie points.

"What is this place?" Mel asked.

"It's a place where people can let go of their inhibitions and explore all of their wildest, darkest dreams," Vanessa said.

Mel's eyes widened. "So, it's some kind of sex club?"

"More of a BDSM club." Vanessa strode into the middle of the empty room. "This is why I'm so private. This is a big part of my lifestyle. Well, not so much these days, but at one point it felt like it was my entire world..."

Vanessa looked off into the distance. For a moment, Mel caught a glimpse of what lay behind Vanessa's veil, but then the usual self-possessed expression returned.

"This is my 'secret.' In addition to a few clubs like The Lounge, I own Lilith's, and several similar establishments in other cities. All separate from my investment firm. I'm not ashamed of my interest in BDSM. But there are a lot of intolerant people out there, especially in my line of work. The gossip and rumors are a distraction. And quite frankly, what I do in my leisure time is no one's business but my own." Vanessa smiled. "So, what do you think?"

"It's nice," Mel liked it more than The Lounge, which she had always found a bit too glitzy. "Really nice."

"Lilith's isn't your average BDSM club. Only the best of everything. Lilith's caters to the same sort of clientele as The Lounge. It's no surprise that the rich and powerful like to exercise their power in other ways."

Mel surveyed the room. There was a set of heavy wooden double doors toward the back of the club. "What's behind those doors?"

"That leads to the private rooms upstairs. And that's where we're headed."

Vanessa took off her coat, revealing a black, form-fitting dress that was cut low enough to be tantalizing while still leaving something to the imagination. And Mel's imagination was running wild.

"But before we go up..." Vanessa looked Mel up and down. "I want to see how my gifts look on you."

Mel untied her coat and slid it off her shoulders. Her skin prickled under Vanessa's smoldering gaze. For a moment, Mel thought that Vanessa was going to tear off the little clothing that Mel still had on and take her then and there.

But Vanessa restrained herself. She wasn't going to deviate from her plans. And it was clear that she did have plans. Mel fiddled with the cuffs at her wrists as Vanessa's eyes did one last lap over Mel's body.

"Follow me," Vanessa said.

Mel followed Vanessa toward the double doors. Half-naked in this huge, empty space, Mel couldn't help but feel exposed. Vanessa pushed open the doors. They made their way up the stairs and were greeted with a long corridor with rows of doors on either side.

Vanessa opened a door at random. "Go ahead. Have a look inside."

Mel peered into the room. The entire floor was essentially one giant bed with pillows thrown around haphazardly. It wasn't hard to figure out what that room was for. Mel opened another door. It looked like a normal bedroom, with a king-sized bed in the middle. But one of the side walls was made up entirely of mirrors.

"They're one-way mirrors," Vanessa said. "There's a viewing room next door. Some people like the taboo of being watched. Others like to watch. All parties have to consent, of course."

Mel wandered down the corridor, opening door after door. There were rooms designed to fulfill every fantasy, from the common to the unusual. There was a classroom, a doctor's office, a jail cell. It was like some sort of kinky hotel.

They reached the end of the hall. Mel stopped in front of a door. Unlike the others, it had a nameplate above it. *The Scarlet Room.* Mel reached out and turned the door handle. It was locked.

"I see you've found The Scarlet Room." Vanessa walked up behind her. She had a key with a red tassel hanging from it in her hand. "You'll get to see what's inside in a moment."

Mel was practically bursting out of her skin. She wanted to see what was behind that door. But she wanted Vanessa even more.

"Before we go in. What's your safe word?"

"Velvet," Mel said.

"Good. Remember, using your safe word isn't a sign of weakness. When you need to use it, use it."

"Okay." The seriousness of Vanessa's expression told Mel that this command was more important than any of the others Vanessa had given her.

"One last thing. Do you trust me?"

"Yes."

"The most important part of all of this is trust. You, trusting that

I will keep you safe. And me trusting you to communicate honestly about your limits and what you're thinking and feeling. Do you promise to do that for me?"

"Yes, Vanessa."

"Good. Trust me. Listen to everything I say. And know that I'll be right there by your side the entire time."

Mel nodded. Vanessa unlocked the door, and they entered The Scarlet Room.

# CHAPTER ELEVEN

"Welcome to The Scarlet Room," Vanessa said.

Mel looked around. The room resembled a Victorian parlor, complete with red vintage wallpaper and ornate furniture, but with the inclusion of a large four-poster bed. What was on the walls told a different story. The shelves, hooks and cabinets, all held a vast array of BDSM equipment.

What interested Mel the most was a rack on the far wall. It was a cornucopia of whips, including a long, thin riding crop. Unlike the others, the crop had a crimson handle. It was the same one that had hung from Vanessa's bed at The Lounge and had haunted Mel since the day she stepped into that room.

"See something you like?" Vanessa asked.

Mel stared at the rack. "Are you going to use one of these on me?"

"Do you want me to?"

Mel nodded, her pulse quickening.

Vanessa sidled up behind her and draped her arms around Mel's shoulders. "Say it. Tell me exactly what you want me to do to you."

"Please, Vanessa. I want you to use the riding crop on me."

"Okay. But I plan to do far more with you than that." Vanessa walked to the center of the room and beckoned Mel with a finger. "Come here."

Mel followed, hypnotized by Vanessa's voice. Vanessa took Mel's hands and brought her wrists together. Out of nowhere, Vanessa produced a short chain and clipped the cuffs to each other.

"Raise your arms above your head," Vanessa said.

Mel looked up as she lifted her arms. She was right underneath an elaborate iron chandelier. A long piece of rope dangled from the center of it. Sure enough, Vanessa reached up and tied the rope to the chain at Mel's wrists, leaving her strung up with her arms stretched almost to their limits. Her feet were flat on the floor, but every muscle in her body was taut.

Vanessa cupped Mel's face in her hands. "How do you feel?"

"Fine," Mel remembered Vanessa's words about honesty. "A little anxious. But not in a bad way."

Vanessa kissed Mel gently on the lips. "Trust me."

Vanessa disappeared somewhere behind her. Mel heard the rustle of fabric and turned her head. Vanessa had slipped out of her dress, revealing a lacy black bra and matching panties. Her lace-topped thigh-high stockings were held up by a garter belt. Just the sight of her made Mel ache.

"Eyes forward. Unless you want me to blindfold you?"

"No, Vanessa." Mel snapped her head back around. There was a challenge in Vanessa's voice that Mel didn't dare to test.

"Stay perfectly still."

Mel heard the click of Vanessa's heels on the floor behind her. When Vanessa came back into view, she had the riding crop in her hand. But instead of coming back to Mel, Vanessa went to sit on the end of the bed.

She leaned back and crossed her legs, admiring her handiwork. "You look delectable tied up and waiting for me like that."

Mel tested her restraints. They held fast. And the sturdy chandelier didn't move at all.

Vanessa smiled. "You've been waiting for this, haven't you?"

"Yes." Mel could feel the blood rushing through her veins.

"Yes? Just 'yes?'"

"Yes, Vanessa."

"That's better." Finally, Vanessa stood up. She circled around Mel, trailing her fingers across the back of Mel's thighs.

Mel felt like an insect caught in Vanessa's web. Only she wanted to be eaten.

Vanessa tapped the tip of the crop against her palm. "Do you know why so many people find the combination of pain and pleasure so irresistible?"

"No, Vanessa."

"It's because pain is a stimulant. Just like a drug, it puts your nervous system on high alert, and makes your body hypersensitive in the best possible way."

Something smooth brushed against the back of Mel's neck. She froze. Was it the tip of the riding crop? What was her safe word again? Violet? Velvet. Mel was nowhere near the point of using it. But she found it reassuring all the same.

"Relax," Vanessa said softly.

Mel breathed the tension out of her body. Slowly, Vanessa snaked the riding crop across Mel's back, lower and lower, all the way down to where Mel's thighs met. Mel inhaled sharply as heat spread through her body. The mixture of anticipation and arousal was a heady cocktail.

Vanessa pulled the riding crop away. Mel squeezed her eyes shut, listening for what was to come. She felt like she was at the top of a rollercoaster, waiting for the inevitable drop.

But instead of a forceful strike, Mel felt a firm tap on her ass. The impact made her jump up onto her toes. But it didn't hurt. Vanessa continued, tapping out a series of short, sharp swats with the tip of the riding crop that left a pleasant tingling behind. Murmurs fell from Mel's lips. Slowly, Vanessa increased the intensity. Slowly, Mel's cheeks began to burn. But it only added to the heat between her legs.

Vanessa pressed her body up against Mel's and ran her hands over Mel's stinging cheeks. "That feeling? That rush? It's your body reacting to the perceived danger. Every stroke brings you closer and closer to an elevated state of awareness." She leaned in and whispered into Mel's ear. "And tonight, I'm going to take you all the way there."

Mel heard the whoosh of the riding crop through the air, then felt the sting of the whip on her ass cheek. She hissed. That was more than a firm tap. Mel reflexively tried to bring her hands down to protect herself, but they were bound above her head. Vanessa snapped the crop against Mel's other cheek. Her skin stung. But it wasn't a bad kind of pain. It was the kind caused her nipples to peak and set her body alight.

"Your skin looks so lovely striped in pink." Vanessa trailed the supple tip of the riding crop over Mel's ass. "How are you doing, Melanie?"

"I'm good," Mel said. "I'm better than good."

Vanessa continued, alternating between gentle brushes of the riding crop and short, sharp stings, gently caressing Mel's body in between. When every inch of her cheeks had been marked by the whip, Vanessa moved on to the back of Mel's thighs. More than once, the crop hit dangerously close to her most sensitive parts.

It was all so delicious. The piercing kiss of the crop. The thrill of not knowing when the whip would fall. The adrenaline coursing through her body. The experience threatened to overwhelm her.

"Do you want more?" Vanessa asked.

"Mmmm." Mel's whole body was alive with energy. "Yes, Vanessa."

"Ask nicely."

"Please, Vanessa. Can I have more?"

"Yes, my pet." Vanessa tipped Mel's chin up with her fingers and kissed her softly. "Don't fight it. Embrace it."

Mel did as Vanessa instructed. She closed her eyes and let everything else fade away. And slowly, she slipped into a state of bliss. She lost track of time. She lost track of everything around her. All that Mel was aware of was her own body, and Vanessa's presence, and the pure, concentrated pleasure that Vanessa was giving her.

The whip disappeared and was replaced by the press of Vanessa's hands. They felt cool against her burning skin. "Do you feel that? The pain has heightened your senses." Vanessa slid a hand up underneath Mel's bra and caressed her breasts. "Every nerve in your body is awake. Every sensation is amplified." She pinched Mel's nipple firmly.

The throbbing deep within Mel intensified. Vanessa's hands roamed her body, teasing, brushing, tickling. Vanessa slid the riding crop between Mel's legs and flicked. Mel gasped. It was like a bolt of lightning shooting straight into her core.

"I'm impressed," Vanessa said. "I thought you'd be begging by now."

Mel's only response was a whimper.

"Do you want me to give you your release?" Vanessa grazed Mel's inner thighs with her fingertips.

Mel nodded. Vanessa slipped her fingers into Mel's panties and between her lips, and strummed her swollen nub, eliciting endless moans from deep within Mel's chest. After going for so long without an orgasm, it didn't take long until Mel was close to the edge.

"Go on," Vanessa said. "Come for me."

Mel convulsed against Vanessa's body, her lips a wide O. She collapsed in Vanessa's arms, overcome by the feeling that she had floated out of her body. "Mmmm…"

Somehow, Mel found herself on the bed, her wrists unbound, Vanessa's arm slung across her small frame. Her body still tingled like her nerves were alight.

"Welcome back," Vanessa said.

"That was incredible," Mel murmured. Was this what Vanessa meant when she said she was going to make Mel come apart? Because she had succeeded.

"That, Melanie, was subspace." Vanessa rolled over to face Mel. "It's a natural high, a rush of adrenaline and endorphins triggered by all the sensations that your body was experiencing. At least, that's the physical side. There's far more to subspace than that. Or so I'm told."

Mel knew exactly what Vanessa was talking about. At that moment when the rest of the world had fallen away was like nothing she'd ever experienced. And the connection she'd felt toward Vanessa had been sublime.

"How are you feeling now?" Vanessa asked.

"I'm good. I'm amazing." Mel reached out toward Vanessa. She was craving the other woman's touch.

Vanessa placed her hand on Mel's side. "Here. Lay on your stomach."

Mel rolled over. Vanessa moved in closer, her body pressed against Mel's side, and ran her hand down to Mel's cheeks. They were covered in angry, red welts. Vanessa traced gentle lines over them with her fingertips while planting soft kisses on the back of Mel's shoulder.

Mel purred. She liked that tender, sweet side of Vanessa. She wondered how often Vanessa let anyone see it. She closed her eyes.

This was by far the best part of her night.

---

Mel and Vanessa sat in silence as Elena drove them back to Mel's apartment. Slowly, Mel's high started to fade and exhaustion set in.

"Are you all right?" Vanessa asked.

"Yeah. I'm just really tired all of a sudden."

Vanessa examined Mel with a frown. "You're dropping. Come here." Vanessa pulled Mel into her. "I should have warned you about this too. Subspace can be intense. It isn't uncommon to feel a drop after coming down from it. A drop in mood, in energy, in everything. It doesn't always happen. But when it does, it's my responsibility to look after you. If you start to feel your mood turn, you need to tell me immediately, okay?"

Mel nodded. The car pulled to a stop outside Mel's apartment. Vanessa got out of the car and open Mel's door. As Mel stepped out onto the sidewalk, Vanessa leaned over to say something to Elena through the window. Elena nodded and turned off the car.

"Come on. Let's go." Vanessa gestured toward the door to Mel's building.

As soon as they entered her apartment, Mel was seized by a

gnawing in her chest. Suddenly, the prospect of being left alone filled her with dread. In minutes she had gone from feeling blissful and content to feeling raw and vulnerable.

Upon seeing Mel's face, Vanessa's expression softened. "It's hitting you right now, isn't it?"

Mel nodded. She felt like her insides were spilling out.

"You're okay." Vanessa gathered Mel in her arms and planted a kiss on the top of her head. "You'll feel better once you're in bed."

Vanessa tugged off Mel's coat. Mel collapsed onto the bed and curled up in a ball. Was Vanessa going to leave her now? And why did that suddenly bother her so much?

Vanessa sat down on the edge of the bed and started typing into her phone. "I'm sending Elena home."

Mel watched in surprise as Vanessa kicked off her shoes and shimmied out of her dress.

For the second time that night, Vanessa hopped in the bed beside Mel. "You didn't think I was going to leave you like this, did you?"

Mel opened her mouth to reply, but there was a lump in her throat that she couldn't get words past.

"Oh, Melanie. I'm not going anywhere." Vanessa wrapped her arms around Mel's small frame. "All of these feelings? It's just subdrop. Okay?"

Mel nodded.

"Don't just nod. Tell me that you understand."

"Yes, Vanessa. I understand." Still, Mel hated herself for turning into such a miserable, needy mess. "I'm sorry, I just..." She trailed off.

"Don't apologize. You have nothing to be sorry for. It's completely normal to feel like this. You made yourself deeply vulnerable to someone else. And now that it's all over and things are returning to normal, it's not unusual to feel a sense of emptiness." Vanessa kissed Mel gently on the lips. "Don't be so hard on yourself. You don't have to be strong all the time."

"Yes, I do," Mel murmured. "I've always had to be strong. I don't know how not to be."

"It's simple. All you have to do is close your eyes and let me take some of the weight off your shoulders." Vanessa pulled Mel in closer. "In fact, I'm ordering you to do that right now."

Mel was too tired to do anything but obey. She shut her eyes and put her head on Vanessa's chest, losing herself in the other woman's warmth and softness. Her eyelids began to feel heavy. "Thank you for staying with me."

"You don't need to thank me," Vanessa said quietly. "I would do anything to keep you from hurting."

# CHAPTER TWELVE

*M*el woke up the next morning wrapped in a cocoon of sheets, the aroma of coffee and cinnamon hanging in the air. Despite her aching muscles, she felt invigorated. She reached her arm out next to her. The other side of the bed was empty. Suppressing her disappointment, Mel rolled over and picked up her phone up from the nightstand. There was a message from Vanessa.

*Had to go. Important meeting. Call me as soon as you wake up. V.*

There was a second message sent ten minutes later.

*Breakfast is on the counter. Eat something.*

Mel sat up groggily and looked across the room to the countertop that functioned as her kitchen. There was a large to-go cup of coffee and a paper bag bearing the logo of the bakery down the road. Vanessa brought her breakfast? Mel backtracked. Vanessa had been here, in Mel's dingy little apartment? And she had stayed the night in Mel's bed?

Mel flopped back down onto her stomach. She twisted her head around to inspect her aching cheeks. Faint bruises were starting to form. The events of last night came flooding back. The car ride. Lilith's Den. The Scarlet Room. And then, Vanessa holding Mel on the bed as she broke down in Vanessa's arms.

Where had all those insecure, needy thoughts and feelings come from? Although Vanessa had said it was normal, Mel couldn't help but feel embarrassed by her momentary weakness. She felt fine now. Amazing, even. She would do it again in a heartbeat, subdrop and all.

Mel looked at her phone. Vanessa's text had been sent less than two hours ago. Would her meeting be over by now? Mel didn't want to interrupt anything, but Vanessa had made it very clear that Mel should call her immediately. Her bossiness should have bothered Mel. It definitely would have, coming from anyone else.

Mel sat up and dialed Vanessa's number.

Vanessa picked up the phone within two rings. "Give me a moment."

Mel heard voices in the background, then the sound of a door closing.

"Melanie. How are you feeling?" Vanessa asked.

"Fine. Is your meeting over?"

"No. But it's nothing that can't wait five minutes."

"I'm sorry, I didn't mean to interrupt," Mel said.

"Don't be. I wouldn't have told you to call me if I didn't mean it. Now, how do you feel? Honestly?"

"Fine. Really. Although I am a bit sore."

Vanessa chuckled softly. It was the first time Mel had heard her laugh. "Well, that's to be expected. How's your mood?"

"Good. I feel great, actually."

"No more subdrop? Sometimes it can linger the next day."

"Nope. I'm back to normal."

"I'm glad." She paused. "I didn't want to leave you alone after last night, but I couldn't get out of this meeting."

"It's okay. I'm fine. Really."

"Have you eaten anything?"

"Not yet, I just woke up."

"As soon as you hang up, I want you to have breakfast. And drink plenty of water. Your body needs to replenish itself after last night."

"Okay."

"I'll talk to you soon."

Mel hung up the phone. The warm, affectionate Vanessa of last night was gone. But she wasn't back to being cool and inscrutable. It was something in between. It made Mel wonder—how much of Vanessa's hard, emotionless persona was an act, and how much of it was actually her?

Mel hopped out of bed and examined Vanessa's breakfast offerings. She didn't know why she was trying to figure Vanessa out. Things between them were supposed to be purely physical. But Mel was beginning to realize that what she and Vanessa were doing together required a level of intimacy that she hadn't anticipated. She remembered Vanessa's words about trust. If life had taught Mel anything, it was that the only person she could rely on was herself.

Mel sighed. Things were starting to spin out of control. If she wasn't careful, it would be too easy for her to lose herself in both Vanessa and BDSM. Because for Mel, the two were inextricably intertwined.

---

The days that followed only left Mel feeling even more conflicted.

"It's been four days, Jess." Mel lay on the lawn with her friend, soaking in the sun between classes. "And nothing!"

"Why don't you just text her yourself?" Jess asked.

"Because it would be weird. She's the one who always contacts me." Mel knew how flimsy an excuse it was.

"So you're supposed to sit around and wait for her to booty call you?" Jess peered at Mel from over her sunglasses. "That's pretty cold."

"It's not like that. She's not like that."

"Then what is it? Are you sure you're not just afraid of putting yourself out there?"

"Well, maybe a little," Mel said. "It's complicated."

"Only because you're making it complicated. Just call her!"

Mel sighed.

"Besides, she could just be busy. Didn't you say she has a demanding job?"

"Yeah. Maybe you're right." In the past, Vanessa had gone for long periods without contacting Mel because of her busy schedule. But after the intimacy of that night at Lilith's, Mel felt like things between them had changed. That they had grown closer. "Honestly? I'm a little worried that I scared her away. Everything seemed fine when I talked to her the next day, but now..." Mel trailed off. It was all too familiar. She'd gotten too close to someone. She'd shown them her vulnerable side. And then they'd discarded her like she was nothing.

Mel banished her thought. Vanessa wasn't Kim. And this was not a relationship.

"Why do you think you scared Vanessa away? Did something happen?" Jess asked.

"It's hard to explain." Mel considered her friend carefully. Jess wasn't shy when it came to her sex life. And Mel trusted her. "There's more to it than what I told you. Promise me you'll keep an open mind?"

"Sure. I'm as open-minded as they come."

Jess listened silently as Mel described the events of that night. When Mel reached the point when she and Vanessa had gone up to Mel's apartment, Jess interrupted her.

"Oh yeah, subdrop." Jess propped herself up on her elbow. "It makes everyone feel needy and depressed. It's totally normal."

Mel gaped at her.

"What, Vanessa didn't explain it to you?"

"She did. I didn't know you were into that kind of thing."

"Don't look so shocked, Mel. Do you think you're the only girl who likes getting tied up and spanked?" Jess grinned. "Anyway, it sounds like Vanessa knows what she's doing. Aftercare, checking up on you in the morning—it's pretty important. So I doubt something as common as subdrop fazed her. You have nothing to worry about."

"You're probably right." Mel turned to her friend. "So you've experienced it before? Subspace? Subdrop?"

"Yeah, a few times. Not for a while though. Unlike you, I don't have some rich Domme lover who owns a BDSM club." Jess sat upright. "Wait. The club Vanessa took you to. Was it Lilith's Den?"

"Yeah. Do you know of it?" Mel asked.

"Of course. Everyone in the BDSM community has heard of it. But it's very exclusive. I've never been inside. Wow. So Vanessa owns Lilith's." Jess looked off into the distance. "I wish I had a girl-friend like her."

"Just don't tell anyone, all right? She is very private about the fact that she owns the place."

"Yeah, no problem."

"And she's not my girlfriend."

"Right. You just have an intense connection with her, you're exclusively seeing each other, and now you're going crazy because she hasn't texted you in a few days."

"It isn't like that," Mel said. Weren't all those things just part of the kinky game that Mel and Vanessa were playing? Mel suddenly remembered something that Vanessa had said as they drifted off to sleep that night. *I would do anything to keep you from hurting.* Had Vanessa really said that, or was it a dream?

"I wish I had someone who I felt as strongly about as you do with Vanessa. I spent most of my weekend dodging Brett's calls."

"What? I thought you two broke up?"

"That was Brendon. I only just started seeing Brett. He's way hotter. Not much upstairs though."

Mel raised an eyebrow.

"What?" Jess shrugged. "He makes up for it in other ways. It's too bad he's as vanilla as they come."

Mel shook her head. Her phone buzzed. A text message. A slow smile spread across her face.

*Tomorrow night. My room at The Lounge. After your shift.* Another message followed shortly after. *I'm sorry that I've been out of touch.*

"Lemme guess? Vanessa?"

"Yep," Mel said. Vanessa hadn't given an explanation. But she had apologized. And something told Mel that Vanessa didn't apologize very often.

"Told you." Jess lay back down and pushed up her sunglasses. "Nothing to worry about."

# CHAPTER THIRTEEN

"*Mmm...*" Mel lay on the king bed in Vanessa's room above The Lounge, her hot, sweaty limbs tangled with Vanessa's. A pair of handcuffs lay discarded on the bed beside them. Mel closed her eyes and let out a long, slow breath.

The last few hours had silenced all of Mel's doubts. She had been right that the night at Lilith's Den had changed everything between her and Vanessa. Only it was for the better. They were more attuned to each other somehow, more connected. It was subtle but unmistakable.

"What are you smiling about?" Vanessa asked.

"I feel like I'm on top of the world right now." Everything in her life was running smoothly. Law school. Work. Even her modest social life. For the first time in as long as she could remember, she was completely stress-free.

Vanessa smiled and got up from the bed. "Drink?"

"Sure." Mel watched Vanessa walk over to the counter. She still found the sight of Vanessa's soft, white curves mesmerizing. Vanessa poured two glasses of whiskey and returned to the bed. Mel loved the taste of whiskey now. The way that every sip flooded her body with a pleasant warmth reminded her of Vanessa.

Vanessa's phone rang. She looked at her cell, then quickly turned it off. She placed it aside and sat back on the bed.

*Again?* This seemed to happen a lot. When it did, it was like Vanessa's mask would slip. She'd get a phone call. She'd ignore it. And she'd continue as if whatever it was hadn't bothered her. But she always seemed slightly rattled afterward. Mel couldn't help but wonder what could possibly shake someone like Vanessa. Despite their growing closeness, Vanessa was still mostly a mystery to Mel.

Vanessa reached out and swept a lock of Mel's unruly hair out of her face. "It's your birthday in a few days."

A knot formed in Mel's stomach. "How did you find out?"

"It's in your employee records," Vanessa said. "I couldn't help but take a look. Do you have anything planned?"

"Not really..." Like every other year, Mel had been planning to let the day pass without telling anyone.

"That means I get you all to myself," Vanessa said.

Mel stared down into her lap.

"What's the matter?"

Mel shrugged. "I don't really like birthdays."

"And why not?"

Mel gathered up the satin sheets around her and pulled them into her lap. "They've always been... disappointing for me. It was just me and Mom growing up, and she wasn't very good at that sort of thing. If she remembered at all."

"I'm sorry. That must have been hard," Vanessa said.

"It's no big deal."

"So your birthdays were disappointing in the past. They don't have to be in the future." Vanessa placed her glass down on the nightstand. "Let me give you the birthday you deserve. Let me spoil you."

Mel hesitated. "I don't know..."

"Please?" Vanessa gave Mel a pleading look. Coming from Vanessa, it looked ridiculous.

A smile broke out on Mel's face. "Okay. But nothing over the top."

"Then I'll cancel the helicopter ride."

"Very funny." Mel smoothed out the sheets in her lap. "That was a joke, right?"

Vanessa shrugged. "Maybe." She placed her hand on Mel's. "I promise you. I'm going to make your birthday unforgettable. You'll love it."

Mel sighed. Vanessa had even more of a disarming effect on her than before. But it seemed to Mel that Vanessa was letting her guard down a little too.

Vanessa took Mel's glass and placed it on the nightstand next to her own. "You're the only person I've ever had to beg to let me spoil them." She pushed Mel down by the shoulders, straddled her body and pinned her wrists above her head. "I think you need a reminder of who you belong to."

---

"Happy birthday, Mel!" James said.

Mel looked at her watch. She hadn't even noticed that it was past midnight. "Thanks," she said quietly. Like Vanessa, James must have found out from Mel's employee records.

"What are you doing to celebrate?"

"Just spending time with… a friend."

"That's all?" James shook his head. "Why don't you come out for drinks with everyone after we close? Consider it an impromptu birthday party."

"I don't think so. I'm not big on birthdays," Mel said.

"Okay, how about this, I won't even tell anyone it's your birthday. As far as the others will know, it'll just be the usual after-work drinks."

Mel hesitated. She had been working hard lately. And she didn't have class until the afternoon. It couldn't hurt to have a little fun.

"Come on, Mel!" James said. "Just this once. Live a little."

Mel held up her hands in defeat. "Sure. Why not?"

"Great." James leaned down against the bar. "So, how do you feel about dancing?"

"Don't push your luck." Mel grabbed her tray and walked off, knowing she was going to regret her decision in the morning.

A few hours later, they had closed up shop, and James, Mel and a handful of her coworkers were hanging out in a seedy bar a few blocks away from The Lounge. It was one of the few places that was still open.

"Mel!" James yelled. "Dance with me. It'll be *fun*."

"How many drinks have you had, James?" Mel asked.

"Not nearly enough." He stood up. "So, are you coming?" He cocked his head toward the 'dance floor' that the group had made by pushing some tables to the side.

"No thanks," Mel said for the tenth time since they'd arrived. "But you should go ahead and join the others."

"Come on, show me your moves, Mel."

Why did James want her to dance with him so much? Mel let out a heavy sigh. "Look, James. You're a great guy, but I'm not interested in whatever it is that you want..."

James looked at Mel blankly. Then he burst out laughing. "Did you think I was hitting on you?"

Mel's face flushed. "Well, you're always so persistent..." Mel frowned. James was laughing a little too hard.

"Oh, man." His chuckles died off. James sat back down. "Sorry. Believe me, I'm not into you that way. I've just been trying to get you to come out of your shell a bit. You don't talk to anyone at work, so I figured you could use a friend. That's it."

He did have a point. Mel wasn't very sociable when it came to her job.

"Besides, I'm gay." James settled back in his chair. "You of all people should have a much better gaydar."

"What? How do you know that I'm gay?" Mel asked.

"I know about you and Vanessa, Mel."

"How? Did she tell you about us?"

"Nope." James grinned. "But you just did."

Mel cursed under her breath.

"I had my suspicions. Vanessa and I have known each other since she opened The Lounge. She hired me herself. After working with her for so long, we've gotten to know each other pretty well. I figured that there was something going on between you two, but she didn't seem inclined to share, so I didn't press her. You know how private she is."

James and Vanessa were friends? Vanessa never talked about her friends, but Mel had assumed that they were more like the kind of people who went to The Lounge, not the kind that worked there.

"But it's pretty obvious." James scratched his chin. "After that incident with that asshole customer, Vanessa became very interested in you. She kept asking me questions about you, and would conveniently only come in on nights when you were working. And then she started sneaking you up to her room above The Lounge late at night."

Mel flushed. She thought they were being discreet.

James smiled. "I think you're good for her. She seems happy. She hasn't been in a relationship since Rose."

"Hold up. We are not in a relationship."

He raised an eyebrow. "If you say so."

"I'm serious! We're just having some fun, that's all."

"Okay, okay. You can call it whatever you want."

Mel scowled at him.

James took a gulp of his beer. "So, is she as bossy in bed as she is at work?"

"I am *not* discussing that with you," Mel said. She was saved from further questioning by the return of two of her coworkers, Ella and Christine. She didn't know them very well, but they seemed close to James.

"So, how are things going with Ben?" Ella asked James.

"Ben?" Mel said. "You mean that Ben?" She gestured toward the other end of the bar where Ben was standing.

"Yep," Christine said. "They've been flirting for months. We all saw it coming a mile away."

How had Mel never noticed that there was anything going on between them? As the conversation continued around her, the handful of drinks she'd drank began to kick in. And Mel realized that she had been walking around with her head down for a long time now. She looked around. What else had she missed? She barely knew her coworkers. Or had any real friends other than Jess. Was Jess right about Mel shutting everyone out?

"So are you and Ben a couple now?" Mel asked.

"Yes. No." James rubbed his beard. "We haven't talked about it yet."

"James? Are you blushing?" Mel asked.

"No." He crossed his arms.

"See, it's not so fun when you're the one getting interrogated, is it?" Mel said under her breath. Apparently, not quietly enough, because the next thing Mel knew, all the attention was on her.

"What does that mean?" Christine looked at Mel. "Do you have a juicy secret to share, Mel?"

"She sure does." James got up. "Why don't you tell them about it while I go find Ben?" He shot Mel a mischievous look and headed to the bar.

Half an hour and several drinks later, James returned. Ella and Christine had finally left Mel alone after she had given them just enough information about her 'mysterious lover' to sate their curiosity.

"I'm going to kill you, James," Mel said.

"Sorry, Mel." He didn't look the slightest bit apologetic. "Those two are relentless when it comes to gossip. I had to get them off my back."

"You owe me big time."

"That's fair." James sat down across from her.

Mel leaned forward. "You can make it up to me by telling me all about Rose."

"Rose? Did I mention her?"

"You said she was Vanessa's ex. What happened between them?"

James lowered his voice. "It was a while back. I don't remember how they met, or how things started. All I remember was that they were hopelessly in love. You could tell just by looking at them."

"Vanessa? Really?" Mel couldn't imagine Vanessa being overly affectionate like that, especially in public.

"Yep." James was oblivious to the hint of jealousy in Mel's voice.

"Vanessa was a different person back then. And they seemed so happy together. But one day, out of nowhere, something happened between them. And then Vanessa basically disappeared for a few weeks. When she came back, she said that she and Rose were done. And that Rose was on her blacklist, and banned from ever coming to The Lounge, or anywhere near Vanessa."

"Wow. Do you know why they broke up?"

"Nope. She refused to tell anyone what happened. But whatever it was, it changed her. She became a bit more reserved, more serious. And since then, she hasn't let anyone get close to her." He took a swig of his drink. "Except for you."

Mel sat back. The world was starting to spin. She tried to sift through everything James had told her in her head, then gave up. She didn't want to think about any of that right now. Mel just wanted to enjoy herself.

Out of nowhere, Ben appeared at the table.

"Hey, Mel." He held out his hand. "Wanna dance?"

Mel grinned at Ben. "Sure, why not?"

"Whoa, seriously?" James said. "I've been trying to get you to dance this whole time, and Ben asks you once and you say yes? I'm crushed, Mel."

Ben sighed. "Should we take him with us?"

"Probably. Come on." Mel grabbed James's arm and pulled him onto the dance floor.

# CHAPTER FOURTEEN

$\mathcal{M}$el picked up a pillow and squashed it over her head. Her ears were ringing, and her limbs felt like lead. She groaned. Why had she agreed to go out last night after work?

The last thing she remembered was dragging James onto the dance floor. Everything after that was a blur. Mel rarely drank enough to actually get drunk. She didn't want to end up like her mother. But she had really let loose last night.

The ringing continued. It wasn't in her head. She rolled over to her nightstand and picked up her phone. "Hello?"

"Happy birthday, Melanie," Vanessa said.

"Thanks, Vanessa."

"Still recovering from last night?" There was a hint of amusement in her voice.

"Ughhh." Mel sprawled out on her bed. "How do you know about that?"

"James. I woke up to a long and interesting voicemail from him. He's quite talkative when drunk."

"I noticed." Everything that James had told her about Vanessa came flooding back. It was all too much to process right now.

"I take it you haven't checked your email today?" Vanessa asked.

"Not yet. I just woke up."

"Well, you might want to take a look. I have to go, but I'll see you in the evening."

Mel stretched out her arms with a smile. She was actually looking forward to celebrating her birthday with Vanessa. Then she remembered. "I'm supposed to work."

"No, you're not. I asked James to write you into the roster for tonight so you'd keep it free. You don't actually have a shift."

"How long have you been planning this?" Mel's work schedule came out a couple of weeks in advance. Vanessa hadn't asked her about her birthday until a few days ago.

"Oh, for quite some time now."

Mel sat up and dragged her hands through her hair. Perhaps Vanessa's comment about canceling the helicopter ride wasn't a joke. And she should have felt uncomfortable about Vanessa manipulating her schedule. But she was becoming used to being subject to Vanessa's whims. And she hated to admit it, but in this case, it was kind of sweet.

"I'll see you this evening," Vanessa said.

"Sure." Mel hung up the phone and checked the time. *Crap.* It was 11:55. Mel had slept through her alarm. She leapt out of bed. Her email would have to wait.

---

Mel made it to campus with a few minutes to spare. It wasn't until the end of her last class that she remembered to check her email. As she and Jess walked out of the building, Mel took her phone out of her bag and scrolled through her emails. They were mostly junk. Nothing from Vanessa. But she had an email from the Financial Aid Office that had been sent this morning. Had she missed a student loan payment? As she read on, she stopped in her tracks.

"Mel? Is everything okay?" Jess asked.

"Yeah…"

"What is it?"

"My student loans. Someone paid them off. Completely."

"Wow." Jess gaped at her. "Do you think it was Vanessa?"

Mel nodded. It could only be her.

"That's amazing, Mel! Right?"

Mel nodded again. But familiar feelings were brewing inside of her. This was too much. There was no way she could accept this.

"Is it a birthday present? I'm surprised you told her about your birthday."

"I didn't. She figured it out herself. And she has this big evening all planned out, but she won't tell me anything about it." Now that Mel thought about it, Vanessa didn't even tell her where they would meet.

"Sounds like she likes to keep you on your toes…" Jess trailed off, her eyes staring out into the distance.

Mel followed Jess's gaze across the lawn. Vanessa had come to pick her up again. And this time, she was holding an enormous bouquet of yellow and white daffodils. Mel had made an offhand comment about how much she loved daffodils once before. She never expected that Vanessa would remember it.

Mel turned to Jess.

"No. You're not running off this time," Jess said. "I want to meet her."

Mel groaned. She was not prepared for Vanessa and Jess to meet. But Jess didn't care. With a confidence that rivaled Vanessa's, she made a beeline for the parking lot. Mel only just caught up with her before she got to Vanessa.

"Happy birthday, Melanie." Balancing the bouquet in one hand, Vanessa pulled Mel into a long, deep kiss.

Jess coughed quietly to the side. Mel broke off, suddenly conscious of all the students walking past the parking lot.

Vanessa gave Jess a warm smile. "You must be Jess. Melanie has told me all about you."

"Oh, really? Good things I hope?" Jess said.

"Yes, she said you're going to be a formidable lawyer one day."

Mel watched Jess's face turn pink. Apparently, Mel wasn't the only one who Vanessa's charms worked on.

Vanessa turned to Mel and handed her the flowers. "These are for you."

"Thanks. They're beautiful." Mel held them up to her nose and breathed deeply. They smelled as wonderful as they looked.

"So, what do you have planned for Mel's birthday?" Jess asked Vanessa.

"Quite a bit. I'm going to spoil her more than anyone ever has spoiled her before." Vanessa said.

"Well, try to keep her out of trouble," Jess joked.

"I can't make any promises." Vanessa shot Mel a suggestive glance.

Jess smirked, a knowing look on her face.

"Don't you have a bus to catch, Jess?" Mel said. "You know, at the other side of campus?"

"Okay, I get the hint. Have fun tonight." Jess turned back to Vanessa. "It was lovely to meet you."

"The pleasure is mine," Vanessa replied.

Jess giggled. "Bye, *Melanie*. Don't forget about brunch on Sunday. I want to hear all about your evening."

"Okay, bye, Jess," Mel said through gritted teeth. She watched Jess disappear around the corner.

Vanessa walked around the car and opened the passenger side door. "Your friend seems nice."

Mel grumbled wordlessly and sat down.

Vanessa took the flowers from Mel's hands and placed them in the back seat. "Let's get out of here."

---

"Mmmm," Mel set down her fork and leaned back in her chair. "This is delicious."

"Isn't it divine?" Vanessa said. "This is one of the best restaurants in the city. It's very hard to get a table. Luckily, I know the chef."

"You went through all this trouble for me?"

"All I did was call in a favor. It's nothing, really."

"This is *not* nothing."

The small, intimate restaurant was finer than any that Mel had ever been to. From the shiny silver cutlery to the crisp, white table-cloths, everything in the room was pristine and rich. Their dinner, which they were halfway through, ran several courses. And there were no other diners. They had the whole restaurant to themselves.

"And I seem to remember saying 'nothing over the top,'" Mel said. "Is booking out an entire restaurant your idea of low key?"

"Trust me, this isn't over the top," Vanessa replied. "If I had my way, we'd be on a flight to Paris right now."

"You're not even joking, are you?"

"Maybe. Maybe not." Vanessa poured them both another glass of wine, hand-picked by the restaurant's sommelier. The bottle was almost empty already.

"Thank you," Mel said. "For all of this." Mel appreciated being able to spend some one-on-one time with Vanessa that didn't involve Mel getting tied to something. Not that she minded that part. But it was a welcome change of pace.

Vanessa smiled. "Didn't I tell you that you would love it?"

"Yes. You were right."

"Aren't I always?" Vanessa reached across the table and placed her hand on Mel's arm. "See? Sometimes it's worth giving something new a chance."

"I know. It's just hard, you know? To be open to anything new and different after being disappointed so many times." Mel picked up her fork and prodded at her food. "It's silly of me, I know."

"Why do you do that?" Vanessa asked.

"Do what?"

"Dismiss your feelings. Pretend that they aren't important."

"I'm not..." Mel sighed. "It's a habit, I guess. When I was growing up, having any feelings at all was a weakness I could never afford to indulge in. I always felt like I had to be strong all the time because I had no one else I could rely on."

"Where were your parents in all this?" Vanessa asked.

"My dad left when I was young. And my mom didn't like how much I reminded her of my dad. So she basically left me to fend for myself. And she was an alcoholic, so she wasn't exactly reliable. She always found new ways to let me down. And even when she was actually around, she wasn't really present." Mel blinked. She had never told anyone that much about her parents. Not since Kim. And Kim had only used it against her.

"That's awful. I'm sorry. No child deserves to be treated like that."

Mel shrugged. "Well, at the very least it taught me to be independent. And it made me want to escape my dead-end life and make something of myself. It's probably why I'm such a control freak. I've always tried to create a sense of stability to cope with the uncertainty that was around me as a kid."

Vanessa gave Mel a small smile. "We're all products of our upbringing, aren't we? My parents? They had high expectations of me, to the point where they were overbearing and controlling." She took a sip of her wine. "My father was a mechanic and my mother was a nurse. They spent their entire lives working themselves into the ground. They wanted me to have a better life than they did, so they put a lot of pressure on me to succeed."

"That sounds hard."

"It was. As their only child, they put all their hopes and dreams on me. They loved me, but their love was conditional on me being perfect in every way. So I ended up internalizing their attitudes. I told myself that I had to excel at everything I did. And I sought to control those around me like my parents did to me. Which I clearly haven't outgrown. We're all hostages of our pasts."

They sat in comfortable silence as they waited for the next course. It arrived with another bottle of wine. By the time they had finished with everything but dessert, they were halfway through the second bottle.

Suddenly, Mel remembered. "Vanessa. You paid off my student loans?"

"Yes. It was nothing, really. To be honest, I wasn't sure if it would make you happy, or mad. I know how independent you are."

"It bothered me a little at first. But then I realized I was being irrational," Mel said. "Either that, or your lavish gifts are softening me up."

"Really? Because I've been holding back." Vanessa said. "Next time I'll have Elena drop off a new car for you. Or keys to a bigger apartment."

"I don't think so," Mel said, trying to look as resolute as possible.

"Suit yourself."

"I'm going to keep working at The Lounge," Mel said. She didn't need to anymore. Without loans to pay off, her scholarships would cover most of her living expenses.

"I expected as much," Vanessa said. "If it were up to me, you wouldn't have to work another day in your life. I'd look after you in every way."

Mel raised an eyebrow. "What, like some sort of sugar baby?"

"You would never allow that, would you? You should know, you're the first woman who hasn't simply let me do whatever the hell I want with you. Outside the bedroom, that is." Vanessa lowered her voice. "You have no idea how infuriating it is. It only makes me want you even more."

Mel suppressed a smile. Knowing that she drove Vanessa crazy in her own way was extremely satisfying.

"I do respect you for it, though. I respect anyone who values independence. Besides, I think your friends would miss you if you quit working at The Lounge. James in particular." Vanessa smiled. "You made quite an impression last night."

"Oh god." Mel buried her face in her hands. "What was on the voicemail James left you?"

"Quite a lot. Including something about you all getting kicked out of the bar. He was quite drunk, it was very hard to understand him."

Mel groaned.

"He also gave me a bit of a lecture about you. He went on and on about how amazing you are and told me never to hurt you. I think he's taken quite the liking to you."

Mel felt warmth rise up her face. She wasn't sure what to make of James' sudden protectiveness.

"I assured him that I would never do anything to hurt you. You know that, right?"

There was a softness in Vanessa's eyes that Mel had never seen before. "I..."

The chef approached the table. He was carrying a small, elaborately decorated chocolate cake with several candles and sparklers sticking out of it. He gave them both a warm smile as he placed it on the center of the table, then disappeared back into the kitchen.

Mel stared at the extravagant creation. "Did you do this, Vanessa?"

"I assure you, that was all Joseph." Vanessa sighed. "He's the chef. I had to tell him it was your birthday for us to get the restaurant for the night, but I made him promise not to make a fuss." She glanced down at the cake. "He's been known to come out singing, so I suppose this is him being discreet."

"It looks delicious," Mel said.

Vanessa pushed the cake toward Mel. "Happy birthday."

Mel blew out the candles and watched the sparklers burn down. "This is definitely the best birthday I've ever had."

"It's not over yet," Vanessa said in a smooth, low voice. "I still have one last present for you."

"Oh?" Mel smiled. "What kind of present?"

"You'll find out soon enough." Vanessa slid her bare foot up Mel's leg under the table. "Now hurry up and eat your dessert."

# CHAPTER FIFTEEN

"*T*his view is stunning." Mel turned on the spot in the center of the enormous penthouse suite. The glass walls gave a 360-degree view of the city beneath them. The twinkling city lights looked like a reflection of the night sky above. Mel examined the room. There were bottles of champagne in ice on the dining table. Soft fluffy robes hung from hooks on the wall. The huge bed was on a raised platform and looked soft enough to drown in.

"It's breathtaking, isn't it?" Vanessa asked. "I remember how much you enjoyed watching the sunset on that rooftop, so I thought you might like the view here. I called in another favor to get this room. It was worth it, just to see your smile."

*Did Vanessa really rent a penthouse suite because she thought I'd like the view?* Mel suddenly found herself overwhelmed.

"What's the matter?" Vanessa sat Mel down on the couch.

All of Mel's emotions poured out at once. "All this. The loans, the dinner, the hotel. It's too much…"

"No, it's not." Vanessa took Mel's hand. "Why is it so hard for you to accept things from others? Or to let them in? Do you think you don't deserve love and happiness?"

"No. I…" Mel trailed off.

"Melanie. Look at me." Vanessa looked deep into Mel's eyes. "You deserve the world. And you don't have to go through life alone."

Mel searched the depths of her heart. Vanessa was right. Sometimes Mel did feel like she didn't deserve to be happy. It was a side effect of a childhood spent alone and unloved. But she knew it was irrational. Maybe just for one night, she could let go of all her doubts and insecurities and enjoy the moment. "You're right. I'm being silly." Mel smiled. "Thank you, Vanessa. This was the perfect night."

Vanessa kissed her. Mel laid her head on Vanessa's shoulder and they sat in silence, sinking into each other.

After a while, Mel peered up at Vanessa from under her eyelashes. "Didn't you say you have one more present for me?"

"Are you sure you're up for it?"

Mel planted a fiery kiss on a very surprised Vanessa. "Yes. Definitely."

"You're insatiable." Vanessa pushed Mel down onto the couch and pressed her lips against Mel's.

A low rumble rose from Mel's chest. Vanessa's lips tasted faintly of wine.

She pulled Mel up off the couch and guided her to an open space in front of a large mirror on the wall. Vanessa grabbed the hem of Mel's blouse and drew it up over her head, then tugged Mel's skirt down to the floor. Vanessa ran her fingers over the cups of Mel's lacy, purple bra. "These were my first gift to you." A light smile crossed Vanessa's lips. "I love seeing you in things that are mine."

That was the reaction Mel had been hoping for when she had chosen to wear that set of lingerie. Vanessa didn't need to tell her what to wear, or what to do anymore. Mel could anticipate Vanessa's every impulse without her speaking a word. But she still delighted in following Vanessa's orders. And she loved the satisfaction that her obedience gave the other woman.

"As lovely as you look in this, it's in my way," Vanessa said. She stripped Mel's bra from her body. "Stay right there."

Mel watched in the mirror as Vanessa strode over to the table and opened up a large leather bag that was sitting on top of it. She pulled out several coils of thick, red rope. All up, it was enough to truss up Mel's body from head to toe several times over.

Vanessa returned to her side. "Close your eyes for me. Keep them shut until I tell you to open them. And put your hands behind your back."

Mel obeyed. Vanessa folded Mel's arms against her back, one forearm on top of the other. She wound the rope around the length of Mel's arms in a series of loops and knots. Mel wriggled her arms. She couldn't move them at all. Mel was no stranger to restraints by now, but this was a far higher level of immobilization. Her pulse quickened.

"Are you all right, my pet?"

"Yes, Vanessa." Mel's nerves were more out of excitement than anxiety.

Vanessa kissed Mel on the back of her shoulder. "This will take a while. Try to relax. You'll enjoy it more if you do."

As Vanessa wound the ropes around Mel's torso, she focused her senses on everything around her. The pressure of the soft rope on her skin, tight, but not constricting. Vanessa's hands and fingers on her chest and back. Everywhere Vanessa touched left a faint tingling behind. It was almost sensual. By the time Vanessa was done, Mel felt light and serene.

"Open your eyes," Vanessa said.

Mel looked at herself in the mirror. The red rope crisscrossed over her chest and shoulders and around her breasts. Underneath her bound arms, her back was a mirror image of her front. A length of rope dangled from the center of her chest.

"It's shibari. Japanese rope bondage. Some consider it an art," Vanessa said. "You make a perfect canvas."

"It's beautiful." Mel turned to each side, admiring the snug rope harness that Vanessa had created.

"It is. And very hard to master. It can be dangerous if you do it wrong. But do it right, and the possibilities are endless." Vanessa picked up the rope attached to Mel's chest and pulled on it gently. As Mel tipped toward her, she planted a long, lingering kiss on Mel's lips. Using the rope like a leash, she led Mel up to the bed.

Then she pressed her hand into the center of Mel's chest and pushed her backward onto it.

Mel tumbled down onto the bed. She shifted onto her side, taking the weight off her arms, and watched Vanessa pull off her blouse and shimmy out of her skirt. The sight of Vanessa's body, out of reach of Mel's bound hands, made Mel hunger for her even more.

"Close your eyes," Vanessa said. "And don't move."

Once again, Mel closed her eyes and lay there in silence, tied up and waiting for Vanessa. She could hear Vanessa rifling around in the bag again. There was a soft thud as something fell to the table, followed by some sounds that Mel didn't recognize. Just when the temptation to peek became too much, she heard Vanessa's footsteps on the plush carpet coming toward her. Vanessa climbed onto the bed and straddled Mel's body. She felt something hard and cool against her stomach.

"Open your eyes," Vanessa said.

Mel opened her eyes. Vanessa was kneeling over her, naked, her pale red nipples standing up on her ivory breasts. And extending out from between her legs was a smooth, black strap-on.

Before this moment, Mel had never understood the appeal of strap-ons. But seeing Vanessa kneeling above her, the ebony cock contrasting against Vanessa's milky white skin, made Mel throb between her thighs. Nervous anticipation welled up inside her. Somehow, the incongruity between the phallic strap-on and Vanessa's feminine curves made it even hotter.

"Don't worry. I'm going to take it very, very slow. When I'm through with you, you'll be more than ready for me." Vanessa's words sounded more like a threat than reassurance.

Mel lay helpless underneath Vanessa as she made good on her promise. She teased Mel with her fingers, her lips, her entire body. She pressed her breasts against Mel's. She wrapped her mouth around Mel's nipples, and sucked, and licked, and bit. She slid off Mel's panties and slipped her fingers down to where Mel's thighs met.

Mel moaned softly. By now, Vanessa could read Mel's body without her saying a word. She knew what drove Mel wild. She knew what pushed Mel toward the edge. And she knew how to get Mel just close enough to make her tremble and cry out, without sending her over it. With Vanessa's fingers and lips on Mel's breasts and her hand between Mel's legs, Mel was quickly reduced to a whimpering, panting mess.

Finally, Vanessa guided the strap-on between Mel's lips and ran the smooth shaft up and down her slit.

Mel pushed herself up toward Vanessa. She couldn't take any more of this. "Please, Vanessa. Please! I need you inside me."

Vanessa stopped. She flipped Mel onto her back and planted three firm spanks on her ass cheeks.

Mel gasped.

"Did I ask you to beg, my pet?" Vanessa brushed her fingertips along Mel's stinging skin.

"No, Vanessa," Mel bit her lip. Like most of Vanessa's 'discipline,' this only turned her on even more.

"For that, I should leave you here on the bed, panting and help-less. Would you like that?" Vanessa's soft, sweet tone was at odds with her words.

"No, Vanessa."

"I didn't think so. Don't forget that you belong to me. I decide when you're ready."

"Yes, Vanessa."

"You're very lucky that it's your birthday." Vanessa grabbed the shaft of the strap-on, and slid the tip down between Mel's cheeks, all the way to her entrance.

Mel's breathing grew heavier and heavier. Slowly, Vanessa pushed herself inside, filling Mel completely. Vanessa grabbed Mel's hip and began to thrust in and out, rocking the whole bed with her movements. Jolts of pleasure shot through Mel's body as Vanessa pushed against that sweet spot inside. Mel rose back to meet Vanessa, every movement making the rope harness pull and roll and dig into Mel's skin. Over the creaking of the bed, she could hear Vanessa's own muted murmurs.

Vanessa withdrew and rolled Mel onto her back. "Look at me," she said.

Mel looked up into Vanessa's dark, piercing eyes. They were filled with need.

"Don't close your eyes," Vanessa whispered. "I want to stare into them and see the moment when you come undone."

Vanessa sank into Mel again, sending a shockwave through Mel's body from her core. She rolled her hips, pushing and grinding in time with Vanessa's thrusts, her arms straining and aching under her weight. Their movements became more and more frantic, more fevered. All the while, Mel resisted the reflex to shut her eyes.

Mel locked her legs around Vanessa's waist. All it took was a few more thrusts, and she lost control. She closed her eyes as the heat in her core flared hot and bright and ripped through her entire body.

They both collapsed on the bed, breathless, sweaty, and satisfied.

---

Hours later, Mel stood by the window, gazing out at the city skyline. Vanessa was in the shower rinsing off the sweat they had worked up. Mel reached out and touched the glass. This wasn't just some wonderful dream. It was real.

She couldn't have asked for a better birthday. Sure, the extravagance of it all had been novel and exciting. But what made Mel happy was the fact that for the entire day, Vanessa had made her feel special. Cherished.

Loved.

Mel closed her eyes. She wasn't a kid anymore. The days of her being tossed aside and forgotten were long in the past. It didn't bother her. But Mel couldn't deny that it had hardened her. That over time, she had put up all these walls to protect herself.

And Vanessa was tearing them all down.

Mel heard Vanessa's footsteps across the floor behind her. She watched Vanessa's reflection get closer and closer.

Vanessa draped her arms around Mel's shoulders and pulled Mel back into her. "What's on your mind?"

"Nothing." Mel reached up and placed her hands on Vanessa's. "I'm just happy."

"I'm glad. Your happiness means a lot to me."

Mel's heart fluttered at Vanessa's words.

"There are still a few minutes left of your birthday. Do you have any requests? Anything that's in my power to do, I'll do it."

Mel turned around and looked into Vanessa's eyes. "I just want to hold you."

A gentle smile spread across Vanessa's face, and she pulled Mel toward the bed.

# CHAPTER SIXTEEN

*M*el entered the restaurant. She spotted Jess sitting at a table in the corner and made her way over to her friend. Mel had barely sat down before Jess started asking her questions.

"How was your evening with Vanessa?" Jess asked. "Who, by the way, is incredible."

"It was good." Mel looked down at the menu with a smile. "Really good."

"What's that supposed to mean? Did she take you out? Did you stay in? I want details."

"Okay, but I'm going to need coffee first."

"Sure. It's my treat. Consider it a late birthday present."

A waiter came over and took their orders. Mel declined Jess's offer of a mimosa. She'd done enough drinking on her birthday to last the whole month.

Mel recounted the events of the night to Jess, skipping over the more explicit part of the evening. Their meals arrived just as Mel was finishing up. "And the next morning, we stayed in bed talking and watching the sun come up."

Jess said nothing. She had a strange look on her face.

"What? What is it?"

"Well, that all sounds extremely romantic. Are things still 'just physical' between you two?"

"Yes," Mel said. "We agreed from the start that this wasn't going to be a relationship. Neither of us wants that."

"Are you sure? How do you know that Vanessa doesn't want something more? She really seems to care about you. Hell, even the way she looked at you when she came to pick you up the other day seemed like a lot more than just physical attraction."

"I doubt it. We have become a lot closer, but she's still so guarded all the time. Especially when it comes to anything personal." Mel wrapped her hands around her coffee cup. "Whenever we get together, it's always at Vanessa's room in The Lounge, or somewhere else. I've never been to her place. I don't even know where she lives. And she rarely tells me about anything that's going on in her life." Mel recalled those phone calls that Vanessa frequently received that would leave her unsettled.

"You could always, I don't know, talk to her about this stuff," Jess said.

Mel shrugged. "It's not a big deal. I don't want to make something out of nothing."

"If you say so."

Mel attacked her French toast, ignoring Jess's skeptical looks. She hadn't told Jess what really made her feel like Vanessa was holding her at arm's length. When it came to the two of them, Vanessa refused to show the slightest hint of vulnerability. Given the nature of their relationship, it was expected to some extent. And Mel didn't want that to change. She liked being submissive. She liked giving Vanessa all the power. Mel liked belonging to her.

But she wanted something of Vanessa in exchange. She wanted real intimacy. Sure, Vanessa would lavish Mel with affection after a scene. But Mel wanted to touch Vanessa in the heat of things, to feel Vanessa's body react under her fingertips. Mel wanted to hold Vanessa in the height of her own pleasure, at the moment of her release. And Vanessa's release, if only she would permit it. She hadn't since that night at The Lounge that started all this.

Mel put Vanessa out of her mind. "How are things with Brett?"

"We broke up," Jess replied. "I'm seeing Brendon now. We have a date tonight."

"Brendon? The boring guy? Didn't you two break up?"

"Yeah, but we got back together again. He showed up at my place with roses and I just couldn't..." Jess looked off into the distance, a faraway look in her eyes. "I think I'm in love with him."

"That's great, Jess," Mel said. For once, Jess sounded like she actually meant it.

Jess smiled. "Plus, he's not as boring as I thought he was. Turns out he was hiding his kinky side."

Mel shook her head. "I'm glad you've found someone."

"Thanks." She was grinning from ear to ear.

Halfway through brunch, they were interrupted by the chime of Mel's phone. She glanced down at it on the table next to her. It was a message from Vanessa. Mel had been waiting to hear from her all morning.

"Let me guess." Jess said. "Vanessa?"

"Yeah. I'll look at it later." Mel silenced her phone. She didn't want to be rude.

"I knew it. You always get this goofy smile when she messages or calls you. Which seems to be a lot these days."

"It's only because she's been away on business again."

"Oh, so she's checking up on you?"

"It's not like that," Mel said weakly.

"Uh huh. It would save you a lot of trouble if you would just admit that you have feelings for her."

Was Jess right? These days, whenever Mel found herself thinking about Vanessa, it wasn't all the kinky things they did together that played in her mind. It was the little things. The parts of Vanessa that made her, well, her. The faint curve of her lips when she was content. The way Vanessa would sweep Mel's hair out of her face. The way Mel's name rolled off Vanessa's tongue.

The way that despite Mel's best efforts, Vanessa had broken through all her defenses.

Mel sighed. This wasn't supposed to happen. She didn't want to get that close to anyone. The last person she'd given her heart to had used her, and manipulated her, then had tossed her aside like she was nothing. But Vanessa was different, wasn't she?

"Just look at the damn message, Mel," Jess said. "I don't mind."

"Thanks, Jess." Mel grabbed her phone and read Vanessa's message.

"Is everything okay?"

"Yeah. Vanessa just wants to know if I'm free next week Saturday."

"And?" Jess asked.

"Well, usually she just tells me to meet her somewhere or says she's going to come pick me up. She never actually *asks*. And not this far in advance."

"Do you think it means something?"

"I don't know." Mel sent back a message saying that she was free.

The reply came almost immediately. *Good. I'll have Elena send some things over for the occasion.*

Mel frowned. *What's the occasion?*

*You'll find out when the time comes. V.*

Mel put down her phone. Vanessa was up to her usual games.

"Wow," Jess said. "You've really got it bad."

———

Mel stood out in front of her apartment building, her hands on her knees, breathing hard. She hadn't been for a run in weeks. Between school, work, and Vanessa, she barely had the time. And she hadn't felt the compulsion to run in a while. As she caught her breath, she noticed a black Mercedes Benz parked out the front of her building.

Mel bounded up to her apartment, ignoring her body's protests. Was Vanessa back from her trip? When she reached the top of the stairs, she saw, not Vanessa, but Elena standing at her door. Her disappointment was replaced by excitement when she saw what was in the woman's arms. Elena held several boxes, shopping bags, and an opaque garment bag.

"Hello, Melanie," Elena said.

"Hi, Elena," Mel said between breaths. "How long have you been standing there?"

"Not long." Elena stepped aside as Mel unlocked her door. "These are for you. From Ms. Harper."

Was that a smile? It was hard to tell with Elena. "Thanks." Mel took the boxes from Elena and placed them on the table inside, then returned for the bags.

"I will be picking you up on Saturday at 8:00 p.m.," Elena said.

"Okay. Thanks." Why didn't Vanessa just tell Mel herself?

Elena lingered at the door. "There's something else. Here." She reached into her pocket and produced a business card. She handed it to Mel. "If you ever find yourself in trouble or in need of anything, give me a call. I will find a way to help you. I'm more than Ms. Harper's driver. I'm also something like her personal assistant. So I'm very resourceful."

Mel stared at the card. It had Elena's name and number on it. "Did Vanessa ask you to give this to me?"

"No. But part of my job includes anticipating Ms. Harper's needs. This is me doing that."

Mel stared at Elena blankly.

"How do I put this? You're important to Vanessa. So if I can help you in any way, she would want me to do so. That's why I'm giving you my number."

"Okay." Mel still wasn't quite sure what was going on.

"Good. We understand each other." Elena gave Mel a courteous nod. "I will see you on Saturday." She walked off down the hall.

Mel rushed back into her apartment and threw the bags down on the bed. She hung the garment bag on the back of the door and drew the zipper down.

"Wow. *Wow.*" Where the hell was Vanessa taking Mel on Saturday?

# CHAPTER SEVENTEEN

"So Vanessa still hasn't told you anything about where she's taking you?" Jess piled Mel's brown curls on the top of her head. How she'd managed to curl Mel's hair was a mystery.

"Nope." Since receiving Vanessa's cryptic message, Mel had tried to get the information out of Vanessa, with no success. Vanessa had sent her 'gift delivery' early in the week, leaving Mel with plenty of time to mull over things. Was this just another of her games?

"Well, it has to be somewhere pretty fancy if it calls for all this." Jess stuck another hairpin in Mel's hair.

Mel winced. "She didn't actually tell me to do my hair and makeup. But based on the outfit she gave me, I definitely need to glam up. Thanks for helping me out, by the way. I'm hopeless with this stuff."

"No problem. You should let me do this more often." Jess had brought her huge collection of makeup and hair products with her to Mel's apartment.

"Don't get your hopes up," Mel said.

Jess placed another pin. "All done."

Mel stood up and went to look in the mirror.

"No! You have to put the dress on first."

"Ok, fine. Can you give me a hand?"

Mel slipped out of her robe. If Jess noticed the modest but sexy lingerie Mel was wearing—bought by Vanessa of course—she said nothing. Mel stepped into the dress.

"I still can't believe she bought you an Elie Saab gown." Jess said.

"Am I supposed to know who that is?"

"God, Mel, you're so clueless. Do you even know how much this all cost?"

"Nope. And I don't want to." Mel had gotten to the point where she no longer thought about how much money Vanessa was spending on her. She wanted to enjoy Vanessa's gifts. And she couldn't when she was thinking about how expensive they were.

Jess tugged the zipper all the way to the top. "There you go."

"Can I look now?"

"Go ahead." Jess had a big grin on her face.

When Mel looked in the mirror, she barely recognized the woman standing in front of her. Her hair was piled up on her head in a neat tangle of curls. Her eyes were dark and smoky, and her lips were a lustrous pinkish red. Her dress was breathtaking. The chiffon gown flowed down her shoulders all the way to the floor. The delicate fabric rippled and fluttered with every movement. It was a deep shade of blue that Mel adored. And it fit her perfectly.

"Wow." Mel twirled around in front of the mirror, something she hadn't done since she was six.

"You look amazing!" Jess said. "Vanessa is going to lose it when she sees you."

Mel smiled. She had to admit, she looked pretty hot.

"What about the jewelry?"

"Oh, yeah, I almost forgot." Mel sifted through the pile of bags and boxes which her outfit had come in. She found the jewelry box. It held a pair of silver sapphire earrings and a matching bracelet. Vanessa herself was always wearing sapphires. Mel put them on.

"Is that it?" Jess picked up the empty jewelry box, frowning. "No necklace? That's weird."

"That's everything." Mel's outfit seemed fine as it was. But Jess was the fashion expert.

There was a knock on the door.

"Elena must be here already."

"Elena?" Jess asked.

"Vanessa's driver." Mel hurriedly put on the pair of strappy heels that Vanessa had sent her.

"Of course she has her own driver. No sports car this time?"

"Nope. Vanessa said she had to go early, so she sent Elena to pick me up. I'm meeting her there. Wherever there is." It was all very mysterious. Mel finally got into her heels. She looked around for her purse.

"Here." Jess handed Mel the clutch. "I'll pack everything up and get out of here. I have so much studying to do." Jess grinned. "I guess we've switched places, huh? I'm glad you're finally letting yourself have a bit of fun these days."

"Thanks, Jess. Wish me luck," Mel said.

"You don't need it." Jess hugged her. "Vanessa is clearly head over heels for you."

---

Mel looked out the car window. They were almost at the outskirts of the city. She located the button to roll down the privacy screen and pressed it.

Elena glanced back at her in the rear-view mirror. "Yes?"

"Where are you taking me?" Mel asked.

"Sorry, Vanessa told me not to say anything. And I'm sure you know how she is about people following her orders." She winked at Mel in the mirror.

Mel flushed, causing Elena to chuckle. Mel decided to change the subject. "How long have you been Vanessa's driver?"

"Five years or so."

"What's it like? Working for her?"

"I enjoy it. She doesn't work me too hard and pays me very well. In exchange, I'm expected to do things that are well outside of my job description whenever she wants me to. Like picking up her dry cleaning. And tracking down things that she wants. Like I said, I'm basically her assistant. But I don't mind. It keeps things interesting."

"You must know her pretty well by now."

"I do. I knew her before I started working for her. Vanessa and my wife are friends."

They chatted away casually. Elena was a woman of few words, but she asked Mel lots of questions and listened intently to her answers. Eventually, the conversation died down and they drove along in silence.

After a while, Elena looked back at Mel. "You know, Vanessa doesn't usually take anyone to these things."

"What things?" Mel asked. They had been driving for almost an hour now. She was getting restless.

"You're about to find out. Look out your window."

Mel rolled down her window. They were on the grounds of a large modern mansion. The white house overlooked a huge, mani-cured lawn that was dotted with fountains and gardens. As they approached the house, Mel saw that there were groups of people milling around at the entrance. All wore evening gowns and tuxes.

The car stopped at the front of the house. Elena got out and opened the door for Mel, holding out her hand to help Mel out. Mel was grateful. Her heels and floor-length dress weren't easy to move in.

Mel stepped out onto the path and scanned the crowd. *There.* Vanessa was standing near the mansion's entrance, deep in conver-sation with a pair of older women. She looked so beautiful. Like Mel, Vanessa wore a floor-length gown, as black as her hair, which shimmered silver in the light. Silver heels and jewelry topped off the look. Her dark eyeshadow brought out the blue in her eyes, and her lips were a rich, deep red. Her loose hair flowed down her shoulders in waves.

"Melanie." Vanessa broke away and strolled over to Mel. She placed her hands on Mel's waist and kissed her lightly on the lips.

"Vanessa. You look beautiful," Mel said.

"And you look exquisite." Vanessa looked Mel up and down, drinking her in.

"It's all thanks to you." Mel smoothed down her dress. "I love this dress. The color is gorgeous."

"I thought you might like it. But I'm not talking about the dress. I'm talking about you."

Mel's face grew hot. She had done all manner of kinky things with Vanessa, yet a simple compliment from her made Mel blush like a schoolgirl. She looked around. "What's all this?"

"It's my annual charity fundraiser. Well, it's my company's fundraiser. The city's rich have deep pockets. This is a way to use it for good for once."

"Why did you bring me here?"

"Because I want you here. By my side."

Mel's heart swelled in her chest.

"Here. I have something for you." Vanessa held out a flat square jewelry box. "Open it."

Mel opened the box gingerly. Inside was a thin silver choker. It had a round ring hanging from the front of it, nestled between two small sapphires. It was subtle enough that it appeared to be nothing more than a fashionable necklace. But Mel knew what it was. A collar.

"Do you like it?" Vanessa asked.

Mel traced her fingertips over the necklace. "Yes. I love it."

"Turn around. I'll put it on for you." Vanessa fastened the choker around Mel's neck, the brush of her fingertips making the hairs stand up on Mel's skin. She spun Mel back around. "A perfect fit. It suits you."

Mel reached up to touch the necklace. The ring at the front sat perfectly in the hollow at the base of her neck.

"Let's head inside." Vanessa held out her arm for Mel to hold and they walked toward the building.

They attracted quite a few stares on the way in. To a crowd filled with wealthy conservatives, two women together was still scandalous enough to turn heads. Vanessa either didn't notice, or didn't care. Mel couldn't stop touching her necklace.

They stepped through the door. The mansion was just as spectacular on the inside. Mel and Vanessa followed the stream of people into a large, packed ballroom. A band played cool jazz from the front of the room. There was a bar to the side, and a silent auction set up in one corner.

Mel didn't get a chance to gawk. As soon as they entered the room, Vanessa was ambushed by guests wanting to talk to her. Vanessa would introduce Mel, then the conversation would move on to business matters. Vanessa occasionally dropped Mel little bits of information, but mercifully didn't expect her to join the conversation. As Vanessa chatted away, Mel simply stood next to Vanessa, luxuriating in it all. The music, the food, the mansion itself. It was magical.

"I hope you didn't find that too boring." Vanessa had fended off the last of the guests. "Politeness requires that I at least make small talk with most of the guests. There are some very important people here tonight."

"I don't mind. I'm happy just being here." *With you*, Mel almost said.

They wandered over to where the silent auction was set up. Mel scanned the prizes. Each was more extravagant than the last. There wasn't a single item going for less than six figures.

Vanessa picked up a brochure for a holiday on a private island in the middle of the Pacific. "How would you like to come on an island getaway, my pet?"

"Seriously?"

"Yes. It's for a good cause after all." Vanessa scribbled an outrageous number on the clipboard. It was by far the highest bid there, and it had to be at least three times what the trip was worth.

Mel's eyes widened. "Vanessa, I couldn't..."

"You can and you will." She put the clipboard back down. "It's already done. We can go during the summer when you're done with your internship."

Mel was both too dumbfounded and excited to reply.

"Come on. Let's go get some air," Vanessa said.

They wandered out through the double doors and into the garden. For what felt like the hundredth time that night, Mel looked around in awe. There were topiaries cut into elaborate shapes and actual marble statues. As they strolled through the garden, they passed an old, worn mirror hanging from a trellis. Catching a glance of her reflection, Mel stopped to admire her necklace.

Vanessa sidled up behind her, her eyes lit with desire. She wrapped her arms around Mel's shoulders, pulling her in close from behind. "You have no idea how long I've wanted to put a collar around your neck." Vanessa's lips brushed Mel's ear as she whispered.

Mel's heart began to race. Vanessa took Mel's chin in her fingers and tilted it to the side. Mel closed her eyes as Vanessa's lips met hers. Vanessa's hot, hungry kisses still made Mel's whole body weak.

"Vanessa? I thought that was you."

Mel opened her eyes. A slender, androgynous looking woman stood next to them. She had delicate, high cheekbones and short blonde hair, and wore a suit that was perfectly tailored to her modest curves. The young woman possessed an air of cool confidence that Mel immediately knew drove every queer woman she came across wild.

"Vicki," Vanessa said flatly. "It's been so long."

"Good to see you too, Vanessa." Vicki raked her eyes down Mel's body and back up again. "Who's your new toy?"

"This is Melanie, my date." Vanessa's jaw was set. "She's not a toy, Vicki."

"Really?" Vicki looked at Vanessa curiously, then turned back to Mel. "Victoria Blake. But you can call me Vicki."

Mel shook Vicki's outstretched hand.

Vicki's eyes fell to the choker around Mel's neck. "That's a very interesting necklace. Did she buy it for you?" Vicki cocked her head toward Vanessa. There was no doubt that Vicki knew exactly what the necklace was.

"Yes, I did," Vanessa said.

"Relax, Vanessa." Vicki flicked a stray strand of hair out of her face. "I'm not going to steal her from you."

"It wouldn't be the first time. Tell me, are you still preying on every new girl who walks into Lilith's?"

"I can't help it. They're just so eager and obedient. It's too easy."

Vanessa shook her head. "You haven't changed one bit, have you, Vic?"

Vicki smiled. "Why would I want to?"

Mel looked from one woman to the other. Were they enjoying this? Mel was beginning to feel very out of the loop. "How do you two know each other?" She asked.

"Your girlfriend here and I are old friends," Vicki said.

*Friends?* Mel raised an eyebrow.

"We used to walk in a lot of the same circles, so it was unavoidable, really. Since there are relatively few lesbians on the BDSM scene, our paths crossed quite a bit."

"Our 'paths crossed?' More like we clashed. A lot. Vanessa here was the lesbian scene queen until I came along. She didn't like having a rival."

"This rivalry of ours only existed in your head, Vic."

"You only say that because you lost."

"No, I simply had no desire to participate in your childish games."

As Vanessa and Vicki traded barbs, Mel tried to process everything that the two women were both saying and not saying. Vicki's comments made Mel even more aware of the fact that she knew very little about Vanessa's life outside of their interactions together. She had no idea if Vanessa was still as involved in the BDSM scene as Vicki suggested she once was. She did own Lilith's Den, after all. Mel wondered if she knew Vanessa as well as she thought.

And more confusingly, Vanessa had been unusually possessive of Mel the whole night, even more so just now in front of Vicki. Until now, Vanessa's games of possession and control never went beyond the bedroom. Was this something else entirely? Mel hadn't missed the fact that Vanessa had made no attempt to correct Vicki when she referred to Mel as Vanessa's 'girlfriend.' For a moment, Mel allowed herself to wonder what it would be like to actually be Vanessa's girlfriend.

Vanessa's phone rang. She pulled it out of her purse. "It's the caterers. I have to take this. I'll be back in a moment." Vanessa hesitated. She turned to Vicki, placed a hand firmly on the blonde woman's shoulder, and said something to her too quietly for Mel to hear. Then she walked off into the garden.

As soon as Vanessa was out of earshot, Vicki flashed Mel a charming smile. "So, Vanessa has finally found a pet she wants to keep." She ran her fingers through her short hair. "I can see why."

Mel fidgeted with her necklace. She didn't like the way Vicki was looking at her.

"How did you and Vanessa meet?"

"At The Lounge. I work there."

"Oh? You didn't meet at Lilith's Den?"

"No," Mel said.

"Has she taken you to Lilith's before?" Vicki leaned lazily against the wall.

"We've been there," Mel said, not mentioning that they had gone there when it was closed.

"It's been a long time since I've seen her there. I guess that's because of you."

As quickly as it had come about, the sliver of jealousy that Mel had felt began to fade.

But Vicki didn't stop there. "I wasn't kidding about her being the scene queen. There was a time when Vanessa went to Lilith's every single weekend. I wasn't the only one who trawled Lilith's looking for subs." Vicki brushed some invisible dust off her pristine jacket. "But I've said too much already."

Mel frowned. She knew when she was being baited. "What did Vanessa say to you just now?"

Vicki shrugged. "Just that you were off limits and to behave myself. For some reason, Vanessa seems to think that I can't control myself around pretty little submissive things like you." Vicki gave Mel a penetrating look that rivaled Vanessa's.

Mel crossed her arms and stared back at Vicki, her eyes narrowed.

"Relax. It's clear that you've only got eyes for Vanessa," Vicki said.

Mel looked across the garden to where Vanessa stood. She had hung up her phone and was walking toward them.

"That's my cue to leave." Vicki turned to the mirror on the fence and smoothed down her hair. "There's a girl over there who has been checking me out all night. The man whose arm she was hanging off has finally left her alone. I'm going to go see if she needs rescuing." Vicki turned back to Mel and flashed her a charming smile. "I'll see you around, Melanie."

"Bye."

Vanessa reached Mel as Vicki was leaving. She glared at Vicki's back as she walked away. "That woman…"

"Is everything okay?" Mel asked.

"Yes. It was a small catering mishap. What did Vicki say to you?"

"Nothing much. She just asked how we met and talked a bit about Lilith's."

Wrinkles formed on Vanessa's forehead. Was she worried that Vicki had revealed something about Vanessa that she didn't want Mel to know?

"Vicki said that you stopped going to Lilith's?" Mel wasn't exactly sure what she was asking.

"Yes, I suppose it has been a while. I haven't gone there since I met you. I haven't needed to. Come on. There are some people I'd like you to meet."

Vanessa's affectionate smile made Mel forget all about Vicki's comments. She took Vanessa's arm again. They ate, drank and mingled a little more. Vanessa introduced Mel to more of her friends. Mercifully she seemed on better terms with them than Vicki. Eventually, the winners of the silent auction were announced. Vanessa won the island getaway, which wasn't surprising considering how much she bid on it.

The rest of the night passed by uneventfully. After what seemed like hours, the party began to die down. Vanessa and Mel sat down on the chairs at the edge of the room, watching the hall slowly empty.

"That was quite the night, wasn't it?" Vanessa said.

"Yes, it was wonderful." Mel slumped back in her chair. Her feet ached, and she was ready to fall asleep right there.

"Melanie?"

"Yes?"

Silence. Then, "Come home with me."

"Sure."

"I mean it. Not to my room at The Lounge. Home. To my apartment."

Warmth sprung up in Mel's chest. "Okay."

# CHAPTER EIGHTEEN

*M*el and Vanessa walked through the door of Vanessa's top-floor apartment. Vanessa flicked on the light. Mel barely even glanced at her surroundings. She was far too distracted by the woman standing next to her.

After a moment Mel realized that Vanessa was being unusually quiet. "Are you okay, Vanessa?"

"Yes," Vanessa replied. "It's been a while since I brought anyone back here, that's all."

*Since Rose?* Mel wondered.

Vanessa turned to Mel. She had a soft smile on her face which seemed to light up her eyes. And for the first time, Mel felt like she could see into their depths. Vanessa drew Mel toward her and kissed her, softly, slowly. It was just like the first time they had kissed, moments before they were swept up in a whirlwind of lust. But this time, there was no urgency. Just a deep longing that only the other could quell.

Their lips and bodies barely parting, they made their way to the bedroom. With a tenderness that Mel had never seen from her, Vanessa slid Mel's dress from her shoulders and let it fall to the floor.

Before Mel could stop herself, her hands were at the straps of Vanessa's dress. "Please?" Her heart thumped hard in her chest. "I want to touch you."

Vanessa touched a finger to Mel's lips and nodded. "Tonight, you don't have to ask."

Mel unzipped Vanessa's dress and slid it from her body. It joined her own on the floor, a heap of black and blue fabric. The rest of their clothing soon joined it.

They tumbled onto the soft bed in a tangle of limbs. Vanessa's scent, rose, and jasmine, and desire, filled Mel's nose. She dissolved into Vanessa's skin, relishing the feel of the other woman's body against her own. Their hands roamed over each other's curves, and their fingers caressed sensitive places.

Vanessa slid her leg between Mel's thighs, and they ground and rocked against each other. Mel's loud gasps were matched by Vanessa's soft ones. It didn't take long for Mel to come apart in Vanessa's arms.

But Mel wanted more. Of Vanessa. Of them. And Mel wanted Vanessa to feel what she felt.

She ran a questing hand down Vanessa's stomach. The way Vanessa's body quivered at her touch was all the encouragement Mel needed. She slid her fingers down to where Vanessa's thighs met, her light strokes eliciting short, sharp sighs from the other woman. The sound was so sweet to Mel's ears. At the same time, Vanessa's own fingers found their way between Mel's legs. It took all of Mel's will to keep her own hand moving.

Mel closed her eyes. It was refreshing to be freed from their roles, if just for a moment. It wasn't that their roles were an act. They were an innate part of both women's being. But this way, they both got to give and take and everything in between. This way, they both got to let go.

Vanessa began to tremble. Then she arched into Mel, her lips parted in a silent scream. Mel soon followed, descending into an orgasm so heavenly that Mel felt like she left her body.

But they didn't stop. They used every part of themselves to bring each other pleasure. Their mouths, their hands, their skin. Mel lost track of how many times they came. Sometimes separately, sometimes together. The walls between them came tumbling down until Mel didn't know where she ended and where Vanessa began. The entire time, neither of them spoke a single word.

———

Hours later, Mel and Vanessa lay in bed, wrapped in the soft sheets. The sun was coming up. They hadn't slept all night. They had spent hours making love, which was the only way to describe what they'd done. Then they lay in silence, basking in each other's presence.

Mel brought her hand up to her neck. She was still wearing the necklace Vanessa had given her. A gentle smile spread across her face.

"Melanie? What are you thinking about?" Vanessa asked.

"Just how lucky I am," Mel said.

Vanessa trailed her finger over the curve of Mel's hip. "And here I was thinking the same thing."

Mel couldn't keep her doubt from showing in her eyes.

"You really don't see it, do you?" Vanessa reached out and stroked Mel's hair. "I've been under your spell since that night I took you into my room at The Lounge. When you sat down on my couch, indignant that I'd helped you. I was telling the truth when I said I believed you could have handled it yourself. But I wanted to rescue you. I barely knew you, but I wanted to be the one to save you from hurt."

Mel's heart fluttered.

"All these things I do, all the lengths I go to. It's all to please you." She pushed Mel's hair behind her ear. Her hand lingered on Mel's cheek. "You have far more power over me than you know. I'm yours as much as you are mine."

Mel's breath caught in her chest. Vanessa looked like she wanted to say more.

But the moment passed in silence.

"I'm going to take a bath." Vanessa climbed out from underneath the covers. "Join me?"

"In a minute. I need a glass of water."

"Okay. Help yourself to anything in the kitchen." Vanessa hopped out of the bed and walked off to the bathroom.

Mel lay there for a moment, face down on the bed. Unlike Vanessa's bed above The Lounge, this one was soft and inviting. And the sheets, and the pillows—they all smelled like her. Mel pulled the covers in closer to her. It was just like being in Vanessa's arms.

Mel sighed. Vanessa was waiting for her. She got up out of bed and walked out into the open living area.

Once again, Mel was in awe. It had been dark when she'd arrived last night, and she had been preoccupied. Now, she saw that the enormous apartment was even more impressive in the daylight. It was decorated similarly to Vanessa's room above The Lounge. Here, however, there were touches of warmth. The floorboards were covered in soft rugs. A recliner sat in the corner, a blanket thrown over one of its arms. A well-read paperback sat on the table next to it.

Mel headed to the kitchen and grabbed a glass of water. She decided to take a look around as she drank. She couldn't help herself. This was Vanessa's sanctuary. Mel wanted to find out what it revealed about the woman who for so long had been a mystery to her.

Mel wandered through the apartment, peeking through doorways and marveling at the rooms. An office with floor-to-ceiling shelves filled with books. Another bathroom that was even bigger than the master bath. Several more bedrooms. Most of the doors were thrown open, inviting Mel in to discover their secrets. Mel learned that Vanessa enjoyed classic literature and that she had a large collection of abstract art.

Finally, Mel came to one last door. Unlike the others, it was closed. It had a heavy deadbolt above the door handle. Mel stared at it. What could be in that room that Vanessa wanted to keep hidden away? She reached out to test the doorknob.

*No.* Mel pulled her hand back. She shouldn't have been snooping in the first place. She wasn't about to try to get into a room that practically screamed 'keep out.' Especially considering that Vanessa was apprehensive about bringing anyone back to her home. Some doors were better left unopened.

Mel made her way to the bathroom. Vanessa was waiting for her in a tub full of fragrant, foamy water. Her damp hair clung to her head, and her skin was glistening wet.

Vanessa beckoned Mel in with a finger. She slipped into the bath in front of Vanessa and leaned back against her. Mel closed her eyes as Vanessa's arms enveloped her.

# CHAPTER NINETEEN

"Hey, Mel. Coming to drinks tonight?" James asked as he passed her.

"Sure." Mel had earned a night off. And it would be her last chance with final exams on the way. Then she'd have to really buckle down.

"Great. By the way, has Ben come in yet?"

"Yep, he's out back."

"Thanks. Do you mind watching the bar for a couple of minutes?"

Mel smiled. "No problem."

James and Ben were now officially a couple, and it was clear from watching them that they were madly in love. They tried their hardest to act professionally at work. But they couldn't help but show their affection for each other. Stolen glances, gentle touches, whispered words. And they lit up in each other's presence.

Did Mel want something like that with Vanessa? The night of the fundraiser had been so perfect. During the week that followed, they'd spent every other night together. What had happened that first night at Vanessa's apartment never happened again. They had gone back to their regular dynamic. But now, everything seemed so much more intimate. So much sweeter.

Mel fingered the choker around her neck. Vanessa was away for business. And Mel was surprised by how much she missed her. They talked almost every day. And at the end of every phone call, there was a silence filled with words unspoken.

Mel sighed. She hadn't intended for this to happen. And she still wasn't ready to admit what 'this' was. Her old doubts still played in her mind.

"Hi there." A short, curvy brunette leaned down over the bar, her crossed arms framing her generous chest. "I'll have a margarita."

"Coming right up." Mel set about making the drink.

"So." The woman twirled a lock of her hair around her finger. "Does your Master ever let you come out and play?"

Heat rose up Mel's face. This wasn't the first time someone had recognized her necklace for what it was. It didn't surprise her, considering what Vanessa had said about the clientele at The Lounge and Lilith's overlapping. The sly smiles, and subtle nods. They weren't suggestive in any way. They were more a respectful acknowledgment that they both belonged to the same secret club.

But this woman clearly had other motives.

"I don't 'play' with anyone." Mel handed the woman her drink. "And I don't have a Master."

"A Mistress then?" The woman asked.

Mel wiped down the bar in front of her, ignoring her question.

"Wait. Don't tell me. You're one of Vanessa's?"

Mel froze. "Uh, yeah." How did she know? And what did she mean by 'one of?'

"Typical. She always liked recruiting subs at the places she owns."

Mel blinked, then continued wiping down the bar in front of her. She didn't know who this woman was, and she didn't care.

"What, did you think you were special? You're just the latest on a long list of names. I bet Vanessa doesn't even remember half of them. She just uses girls like you until she gets bored and moves on to the next one."

Mel stopped. "What are you talking about? Who are you?"

"I'm Rose. Vanessa and I? We have a long history."

This was Rose? She wasn't what Mel expected. She was older than Vanessa. And Mel couldn't imagine her as a submissive. Everything about her seemed predatory.

But none of that mattered. She was banned from the club.

"You shouldn't be here," Mel said.

"Oh? So you have heard of me? Did Vanessa tell you what happened between us?"

Mel didn't respond. But she didn't call security either.

"She hasn't told you? I'm not surprised, considering what she did to me." The woman took a sip of her drink, never taking her eyes off Mel. "I was just one of her submissives at first. It was nothing serious. But then Vanessa decided that she wanted me all to herself permanently. She even gave me a pretty collar, just like yours. We were together for two years. We were happy. We were in love. At least I thought we were."

Mel waited for Rose to continue. She seemed to have a flair for the dramatic. Which made Mel wonder if she should believe a word that she said.

"But one day, something bad happened to me. Something traumatic. And Vanessa? She couldn't handle it. Or didn't want to." Rose lowered her eyes, her voice cracking. "So she ran. She disappeared. She cut me out of her life like I meant nothing to her."

Mel felt a gnawing in her stomach. Rose's story matched up with what James had told Mel.

"Vanessa abandoned me when I needed her the most. When I was hurting and broken." Rose looked into Mel's eyes. "You know what this kind of relationship does to you. Giving yourself to someone, mind, body, and heart. Trusting them with your entire being. It leaves you fragile and vulnerable. And for Vanessa to take advantage of that, to rip me open and take me apart time and time again, only to leave me to deal with the aftermath all by myself. It was heartless."

Mel spoke up for the first time during Rose's story. "Vanessa would never do that."

"That's what I thought too, until she left me. I don't think she ever loved me, really." Rose's eyes were filled with pain. "She showered me with gifts and said sweet things to me so that I would be her perfect little submissive and satisfy her interminable need for control. She gave me just enough attention so that I felt like she cared about me. But she never really gave me any of herself."

Mel's stomach lurched. Hadn't she had that same thought a million times before?

"She's doing the same to you, isn't she?"

Mel didn't respond.

"Have you ever been to her apartment?"

Mel nodded without thinking.

"That's further than most of the others then. How about her playroom? Has she shown it to you yet?"

Her playroom? Was that what was behind that locked door in her apartment? Mel had been back to Vanessa's apartment a handful of times since the night of the party, and the door had always been shut. Her surprise must have shown on her face.

"Didn't think so. Guess you're not that special to her after all," Rose said.

The sudden edge in Rose's voice shook some sense into Mel. "You need to leave. Now."

"I'll be out of your hair in a second. I just thought that I should warn you." Rose downed the last of her drink. "Vanessa ditched me at the first sign of trouble. And she'll do the same to you."

"Rose?" James's voice rang out from behind Mel. "What the fuck?"

Rose put down her glass, shot Mel a cheeky smile, and disappeared into the crowd.

"Dammit!"

Mel watched James chase after Rose. Was everything that Rose said true? Vanessa never spoke about her exes or her past in general. Was it because she had something to hide?

Was Mel just the latest of Vanessa's disposable subs? She thought back to her encounter with Vicki at the charity fundraiser. Vanessa had been reluctant to leave Mel alone with Vicki. Was it because she feared Vicki would expose her? Mel remembered Vicki's words.

*Vanessa has finally found a pet she wants to keep.*

James returned to the bar, his fists clenched at his sides. "I don't know how Rose got past security, but she's gone now. Did she give you any trouble, Mel?"

"No," Mel said. "She just ordered a drink."

"Goddammit. This is the second time that she's gotten in here recently. Vanessa will be pissed."

"Is she really that touchy about Rose?" Mel asked.

"Let me put it this way. Last time Rose got in here, I had to talk Vanessa out of firing the entire security staff. Now I regret not letting her."

Did Vanessa's hostility toward Rose stem from guilt?

"I'm going to have to tell Vanessa about this." James pinched the bridge of his nose. "Look, do you think you could not say anything to Vanessa until I've talked to her? I know you two are close, but I think she should hear it from me since it happened under my watch. I'll call her as soon as she gets back from her business trip."

"Sure." Mel didn't feel good about keeping something from Vanessa. But if Mel told Vanessa that she had met Rose, Vanessa would want to know what Rose had said to her. And Mel wasn't prepared to talk to Vanessa about that. Not until she'd had a chance to process it all.

"Thanks, Mel. I won't mention to Vanessa that Rose spoke to you, I'll leave that to you. I don't want to get in the middle of anything. Just let me talk to her first."

"Okay."

"Thanks, Mel. I'm sorry for putting you in this position." James sighed. "I'm going to go have a chat with security."

Mel watched James disappear into the crowd, a sinking feeling in her stomach. Surely Rose's words were just the angry rantings of a jilted ex?

But Mel couldn't help but think about how everything that Rose said sounded all too familiar.

# CHAPTER TWENTY

*I*t had been a month or so into Mel's freshman year. She was at the top of the world. She'd finally left her old life behind. She'd had lots of new experiences. Living in a dorm, going to wild parties, finding friends who she actually fit in with. No one cared that she was gay here. And she wasn't the only one. She'd had her first of many kisses. One of which led to several other firsts, most of them involving the girl in the bed next to her.

Mel turned her head to look at Kim. Her blonde locks were in disarray, and her eyes were closed. She had a satisfied smile on her face. Mel watched Kim's chest rise and fall under the covers.

Kim was Mel's roommate. Over the past few weeks, they had become exceptionally close. And an alcohol-fueled hookup one night had led to them falling into bed with each other over and over again. Mel was infatuated with her.

The problem? Kim was straight as an arrow. At least, that was what Kim said.

Mel sighed. "We can't keep doing this, Kim."

"Why not?" Kim asked, her eyes still closed. "I'm having fun. Aren't you?"

"Well, yeah." The last few weeks had been incredible. But it wasn't because of the sex. It was the little things. The quiet moments that Mel had shared with Kim. Having Netflix marathons in their PJs that lasted until the early hours of the morning. Cuddling in bed and sharing secrets under the covers. Waking up to a gentle kiss from Kim.

"Then what's the problem?" Kim burrowed in close to Mel and pulled the sheet up over them both.

"What is it that we're doing? Do you even like girls?"

Kim shrugged. "I don't know. Does it matter?"

"It does to me," Mel said. "I like you, Kim. A lot."

"Look." Kim looked up at Mel with her big, pale eyes. "I don't know if I like girls, but I do know that I like you. Isn't that what's important?"

"I guess. But is this ever going to go anywhere?"

Kim kissed Mel on the lips. "We don't have to worry about any of that right now. We're young, Mel. This is college. Let's just enjoy ourselves."

Before Mel could respond, Kim pushed her shoulders down onto the bed and straddled her body, leaning down to kiss her again. And within moments, Mel's complaints were forgotten.

---

Kim woke Mel up with a soft kiss. "Good morning, beautiful."

"Morning," Mel grumbled, still half asleep.

"Aww, did I wake you? Let me make it up to you." Kim slipped her hand into the bottom of Mel's shirt.

Mel's eyes flew open. "No, Kim. Stop." Mel pushed her away.

"Jeez, what's the matter with you?"

Mel sighed. "I've told you, I don't want to keep doing this."

"That's not what you said last night."

"Last night was a mistake."

Kim pouted at her.

"I'm serious, Kim. I don't want to be your fuck buddy. I want a girlfriend."

"Ugh, that again." Kim rolled her eyes. "Why are you always going on about this, Mel?"

"Because it's important to me."

"But why? What's wrong with the way things are now?"

"Nothing. Nothing has to change, Kim! All I want is for you to acknowledge what this is. Look at us! We're basically a couple already."

Kim didn't deny it. "If you don't want anything to change, then what's the problem?"

Mel wanted to scream. Kim always seemed to miss the point. Or simply refused to see it. "The problem is that I'm falling in love with you, Kim!" There. She said it. "I can't fall in love with someone when they don't even like me enough to want to be my girlfriend! And you can't tell me that you don't have feelings for me too." Mel's confidence was feigned. She wasn't actually sure if Kim shared her feelings. But she hoped that she was right.

"Look, I really like you, Mel. I care about you. And I want to be with you. Isn't that enough? Aren't I enough for you?"

"Kim..."

"If you really cared about me, then something as stupid as a label wouldn't matter."

*No.* Mel wasn't going to let Kim turn this on her again. Mel steeled herself. "I can't do this anymore, Kim. I'm sorry, but I can't be with you without really *being* with you." Mel got up. "I'll go see the RA tomorrow about moving to a different room."

"Wait, don't leave."

Kim's voice tugged at Mel's heartstrings. She almost lost her resolve. But Mel had caved to her too many times before. She opened the door and left the room.

Mel was sitting in the common room a few hours later when the text came. *Will you be my girlfriend?*

---

Kim rolled over onto her side and faced the wall. Mel's stomach sank. Kim was in one of those moods again. This seemed to happen more and more these days.

"Is everything okay, Kim?" Mel asked.

"I'm fine." Kim curled up into a ball. "God, why are you always asking me that?"

"Because you don't seem fine. And you're shutting me out again."

"I'm not shutting you out. You're just too suffocating. God, why are you so needy all the time?"

"I'm not-" Mel sighed. "It's just that, you say you love me, but you don't act like it. Sometimes it's like you're only using me for sex. Which doesn't even make sense since the way that you act after we have sex makes me think you hate it. And you hate me." Mel's voice quavered.

"How can you even say that? I'm the only person who has ever stuck by you, who has ever loved you, and this is how you repay me? After everything that I've done for you? I agreed to be your girlfriend just for you, for god's sakes."

"You won't even let me tell anyone that you're my girlfriend. We've been together for six months! And our friends don't even know about us," Mel said.

"We've talked about this. You know how my parents are. If they find out, they'll disown me! Or worse. Is that what you want?"

"No, but-" Mel took a deep breath. "I'm tired of this, Kim. I'm tired of all the fighting. I'm tired of you lashing out at me. I'm tired of all the guilt trips."

"Me? You're the one who's always trying to make me feel guilty. You're the one who's saying that I don't love you. How do you think that makes me feel? I'll never be enough for you, Mel."

"Is it really asking that much to have my girlfriend tell me she loves me once in a while? Or god forbid, show me some affection? I have needs too, you know."

"You want me to tell you that I love you every minute of the day and dote on you all the time? I'm not your mother, Mel. It's not my problem that she never did all those things." Kim scoffed. "And these 'needs' of yours? You mean all that perverted shit you're into? It doesn't take a shrink to figure out why you're so messed up."

Mel winced. This wasn't the first time Kim had used things that Mel told Kim in confidence against her. "That has nothing to do with this!" She threw her arms up in the air. "This is pointless. I'm not putting up with this anymore." Mel turned to leave.

"If you walk out that door, it's over. You'll never be able to find anyone who loves you like I do."

Kim's words hit Mel hard. But she held firm. Mel stormed out the door and slammed it behind her.

She spent the next few days avoiding Kim. Which meant going back to their dorm room as little as possible. When they did run into each other, Kim simply pretended that Mel wasn't there. That was fine with Mel. She wasn't surprised by Kim's behavior. Kim probably thought it was only a matter of time until Mel came crawling back. But as far as Mel was concerned, it was over between them for good.

One night, she came back to her dorm after spending most of the day in the library. She hoped that Kim was asleep since it was so late. But when she opened the door, Kim was sitting on Mel's bed. Her eyes were red and her cheeks were wet with tears.

"I'm sorry Mel," Kim said, her voice cracking. "I didn't mean those things I said."

Mel stood rooted in the doorway. "Kim, I-"

"I need you, Mel!" Kim began to sob. "You're not going to leave me, are you? I can't live without you."

As Mel looked into Kim's pleading eyes, her resolve shattered. "Kim." Mel sat down on the bed next to her girlfriend. "I'll stay. But things have to change. We can't go on like this forever."

"I'll do better, I promise." Kim buried her face in Mel's chest. "I love you, Mel."

"I love you too." Mel hugged her tight.

---

Mel watched Kim pack the last of her things. Summer was finally here. Everyone was looking forward to it, except for Mel. She was anxious about being away from Kim, especially considering how strained things had been between them for the past few days.

Kim cleared everything from the top of her desk and dumped it into a box with a loud thud.

"Is everything okay, Kim?"

"Yes," she snapped.

They sat in silence as Kim packed the last of her things. Mel had felt like she was walking on eggshells all week. Was Kim upset about going home to her overbearing, conservative family? Or had Mel said or done something to set her off?

"So you're still coming to visit over the summer, right?" Mel asked. Mel wasn't looking forward to going 'home.' Kim's visit was the only thing she had to look forward to.

"Yeah, about that…" Kim sat down on the bed a few feet away from Mel. "I don't think we should do this anymore. We've let things go far enough."

"What? What do you mean?"

"You know, *this*. It was fun while it lasted, but it's run its course."

Mel at Kim blankly.

"Come on, Mel. This was never serious. You had to know that."

Mel's stomach dropped. She knew where Kim was going, but she refused to believe it.

"Of course you didn't." Kim rolled her eyes. "You only saw what you wanted to see. Think about it."

Was she right? Mel thought about all the times Kim had been hot and cold. How she'd pushed Mel away over and over. How she seemed to only care about sex. Had Mel had ignored all the signs because she was in love with Kim? "No." Mel finally spoke. "No. You told me you loved me a hundred times. You can't tell me that wasn't real."

"I only told you that to get you off my back. Hell, I only agreed to be your girlfriend so you'd stop bothering me about it. It was just so hard to say no to you when you were always so sad and needy all the time. I didn't feel like I had a choice."

5

"Are you saying you were with me out of pity?"

"Don't look at me like that, Mel. Like I said, it's college. I wanted to experiment. Everyone does this. But I'm not actually into girls. Not that way. You'll probably grow out of it too."

"You're wrong, Kim. This isn't a phase for me. I like girls. I always have. And I love you!"

"Maybe you really do love me. But I never loved you. You knew that. You even said it to me yourself."

*No.* Could it be true? Had their entire relationship been a lie?

"I'm really sorry, Mel…"

Kim's words all hit Mel at once. She started to cry. Kim was the first girl she'd ever loved. And now, like everyone else in Mel's life, Kim was throwing her away like she meant nothing.

"I gotta go, my ride is leaving soon. I'll see you around, okay?" Kim got up from the bed and left Mel sobbing in their empty dorm room.

# CHAPTER TWENTY-ONE

*M*el sat next to Vanessa in the back seat of Vanessa's Mercedes. As soon as she'd returned from her trip, Vanessa had taken Mel to dinner at one of the restaurants she owned. Now, they were on their way to Lilith's Den, for the first time since that night so long ago.

Butterflies filled Mel's stomach. She was excited. But at the same time, she felt a sense of unease. Since Mel's conversation with Rose, the woman's words had played over and over in her head. The time and distance from Vanessa had only made her insecurities fester.

"Are you all right, my pet?" Vanessa asked.

"I'm fine," Mel said. The way Vanessa called her 'my pet' rankled her now.

Vanessa's phone rang. Mel tensed. Was it James calling to tell Vanessa about Rose? Mel had kept her word to him and hadn't said anything about it to Vanessa. Had James called to tell her already? Even if he had, Mel doubted that Vanessa would mention it to her.

Vanessa looked at her phone. She silenced it and shoved it back in her purse. It definitely wasn't James. Vanessa always picked up his calls. It had to be another of those mysterious phone calls that Vanessa always ignored. It was happening a lot lately. And they seemed to get to her even more. At times Mel would find Vanessa gazing off into the distance, her forehead lined with concern. Like right now.

"Is everything okay?" Mel asked.

"Yes." Vanessa snapped out of her trance. "Everything is fine."

"Are you sure? You seem worried."

"Yes. I'm fine." Vanessa's lips were pressed together in a straight line.

Mel wasn't surprised. Vanessa never confided in her in the past. Why would things be any different now?

Vanessa turned to Mel. Her worried expression had been replaced by a hungry look. "I have quite the night planned for us." She slid a hand along Mel's thigh.

Vanessa hadn't told Mel what this elaborate scene she had planned involved. Keeping Mel in the dark was all part of Vanessa's game. And Mel couldn't deny how much the suspense thrilled her.

But Mel couldn't help but notice the timing of Vanessa's shift in mood. Did Vanessa only need Mel to satisfy her need for control? Mel could think of someone else who only needed her for sex. Kim.

Mel pushed the thought out of her mind. Kim had been abusive. Mel knew that now. And Vanessa definitely wasn't. But Vanessa had said from the start that she wasn't looking for a relationship. Neither was Mel at the time. But as they'd gotten closer, Mel had found herself wanting more. And Mel thought Vanessa did too. What if she was wrong? What if she really was just a toy to Vanessa?

They pulled up out the front of Lilith's. Once they were inside, Vanessa took Mel up to The Scarlet Room. She gave her usual spiel about safe words and trust, and they went inside.

The room looked the same as the last time. But now, there was a high-backed wooden chair in the middle of the room. A small table sat next to it, with a black leather bag on top. Mel recognized the bag. It was the same bag of toys that Vanessa had taken to the hotel room on Mel's birthday.

"Take a seat." Vanessa gestured toward the chair.

Mel sat down. Vanessa pulled a long piece of black cloth out of the bag. Within seconds, it was around Mel's eyes. Vanessa drew the

BEING HERS

back of her fingers down Mel's cheek. Mel could feel Vanessa's breath and the heat of Vanessa's face, just inches from her own. Her lips parted. Vanessa brushed them with her fingertips, then pulled away.

So it was to be a night of mind games designed to drive Mel into a state of frustration. It was working—but not the way Vanessa intended.

Vanessa traced a finger down to the collar around Mel's neck. "You're all mine tonight. What should I do with you?" Vanessa rifled around in the bag, then dropped something onto the table with a metallic clink. "First, I'm going to make sure you can't escape from that chair. But what then?" Vanessa reached into the bag again.

A buzzing filled the air. A vibrator? Vanessa drew it down Mel's thigh, sending vibrations through her. Mel's hairs stood up on her skin.

"I could torture you with pleasure until you begged for mercy. Or—" Vanessa brushed something along Mel's arm "—I could punish you with this."

Was it a flogger? Mel liked the sound of that. She wanted something physical. Something visceral. Something to drown out everything else she was feeling. She knew it was wrong. But she didn't stop Vanessa. She wanted to feel the rush to take her mind off everything.

"Is that what you want?" Vanessa trailed the flogger along her thigh.

"Yes," Mel replied.

"'Yes?' Yes, who?"

"Yes, Vanessa."

Silence filled the room. Neither of them moved.

"No." Vanessa pulled the blindfold from Mel's eyes.

Mel squinted in the light. "I didn't say to stop."

"I don't care."

Mel let out a frustrated groan.

"Velvet," Vanessa said.

Mel froze. She had never once used her safe word. But it had been drummed into her head that it meant that everything stopped.

She sighed. She knew that Vanessa had been right to end things. This all felt so wrong.

Vanessa went over to the bed and sat down. "Come. Sit."

Mel obeyed. Tension hung in the air. And now, it wasn't just coming from Mel.

"Melanie." Vanessa's voice shook. "What the hell is going on?"

"Nothing." Vanessa wasn't the only one who got to refuse to share her feelings.

"Fine. If you don't want to talk, then you're going to listen. Because this? Whatever it was that you just pulled? It's unacceptable."

"Unacceptable? I'm not a child, Vanessa," Mel snapped. "Don't speak to me like one."

"Are you sure? Because you're behaving like a child right now."

Mel knew Vanessa was right. But she remained silent.

"Christ, Melanie!" Vanessa got up and started pacing next to the bed. "This isn't a game! You know better than to come in here like this. Angry. Reckless. Do you have any idea how dangerous all of this is? Especially if you're in the wrong state of mind?"

All the feelings that had been festering inside of Mel began to boil over. "You're the one who's always using this as an outlet for dealing with your own goddamn problems, whatever they are. Do you think I haven't noticed that every time you get upset, you assert your dominance over me in order to feel better?"

Vanessa's face turned red. "That's different, Melanie, and you know it. I'm in control of myself at all times. Right now? You're clearly not. And that makes people do stupid things. Like push themselves harder than they should. Like ignore their limits. That's how accidents happen, Melanie. That's how people get hurt."

Mel felt a pang of guilt.

"And you do not pull this shit on me. Do you have any idea the position you're putting me in? I was about to cuff you to a chair for god's sake. I had a whip in my hands, Melanie. Do you have any idea how easy it is for me to hurt you if we're not careful?" Vanessa's voice shook. "Do you have any idea what it's like to live with that sort of guilt?"

"I just-"

"Just what, Melanie? What could possibly make you behave this way?" Vanessa crossed her arms. "Well? Tell me."

"Is that an order, or do I have a choice?"

Vanessa's eyes filled with hurt. "When have I ever made you feel like you don't have a choice?" Vanessa sat down. "Melanie. Talk to me. What's the matter?"

Mel spat out the first thing that came into her head. "Those phone calls you keep getting. Why won't you tell me what they're about? Why are you so touchy about them?"

"What? That has nothing to do with you." She looked at Mel with narrowed eyes. "What's this really about?"

"You're always keeping me at arm's length. You never let me in. And you expect me to become vulnerable to you time and time again, but you never give me any of yourself." Mel couldn't stop her thoughts from spilling out. "You're always going on and on about trust. Do you even trust me?"

"Melanie-"

"Or is this all just a game? Do I mean nothing to you?"

"What makes you think that? Where is this coming from?"

"Do you care about me at all? Or am I just some toy, like Vicki said? Something for you to use up and throw away? Just like all the others?"

The color drained from Vanessa's face.

"Just like Rose?"

Vanessa recoiled.

And Mel knew that she had gone too far.

"Get out," Vanessa said coldly. "Now."

Mel ran out of the room, slamming the door shut behind her. Somehow, she found herself out on the street. Elena was waiting outside for both of them. Mel streaked past her, her eyes full of tears, ignoring Elena's yells.

When Mel got home, she took off the necklace that Vanessa gave her and tossed it deep into the bottom drawer of her dresser.

# CHAPTER TWENTY-TWO

*M*el stood by the bar at The Lounge. It had been two weeks since that fight with Vanessa. Two weeks, and Mel hadn't heard a thing from her. That was long enough for Mel to know that things between the two of them were damaged beyond repair.

Mel didn't even want to repair them. Not after the way Vanessa had treated her. Mel knew she wasn't innocent in all of this. But Vanessa? She had kicked Mel to the curb, then had disappeared. After three days, Mel's regret overwhelmed her. She'd pushed her pride aside and called Vanessa, fully prepared to apologize and talk things out. But it rang and rang until it went to voicemail. Mel didn't try to contact her again. If Vanessa wanted to talk to her, she would. But she didn't even try.

Mel should have known that it was all too good to be true. She was done. She'd gotten this far in life on her own. She didn't need anyone else.

"That's it," James said. "I can't stay out of this any longer."

Mel crossed her arms. "Do you really have to do this, James?" Mel knew that James didn't deserve her ire. But she didn't care.

"Yes. We do." He threw his arms up in the air. "What the hell happened between you and Vanessa, Mel? You've been moping around here like a piece of you died. And I haven't seen Vanessa like this since, well, Rose."

So James had seen Vanessa. That meant that Vanessa hadn't completely disappeared. She was just avoiding Mel.

"Look, I know that you two had a fight. But have you even talked about whatever it is that happened?"

Mel shrugged.

"Wait. Don't tell me that Rose caused this. Did something happen the day that she came in?" James took Mel's silence as confirmation. "Look, I still don't know what happened between Rose and Vanessa, but I pieced together enough to know that you can't trust her. Especially when it comes to Vanessa."

"It wasn't Rose." It wasn't only Rose. Vicki had said the same thing. And Vanessa hadn't denied any of it.

James let out a frustrated groan. "Don't you see it, Mel? You're both exactly the same. Too stubborn to say what you're really feeling. Afraid of getting your heart broken. Just talk to her, Mel. I'm sure you can work things out."

"It's over between us, okay, James?" Mel yelled. "I don't want to work things out. I don't want to talk to her. I don't want to see her ever again!"

"Looks like you don't have a choice." He was looking over Mel's shoulder.

Mel turned. Vanessa was walking toward them. Mel sighed.

"Talk to her, Mel. Your shift is almost over, anyway. Go." James walked off into the back.

Vanessa reached the bar. "Hi," Vanessa said. "Can we talk?"

"There's nothing to talk about." Mel turned away and began tidying up behind the bar.

"I need to tell you the truth, Melanie. About everything. About Rose."

Mel hesitated.

"Please, Melanie."

Mel balled her fists. She had never been able to resist Vanessa's pleas. "Fine."

141

A few minutes later, they were seated at a booth at the quieter end of the club. A generous glass of whiskey sat before each of them. Vanessa had insisted on it. Mel was begrudgingly grateful.

Vanessa took a long drink. She placed her glass down on the table. "I'm so sorry, Melanie. For the way that I treated you that night. For disappearing." She paused. "I'm sorry. I'm...not very good at this. This is hard."

"This is hard? For you?" Mel's voice cracked. "It's been two weeks, Vanessa. Two fucking weeks since you yelled at me and told me to leave. And then nothing!"

"I know. I'm sorry."

"I tried to call you." Hot tears formed in the corners of Mel's eyes.

"I know. I'm so sorry, Melanie. I was in a bad place and..." Vanessa closed her eyes for a moment. "I can explain. Or at least, I can try to."

Mel crossed her arms. Nothing that Vanessa could say would make her change her mind.

"James told me that Rose came in here. He omitted the fact that she'd spoken to you until I pressed him. You never said anything." She looked into Mel's eyes searchingly, but Mel's face was stone. "It was no coincidence that Rose came in here and spoke to you. She must have heard about you after I took you to the fundraiser. People gossip. Word gets around. She probably got jealous and decided to sabotage things. She's like that. And for the past few weeks, she's been... well, she's the reason I've been so distracted lately."

For the first time, Mel noticed that Vanessa looked different. She was wearing jeans. A plain blouse. No makeup. Her hair was pulled back into a messy ponytail instead of loose over her shoulders like usual. It was a far cry from the impeccably put-together woman Mel knew.

"I'll start at the beginning. I'll start with what really happened with Rose. I didn't abandon her, Melanie. I ended things because she was careless about her limits. And it nearly killed her."

Mel watched Vanessa take another drink. She was clearly struggling with this. Mel owed it to Vanessa to hear her out.

"I met Rose years ago at Lilith's Den. We were instantly drawn to each other. We were both deep into the BDSM scene at the time, her even more so than me. She was older and more experienced, which was why I never expected that things could go so wrong..." She trailed off, a distant look in her eyes. "It started as the two of us just having fun together. Then, she became my submissive. And eventually, we fell in love, and she became my girlfriend too. It was the first and last time I had ever mixed love and BDSM."

Mel felt a twinge of jealousy, but pushed it away.

"Rose was a BDSM junkie. She was always chasing that high. She loved bondage more than anything. I learned shibari for her."

Mel thought back to her birthday when Vanessa had bound her up in all those knots. It only aggravated her even more.

Vanessa pressed on. "Over time, the things that she wanted us to do together became more and more extreme. There were many occasions when I refused to do something she wanted because I felt it was too risky. But Rose would keep pushing. Sometimes I held firm, but occasionally I gave in." A wistful look crossed her face. "I've never been good at saying no to the people I love. I just want so much to make them happy."

Vanessa's words from that night after the fundraiser echoed in Mel's mind. *All these things I do, all the lengths I go to. It's all to please you.*

"There were so many red flags. Rose was irresponsible and reckless from the start. She was always pushing limits in every area of her life and our relationship. She didn't take things seriously. Didn't respect my boundaries or her own. But I ignored the signs because I was in love with her."

Mel couldn't help but empathize. She knew what it was like to be blind to someone's faults because of love.

"It's no excuse, of course. Her safety was my responsibility. I should never have done anything I felt uncomfortable with. But one day, I agreed to do a very complex scene with her. Rose wanted to be tied up, gagged, and suspended from the ceiling. Suspension bondage is not for beginners. By then, I was experienced enough that I felt confident doing something like that. But no amount of experience changes the fact that if anything goes wrong, getting out of all those bonds is a long and difficult process. And it requires an incredible amount of trust on both sides. Which, until that point, I thought we had." Vanessa stared down into her glass. "But there was something that Rose had kept from me. And I found out about it in the worst possible way."

Mel watched Vanessa as she gulped down the last of her drink.

"We were at my apartment. In the playroom. I had tied Rose up in a way that immobilized her entire body, and I suspended her from the ceiling, just like she wanted. I was teasing her with a flogger. She had a gag in her mouth which made it difficult for her to communicate. But we had come up with signs for situations like that. Simple signs she could make with her hands, for things like 'I'm okay,' 'stop,' and her safe word. Rose had given me the okay several times. Everything was going well. Suddenly, she started gasping for air. Like she couldn't breathe. And she was shaking, and crying, and..." Vanessa's voice was so quiet that Mel could barely hear her. "I'll never forget the look in her eyes. She thought she was going to die. And maybe she would have if I hadn't acted quickly. I took the gag from her mouth and cut her down. I always kept scissors nearby just in case, but I didn't think I'd ever need them. It took far too long to get her out of all the ropes. Those seconds, they felt like hours. I didn't know what was happening to her. I called 911, frantic. And I held her until the ambulance arrived."

The pain in Vanessa's voice made Mel's heart ache.

"They took her to the hospital. They treated her. She was fine in the end. But I didn't know this at the time because I was detained by the police at the hospital. The scene that the paramedics were faced with when they walked into my apartment must have looked suspicious from the outside. Not to mention all the marks on Rose's body. The police had questions for me. They interrogated me about my relationship with Rose as if they didn't believe that I was her girlfriend of two years. They took the fact that I didn't even know about Rose's condition to mean that our relationship wasn't what I said it was. Because I should have known if I was that close to her. It took several hours and a phone call from my lawyer to clear it all up. And once I was released, Rose told me the truth."

"She'd had asthma her entire life. Serious asthma that had her in and out of the hospital. No one ever thinks of asthma as something that can be life-threatening. But it was for Rose. It almost killed her as a child on a few occasions. It was very traumatic for her. I think those memories are what had her so afraid that day in my playroom when she started to have trouble breathing…" Vanessa gripped her empty glass, her knuckles white. "Rose said that her asthma improved as she got older. She still had to take medication for it daily. And she still occasionally had attacks. But she hid it from everyone, including me. I don't know why. Perhaps she deliberately kept it from me because she knew that I would never do anything extreme with her if I knew. Or perhaps she was just in denial about how serious her condition was.

"But her secrecy made everything so much worse. She had an inhaler in her purse the entire time. It was on the coffee table, just a few feet from the playroom door. But I didn't know it was there. And she was too incoherent to tell me about it. It wasn't just the asthma. All the adrenaline running through her veins seemed to trigger a panic attack, which made everything worse. Not to mention she was already deep in subspace. You know what it's like when you're there. How detached you feel from reality, how hard it is to think, to feel."

Mel knew Vanessa was right about that. It would be terrifying to have something go wrong while in that headspace.

"That incident shook us both to the core. I know in my head that what happened wasn't my fault, but in my heart I can't stop feeling like I failed to protect her." Vanessa's eyes were wet with tears. But she wouldn't let them fall. "Rose wanted to keep going. To continue with our life, our relationship, like nothing had happened. I tried. But I just couldn't do it. Every time I looked at her it was a reminder of how I let love cloud my judgment and nearly killed someone I loved. So I ended things with her.

"She didn't take it well. She'd show up at all the places she knew I'd be and beg me to take her back. But I couldn't let it happen again.

So I locked that playroom door forever. And I locked up my heart forever. I banned her from all the places I owned, hoping it would keep her away.

"But it didn't stop her. She kept calling me, begging me to take her back. Eventually, she stopped. I thought that was the end of it. But now and then, for whatever reason, she starts again. The phone calls I keep getting that I never answer? They're not from work. They're from her."

Mel spoke for the first time during Vanessa's long confession. "Why do you put up with it? You could have changed your number, you could have blocked her. You don't even answer her calls." Mel didn't mean to sound like she was blaming Vanessa, although she likely did. She just couldn't understand why someone as strong as Vanessa would allow Rose to hold her hostage all this time.

"Because I know her. I've seen firsthand the lengths she was willing to go to get me back. It bordered on stalking. So when it stopped, and all that was left was her calling me once in a while? I was relieved. I figured that if this was all I had to deal with I could handle it. And I think there was a part of me that saw it as a kind of penance."

Mel's surprise turned into empathy. She knew what it was like to feel the guilt of something that wasn't your fault. Her father leaving. Her mother's resentment toward her. Kim's unpredictable anger. She knew now that none of it was her fault. But it didn't stop her from feeling like it was.

Vanessa picked up her glass to drink and saw that it was empty. She placed it back down and sighed. "It doesn't matter. Rose ended up escalating her behavior again in the end. The night that she came into The Lounge and spoke to you wasn't the first time she'd tried to slip past security recently. That night long ago when I came in to see you and ran off after talking to James? It was because she'd tried to get into the club just hours before. I was far too shaken to talk to you for the rest of the night. I never did apologize to you for that." Vanessa smiled weakly. "It seems silly in comparison now."

Mel didn't know what to say. She had no idea that any of this was going on.

"Everything with Rose? It happened years ago. And it took a long time for me to get over it. Initially, I stayed away from BDSM altogether. But eventually, I found myself back at Lilith's. And since then there have been other women, some of them submissives. And yes, there were a lot of them. I suppose I gained a reputation because of it, which is what Vicki hinted at when she spoke to you. I'm not proud of the way I behaved. But it was all because I didn't want anyone to get too close. I felt that if I developed feelings for them, I couldn't trust myself to be responsible. So I cut them loose before they could get too attached." Vanessa looked up at Mel. "But then I met you."

Mel's heart skipped a beat. The sudden affection in Vanessa's eyes made her resolve waver.

"I never intended to start anything with you. But I couldn't help it. I was drawn to you. That night in the Scarlet Room, the first time I took you to Lilith's Den? That was when I realized I was falling for you. And it terrified me. I considered ending things. But I couldn't stay away."

Mel thought back to when she had been agonizing over whether she had scared Vanessa off. She had been wrong about the reason, but at least now she knew it wasn't all in her imagination.

"And that night two weeks ago at Lilith's when you were angry with me. It reminded me far too much of the way Rose used to push boundaries. And once again, I found myself in a position where someone I cared about was behaving recklessly in a situation where I could potentially hurt them. That's why I reacted the way I did. And when you said Rose's name? I fell apart. I couldn't handle being reminded of how I'd failed to keep her safe."

Mel suddenly remembered something that Vanessa had said the night of their fight at Lilith's. *Do you have any idea what it's like to live with that sort of guilt?* Mel felt sick to her stomach. She hadn't caught it back then, but now it all made sense. And she'd made it so much worse by throwing Rose's name at Vanessa without knowing the gravity it held. The horror of what she'd done and said hit her at once.

"So I pushed you away. I shut the world out. I got lost in my own head. Which is why it took me so long to realize that I'd done the one thing you feared more than anything."

Mel looked down, her vision blurring with tears.

"Oh, Melanie. I'm so sorry. For lashing out at you, for disappearing when I should have been there. I never meant to abandon you. I need you to know that." Vanessa took Mel's hand across the table. "I will never leave you again, Melanie. You mean more to me than you could ever know."

Mel's heart slowed. Vanessa's hand felt heavy in hers. She looked into Vanessa's eyes. "I'm sorry, Vanessa. All those things that I did, all those things that I said to you—I had no idea. I should never have said any of it. I was angry, and careless, and stupid." Mel wanted to say that everything was fine now. That they could just go back to the way things were. But Mel was far too overwhelmed by everything. So she did what she always did. She retreated. "I just... I can't. I'm sorry. I can't do this." Mel pulled her hand away.

"Melanie, wait..."

"Goodbye, Vanessa." Ignoring the pleading look in Vanessa's eyes, Mel stood up and walked away.

# CHAPTER TWENTY-THREE

"That's it for the day, everyone," Professor Carr said. "And for the year. Congratulations on making it through your first year of law school." She crossed her arms and leaned back on her desk. "Don't get too excited. Your second year will make this year seem like kindergarten."

The class broke out into chatter. Mel gathered her things and followed Jess to the door absently. Now that school was over for the year, she had nothing to distract her from what was really on her mind.

"Melanie, can I see you for a moment?" Professor Carr waved Mel over to her desk.

"Sure." Mel told Jess she'd catch up with her later.

"Melanie. How would you like to be my intern this summer?" Professor Carr asked.

"What?" A smile broke out on Mel's face. "Seriously?"

"Yep. Your performance in class impressed me. Plus, you aced your final exam. Top of the class by the way. Congratulations."

"Thanks, Professor."

"So is that a yes?"

"Yes," Mel said. "Of course."

Professor Carr smiled. "I'll be in touch over the next few days. Enjoy your free time while you have it because you're going to be working hard all summer."

"Okay. Thanks, Professor."

Jess was waiting for Mel out in the hall. "So? Did you get the internship?"

"Yep," Mel replied.

"That's great, Mel!"

"Yeah. I guess so." Mel gave Jess a weak smile.

"That's more like it! Let's go out to celebrate. Now that school is over, you have no more excuses. And I know you don't have work tonight."

"I don't know," Mel said. "I just want to go home and relax."

"By relax, do you mean 'sulk about Vanessa?'" Jess asked. "When was the last time you left the house for something other than work or school?"

"I went for a run yesterday." Mel had taken it up again in the past few weeks. She needed the distraction.

"Come on, one drink. I'm not letting you sit around and mope any longer."

"Fine." Mel didn't have the energy to argue.

Half an hour later, Mel and Jess were sitting in a bar a few blocks from campus.

"I can't wait to start at the DA's office," Jess said. She too had gotten the internship she wanted. "It'll probably be lots of paperwork and case research, but I hope I get to see some interesting trials…"

Mel stared into her glass as Jess chatted away. Mel had gotten everything she wanted. She'd ended the year with an amazing GPA, and she'd gotten an internship that most law students would kill for under a woman she idolized. A few months ago that would have made her happy. But instead, she felt empty.

"I need to go shopping," Jess finished the last of her cocktail. "My wardrobe is nowhere near professional enough. Wanna come, Mel?"

"Sure," Mel replied.

"I think I'll go for a whole new look. New clothes, a new hairstyle. The works. I've been thinking about trying a shorter style, what do you think? I asked Brendon, and he just said 'whatever makes you happy.' I appreciate the sentiment, but sometimes I wish he had opinions of his own..."

Mel swirled her drink around in her glass. Whiskey. She'd ordered it without thinking. She pushed her drink away with a sigh. It should have been Vanessa she was celebrating with. Vanessa had asked Mel if she could treat her when she got the internship. Mel had agreed to it, with the caveat that it was 'nothing over the top.'

Mel almost laughed now at the idea of giving Vanessa 'permission' to do something. She felt a tinge of sadness when she thought about the fact that she'd never experience Vanessa spoiling her again. And that she'd never get to go on that island getaway with Vanessa. She'd actually been looking forward to it.

"Still thinking about Vanessa, huh?" Jess said.

Mel nodded.

"What really happened between you two? It might help to talk about it."

"It won't." Mel downed the rest of her whiskey. She hadn't told Jess the details of what happened between her and Vanessa. Not because it was hard to talk about. But because Mel was afraid that Jess would confirm what Mel was now starting to feel. That she was an idiot for walking away from Vanessa.

"Okay. I won't push you." Jess got up. "I'm going to the ladies' room. I'll be back in a minute."

As Jess disappeared into the crowd, Mel pulled out her phone to pass the time. She opened up her social media feed and started to browse. Among the notifications was a friend request.

From Kim Roberts.

Mel's stomach dropped. After Kim had broken up with Mel, she had cut off all ties, deleting Mel from everything as if trying to erase their entire relationship. When they had crossed paths at college the following year, Kim had acted like Mel wasn't even there.

ANNA STONE

So why did she send this friend request? Why now?

Mel's curiosity got the best of her. She tapped 'accept' and scrolled through Kim's profile. It was mostly pictures of her, looking almost the same as in college. Most of them seemed to be with the same woman. As she scrolled down, the woman showed up over and over again. Mel reached a post announcing Kim's engagement. Kim was getting married to someone named Alex. The post was accompanied by a photo of Kim and the woman who kept popping up in all those photos. Alex. Mel's mouth dropped open. Kim was marrying a woman.

Anger prickled inside her. Kim had dumped Mel claiming she wasn't into girls, and here she was, marrying another woman? *That hypocrite.*

Mel put her phone down and took a breath. It was unfair to be mad at Kim for that. Kim wouldn't be the first person who had struggled with their sexuality. And it made sense. Kim had grown up with a conservative family. And she'd always seemed to feel guilt and shame when it came to sex. Did this mean that Kim had lied all that time ago when she said she wasn't into girls? And if so, was she lying to Mel or to herself?

As Mel mulled over everything in her mind, something else occurred to her. What other lies had Kim told her? *I'm not into girls. This was never serious.*

*I never loved you.*

Mel had never gotten over the things that Kim had said to her that day. Not to mention how Kim had treated her throughout their entire relationship. Kim's constant emotional manipulation had made Mel second-guess herself even more than she already did when it came to her feelings. Every time she got close to anyone, she would wonder: *do they actually love me? Will they just leave me like everyone else? Is this what I deserve?*

And Mel had let those stupid, baseless insecurities ruin everything with Vanessa.

She sighed. Mel turning her back on Vanessa after she'd poured her heart out was the final nail in the coffin. It was too late to fix things. And clearly, she was too broken to be in a relationship. Vanessa was better off without her.

Jess returned to the table. Mel turned off her phone and stuffed it in her bag.

"Everything okay?" Jess asked?

"Yep." Mel pushed it all out of her mind. "Let's get another drink."

# CHAPTER TWENTY-FOUR

*M*el opened her dresser drawers one by one. Nothing. She let out a groan of frustration. She had to have a few pairs of pantyhose lying around. Her internship started tomorrow, and she needed to look professional. She had to make a good first impression. This internship could lead to a job when she graduated in a few years. She was not going to squander the opportunity.

She smiled to herself. Things were starting to look up. Mel had a chance to do some good at The LSP, even if that just meant going on coffee runs for the lawyers who were doing the real work. And working with Professor Carr outside of the classroom would be an invaluable experience. There was a world of possibilities ahead of her.

If only she could find that pantyhose. Mel tugged open the bottom drawer of her dresser and dug around inside. Sure enough, there were several pairs of pantyhose balled up in the corner. Mel grabbed them, and froze.

Buried beneath all her junk was the silver and sapphire choker with a ring at the front.

Mel's hand hovered over the necklace as she fought the urge to pick it up. It had been weeks since she'd taken it off, yet she still found herself reaching up to touch it, only to find her neck bare. Mel pulled it out of the drawer and held it up before her eyes. Before she knew it, she had unclasped the back and was fastening it around her neck.

Mel looked at herself in the mirror. The ring sat perfectly in the hollow at the base of her throat. The familiar weight of it was comforting.

Mel sighed. After all this time apart from Vanessa, she couldn't help but feel like she had made a mistake. All this had started because Mel had been afraid that Vanessa didn't truly care about her. But hadn't she shown Mel time and time again that she did? It wasn't the gifts and the extravagant gestures. It was the little things. Remembering small, seemingly insignificant details about Mel, like how she loved daffodils and the color blue. Listening to Mel talk for hours while they lay in bed together. Letting Mel see that softer side of her that Vanessa didn't show anyone.

Despite the nature of their relationship, they were always equals. Unlike Kim, Vanessa had respected Mel and her feelings. Vanessa did everything she could to make Mel happy. And that night that she'd told Mel about Rose, Vanessa had admitted that she was falling for Mel.

As Mel fingered the choker around her neck, something that Vanessa had said that night she had given Mel the necklace came back to her. *I'm yours as much as you are mine.* It was all so obvious now. Vanessa had felt the same way about Mel that Mel felt about her.

And Mel loved her.

Mel had been in love with Vanessa for god knows how long. But fear had kept her from admitting it, even to herself. As she stood there, staring into the mirror, all those fears came rushing back.

*No.* No more excuses. No more self-pity. Mel steeled herself. Vanessa had always been the dominant one in their relationship. But that didn't mean that Mel was powerless. It was time for her to take control. She hoped that it wasn't too late.

Mel looked at the clock. She needed to see Vanessa, face to face, before she lost her resolve. But it was getting late. And Mel didn't even know where to find her. Unless...

Mel opened her wardrobe and dug out the clutch that Vanessa had given her for the charity fundraiser. In a small pocket in the lining, right where Mel had put it, was a white business card.

Mel picked up her phone and dialed the number.

"Elena? I need a favor."

---

Half an hour later, Elena pulled up at the front of Mel's building. Within seconds, they were on their way to Vanessa's apartment.

"Thank you so much for this, Elena," Mel said.

"Not a problem," Elena replied.

"I wasn't sure if you'd want to help me since Vanessa and I... you know."

Elena shrugged. "It doesn't matter. She still cares about you."

Elena's words buoyed Mel. She didn't know if Vanessa would take her back. But she needed to speak to Vanessa, if only just to apologize, and to tell Vanessa how she felt. She just hoped Vanessa still felt the same way.

"Don't worry." Elena glanced at Mel in the rear-view mirror and shot her a warm smile. "I wouldn't be helping you if I didn't think Vanessa wanted to see you. She misses you."

All Mel could manage in return was a nervous smile. The rest of the car ride passed in silence. When they finally arrived at Vanessa's apartment, Elena parked the car and got out.

"I'll let you into the building." Elena held up a keycard. "After that, you're on your own."

"Thanks." Mel was grateful that she didn't have to ask Vanessa to buzz her up through the intercom.

Mel raced toward the building, Elena on her heels. Elena swiped her into the lobby.

"Thanks again, Elena," Mel said. "I owe you one."

"Any time." Elena gave Mel a farewell nod. "Good luck."

The elevator ride up to Vanessa's apartment seemed to take

forever. When Mel reached the top floor, she dashed to Vanessa's front door.

Mel took a deep breath and knocked. Moments later, the door swung open.

"Melanie?" Vanessa stood in the doorway in a silky robe. She had a towel over one arm and her hair was damp.

"Vanessa," Mel said. After all this time, Vanessa was still able to take Mel's breath away.

For a moment, they stood there, on opposite sides of the doorway, their gazes locked.

Vanessa's eyes fell to Mel's neck. Seeing her choker there broke her out of her trance. She opened the door wide. "Come in."

As soon as Mel was inside, everything spilled out. "I'm so sorry, Vanessa. For everything. I'm sorry that I behaved the way I did. I'm sorry that I said all those horrible things. I'm sorry that I walked away from you-"

"Melanie," Vanessa said. "Sit down."

Mel obeyed.

"You don't have to apologize. I understand."

"No, I do. And I want to explain myself," Mel said. "All my life, everyone I've ever loved has abandoned me. My father. My mother. She would leave me alone or forget about me, time and time again, and she was never really there when I needed her. So, all that time ago, I told myself I didn't need anyone else. I told myself I didn't need love. And after a while, I began to believe it." Mel felt a torrent of emotions rising up.

Vanessa reached out and placed her hand on Mel's.

A sense of calm washed over her. Mel continued. "But you? You made me remember what it was like to feel loved. And it terrified me. The only other person who made me feel like that was Kim. I think she loved me too in her own twisted way. But she manipulated me and toyed with my emotions until I didn't know what to feel anymore. And in the end, she abandoned me too. And she told me she never loved me and that none of what I felt was real. It crushed me. So when Rose came along and said all those things, it reawakened all those doubts and fears. I was scared of getting hurt again, so I pushed you away. And I did it in the most destructive way possible, and I'm so sorry..."

"It's all right, Melanie," Vanessa said. "I understand."

"But that's not all. After everything that happened, I realized that I can't let my past hold me hostage. And I realized that what we had was too precious to give up on. And I realized that I couldn't hide from my feelings. Vanessa—" Mel's pulse was racing "—I love you."

Vanessa smiled. She wrapped her arms around Mel and pulled her in close. "Oh, Melanie. I promise you, I feel the same way. I always have. From the start, I never thought of you as my submissive because I always hoped for more. It took me a while to admit it to myself. I was afraid that if I held you too tightly I'd hurt you like I did Rose. But I couldn't help myself. I did everything I could to make you mine, but I never told you how I really felt. It's the biggest mistake I ever made. So I'm telling you now." Vanessa took Mel's hands in hers. "I love you, Melanie."

Mel's heart sang in her chest. She leaned over and kissed Vanessa, soft and slow, gentle and sweet. Mel had missed those lips. They seemed to fit perfectly with her own.

"It's time we made another rule," Vanessa said. "Next time one of us has a problem? We talk about it. And face it together. No lies, no keeping everything inside. No lashing out. And no disappearing acts. How does that sound?"

"Okay." They had been given a second chance at this. Mel was not going to mess it up. She closed her eyes and nestled in closer to Vanessa, and they sat there together, silent and still.

"Melanie?"

"Yes?" Mel could feel Vanessa's heartbeat pulsing through her body.

"I want to show you my playroom."

# CHAPTER TWENTY-FIVE

*V*anessa unlocked the door to the playroom and flicked
on the light. Mel followed her inside. She was immediately reminded of The Scarlet Room at Lilith's Den. Was The Scarlet
Room inspired by Vanessa's playroom or the other way around?
The only difference was that this room seemed more intimate and
personal. It was packed to the brim with every toy and tool imaginable, each carefully organized and lovingly cared for. A rack on the
wall displayed a collection of whips, crops, and canes, all with
crimson leather handles like Vanessa's riding crop. At the end of the
room was an elaborate iron four-poster bed with rings all along the
frame. Tie points. The smell of leather hung in the air.

Vanessa walked to the center of the room, her bare feet padding
on the floorboards. She looked around, an undecipherable expression on her face.

"Are you all right, Vanessa?" Mel asked.

"Yes. It's the first time I've been in here with someone since
Rose."

Mel took Vanessa's hand. "We don't have to do this."

"I know." She squeezed Mel's hand back. "But I want to share
this with you."

Vanessa pulled Mel in close and kissed her. Mel pressed her body up against Vanessa's, returning the kiss with double the intensity. It had been so long since she'd held Vanessa like this. Vanessa's soft, full lips seemed to melt against hers.

Vanessa pulled away. "Slow down, my pet. We have all the time in the world. And we have all of this at our disposal." She gestured around the room. "Within these four walls, the possibilities are endless. So tell me, Melanie. What do you want me to do for you tonight? What is it you desire more than anything?"

Mel looked around her. The playroom was well stocked. There was so much that she wanted to do with Vanessa. So much that she wanted to try. But right now, she only wanted one thing. "I want you, Vanessa. But I want all of you. I want the dominant, commanding you who can bring me to my knees with no more than a look. I want the sweet, tender you that I saw that night after the fundraiser. I want to serve you. I want to be yours in every sense of the word. But I want to be able to touch you and make you feel the way that I feel when you touch me. I want to see that vulnerable side of you that no one else gets to see."

Vanessa's face wore a strange expression. She pulled Mel over to the bed, and they sat down. "The night that we fought, you said that to me," Vanessa said. "That I kept you at arm's length. That I never gave you any of myself."

"I'm sorry, I didn't mean all of that. I was angry, and Rose's words were in my head, and-"

"It's all right, Melanie. You were right. I expected you to give me your everything when I gave you very little in return. I'm sorry."

"All I want is for you to feel like you can open up to me," Mel said. "Like you can become vulnerable with me."

"I understand," Vanessa said. "I was never good at opening up, and after everything with Rose, I closed myself off even more. I've been that way for so long now that I've forgotten how to let people in. But I want to let you in. I won't hold any part of myself back from you any longer."

Mel smiled. "Thanks, Vanessa. That's all I want."

Vanessa kissed Mel again, hard. Her lips were overpowering. "You also said you want to make me feel the way you feel when I touch you." She drew a hand down Mel's cheek. "How do I make you feel?"

"Like you're my everything," Mel said. "Like I'm the center of your world. Like I'm safe with you."

"I already feel like that, Melanie. But if you want to show me what that's like, I'll let you." Vanessa had a familiar gleam in her eyes. "But we're going to do it my way."

Mel's pulse sped up. In an instant, Vanessa had transformed into the self-possessed, domineering woman who had captured Mel's attention from the first time Mel laid eyes on her. Mel now understood that it wasn't a mask. It was just one of Vanessa's many facets.

"Stand up for me, Melanie," Vanessa said. She waited for Mel to obey. "Take off your clothes. All of them."

Mel began to strip slowly, piece by piece, peering at Vanessa from under her eyelashes. To Vanessa's credit, she didn't break her gaze until Mel stood before her in nothing but the collar around her neck. Then Vanessa looked Mel up and down, drinking Mel in with her eyes. There was a slight chill in the room, causing tiny goosebumps to sprout on Mel's skin.

"There's a blindfold in the chest over there." Vanessa pointed across the room. "Bring it to me."

Mel went over to the chest and dug around for the blindfold. When she returned to the bed, Vanessa had removed her robe and was reclining in the center of the bed, her back propped up on a mountain of pillows. Mel traced her eyes over Vanessa's naked figure unashamedly as she handed Vanessa the blindfold.

Vanessa patted the bed next to her. "Come. Kneel."

Mel hopped onto the bed and knelt beside Vanessa.

The moment the blindfold went over Mel's eyes, Vanessa became her world. She listened carefully to the sound of Vanessa's breath and inhaled the clean scent of Vanessa's freshly washed skin. Mel wanted to reach out and touch her, but she didn't dare to do so without permission.

"So you want to serve me?" Vanessa asked, her voice low and hypnotic.

"Yes, Vanessa. More than anything."

"Then make me feel like your queen. Worship every inch of me. Show me that you're mine."

"Yes, Vanessa." Mel reached toward where she sensed Vanessa was, until her fingertips touched Vanessa's soft skin. She traced her fingers down the length of Vanessa's body and slithered down to Vanessa's feet.

Mel took Vanessa's command to worship every inch of her literally. Mel worked her way upwards, exploring every part of Vanessa's body as if touching Vanessa for the first time. Her lips followed the trail made by her fingertips. When she reached the insides of Vanessa's thighs, she lingered. Vanessa's scent tempted Mel to taste her then and there. But Mel wanted to draw everything out, to savor every moment, to map every stretch of Vanessa's skin.

She kissed her way up Vanessa's smooth, flat stomach, caressing the other woman's curves with her hands. When Mel drew her hands over Vanessa's breasts, she found that Vanessa's nipples had already formed into tight peaks. Despite the blindfold, Mel could see Vanessa's rosy pink buds clearly in her mind. As soon as Mel's lips touched them, Vanessa's whole body tremored. Mel showered attention on Vanessa's breasts and nipples, reveling in the soft sounds she elicited from deep within Vanessa's chest.

As Mel kissed her way up Vanessa's neck, Vanessa took Mel's face in her hands and kissed her hungrily. "I want you to devour me," she said.

Mel slid a probing hand down between Vanessa's legs. Her fingers slipped easily into Vanessa's silky, wet folds. She crawled back downward, painting kisses down Vanessa's stomach. Mel wanted to take it slow, to tease Vanessa like Vanessa had teased her so many times before. But her own lust got the better of her.

Slowly, Mel parted Vanessa's lips with her tongue and ran it up and down her folds. Vanessa's hands fell down to the back of Mel's head, holding her in place. Mel licked and stroked and flicked away, drunk on Vanessa's taste. Vanessa rocked her hips against Mel's mouth, taking charge of her own pleasure. Muted cries sprung from her lips.

"Melanie," Vanessa said between breaths. "I want you inside me."

"Yes, my Queen." As soon as the words left Mel's lips, Vanessa's body shivered and her breathing grew heavy. Mel had always been aware of the power Vanessa's words had over her. But until now, she hadn't known that her own words could have the same effect on Vanessa.

Mel slipped a finger inside her, then another. Vanessa gasped, her walls clamping around Mel's fingers. Slowly, Vanessa yielded, and Mel began to dart her fingers in and out. She crawled back up the bed and pressed her body against Vanessa's. Mel wanted to be close to her through this, to dissolve into Vanessa so deeply that she felt everything Vanessa was feeling.

Vanessa let out a low purr as Mel slid her thumb up to Vanessa's swollen nub. Her hands grasped for Mel's body, pulling her in tighter. Mel could feel how close Vanessa was. Finally, Vanessa's body began to quake. Her walls pulsed around Mel's fingers, her wild howl echoing through the room.

Vanessa's scream only emboldened Mel. She thrust away, coaxing out every little part of Vanessa's orgasm. But Mel didn't stop. Another orgasm quickly followed. And another, until finally, Vanessa shattered in Mel's arms.

"Melanie…" Vanessa murmured, breathless.

Mel snuggled into the side of Vanessa's body and threw her arm across Vanessa's chest. Still blindfolded, Mel could feel Vanessa's body slacken and her breathing slow down. Vanessa showed no sign of stirring from her post-orgasm daze.

Mel smiled to herself. This was exactly what she wanted. To give Vanessa everything that Vanessa had given her. To make Vanessa lose herself in Mel and surrender to the pleasure that Mel was giving her. And she had succeeded. More than once.

When Vanessa finally recovered, she pulled off Mel's blindfold. "You served your queen well," Vanessa said. "You've earned yourself a reward." Her lips curved up into a slight smile.

Mel's heart sped up. She knew what that smile meant. Vanessa had relinquished control to Mel, if only for a moment.

Now it was time for her to take it back.

---

Ten minutes later, Mel was on all fours on the edge of the bed. Her body was positioned so that her ass was thrust up in the air, and her feet hung off the side of the mattress. Her ankles were bound to the bed frame, spreading her legs shoulder-width apart. Her wrists were bound together by a long rope attached to the other side of the bed.

Vanessa double checked her knots, then knelt on the bed in front of Mel. "Now that you're mine again, mind, body, and heart, I'm going to remind you what it means to belong to me." She took Mel's chin in her hands and tipped Mel's face up toward hers. "I'm going to unravel you bit by bit until all that's left is pure unbridled desire, and you're unable to do anything except lose yourself in a haze of ecstasy."

Mel's breath quickened. Vanessa's words alone were enough to make her ache.

Vanessa disappeared somewhere behind her. The position Mel was in left her unable to see most of the room, so she closed her eyes and listened to Vanessa's soft footsteps. Mel had no idea what Vanessa was going to do with her. But instead of anxious anticipation, Mel felt completely calm. Vanessa knew her deeply. Sometimes it felt like Vanessa knew Mel better than Mel knew herself. And she trusted Vanessa unconditionally.

Vanessa returned to the bed and stood behind Mel. Mel twisted around to look at her. Vanessa held one of her crimson-handled whips in her hand. It was a short flogger with countless leather tails.

"I'm going to introduce you to my favorite toy. It's this flogger here. It has so many uses." Vanessa draped the flogger over Mel's back. "It can be used to tease."

The soft tails of the flogger brushed along Mel's back and down the backs of her thighs. She shuddered with delight.

"With a bit of force, it makes a lovely, solid thud."

Mel felt a firm swat on her bare ass. The impact made her jump.

"Turn it on its side, and it stings just as much as a riding crop." Vanessa whipped Mel again.

Mel hissed. It was like a hundred tiny needles had pierced her skin.

"And once you get into a rhythm, it can be almost hypnotic." Vanessa brought the flogger down on Mel's thrust out ass over and over, one cheek then the other, firmly but not hard enough to really hurt.

"Mmmm..." Mel closed her eyes as Vanessa drew stripes across her skin with the whip. She embraced the sensations, pushing herself out to meet the flogger, losing all sense of time. The next thing she knew, Vanessa was massaging her tender, hot cheeks.

"That was just the warm-up," Vanessa said. "Now it's time for the real thing."

Mel shifted in her bonds, anticipation brewing inside of her. The ropes barely allowed her to move an inch.

"I'm going to flog you ten times. Harder this time. I want you to count them out loud for me."

"Yes, Vanessa," Mel replied.

Vanessa took a few steps back. Mel tensed, waiting for the inevitable. Silence hung in the air. But the flogger didn't fall. After what felt like minutes, Mel relaxed her body.

*Slap!* Mel cried out. The flogger stung like hell on her already raw skin. But it left behind a pleasant burning feeling.

"Count," Vanessa said.

"One." *Slap!* Mel's fingers curled around the silk bedsheets beneath her. "Two."

Mel continued to count, the heat of the blows spreading across her cheeks and the backs of her thighs. When she reached five, Vanessa slid the flogger down between Mel's legs, teasing her lips with its tails. Mel murmured softly and spread her knees apart as far as she could in her restraints.

Vanessa's response was a sharp, stinging strike.

Mel gritted her teeth. "Six."

Vanessa alternated between stinging lashes and gentle brushes of the flogger against Mel's swollen lips. As the conflicting sensations flooded Mel's body, she found herself slipping into that state of bliss. As soon as the word ten left her lips, Mel closed her eyes and surrendered completely, allowing herself to fall, knowing that Vanessa would be there to catch her. The walls fell back, and the room faded into nothing. The world disappeared. All that remained was Vanessa.

Vanessa removed the ropes from Mel's wrists and ankles and laid her down on the bed. Mel's lips sought out Vanessa's lips, her hands grasped at Vanessa's curves, her body arched toward Vanessa's. And Vanessa's hands were all over Mel's body, seemingly on every part of her electrified skin at the same time. And Vanessa's lips, soft and wet, roamed down her neck, and across her breasts, and over her tiny pebbled nipples.

"Oh god, Vanessa." Mel was drowning in her. "I need you. Please!"

Vanessa pushed Mel's knees apart. The moment Vanessa slipped her fingers inside, Mel crumbled. Her heavy breaths turned into gasps, and her gasps turned into moans. Vanessa's thumb worked Mel's clit while her fingers plunged in and out, her whole body pushing against Mel's with every thrust. Mel whimpered. She felt like she was going to burst.

"Do you want me to let you come?" Vanessa asked.

Mel nodded.

"Then tell me." Vanessa leaned down and spoke into Mel's ear. "Who do you belong to?"

"You, Vanessa," Mel whispered. "I belong to you."

Only then did Vanessa allow Mel her release. Mel cried out as pleasure overtook her. Vanessa held her close, still inside her and all around her at the same time, as she rode out her orgasm like a wave.

When Mel came back down to her body she was wrapped in Vanessa's arms underneath a pile of soft blankets. The floral scent of Vanessa's damp hair hung in the air. The press of Vanessa's body against hers felt familiar and comforting.

Mel let out a sigh. "This was always my favorite part."

"Mine too," Vanessa murmured. "Every time I put my arms around you, I didn't want to let go."

"You never have to. I'm not going anywhere." Mel said. "I'm yours, after all."

Vanessa kissed Mel softly on the lips. "You're mine," she said. "And I'm yours."

# EPILOGUE

## VANESSA

anessa awoke in an unfamiliar bed. Sunlight streamed through the window, warming her bare skin. The air was filled with the scent of daffodils. Mel's favorite. Vanessa turned her head to the side. Mel lay next to her, fast asleep. She was still wearing that necklace that Vanessa gave her. She never seemed to take it off.

Vanessa smiled to herself. It was the first day of their island getaway, the holiday that Vanessa had 'won' for Mel at the fundraiser. They'd only just managed to squeeze it in before summer ended. Although they were only here for a few days, Vanessa had a great deal planned, most of which didn't involve them leaving their suite.

Vanessa watched Mel's chest rise and fall. She looked so serene. Vanessa would never get tired of watching Mel sleep. She had almost let Mel slip away. She would never make that mistake again.

Mel's eyelids fluttered open.

"Good morning." Vanessa leaned down and kissed Mel on the lips.

"Mmmm…" Mel closed her eyes again. "What time is it?"

"Late," Vanessa said. "We slept in."

Mel yawned. "I should check my email."

Vanessa nodded. After Mel's summer internship at The LSP, she had been hired part-time as a legal secretary. Her superiors had come to rely on her to the point where they would email and call her even on her days off. But Mel didn't seem to mind. She believed in the work they were doing.

Mel rolled onto her back and scrolled through her phone. After a few seconds, she scrunched up her face, her finger frozen above the screen.

"Is everything all right?" Vanessa asked.

"Yeah. It's fine."

"Melanie." It was clear to Vanessa that Mel was not fine. "No lies, remember? No keeping things to ourselves."

"Sorry." Mel placed her phone down next to her on the bed. "It's a hard habit to break."

"It is for me too. But we can't be solitary creatures anymore." Vanessa propped herself up on her arm. "You don't have to tell me everything. Just know that you can if you want to."

"I know," Mel said. "It's just, I got a message. It's from Kim. She hasn't tried to contact me all this time…"

"What does she want?" Vanessa tried very hard to keep her displeasure from showing. She hated Kim because of how Kim had treated Mel. And the last thing the two of them needed was another ex causing trouble. The first thing that Vanessa had done after she and Mel had gotten back together was take out a restraining order on Rose. She was finally out of Vanessa's life for good.

"I don't know," Mel said. "And I don't want to know. It's all in the past." Mel tapped the screen a few times and set down her phone. "There. I deleted it. And blocked her."

"Are you okay?"

"Yeah." Mel smiled and closed her eyes. "I am. Because you're here."

"Good. I want you all to myself this weekend." Vanessa said. "With all the business trips I've been going on, and work and law school for you, it seems like we barely get to see each other anymore."

"I know. It sucks." Mel yawned and settled in closer to Vanessa. "I don't want this trip to end."

Vanessa thought for a moment. "Well, we can't stay here forever, but I think I have a solution."

"Hmmm?"

"How would you like to move in together?"

"What? Are you serious?"

Vanessa nodded. She wasn't the type to make spontaneous decisions, but this felt right. "You could move into my apartment. Or we could get a place of our own if you'd prefer it. Somewhere new..." Vanessa trailed off. She was unable to read the expression on Mel's face. "What do you think?"

"Yes." A smile spread across Mel's face. "Of course. I would love that, Vanessa."

"That's settled then." Vanessa planted a firm kiss on Mel's lips. Then in one swift motion, she pinned Mel's shoulders to the bed and straddled her body. "Now I can have you all to myself whenever I want. Do you like the sound of that, my pet?"

Mel was definitely awake now. "Yes, my Queen."

Heat rose up inside Vanessa's body. She still wasn't used to Mel addressing her like that. And it was becoming apparent that Mel knew exactly how much it turned Vanessa on.

Mel squirmed underneath her playfully. Vanessa had been gazing down at her girlfriend like a lovesick teenager for far too long. She was getting soft.

And Mel was getting far too bold.

"Don't think I don't know what you're doing. You've been forgetting your place lately." Vanessa reached over to the nightstand and picked up a pair of handcuffs they had used the night before. She dangled them over Mel's body. "Now that we're going to be living together, I'm going to remind you of it. Every. Single. Day."

Mel stopped moving. Her eyes were fixed on the handcuffs. *Not so bold anymore, are you?* Vanessa grabbed Mel's wrists and pulled them above her head. She looped the cuffs around a post on the headboard and fastened them around Mel's wrist.

Vanessa got up from the bed and picked up her phone. "Looks

like I missed a few work calls while we slept. I should go deal with them." She watched the expression on Mel's face shift from excitement to disbelief. Vanessa only had one call to make. It wouldn't take her more than two minutes. But she wanted to make Mel squirm.

"Are you really going to leave me here like this?" Mel asked.

"Yes. Is that a problem?"

Mel bit her lip. "No, Vanessa."

Vanessa sighed. The look of dismay on Mel's face was almost too much to bear. Vanessa leaned down to give Mel a reassuring kiss. However, as soon as Vanessa's lips touched Mel's, it became clear that Mel didn't mind her predicament one bit.

"Don't go anywhere," Vanessa said.

Mel smiled. "Yes, Vanessa."

# HER SURRENDER

# CHAPTER ONE

"*I* can't believe she broke up with me over text." April scowled and placed her phone on the table next to her plate. "Who does that?"

"That's pretty cold," Lexi said between mouthfuls. "Did she say why?"

"No, but I have a few ideas." Actually, it was more like a long list of ideas. At the very top of it was the fact that April and Christie had fought constantly. "We were only together for six weeks, but the least she could do was call me!"

"No one makes phone calls anymore." Lexi pushed one of her dark curls out of her face. "At least she didn't just ghost you."

"You're not helping, Lex." April's long-time friend and coworker had a cavalier attitude when it came to relationships.

"Sorry," Lexi replied. "I know it sucks, but just last week you were saying that you weren't that into her. Admit it, you were going to break up with her anyway."

"*If* I was going to break up with her, I would have done it in person."

"Look at it this way. She saved you the trouble of an uncomfortable conversation."

"I guess." April rested her chin on her hand. "I'm never getting back that book I lent her, am I?"

"Probably not," Lexi shoveled the last of her lunch into her mouth.

April wasn't that upset, not really. Christie had been nice, and they had a lot in common, but there were no sparks between them. What bothered April was that this was just the latest in a string of short relationships that had fizzled out, mostly because of personality clashes. April, as one of her exes put it, was "strong-willed". She was pretty sure that meant that she was hard to get along with.

April sighed. She was twenty-eight now. She knew that it was silly, but she was beginning to feel like she was doomed to spend the rest of her life alone. All her friends were pairing off and getting married, then moving away to start new lives, and April was being left behind.

"We should head back," April said. Their lunch hour was almost over.

"Yes, boss," Lexi said.

Waving goodbye to the cook, April and Lexi left the diner. It was a short walk from the library where they both worked, so they went there regularly for lunch. The diner had been there for as long as April could remember, and it was one of the few remaining local, family-run businesses in the area. But with rent prices going up as they were, April wondered how much longer the diner would last.

April and Lexi made their way back to work, chatting as they walked. Their workplace, the Oakmont Street Library, was just a few blocks away. The library was more than a library. It doubled as a community center and a meeting place for everyone who lived in this part of the city.

April was the library's director, but only for the last few months. She'd worked at the library for years and had been promoted to the top spot after the old director's sudden resignation. The timing couldn't have been worse. As soon as April had taken over, all of Oakmont Street, including the library and the surrounding apartments, had been bought by a multinational property development company. Oasis Developments had big plans for Oakmont Street. And those plans didn't involve leaving the library standing.

Lexi and April reached the library and headed to their small shared office in the back. Lexi was the library's event coordinator, which had been April's position before her promotion. The two of them, along with a few others, made up a bare-bones staff that barely kept the place running. Somehow, the library scraped by despite all the funding cuts.

But now, its time was running out.

April picked up the bundle of mail that had been left on her desk and flicked through it. She reached an envelope with a familiar logo. Her heart stopped.

It was a letter from Oasis Developments.

Ever since Oasis bought the building, April had been trying to get in touch with them to talk about the library, but all of her phone calls and emails had been ignored. This was the only piece of correspondence the library had received from Oasis in months.

April ripped open the letter and scanned the page. Her stomach sank.

"Everything okay, April?" Lexi asked.

"It's from Oasis. We have 90 days to vacate the building." April collapsed into her chair. She'd known this was coming since Oasis bought the building. The city didn't have the funds to relocate the library, so they were on their own. Unless April could come up with a way to save it, the library would be forced to close its doors. "It's official. This is really happening."

Lexi placed a hand on April's arm. "Sorry, April. I know how much this place means to you."

The library was special to April, for reasons that ran deeper than the fact that she worked here. It was *her* library. She'd always thought of it as hers, even before she became director, even before she started working here as a page in high school.

"They can't just tear it down," April said. "Half of West Heights has already been torn down by developers. Soon there's not going to be anything left." April dropped the letter onto her desk. "It feels like everything is changing so fast, and there's nothing I can do to stop it."

"I know," Lexi said. "It sucks."

April sighed.

"Do you know what would cheer you up?"

April raised an eyebrow. "Does it involve getting drunk?" That was usually Lexi's go-to suggestion.

"No," Lexi said, feigning offense. "Well, yes, it involves alcohol, but that's not the point." She sat down in her chair and rolled it over to April's desk. "Come to The Sapphire Room with me tonight."

April groaned. The Sapphire Room was the city's lesbian bar. April hadn't been there in years. Lexi, however, went there on a regular basis, usually to pick up women.

"Come on," Lexi said. "It'll be fun. And you never know, you might meet someone."

"I've had enough of relationships for a while. I'm not looking to start another."

"Who said anything about a relationship?" Lexi asked. "Nothing like a mindless one-night stand to help you forget about all your problems."

"I don't know," April said. "That's not my thing."

"Come on, it'll be fun. I'll be your wing-woman."

"I guarantee that you'll be the one dragging some woman home with you within an hour."

"Then you won't have to stay for long, will you?" Lexi said. "Just a few drinks. If you're not having fun, you can go home."

"All right," April said. "Just a few drinks."

---

April leaned back against the bar, sipping the mojito she'd been nursing since they arrived. It was loaded with sugar, probably to mask the taste of the cheap rum.

As soon as she'd walked through the door, April remembered why she hadn't been to The Sapphire Room in years. The bar, which was decorated in an eclectic mix of shabby chic styles, was too loud, and much too crowded.

"Anyone catch your eye yet?" Lexi asked, scanning the crowd.

"Not really," April replied.

They'd been here for almost an hour, drinking and chatting. Lexi was making a valiant effort to stay with April, but April could tell that her friend was losing her resolve with every woman who shot her a flirtatious glance. April didn't understand why, but women practically threw themselves at Lexi. She seemed to be seeing a different woman every week. To her credit, Lexi was always upfront with the women she met about her casual approach when it came to dating. It didn't deter them.

"You know, you'd have more luck if you didn't glower at every woman who looks your way," Lexi said.

"I am *not* glowering." Nevertheless, April tried to look more relaxed. "It doesn't matter. I'm not interested in anyone anyway."

"It might help you get over Christie," Lexi said.

"Is sex your solution to all of life's problems?"

"Not all of them. Just most of them. Besides, I seem to remember you complaining about how boring your sex life was even when you were with Christie. When was the last time you actually had good sex?"

"God, I can't even remember." April's last few relationships had lacked any excitement in bed. Pretty much every part of her life was lacking in excitement right now.

Lexi shook her head. "Life is too short for bad sex. Or worse—no sex." She downed the rest of her beer. "I'm going to the ladies' room, I'll be right back."

"Okay."

April placed her drink on the bar and pulled down the hem of her dress. She didn't know why she'd bothered to dress up. It wasn't like she was trying to impress anyone.

Her mind wandered back to the library. There were ninety days until the library had to close its doors. Ninety days to come up with a way to save it. April spent the next few minutes brainstorming ideas but came up empty.

When Lexi returned, she had a guilty look on her face. "So, I know I kind of forced you to come here…"

"Seriously?" April said. "You're going home with someone?"

"*Someone* is coming home with me. I hate sleeping in another woman's bed."

"How did you meet someone in the five minutes you were gone?"

Lexi shrugged. "There was a line for the bathroom. I started talking to the woman in front of me. We had a very interesting conversation." Lexi cocked her head toward a gorgeous long-haired woman standing near the door, typing away on her phone. She was exactly Lexi's type.

"I'm sure it was her conversation that won you over," April said. "It's okay, I was getting bored anyway. I'll probably just go home. Have fun."

"Have I ever told you that you're an amazing friend?"

"Only every time something like this happens."

Lexi grinned. "I'll see you on Monday."

April watched Lexi walk over to the woman, smoothly slide her arm around the woman's waist, and lead her out the door. April finished off the last of her drink. If she left now, she could be in bed by eleven-thirty. Perhaps a good night's sleep would help her tackle her problems in the morning.

As April turned to leave, she noticed a woman standing at the other end of the bar, waiting to order a drink. She looked older than April, but not by much. She was tall and slender, with high cheek-bones, and short, feathery blonde hair that was swept back from her face. She was dressed in a way that seemed effortless and stylish at the same time. Dark skinny jeans. A black blazer with the sleeves rolled up. Heeled ankle boots. She possessed an androgynous air while still seeming utterly feminine.

Had the woman been here all along? The bar was small, and April had been idly watching the crowd all night. April definitely would have noticed someone like her. She simply radiated this cool confidence that made it impossible for April to tear her eyes away.

Suddenly, the woman turned toward her. Her eyes locked onto

April's across the bar. The woman smiled, an enchanting smile that made April's whole body weak. A smile that whispered a suggestion into April's ear.

April looked away, her heart racing. The woman at the other end of the bar had turned April's legs to jelly with no more than a look. What could she do with a word?

A touch?

April's skin grew hot. She had barely shared a glance with this woman, yet her mind was going off to indecent places. What was wrong with her? It was time for her to get out of here. She fished around in her purse, looking for her phone so she could order a ride.

"Hi."

April looked up. The woman was standing right next to her.

"My name is Victoria." She smiled. "But you can call me Vicki."

# CHAPTER TWO

"*A*nd you are?" Vicki asked.

*Where did she come from?* April had been so lost in her head that the slim blonde had seemed to materialize next to her.

"April," she stammered. April, tongue-tied over a woman? If Lexi could see her right now, she'd have a field day.

"What are you drinking, April?" Vicki had to lean in so that April could hear her voice over the noise of the bar.

"A mojito," April replied.

Vicki waved over the bartender. "Two mojitos."

*Wait, what?* This woman was buying April a drink now? This wasn't part of the plan. April was supposed to be going home.

Vicki turned back to April. "Did that friend of yours abandon you?"

April nodded. "She picked up someone in the bathroom," she said, finally regaining the ability to speak in full sentences. Wait, how long had Vicki been watching her?

"I'm glad she did," Vicki said. "I've been waiting to get you alone."

"And why is that?" April's wits were returning now. And suddenly, Vicki's smile seemed more arrogant than alluring.

"I wanted to talk to you," Vicki replied.

"About what?"

"How about we start with why you're here tonight?"

"I'm here because my friend dragged me along with her," April said. "But since she's gone, I was planning to go home."

"Was? Does that mean you're not planning to go home anymore?"

April hesitated. "That depends if I can find a reason to stay."

"Here's one right now." Vicki tilted her head in the direction of the bartender. She'd just finished making their drinks. She placed them on the bar in front of them. Vicki slid one of the glasses over to April. "Now you have a reason."

April picked up the drink and sipped it nonchalantly. She didn't want Vicki to think she was interested. Because she wasn't. Even if she was, it was only because Vicki was outrageously attractive. Those cheekbones of hers could cut glass, and her eyes were a striking green. And she was so tall; although, everyone was tall compared to April.

Everything about Vicki seemed too perfect. Even though her outfit was casual, her clothes were fine, almost too nice for a place like this. And she smelled divine, a sweet, citrusy scent that could only have come from a very expensive bottle.

April realized that neither of them had spoken in a while. "Why are you here tonight?" she shot back.

"I was hoping someone exceptional would walk through the door." Vicki ran her fingers through her short hair. "I'd given up until I saw you."

If those words had come out of anyone else's mouth, April would have rolled her eyes and walked away. But somehow, coming from Vicki's lips, they made April want to melt.

"Judging by the way you were looking at me earlier, you were thinking the same thing," Vicki said, never taking her eyes off April's.

"Can't a girl just admire the view?" April asked.

"You're admitting it then? That you were checking me out?"

"I didn't say that," April said, twirling a lock of her long brown hair around her finger. When she realized what her hands were doing, she stopped. She was not some flirting teenage girl.

"You never did answer my question." Vicki leaned down on the bar. "Why did you really come here tonight? It can't be just because of your friend."

"Do I need a reason to come to a bar? Maybe I just wanted a drink."

"You're not here to drink. You can't have had more than a couple of drinks, or you'd be at least tipsy. And you're not the type to come to a place like Sapphire for no reason."

"How do you know that?"

"I can tell," Vicki said. "And, I would have seen you here before if you were."

"Spend a lot of time here hitting on women, do you?" April had been friends with Lexi for years. She knew a player when she saw one.

Vicki placed her glass down on the bar. "It's my turn to ask questions."

"Excuse me?"

"You heard what I said," Vicki replied. "But since you don't seem inclined to answer me, I'm going to make an educated guess."

April crossed her arms. "Go ahead."

"You're here to take your mind off your problems."

April shrugged. "Maybe."

"And what would those problems be?"

"The usual. Work. Women. Everything."

"I can't imagine you having problems with women," Vicki said.

"Are you kidding?" April said. "I have nothing but problems with women. And it's not like they're lining up to date me."

"Of course they're not. They're all intimidated by you."

"*I'm* intimidating?"

"Extremely," Vicki replied. "Not to mention you're the hottest woman in the room. That's intimidating."

"That didn't stop you."

"Because I like a challenge."

184

April shook her head. "It's a game to you? Finding a woman at a bar and seeing if you can get her to go home with you?"

"I do enjoy playing games," Vicki said. "But that part comes later."

April gaped at her. What exactly was Vicki suggesting? A number of naughty images sprang up in April's mind.

"How about we ditch this bar and go somewhere nicer?" Vicki asked.

April narrowed her eyes. "Somewhere nicer?"

"Yes. A different bar, for example."

"I'm sure that's what you meant."

"Why, did you have somewhere else in mind?" Vicki propped her elbow up on the bar and crossed her ankles. "I'm open to suggestions."

April couldn't believe Vicki's nerve. Did she really think that it was a given that April would go home with her? That as soon as they stepped through the door Vicki would have April up against the wall and begging for Vicki to…

*Wow.* Where had that thought even come from?

"So, what do you say?" Vicki asked.

April bit the inside of her cheek. Her mind was telling her to put her drink down, and walk out the door, to go home to the comfort of her bed. But the rest of her body was screaming something completely different.

"I know what you're doing. You're trying to find an excuse to walk away. You're telling yourself that you shouldn't do this, you shouldn't want this." Vicki leaned in closer. "It's only one night. Give in to temptation just this once."

There was something hypnotic about Vicki's smooth voice, and her perfect skin, and her dark green eyes. They seemed so endless, so easy to get lost in.

Or maybe those mojitos were stronger than April realized.

Vicki straightened up. "Of course, if you're not interested, just say the word and I'll leave you alone."

Vicki drummed her fingers on the bar next to her. With every tap, April could feel her reservations falling away. Her eyes wandered down to Vicki's full, coral red lips...

"Kiss me," she said.

"What?" For the first time that night, Vicki's composed facade wavered.

"Kiss me." April gave Vicki a tantalizing smile. "I want to know what I'm getting myself into."

Something ignited in Vicki's eyes. Without hesitation, she reached out and cupped April's cheek in her hand, drawing her into a searing hot kiss.

At once, April crumbled. She closed her eyes and let Vicki's mint-tinged lips and heady scent overwhelm her senses. Her head began to spin, and the floor seemed to slip out from under her.

April pulled back, breathless. "Okay."

"Okay, what?" Vicki asked.

"Okay. I'll come home with you." It was just one night after all. One night, no strings. And April was going to keep her head.

Not five minutes later, they were in the back seat of a cab on the way to Vicki's apartment, their lips and arms locked together in a tempest of lust.

---

April and Vicki walked down the hall to Vicki's apartment. They had ended up in a nice part of the city, in a fancy apartment building. April didn't have a chance to comment before Vicki pushed her up against what April hoped was her front door.

April grabbed onto Vicki's waist, pulling her in closer. Vicki pressed her lips to April's in an insistent kiss. April struggled to keep herself from dissolving into Vicki's skin. She wasn't doing a very good job of keeping her head.

"Mmph." April shoved Vicki away playfully. "Shouldn't we wait until we're inside? Do you really want to give your neighbors a show?"

"They're going to get a show either way," Vicki replied. "The whole building is going to hear us later."

"You're a lot of talk, but I'm not seeing any action."

"Oh, I'm going to make you regret saying that." Vicki unlocked the door. "Inside."

As soon as Vicki opened the door, her expensive clothes and perfume made sense. A place like this, in this part of the city, would cost a fortune. The spacious loft was sleek and open, with high ceilings and big windows. It was all pale wood and glass, clean and white, while still feeling warm and welcoming.

"After you," Vicki said.

April stepped inside. A small black cat stood up on the arm of the couch, yellow eyes glinting in the light. He looked at her and arched his back, his fur standing up, then darted off into the kitchen.

"That's Sebastian," Vicki said, flinging her blazer over the back of a chair. "Ignore him, he gets jealous."

April turned in a circle in the center of the room. "This is a nice place."

Vicki appeared behind her, wrapping her arms around April's waist. She kissed the side of her neck. "If you think this is impressive, you should see the bedroom."

"In a hurry to get me out of this dress, are you?" April asked.

"What can I say? I'm simply dying to see what's underneath it."

"Do your corny lines ever work on anyone?"

"You're standing in my apartment right now, aren't you?" Vicki said, running her fingers through her blonde locks. "You tell me."

God, it was so sexy when she did that. "Show me the way to your bedroom and I'm yours."

Vicki grabbed April's hand and pulled her down the hall and into her bedroom. It looked much the same as the rest of the house, but not as bright. It was decorated in various shades of gray, with hints of red. There was a huge closet built into one wall. Apparently, the stylish woman owned a lot of clothing.

Vicki kicked off her boots. "You have twenty seconds to get out of that dress."

A smile spread on April's lips. She liked a woman who took

charge in the bedroom. "Why don't you come here and take it off me?" April asked.

Vicki answered April's challenge by backing her toward the bed, unzipping April's dress, and yanking it over her head in the space of a few seconds.

She pushed April onto the bed and raked her eyes down April's body. "Where have you been all my life, April?"

"Just shut up and get over here," April said.

Vicki raised an eyebrow. "I don't take too kindly to being ordered around."

"What are you going to do about it?" April asked.

Without taking her eyes off April, Vicki stripped off her clothing until she was left in only a pair of black panties. Then she dived onto the bed and tore off April's bra, flinging it to the side, and kissed April greedily. Her hand skimmed down to April's chest, caressing the curves of her breasts and the peaks of her nipples.

April let out a soft murmur, drawing Vicki down to her. Vicki's thigh slipped between April's, pressing against her panty-covered mound. April ran her palms up Vicki's smooth stomach and over her breasts. Above her, Vicki let out a halting breath.

She straightened up, kneeling over April with one leg at either side of her. "Why don't we have a little fun?"

"Oh?" April bit her lip. "What kind of fun."

"Stay right there."

"Yes, ma'am."

Vicki got up and walked over to a chest at the end of the bed. She opened the lid and began to dig through its contents, seemingly searching for something in particular. A toy of some kind? Vicki had mentioned that she liked to play games.

Whatever Vicki was looking for, it was taking far too long. April crawled to the end of the bed and peered into the chest.

"What's... oh!"

Inside the chest was a large collection of toys. Sure, there was a strap-on and a vibrator. But on top of that, there were handcuffs, ropes, a blindfold—even some kind of whip.

Vicki gave April a firm stare. "Didn't I tell you to stay there?"

April frowned. "Yes, but-"

"Then why didn't you?"

"Because I wanted to see what you were doing." April paused. "Is that a whip?"

"It's not a whip," Vicki said. "It's a riding crop."

April raised an eyebrow. "How do you know so much about that?"

"Let's just say what's in this chest isn't even half of my collection."

"Where's the rest of it?"

Vicki shut the lid. "Wouldn't you like to know?"

"Come on," April said. "You can't say something like that and not show me."

"I don't think so. There's a reason I keep it all hidden away. The rest of my collection isn't for the faint of heart."

"I'm no stranger to that kind of thing," April said. "It doesn't scare me."

"Let me guess. Someone tied you to a bed once and now you're an expert in all things kinky?" Vicki said.

April's cheeks grew warm. "Are *you* an expert in all things kinky?"

"You didn't answer my question."

"They were handcuffs. Someone handcuffed me to the bed." It was an old girlfriend of hers, one of her many relationships that didn't last. "It doesn't matter. Nothing that you could show me would shock me."

"I wouldn't be so sure about that," Vicki said.

April folded her arms across her chest. "Try me."

For a split second, Vicki's eyes flicked over to the closet built into the wall.

That was the only hint April needed. She leaped off the bed and made a beeline for the closet. Vicki made a half-hearted attempt to stop her, but not before April reached the closet and flung the doors open.

Her jaw dropped. "What the hell?"

"Do you still think nothing could shock you?" Vicki asked.

April scanned the contents of the enormous closet. It didn't contain clothing. Instead, illuminated by bright lights, were racks and shelves full of every kind of kinky toy imaginable.

Her eyes fell on a series of silver chains, all with different types of clips at the ends. "Are those..."

"Nipple clamps?" Vicki said. "Yes."

April pulled her hand away. Moving on, she ran her hands along a rack of various leather implements. She picked one up, a short black whip with dozens of tails, and held it before her. "Why do you have all this?"

"Because I'm a Domme." Vicki held out her hand and stared at April until she placed the whip in it. She slipped it back into its place on the rack. "I can tell by the look in your eyes that I don't have to explain to you what that means."

April knew what it meant, in a general sense at least. "Do you do this for a living?"

"It's more of a hobby," Vicki replied. "Something I enjoy."

"You get turned on by this?"

"Do you?"

April hesitated. She had never been interested in anything like this. At least, not anything this extreme. But for the past few minutes, the heat between her thighs had been steadily increasing.

"Of course, I enjoy all things vanilla too," Vicki said. "I wouldn't have invited you over if I didn't." She shut the closet doors, hiding everything from view. "Why don't we-"

"Show me." The words flew out of April's mouth before she knew what she was saying.

"Show you what?"

"Show me what you do as a Domme. Show me how you use all of this." April gestured toward the closet.

"Those are just tools. And they're not for beginners." Vicki led her back to the bed and sat down next to her. "Besides, that's not how it works. An interaction between a Domme and her submissive isn't about whips and chains. It goes far deeper than that."

"Then show me what it's really about." April rearranged herself so that she was kneeling on the bed with her legs tucked underneath her. "Please?"

Vicki studied April silently for a moment. "Did you like it?"

"Like what?" April asked.

"Being handcuffed to the bed."

"Yes," April said. The memory of that night had stayed seared in her mind. "I liked it."

"Why?" Vicki asked. "What did you like about it?"

"I'll tell you if you agree to show me what you do."

"I don't make a habit of letting submissives dictate terms."

"Can't you make an exception?"

Vicki searched April's face, her green eyes probing into April's. April held her gaze. She didn't know why, but she wanted this so badly.

Vicki shook her head. "All right," she finally said. "I'll show you."

# CHAPTER THREE

"Strip off your panties and come here," Vicki said.

April did as she was told, moving to stand in front of Vicki in the center of the rug. "What are you going to do?" she asked.

"You'll see. Don't worry, I'm not going to use any of my toys."

"Then how are you going to show me what you do?"

Vicki didn't answer her. "You need to choose a safeword. Something you're unlikely to say accidentally."

"Why do I need a safeword if you're not going to use your toys?"

"Safewords aren't just for physical play," Vicki said. "Your safeword?"

April thought for a moment. "Cinnamon."

"Cinnamon it is. Say the word, and everything stops."

April nodded. "Okay."

Almost immediately, there was a subtle shift in Vicki's demeanor. The green in her eyes darkened, and her physical presence grew to fill the room. It was like she slipped on a mask, one that amplified a certain side of her. It was the side of Vicki that had made April fall to pieces the moment their eyes had met in the bar.

"You seem to have this idea that BDSM is all physical," Vicki said. "In reality, it's all in the mind. Everything in my closet? It's all window dressing. I don't need any of it to gain your submission. I'm going to show you that right now."

"How?" April asked.

"I'm going to peel back all your defenses and work my way deep inside you until you're truly vulnerable," Vicki said. "Until you have no choice but to surrender."

A shiver rolled down the back of April's neck. She kept her face blank, not letting Vicki see how much she was getting under her skin.

"And then," Vicki said, a smile playing on her lips, "You're going to beg me for release."

April smirked. "You can try."

"I'm very good at what I do. If I say you're going to beg, then you're going to beg. That brings me to the rules of the game." Vicki began to pace in front of her slowly. "You will obey every instruction that I give you. You will remain perfectly still otherwise. And you will remain silent unless I ask you a question. When I ask you a question, you will answer me honestly."

"Are you going to make me call you 'Master' too?" April asked. "Or is it Mistress?"

Vicki's face remained impassive. "You've already broken a rule."

"You didn't say that we'd started."

"We've started," Vicki said firmly. "Talk back to me again, and this ends."

April bit back a retort.

"Good, you're learning. Now close your eyes."

April hesitated.

"Is there a problem?" Vicki asked.

"Why do I have to close my eyes?".

"Because in the darkness, there's nowhere to hide."

April glanced over at the closet. Although it was shut, she had a clear picture in her mind of what it contained. It suddenly hit her how crazy this was. She was alone in an apartment with a stranger who had a closet full of what was essentially torture equipment.

Vicki said she had no intention of using any of it but that didn't stop April's pulse from racing.

"Look," Vicki said, "If you're uncomfortable with any of this, we can stop."

"No," April said. "I don't want to stop."

"Then choose." Vicki took April's hand. "Choose to hand control over to me. If you want to do that, close your eyes and trust me. You can feel safe with me."

*Safe.* Although she hadn't realized it, that was what she'd been wanting to hear. She took in a breath and shut her eyes.

April's senses took a moment to adjust. Then she could hear the near silence of the room, and could feel the soft fibers of the rug between her toes. Vicki let go of her hand, but April could still feel the woman's presence beside her, and the electricity radiating between them.

Vicki circled behind April and hooked her arms around April's body, pulling her gently back against her chest. "Now, I'm going to ask you some questions," Vicki said. "Let's start with something easy. What's your name?"

"April Reid," she replied.

"Why did you come home with me tonight?"

"Why did you bring me home with you tonight?" April couldn't help herself.

Vicki's arms tightened around April's body. "Do I need to tell you the rules again? *I* ask the questions. *You* answer them." Vicki's voice was soft but firm. "Why did you come home with me tonight?"

"I don't know," April said. "I wanted to get laid."

"But why me?" Vicki asked. "I was watching you. There were plenty of other women who were interested in you. You didn't give them a second glance. Why me and not someone else?"

"You looked like you could show a girl a good time," April said.

Vicki let out a faint chuckle. "Flattery will get you nowhere. Try harder. *Why are you here?*"

"Because I want you to fuck me."

"Close," Vicki slid a hand down the center of April's stomach, stopping just below her bellybutton. "But we're not quite there yet. How about this? Why did you ask me to show you what I do?"

"Because... I was curious," April said.

"Once again, you're close but not quite there."

April let out an exasperated sigh. "I don't know."

"I do." Vicki pulled her in tighter. "I could tell from the moment I saw you what kind of woman you are. Strong. Fierce. Wild. You came home with me because you wanted someone who could handle you. Someone who can take you, and tame you, and tear away your tough exterior to get to what's beneath it. To get to that part of you that's just pure, unbridled lust."

One of Vicki's hands crept down to the inside of April's thigh, the other, up to her chest. She brushed her fingers over April's nipples. "And when you found out that I'm a Domme, you wanted more than to give in to lust," she said. "You wanted to give in to all those dark desires that you barely even knew you had. Does that sound right?"

April let out a breathy whimper. With Vicki pressed against her, and Vicki's hands all over her body, she was finding it difficult to think. But her whole body told her that the answer to Vicki's question was yes.

"Let's try this another way," Vicki said. "Tell me about the time you were handcuffed to the bed."

April thought back to that night. "It was years ago, with an old girlfriend."

As soon as April started talking, Vicki slid her hand up April's thigh and into her slit, gliding her fingers up and down with the lightest of touches.

A moan fell from April's lips. "We... we got these cheap handcuffs from a bachelorette party," April said. "Afterward, we were in bed together, and we wrestled a bit, and she pinned me down and cuffed me to the bedpost." Just recounting the night made April even hotter.

"Why did you wrestle her?" Vicki asked. "Why didn't you just let her handcuff you?"

"I don't know," April said.

"Yes, you do. Think about it."

Vicki circled April's swollen clit with a fingertip. April's breath hitched. Her legs would have given out if she didn't have Vicki there to hold her up.

"Because... I didn't want to give up so easily."

"What's so bad about giving in, allowing yourself to be vulnerable?" Vicki asked. "Why is that so hard?"

April tensed. This was a little too personal.

"You don't have to answer that. Why don't you tell me what you liked about being handcuffed to the bed?"

April searched her mind. "I liked having that power taken away from me. My free will taken away from me. I liked that it forced me to..." How could April explain what that night had been like for her?

"Succumb to your desires?" Vicki whispered.

"Yes." April was unable to keep the desperation from her voice. She had no idea how long it had been, but she'd been ready for Vicki the moment she walked through the door to her apartment. Her body craved release. Her body craved Vicki.

"And what did that feel like?" Vicki asked, her fingertips still strumming April's bud.

"It felt so liberating."

For a while, Vicki didn't speak. All April could hear was the faint sound of Vicki's breath in her ear.

"Keep your eyes closed." Vicki took April's hand and pulled her across the room. "The bed is behind you. Sit down on the edge and lay back."

April obeyed. Vicki guided her hand back down to the crease of April's thighs, skimming her fingers up April's wet folds. April quivered on the bed.

"Had enough?" Vicki asked. "Do you want to come?"

"Yes," April murmured.

"All you have to do is ask."

April groaned. She had forgotten about Vicki's vow. She sealed her lips shut, determined not to give in. But she already knew it was futile.

"I can see how worked up you are," Vicki said. "How every stroke of my fingers drives you closer and closer to the sweet release." Vicki stilled her hand. "But I'm not going to allow it until you say please."

April covered her mouth with her fist, biting back a moan. She couldn't take much more of this torment. She needed Vicki so badly that it hurt.

"All you have to do is say the word."

Vicki slid a finger down to April's entrance and dipped it inside her. A single finger, only shallow enough to tease, nothing more. April whimpered again, her body screaming for the release that Vicki was keeping just out of reach.

"Please." The word fell unbidden from April's lips.

"What was that?" Vicki asked. "I didn't quite hear you."

"Please." April didn't care anymore. She needed to come right now or she would lose her mind. "Please!"

"Now that wasn't so hard, was it?"

The next thing April knew, Vicki plunged her fingers inside her. Then Vicki was on top of her, kissing her furiously. April's whole body began to quake. With Vicki's thumb on her clit and two fingers inside her, the ache in April's core began to build and build...

April cried out as pleasure burst from deep within and spread through her. She trembled with the aftershocks, her head thrown back.

But even as her orgasm faded Vicki didn't stop. Removing her thumb from April's sensitive bud, she continued to pump her fingers in and out, pushing against that spot inside which drove her wild.

"Oh god!" Soon, another orgasm followed, even more powerful than the last. April clutched at the bedsheets as wave after wave crashed through her.

Finally, Vicki withdrew and kissed April again, more gently this time. April let the soft bedsheets engulf her. She wanted nothing more than to lie there forever, sinking into Vicki's lips.

But eventually, she had to come back to reality. "That was... wow."

Vicki collapsed next to her. "It wasn't bad for me either."

"But I barely even touched you."

"You didn't need to. Your submission is its own reward." Vicki traced a meandering line down April's thigh with her fingers. "Don't get me wrong, I'm not one of those types who doesn't like to be touched. But not tonight."

"Some other night, then?" April blurted the words out before realizing what she was asking.

"Sure. As long as it's vanilla only."

It wasn't hard to figure out what Vicki meant by 'vanilla.'

"Why?" April asked. "I don't want vanilla. I want more."

Vicki groaned. "Don't say that. You have no idea how much I want to say yes."

"Why don't you?"

"Because I don't do bratty submissives."

"What does that mean?" April asked.

"It means I don't mess with submissives who like to push back and test my authority," Vicki said. "I like my subs obedient and eager to please me. You are neither of those things."

April sat up and looked down at Vicki. "Sounds to me like you're afraid of a challenge."

"You're proving my point with every word you say."

"Teach me, then," April said. "Teach me how to be your submissive."

"I'm not looking for someone who needs to be tamed," Vicki said.

"I don't need to be tamed. I can be good."

Vicki laughed. "I've only known you for a few hours and I know that's not true."

"Please?" April asked as sweetly as she could.

Vicki scrunched up her brow. "You're serious about this?"

"Yes, I am."

"It isn't all fun and games. There are rules. Conditions."

"I can handle it," April said.

Vicki folded her hands behind her head. "How about this? There's a club downtown that a friend of mine owns. It holds a ladies-only night every other Tuesday. I'll meet you there the

Tuesday after next and give you a real taste of what it means to be my submissive."

"A real taste?" April glanced over at the closet full of toys. "What exactly does that involve?"

"You'll have to wait and see," Vicki said. "And you're going to have to prove to me that you can behave."

"Okay."

"I'll write down the address for you."

"Can't you just text it to me?" April asked.

"I could if I wanted to," Vicki replied.

"What, I don't even get your phone number? You expect me to go to some club and just wait for you to turn up?"

"If you want to play the game, you have to prove to me how much you want it."

So, Vicki wanted to keep her on a string? April was starting to regret her promise to be good. If Vicki was going to toy with her, it was only fair that April could toy with her back.

But for now, she would play by Vicki's rules.

"Okay," April said. "Write down that address for me."

# CHAPTER FOUR

*W*hen April arrived at the library on Monday morning, Lexi was already there with her head on her desk.

"Good morning, Lexi," April said.

"Not so loud," Lexi mumbled.

"Don't tell me you went out again last night?"

"I did. I'm too old for this. Getting drunk, spending the night in some other woman's bed."

"I've been too old for that for years," April said. "And I'm younger than you."

Lexi looked up at her. "Why are you so cheerful today?"

April shrugged. "Because I didn't spend my Sunday night getting drunk."

"No, that's not it." Lexi studied April's face. "No way. Did you get laid?"

April sat down at her desk. "Maybe."

"I knew it! Was that on Saturday night?"

April nodded.

"What happened?" Lexi asked. "I thought you left after I did."

"I was going to, but then I met someone."

"And?"

"And I went to her place," April said. "It was a really nice place."

"Come on, you've got to give me more than that," Lexi said.

"You know how it is. One thing led to another, and..." Just thinking about it made April burn inside. "It was really, really hot. And kind of kinky."

"Oh? Are we talking 'furry pink handcuffs' kinky, or 'chains and leather' kinky?"

April flushed. "I'm not going into detail." Besides, truth was, it was something different altogether. But she couldn't explain that to Lexi. "Anyway, I'm meeting her again next week."

"Oh? Like a date?"

"I don't think so," April replied. "It sounds like she just wants a repeat of the other night." And so did April.

"I thought hook-ups weren't your thing?" Lexi said.

"This is the exception."

"Good for you. Didn't I tell you that it'd be fun? You've forgotten all about Christie too, haven't you?"

"Fine, you were right." April had barely thought about Christie all weekend. And she hadn't been worrying about all the problems with the library as much as she should have been.

"I'm glad one of us got something out of Saturday night," Lexi grumbled.

"What happened with the woman you took home?"

"She was a total pillow princess. I made her come four times, but when it was her turn, she gave up after a few minutes. Who can come in three minutes?"

April had come in three minutes on Saturday night. Well, at least she had the second time. She hadn't even known that she was capable of orgasming more than once.

She felt so conflicted. She hated that Vicki was able to command her body like that. She hated even more that Vicki was able to get into her head, to turn her into a begging mess. April didn't beg. She didn't let others control her. Yet, Vicki had wrested control from her effortlessly. And April had enjoyed every moment of it. All those presumptions Vicki had made about what April really wanted? They were completely true.

April had tasted submission. She wanted more.

But next time, she wouldn't give in quite so easily. Next time, she'd make Vicki work for it. It was bad enough that Vicki had her on a leash, making April wait over a week to meet her at some club without so much as a phone number.

"Are you still thinking about the other night?" Lexi asked. "You're not falling for this woman, are you?"

"God, no," April said.

After she had left Vicki's apartment and the excitement of the night had faded, April had remembered what Vicki was really like. Cocky. A player. Vicki probably saw April as nothing more than another conquest. She could tell that Vicki's dominant personality wasn't limited to the bedroom. April had no interest in a relationship with someone as stubborn as herself. It would be a disaster.

"It's all just raw physical chemistry," April said. "We are completely incompatible otherwise."

"Well, be careful," Lexi said. "I know you haven't done the 'casual' thing before, but there's a risk of one of you developing feelings. It happens a lot, and it never ends well. Someone usually ends up getting their heart broken. Or worse, they end up falling in love and moving in together."

"You don't have to worry about that," April said. She switched on her computer. It was time to get to work.

"By the way, you might want to check your inbox," Lexi said. "The mayor's office sent out an email about the town hall meeting tonight."

The meeting had been called to give the community a chance to voice their concerns about the impact of all the new developments in West Heights. April was planning to attend on behalf of the library, but she had low expectations. The mayor and the city council supported all the new developments in West Heights because of the money that was coming in with them. The concerns of the existing residents were barely on their radar.

"Apparently, a representative from Oasis Developments is coming to speak to everyone," Lexi said. "It's probably some PR person whose job it is to convince the locals that bulldozing

Oakmont Street to make room for luxury apartments is a good thing."

April found the email in question and skimmed through it, confirming what Lexi had said. "Maybe this is our chance to make Oasis listen to us about the library."

"I wouldn't hold my breath," Lexi muttered.

April ignored her. This could be April's last opportunity to save her library. Oakmont Street Library had been struggling for a while now. The library was unusual in that it relied more heavily on private funding than money from the city. The building itself had belonged to a wealthy philanthropist who leased it to the city for a token amount. But when the owner had passed away unexpectedly, his family had put his estate up for sale.

In the ensuing months, April had scrambled to save the library. Fundraising, soliciting donations, applying for state and federal grants. It wasn't enough. Property in West Heights was now at a premium. And so, Oasis Developments had snapped up the building.

Now, they had 90 days to leave the premises. Because the city didn't have the funds to buy or rent a space for the library in West Heights, they would be forced to close their doors. There were no options left.

Unless April could somehow convince Oasis Developments not to tear the building down.

"I'm going to that meeting," April said. "Whoever this representative is, I'm going to make them understand how important a role the library plays in the community. They can't just demolish it. They've already torn down half of West Heights. Corporations are taking over, people who have lived here for decades are being forced out because rent is too high. I may not be able to save the entire suburb, but I'm not going to give up on the library."

"Look, I'll come to the meeting tonight too," Lexi said. "But do you really think you can fight a corporation like Oasis?"

"I don't know, but you bet your ass I'm going to try."

"I know this place means a lot to you, but you have to be realistic. West Heights has already been changing for years."

What Lexi was saying was true. Fifty years ago, the historic suburb of West Heights had been mostly working-class families and immigrants. Fifteen years ago, the artists, musicians, and students started moving in. Everyone had quickly learned to coexist, creating a diverse melting pot. But with corporations like Oasis taking over, all of those people would be pushed out, and West Heights would never be the same.

"This is different," April said. "I'm not going to let West Heights be taken over."

"Well, no matter what happens, I'll be there to back you up," Lexi said.

April settled into her chair. She had to prepare for the meeting. Tonight, April was going to stand before this representative from Oasis Developments and present her case for why the library needed to remain open. She didn't know if it would make a difference. But one thing was certain.

She wasn't going down without a fight.

That evening, April left her apartment and headed to the town hall meeting. It was being held in the auditorium of the local high school. She gazed wistfully around at the neighborhood as she walked. This place that she'd called home for so long was changing right before her eyes.

A few people greeted April as they passed her on the street. April had worked at the library for years, so she knew everyone who came in. Most of the community went to the library for one reason or another. To borrow books, to use the computers, to meet up for activities and clubs.

West Heights needed the library. April wasn't going to let it get torn down.

When April reached the hall, the meeting had just begun. Mayor Collins was speaking on the stage, and a handful of council members were seated behind her. April was surprised that the Mayor had come in person. She was even more surprised that the hall was packed. She'd been to a few of these meetings before when there were matters relating to the library on the agenda, and the room was usually half empty.

It made sense. The library wasn't the only thing being displaced by Oasis. Not only had Oasis bought the library, but they had also bought all the surrounding apartments and houses. Even a small park, the only one for miles, was on the firing line. Most of the attendees appeared to be older people who had lived in the area their whole lives. They likely felt even more strongly about the changes taking place in their home than April did.

April scanned the seats looking for Lexi's black curls, which she always wore piled up on her head. Spotting her, April crept down to the aisle and took a seat next to her a couple of rows from the front.

"What did I miss?" she whispered.

"Not much," Lexi replied. "Collins is talking about new building regulations."

Mayor Collins was one of April's least favorite people. It was clear that she cared more about the more affluent parts of the city than West Heights. She was responsible for the funding cuts to the library over the past few years, and she supported all the new developments that were going up around the city, including on Oakmont Street.

Mayor Collins seemed to dislike April just as much as April disliked her. They had clashed a few times over the library, even before Oasis bought the building. April suspected Mayor Collins was glad that it was being shut down.

April tried to settle in and listen to the mayor, but she found herself getting restless. After a sleep-inducing explanation of the height limit changes for new buildings on King Street, Mayor Collins moved on to the final topic of the night.

"Now," she began. "The main reason I called this meeting was to give everyone a chance to discuss the effects of some of the upcoming development projects on the community. I've received a truckload of submissions about the proposed development on Oakmont Street, and I thought it could be helpful to have an open conversation about it. I invited Oasis Developments to join the discussion, and they've sent a representative to come speak with us." The mayor looked down at a sheet of paper in front of her. "She's the Vice President of Project Development. Hopefully, she will be able to address your concerns."

April frowned. With a title like that, this woman had to be high up in the chain of command. On one hand, it meant that she was someone who actually had the power to change things. On the other hand, she was probably some stuffy middle-aged woman in a suit who earned more in a day than April did in a month. She couldn't expect someone like that to be sympathetic to the residents of West Heights.

"Ms. Blake, was it?" Mayor Collins looked down toward someone sitting in the front row.

A tall woman with short blonde hair stood up and walked toward the stage. Her back was to the crowd, her face hidden from view, but the upright, self-confident manner in which she held herself was very familiar to April.

Her stomach dropped. *No.* It couldn't be.

The woman climbed the stairs up to the stage and took her place next to the Mayor. "Please," she said. "Call me Vicki."

# CHAPTER FIVE

*T*his is not happening.

April simmered inside. There was no denying it. She had traded her jeans and blazer for a stylish, tailored pantsuit and heels, but otherwise, it was the same Vicki. Suddenly, the room felt too hot.

"Vicki it is," Mayor Collins said. "Vicki is in charge of the Oakmont Street project. She's going to tell us a little about the development, then we'll open the floor for questions. Vicki?" The mayor handed the microphone to Vicki and sat down on a chair behind her.

Vicki began to speak, but April didn't hear a single word. She was too busy trying to calm the emotions warring inside of her. Disbelief. Betrayal. Anger.

Desire.

Why, despite everything, did Vicki still provoke this reaction in her? In April's mind, it was clear—Vicki was the enemy. But her body said otherwise. Even though Vicki was more than twenty feet from where April sat, just being in the woman's presence stirred something deep within her. Hearing Vicki's compelling voice brought back the memory of her lips on April's ear. Watching Vicki command the stage made April feel breathless.

Lexi nudged April in the ribs.

April blinked. "Huh?"

Lexi cocked her head at the stage where to where Vicki sat next to the Mayor. When had she finished speaking? Why was it that whenever Vicki was in the room, April would lose awareness of everything around her?

"Anyone?" Mayor Collins asked. "Based on the number of emails I get, I know you all have questions. Vicki is here to answer them. The floor is open."

The room remained silent. Clearly, no one wanted to be the first to go head to head with this corporate heavyweight. April didn't blame them. But she refused to be intimidated by Vicki.

She stood up.

"Ah, Miss Reid." Mayor Collins failed to keep her disappointment from showing in her voice.

Someone walked over to April and handed her a microphone. April's palms were sweaty. She usually didn't have a problem speaking in front of people. But her mind was awhirl with thoughts of Vicki.

She looked up at Vicki. If Vicki was surprised to see April standing there, she didn't show it. Maybe she didn't recognize April with the bright lights of the stage in her eyes.

Or maybe April was just a forgettable one-night stand to her.

"When you're ready, Miss Reid," Mayor Collins said.

Pulling herself together, April began. "I'm speaking on behalf of the Oakmont Street Library, and all its staff and patrons." She had gone over these words in her head countless times, but she stumbled over them, her voice trembling. "It's been an important part of West Heights and the surrounding suburbs since the sixties. The library building is over one hundred years old. It's been a part of West Heights longer than any of us."

April took a deep breath and continued, her voice echoing through the hall. Slowly, she regained her focus. She had a job to do.

She was not going to let her feelings about Vicki distract her from her goal. She was not going to let Oasis win.

She was not going to let Vicki win.

April finished her prepared points about the library, but she didn't stop. She was all fired up now. And she had so much to say. "This isn't just about the library. Other important, historic buildings and landmarks are being demolished all over West Heights. People's homes are in the firing line too. It's been happening the same way, over and over. Some rich developer will buy a block of apartments, then double, even triple the rent, sometimes illegally, until the tenants can't afford to pay anymore. They end up getting evicted, tossed out onto the street, unable to find anywhere to live because everywhere else in the area has had their rent raised too. Meanwhile, developers like Oasis will come in and bulldoze the buildings so they can build high rises, pocketing millions of dollars. They're destroying our beautiful suburb, our community, and the library is just a small part of that."

When April finished, her heart was pounding. She dropped her arms to her side, microphone in hand.

To her surprise, the entire audience started clapping.

Buoyed, April fixed her gaze on Vicki, her glare containing all her anger toward Oasis Developments, and all the other corporations taking over her suburb, and Vicki for being a part of it.

"Thank you, Miss. Reid," the mayor said. "Passionate as always." She turned to Vicki. "Vicki, is there anything you'd like to say?"

"Yes. Miss Reid, was it?" Vicki asked, a hint of amusement in her voice. "I agree, that was a very passionate speech."

There was no mistaking it—Vicki recognized her. She knew April was the woman she'd seduced and tormented. The woman who had been more than willing to yield to her command. And even now, Vicki's devilish smile—the very same one that had lured April to her that night at the bar—almost made April's legs give out from under her.

April stood up straighter.

"You should know that Oasis is taking all of this into consideration," Vicki said. "We're aware of the valuable services Oakmont

Street Library provides, and we're arranging talks with the library's leaders to discuss how we can minimize the effects of the new development on the community."

"That's funny," April said. "Because I run the Oakmont Street Library, and I haven't heard a thing from Oasis since you bought the building."

Vicki tensed, a flicker of surprise crossing her face.

*Not so smug now, are you?* April thought.

But it didn't last. Vicki pulled at the front of her jacket, straightening it out. "You'll be receiving an email from my assistant first thing in the morning so that we can organize a meeting," she said. "I'd like to open up a discussion with all the staff at the library so we can figure out a suitable resolution."

"The only suitable resolution is one that doesn't involve destroying a hundred-year-old building and cutting people off from important resources that they need," April said.

"Let me assure you, Oasis is committed to minimizing the impact of this project on the community."

"You already used that line. How exactly are you going to do that?" April asked.

"That remains to be seen. It's why I'm going to work with you to make sure that the community is heard," Vicki said firmly.

"So we're going to sit down and have a chat, and then you're going to bulldoze the place anyway?"

"I will pass on your recommendations to the appropriate-"

"What, so that Oasis can just ignore them? Just like you people have been ignoring my attempts to contact you for months now?"

"You've made your point, Miss Reid," Mayor Collins said. "Why don't we hear from someone else now?"

April handed the microphone off and sat down. Vicki turned her attention to the rest of the audience. Although Vicki had lost her cool a moment ago, her infuriatingly self-assured demeanor had returned.

However, April had gotten everyone fired up. Hands were going up all around her. It seemed like everyone had something to say now. April's jaw almost dropped when Mrs. Evans, a quiet old lady who lived down the street from the library, launched a scathing tirade about how the Oakmont Street development project was pushing her friends out of the homes they'd lived in for decades.

April sat back and watched the proceedings with glee. To Vicki's credit, she handled it like a pro. But as the questions continued, she showed almost imperceptible signs of frustration. Vicki would cross her legs, then uncross them again a moment later, or would run her fingers through her hair a little too compulsively. Now and then, she would look in April's direction. And April would be staring right back at her, defiant.

After over an hour of this, Mayor Collins called an end to the meeting. It had already gone over time.

"If you have any further feedback, you can contact my office," she said. "We'll pass it along to Oasis. Thank you for coming, Ms. Blake."

"Please, it's Vicki," she said firmly. She turned, addressing the audience. "And please, feel free to contact me directly if you have any concerns."

April scoffed. She had no doubt that any emails sent Vicki's way would be palmed off to someone less important.

As everyone started to file out of the hall, Vicki and the mayor remained on stage, chatting with each other. Vicki glanced at April as she got up to leave, but April simply turned and marched toward the door.

"Whoa," Lexi said. "Wait up. Why are you in such a hurry?"

"I don't want to be in the same room with that woman any longer than I have to."

"Huh? You mean Vicki Blake?"

"Yes, her," April replied. "She's so... ugh! I can't stand her!"

"Well, you really showed her," Lexi said. "It was pretty awesome. We'll see if she follows through with her promise to work with us."

"I'm not holding my breath." April didn't trust Vicki as far as she could throw her, and she had no doubt that any meeting with Vicki would be fruitless. Right now, April never wanted to see or speak to Vicki ever again.

She would never work with Vicki Blake.

# CHAPTER SIX

*A*pril refreshed her email inbox for the twentieth time that Tuesday. Here it was, almost time to go home, and nothing. "I knew I shouldn't have trusted that woman," she muttered.

Lexi looked across to April's desk. "Hmm?"

"Vicki! She said she was going to work with me. She said she'd be in touch. It's been a week now. I've called, I've emailed, I've left messages with her assistant, and nothing!"

"I'm not surprised," Lexi said. "I didn't know whether I should say anything or not because this isn't very professional, but I know a little about her."

April swiveled her chair to face Lexi. "What is it?"

"Well, in case you didn't already guess, she's a lesbian. So naturally, I've heard things." Ever the social butterfly, Lexi seemed to know every queer woman in the city. She always knew who was dating who, who was sleeping with who, and the latest in lesbian drama. "Vicki Blake has a reputation for being a player. And not in a good way."

April held back a curse. Her initial instincts about Vicki were right. Although Lexi liked to gossip, she rarely spoke badly about anyone.

"She's either out causing trouble with some girl on her arm, or she's at Sapphire looking for someone to take home," Lexi said. "Not that there's anything wrong with that, obviously. But it's the way she goes about it. She charms women with her money and sweet words, then ditches them when she gets bored. It's like everywhere she goes, she leaves a trail of brokenhearted women in her wake."

April knew it. She never should have gone home with Vicki. That whole act Vicki pulled about not giving April her number was probably so that she could disappear without a trace. Today was the day that April was supposed to see her again. If none of this had happened and April went to that club tonight like Vicki had told her to, would the Vicki even show up?

It didn't matter. There was no way April was going to that club to meet Vicki. Not after all this.

Besides, even if Vicki had been telling the truth about seeing April again, she definitely would have changed her mind after the town hall meeting.

They were adversaries now, and Vicki knew it.

"I'm not surprised she works for a company like Oasis," Lexi said. "And I'm not surprised she hasn't kept her word."

"I can't believe her," April said. "Was she lying about wanting to work out a solution? Was she just trying to get me to lay off her at that meeting?" April's hands balled into fists on the desk. "If she doesn't get back to me soon, I'm going to go down to her office and confront her myself. She can't just make all these promises and then disappear!"

"Whoa, slow down," Lexi said. "Whenever you get all fired up, your first instinct is to go nuclear. That's not always the best idea."

"I'm just thinking about the library," April grumbled. "How else am I supposed to get her to listen to me? What else am I supposed to do?"

Lexi shrugged. "I don't know. That's why Eliza left you in charge, and not me."

*Eliza.* Lexi's words gave April an idea. She could pay Eliza a visit after work and ask for advice. Eliza had been the director of the library before April, and she had plenty of experience dealing with these kinds of issues. Eliza was both a mentor and a friend to April, and her cool demeanor meant that her perspective was always different from April's.

"I'd love to stay and help you work this out, but I have plans later," Lexi said.

"Let me guess," April said. "These plans involve a woman?"

"They might." Lexi gathered her things. "Hey, what happened with that woman you met at Sapphire? What was her name again?"

April's face grew warm. "I didn't say. It doesn't matter. I've decided not to see her again."

"Why not? Last week you were convinced she was some sort of sex goddess."

"I also said that we weren't remotely compatible. It's becoming more and more clear."

"That's too bad. Sorry it didn't work out." Lexi grabbed her coat from the back of her chair and headed for the door. "I'll see you tomorrow."

April remained at her desk, intending to get a little more work done. But her mind kept drifting back to Vicki. She opened up her web browser. Maybe she could find some other way to contact Vicki about the library. For the past few days, she had resisted the temptation to look Vicki up, to try to find out something about the woman who had been driving her crazy all week. But this was for the library after all. It had nothing to do with April satisfying her personal curiosity.

She typed "Victoria Blake" into a search, not expecting much. It was a common enough name. But to April's surprise, the whole first page of results appeared to be about Vicki.

*That's odd.* Abandoning her quest to find Vicki's contact information, April decided to dig. After all, it was important for her to know just who she was dealing with. She clicked through some articles about Vicki, most to do with her professional achievements. Several of them referred to her as the daughter of Harold Blake.

Naturally, that was a thread April had to follow. She searched for 'Harold Blake' and was met with even more results than she had gotten on Vicki. Harold Blake was the head of an international property development company that was worth billions and had been in his family for generations. Vicki's family.

That explained Vicki's fancy apartment, as well as Lexi's accusation that Vicki threw her money around to get women. Although April hadn't been seduced by Vicki's money, she was just another woman taken in by Vicki's charms.

It also explained Vicki's arrogance. With a family like that, Vicki had probably lived a cushy, privileged life. No wonder she didn't give a damn about the people of West Heights.

As April stared at the screen, something caught her eye. The page on Vicki's father described Blake International as one of the biggest property development firms in the world. A company like Oasis had to be one of Blake International's competitors.

Why, then, was Vicki working for Oasis?

It didn't matter. Watching West Heights change over the past few years had proven to April that all those big multinational development companies were the same. They wouldn't rest until every square inch of land, including national parks the world over, was covered with luxury high-rises, shopping malls, and office buildings.

April returned to her search for Vicki's contact information. All that came up was the same work email and phone number that April already had. Sighing, April sent off another email. She didn't know why she bothered. She would just get another canned response back saying that 'Ms. Blake would contact her as soon as possible.'

It aggravated her to have to chase Vicki for this. April hated the idea of begging Vicki for attention. But this was for the library.

And April would do whatever it took to save it.

---

After locking up the library, April made the short walk to Eliza's house. Too late, she remembered that Eliza had been away visiting her sister. April hoped she'd returned.

She reached Eliza's address. The small townhouse was one of the few remaining houses in the area that hadn't been bought out and torn down in preparation for new developments. The red brick facade was crumbling, and the door needed a new coat of paint, but April liked the familiarity of it. She'd grown up in one just like it. Of course, April's old family home had been replaced by a block of apartments several years ago.

April knocked on the door.

"I'll be right there," a voice called from inside. After almost a minute, a short, dark-haired woman with bright brown eyes opened the door. "April. Come in."

April followed her inside. The interior of the house matched the outside. The wallpaper was peeling off, and the floorboards creaked under April's feet.

Eliza walked slowly down the hall. She was barely forty, but the measured way she held herself made her seem decades older than she was. It was the result of a recently developed autoimmune condition that left her joints stiff. It was the reason Eliza had to quit her job as director of the library. April helped her out by picking things up for her from the store every now and then, but Eliza was too stubborn to accept anything more.

"Would you like something to drink?" Eliza asked. "I'm about to make tea." She was always drinking tea.

"Sure." April sat down at the kitchen table. "How was your trip?"

"It was great."

Eliza filled April in as she made tea in the kitchen. April wanted to help her, but she knew better than to ask. Still, it pained her to see someone she cared about struggling. Eliza had been there for April since the day they had met fourteen years ago. Eliza was a librarian at the time. She and a teen-aged April formed an unusual friendship, which April had sorely needed. Now that Eliza needed her, she wished she could repay the favor.

When Eliza was finished, she handed April a cup and sat down at the table across from her. "How did that town hall meeting go? I heard someone from Oasis came to talk to everyone."

"The meeting itself was great," April said. "Half the neighborhood showed up. But it didn't do much good in the end."

April recounted the events of the last week. Naturally, she left out the part about having sex with Vicki. Eliza listened calmly and silently, showing no reaction to April's growing frustration.

"It's been over a week now!" April said. "And I still haven't heard back from Vicki."

Eliza took a slow, thoughtful sip of her tea. "That woman sounds exactly like every other corporate big-shot I've had to work with," she said. "All evasive language and empty words. Unfortunately, these things always take time. A week is nothing. You've just got to keep on pressuring them."

"Keep pressuring them?" April said. "I don't have time for that! We have less than three months before they tear the place down, and I'm just supposed to keep sending them polite emails and phone calls?"

"April. You need to stop putting your heart before your head. That's not always a bad thing, but right now, you're letting your emotions control you. You look like you're ready to pick a fight."

April crossed her arms. Lexi had said something along those lines too.

"I understand more than anyone why you feel like you have to stand up for the library," Eliza said. "But sometimes, you have to slow down and think, and allow time for diplomacy to work."

"Okay. I'll be patient. But the moment I get Vicki on the line, I'm going to do everything I can to stop Oasis taking over."

"April," Eliza said. "You should be prepared for the fact that you might not be able to stop this."

"Why are you being so calm about this?" April asked. "You worked at the library for longer than I have. You've lived in West Heights longer than I have. The whole neighborhood is being taken over. It's not fair!"

"Life isn't always fair. And change is a part of life."

April huffed.

"You need to be more open to compromise. When the woman from Oasis finally gets back to you, don't just bully her into doing what you want." Eliza held up her hands defensively. "Sorry. Poor choice of words. What I mean is you should stay calm and talk with her civilly. Try to meet her halfway."

"Fine," April said. "I'll try."

"Look, since you're here, there's something I need to tell you," Eliza said. "When I was visiting my sister, she asked me to come and live with her." She placed her cup of tea down on the table. "I said yes."

"What? You're moving away?"

Eliza nodded.

"But you can't leave!" April said. "You've lived here your whole life. You love it here."

"I do. But as you know, my health isn't great. It would be good for me to have people around who can help me out a little. Plus, I can barely even get up these stairs anymore."

"But you have me here to help you," April said. "And all your other friends."

"I can't rely on all of you forever," Eliza said. "Also, my medical bills are starting to pile up. The developers who bought the place next door have been offering to buy my house for years now. I've always turned them down, but they recently made me an offer that's hard to refuse. April, it would mean that I'm set for life."

"But..." Tears began to form at the corners of April's eyes. She wasn't the type to cry at the drop of a hat. But she had known Eliza since she was fourteen. She had opened up April's world and introduced April to the sanctuary she needed so badly at the time. She had taught her how to stand up for herself and fight for what she believed in. She was April's guiding star.

And now she was moving away.

"You can always come visit me. It's only a short flight away." Eliza placed her hand on April's. "I'm sorry. I wish it didn't have to be this way."

"I understand." April blinked away her tears. "I should go. Thanks for the tea."

"Okay." Eliza gave her a sympathetic smile. "Try to remember what I said. Be open to compromise."

April nodded. As soon as Eliza let go of her hand, she fled out the door.

April stood on the sidewalk, wiping the tears from her eyes. She wasn't being fair to Eliza. But she was just so angry at the world right now. Everything was changing. Everything was out of her control. And there was nothing she could do about it.

But that didn't mean that she wasn't going to try.

She would take Eliza's advice about being open to compromise. But she wasn't going to sit around and wait for Vicki any longer. April needed to track her down, figure out a way to see her face to face. It wouldn't be easy, with Vicki ignoring April's attempts to get in touch.

There was one option. It was Tuesday night, and April knew exactly where Vicki was supposed to be.

It was a long shot. But April had to take it.

# CHAPTER SEVEN

*W*hen April got home from Eliza's, she only had an hour before she was due to meet Vicki at that club. After a quick shower, she looked up the address that Vicki had given her, hoping to find out the name of the club. However, there was no information about it online at all. It was like it didn't even exist.

Was this some kind of joke? Had Vicki been messing with her all along? April sighed. It wasn't like she had any other options. She threw on a simple black dress that was somewhere between casual and dressy, and headed straight to the club before she lost her resolve.

April arrived at the address with a few minutes to spare. She double-checked the number next to the small, black door in front of her. *This is it.* Once again, she wondered if Vicki was messing with her.

April looked up at the sign above the door. It read *Lilith's Den* in red cursive script.

*Lilith's Den?* April had taken a class on mythology at college, and although she had forgotten most of what she'd learned, she was pretty sure that Lilith was a demonic seductress from Jewish folklore.

And April was marching right into her den.

Two women walked around April to get to the door. They were both dressed in long black coats. One was wearing thigh-high leather stiletto boots with laces all the way up the front. The other wore a spiked leather choker around her neck that resembled a collar.

*What the hell is this place?* When Vicki mentioned a club, April assumed she meant a nightclub. What if this was a different kind of club entirely?

It didn't matter. April wasn't planning to stay. She would go in, find Vicki, and make her set a meeting there and then. That was it.

Steeling herself, she followed the couple through the door.

April was met with a small lobby, all painted black. A large, burly woman in a suit stood by a set of doors which led to the club inside. Another woman sat behind a small desk beside the door, a tablet in her hand.

The woman at the desk greeted the couple in front of April, waving them through. The bouncer opened the door and let them inside. April caught a glimpse of the flickering lights beyond before the bouncer pulled the door shut.

"Can I help you?" the woman at the desk asked.

"Someone invited me here," April said. "A friend."

"Are you on the list?"

*Great, a list.* Vicki hadn't said anything about a list. "I don't know."

The woman looked her up and down skeptically. "Name?"

"April Reid."

The woman tapped at the screen on her tablet, frowning.

April's shoulders sagged. It was unlikely that Vicki had bothered to put her on the list, especially after everything that had happened. Coming here was a stupid idea.

"There," the woman said. "April Reid. You were invited by Victoria Blake?"

"Yes," April stammered.

"Then she's responsible for you while you're in here. You'll need to sign these." The woman grabbed a clipboard from under the desk and handed it to April.

"What is all this?" April asked, flicking through the pages.

"Club rules, waivers, a non-disclosure agreement. The usual."

*The usual?* What had April gotten herself into?

"A first-timer, huh?" The woman asked.

April nodded.

She smiled. "I know how scary going to a BDSM club for the first time can be. Don't worry, you're in good hands with Vicki. She's one of our regulars."

*A BDSM club.* Of course Vicki would spring this on her. Was this supposed to be some kind of test? Was Vicki trying to scare her, to see whether April was serious about being her submissive? It didn't matter. April wasn't interested in that anymore. She did not want a repeat of the other night, no matter how much the thought of it turned her on.

Maybe this was a bad idea.

"Is everything okay?" the woman asked.

"Yes," April said. "It's fine."

She sighed. She was going to regret this. Without even reading the documents, she scribbled her signature at the bottom of each page and handed the clipboard back to the woman.

"Great." The woman gestured toward the door. "Welcome to Lilith's Den."

The bouncer opened the door wide. Focusing her mind on her goal, April strode into the club.

Music assaulted her ears. The dimly lit room was filled with women, drinking, talking, dancing. It almost looked like any other club. However, the patrons were mostly dressed in black, with only flashes of other colors to be seen. Some, like April, wore dresses. A few wore suits. Others wore lacy corsets or elaborate contraptions made of straps and leather. April's jaw dropped when a woman edged past her wearing nothing but latex pants and duct tape over each nipple in the shape of an X.

The club itself? It contained the usual tables and chairs, and there was a bar at one end. But around the room were all sorts of unusual pieces of furniture, some of which had people tied to them. A large wooden cross, a horse-shaped bench. Most of the crowd's attention was turned toward the large stage at the far end of the room where a woman was being led around on a leash.

April stood rooted on the spot, staring at everything. For the second time that night, she felt the urge to turn around and walk out the door.

Then, she spotted Vicki.

*Wow.* Vicki looked even hotter than she did the night April had met her at the bar. She was sitting in the corner, lounging lazily on a chair, her legs crossed. She wore tight leather pants and a matching jacket, with a loose black top underneath and heeled leather boots. She wouldn't have looked out of place on the cover of a high-end fashion magazine.

Vicki sat alone, a martini glass in her hand. There was this empty zone of space around her as if no one dared to approach her. But more than one woman in the crowd was looking Vicki's way, eying her with either jealousy or adoration. Vicki didn't pay them any mind.

She tossed back the last of her drink, placed the glass on the table, and sat back, scanning the room idly. Almost immediately, Vicki's eyes fell on April.

*Shit.* There was no turning back now.

Summoning all her strength, April marched purposefully toward Vicki. As she approached, Vicki's lips curved up into a smile, one that seemed to say, *I knew you'd come.* But April hadn't come for Vicki. This was purely about the library.

"Hi April," Vicki said.

"Don't 'Hi April' me." April put her hands on her hips. "I've been trying to get hold of you all week!"

Vicki stretched her arm out over the back of the chair. "Miss me that much, did you?"

April scowled. "You said you'd contact me. About the library, I mean."

"I did say that. But I've been busy."

"Busy? So busy that you couldn't even send a single email?"

"I was out of town dealing with a work emergency. I wouldn't have been able to meet with you anyway."

"You could have told me that instead of leaving me in the dark," April said. "I guess the library isn't high enough on your list of priorities."

"Look." Vicki stood up to face April. "I didn't forget. I wasn't ignoring you. I've simply had my hands full all week."

"Are you sure that's why?" April asked. "It wasn't because you found out that the woman you slept with is the same one standing in the way of your development project and you didn't want to face me?"

"Although it was quite a surprise, I don't let business get in the way of pleasure," Vicki said.

April let out an exasperated sigh. "I don't have time for your games."

"I mean it. And I'm being honest. I was always going to meet with the head of the library. Public opposition to this project is high, so it's something Oasis needs to address. But I haven't had a spare moment for the past week."

"You weren't too busy to come here tonight," April said.

"That's because I told you I'd be here," Vicki replied. "I came here for you."

April felt a twinge of desire at Vicki's words. Her stupid, traitorous body. "You didn't seriously expect me to come here after everything that's happened?"

"You're here, aren't you? You came here for me too."

"Yes, but… No! I came here because you've been dodging my calls and emails. I decided I needed to find you and speak to you in person."

"I'm very glad you did, April." April's name seemed to roll off Vicki's tongue.

"Don't use your seductive bullshit on me," April said. "I saw through that smile of yours the moment we met. And I came here because I wanted to talk to you about the library. That's it."

"Really?" Vicki asked. "So this has nothing to do with the other night and how incredible it was?"

Heat rose through April's body. "No, it doesn't. I came here to try to see if we could work together to come up with a solution for the library. But it's clear that your mind is only on one thing."

"Can you blame me? You're not the only one who enjoyed the other night."

"Dammit, Vicki, can't you take this seriously?"

"Okay, fine." Vicki combed her fingers through her hair. "Here's the deal. This project is going ahead. There's nothing you can do to stop it. But I meant it when I said I will work with you to try to minimize the impact-"

"That's not enough!" April said. "We both know that's not going to be enough. If you're going to go ahead with this project, I'm going to do whatever it takes to stop you."

"You can try, but it's not going to change anything," Vicki said. "Be reasonable. Work with me here."

"I'll never work with you."

"Look, I get it. You're feeling betrayed because you found out I'm on the opposite side of this crusade you're on."

"I'm not on a crusade!" April glanced around. They were attracting more than a few stares. She lowered her voice. "And I don't feel betrayed. I never felt anything toward you to begin with."

"All right, you keep telling yourself that," Vicki said. "Whatever it is that you feel or don't feel toward me, don't let your emotions get in the way of us working together to do what's right for the library."

April cursed under her breath. As much as April hated to admit it, Vicki was right. Her anger toward Vicki was clouding her judgment. Maybe Lexi and Eliza had a point about April's tendency to act on her feelings without thinking.

"How about we meet next week?" Vicki asked. "I'll come by the library, and we can have a meeting with all the staff. Wednesday morning. It's the earliest I can do. How does that sound?"

April took a deep breath, attempting to settle the emotions roiling inside her. "All right. Next Wednesday morning."

"I'll have my assistant call you in the morning to confirm. I promise."

April nodded. Almost at once, a huge weight fell from her shoulders. But the turbulence within her remained.

April had been afraid of this. Afraid that it wasn't really the situation she was angry about. It was Vicki. And maybe it wasn't just anger that April was feeling toward her. Her eyes traveled down Vicki's body. April couldn't deny how incredibly sexy she looked in all that leather.

Vicki smiled. "Is that all you want from me? Because my offer still stands?"

"Your offer?" April asked.

"You know, the real reason you're here."

April scoffed. "I don't know what you mean."

"Yes, you do," Vicki said. "You want me to show you what a Domme can do."

April's said nothing.

"Or maybe I'm mistaken," Vicki said. "Maybe there's some other reason your cheeks are that lovely, rosy shade of pink. Some other reason you can barely meet my gaze. Some other reason you're still standing here with me."

"I..." April's tongue seemed stuck to the top of her mouth.

"Vicki?" A voice said from next to them. "I hope I'm not interrupting."

April turned to see a woman with pale skin and long, wavy black hair standing beside them. She, like April, was dressed in a simple black dress, but she somehow managed to look far more glamorous than April and anyone else in the room.

"Vanessa." There was a flicker of annoyance in Vicki's eyes. "I didn't know you were coming tonight."

"I thought I'd check up on the place," Vanessa said. "Make sure that no one is getting into trouble." She gave Vicki a pointed look.

"Trouble? Just because you've settled down doesn't mean the rest of us can't have any fun." Vicki seemed to remember April's presence. "April, this is Vanessa. Vanessa, this is April."

"A pleasure to meet you, April," Vanessa said. "So, this is who begged me to put on the list, Vic?"

*Begged?* April got the impression that this woman was trying to embarrass Vicki. April looked from one woman to the other. She couldn't quite tell if this was friendly banter or veiled hostility.

Vicki ignored Vanessa's comment and addressed April. "Vanessa owns Lilith's Den. She used to be the queen of this place too, until she got a girlfriend."

"I assure you, I'm still the queen of this place. And my girlfriend is right over there." Vanessa cocked her head toward the bar. "I'd be very careful what you say about her."

"I'm surprised you left her alone for a few seconds," Vicki said. "You two are usually joined at the hip. Aren't you scared someone's going to steal her?"

"You're the only person I've ever had to worry about trying to steal her. You know, she still hasn't forgiven you for stirring up trouble at that fundraiser. And neither have I."

"That was last year," Vicki said. "How many times do I have to apologize?"

"As many times as it takes," Vanessa replied.

April stifled a grin. It was satisfying to see Vicki thrown.

"I'd love to stay and chat, but we reserved a room upstairs," Vicki said. "Say hi to Mel for me."

"I'll pass along the message," Vanessa replied. "It was lovely to meet you, April."

"Likewise," April said.

Vicki's eyes followed Vanessa as she walked away.

"What was that about?" April asked.

"Vanessa?" Vicki replied. "Don't worry, that was just her being friendly."

"Friendly? I'm pretty sure she accused you of trying to steal her girlfriend." April remembered what Lexi had told her about Vicki's reputation for causing drama.

"I didn't try to steal her girlfriend. Vanessa can be possessive."

"Sure." April didn't believe Vicki one bit.

However, something about watching Vicki being dressed down by Vanessa had defused April's anger. And she couldn't help but wonder what kinky delights Vicki had in store for her.

April's curiosity got the better of her. "What did you mean about reserving a room?" she asked.

"I only said that to get rid of Vanessa," Vicki said. "I did reserve a room upstairs. But you've made it clear you're not here for that."

April hesitated. "What's upstairs?"

"Upstairs is where I teach you about being my submissive."

April's heart thumped. She had told herself that all she was going to do was talk to Vicki, then leave. She'd told herself that she wasn't going to do this. But as she looked into Vicki's jade eyes, she found herself wishing that Vicki would yank her in close and devour her with her lips like she had the night they met.

"So I wasn't mistaken," Vicki said. "You're still interested."

"I… might be," April said.

"It's simple." Vicki leaned in and spoke into April's ear. "Yes? Or no?"

With Vicki so close, April could feel the electricity sparking between their bodies. It would be so easy right now for April to just close her eyes and kiss her.

April exhaled slowly. She had gotten what she came for. She had gotten Vicki to listen to her. She had no reason to stick around. No reason not to walk out the door.

No reason not to give in to temptation.

"Yes," April whispered.

At once, Vicki's lips were on April's. The deep, overpowering kiss made April's world spin. *Vicki* made April's world spin. April knew this was dangerous, but she had no chance of resisting now.

Vicki broke away. "Let's go upstairs."

# CHAPTER EIGHT

"So," Vicki said. "What do you think?"

April looked around the room. If the club downstairs looked like some sort of kinky dungeon, this room was much more imposing. It was painted a deep purple and was filled with more of the same strange furniture as downstairs, along with a bed. Arranged around the room on shelves and racks was a collection of BDSM toys that rivaled the contents of Vicki's closet.

April's stomach fluttered. The other night, when the two of them were recovering in Vicki's bed, Vicki had asked April which of the toys in the closet appealed to her. She hadn't known where to start. The restraints, those formidable looking whips—April wanted to try it all. As much as everything in this room intimidated her, it turned her on even more.

Vicki spoke again. "It's not too late to back out."

April turned to face her. "A minute ago, you were practically begging me to come up here with you. Are you sure you're not the one losing your nerve?"

"I mean it," Vicki said firmly. "If you're not comfortable with any of this, you can back out at any time. Or use your safeword."

"I know," April replied. "I wouldn't be here if I didn't want this."

"Remember," Vicki said. "A Domme's first priority is looking after her submissive. You're always safe when you're with me. I'll never push you further than you can handle."

April nodded. "Okay." She found Vicki's seriousness reassuring. "What are we going to do?"

Vicki smiled. "Since you were so interested in the toys in my apartment, we're going to play with some of them."

April folded her arms across her chest. "I thought you didn't need tools?"

"I don't. But they have their uses," Vicki said. "Especially when it comes to making unruly submissives more amenable."

Goosebumps sprouted on April's skin. What had she gotten herself into?

Vicki walked over to over to a padded leather table near the end of the bed. "Get onto the table on your hands and knees."

April looked at the sturdy black table. It was about waist height, and almost looked like a massage table, but it was clearly meant to be used for something more sinister. There were rings all around the edges that looked like something could be tied to them.

April glanced at the toys arranged around the room again. She and Vicki had briefly discussed what Vicki referred to as "limits" before they'd come inside. April knew that Vicki wouldn't cross any lines, but she wanted to know what the other woman had planned. "What are you going to do?"

"April," Vicki said. "What was my first rule?"

April thought back to that night in Vicki's apartment. "To obey your instructions."

"Get onto the table, before I make you crawl here."

April opened her mouth to retort, but Vicki gave her a frosty look that compelled her into action. "Fine." Without taking her eyes off the other woman, April walked purposefully to the table and climbed onto it on all fours.

Vicki took April's chin in her fingers. "What was my second rule?"

"To remain silent unless spoken to," April said.

"Do not break my rules again."

April nodded. The weight of Vicki's stare made her want to crumble.

Vicki brought her lips to April's in a knee-melting kiss. "Good," she said.

After the other night, April was starting to see a pattern in Vicki's behavior. Obey her, and Vicki would reward April with the kind of sweet, hot passion that made April weak. Disobey her, and Vicki would show April her much darker side. April couldn't help but wonder—what would Vicki do if April continued to defy her? How far could April push her?

Was she brave enough to try to find out?

"As for what I'm planning to do?" Vicki continued. "It's exactly what I told you the other night. I'm going to show you what it means to be my submissive. It's not all fun and games. And it's not all about sex, and pleasure. It's about power. It's about control. It's about you relinquishing both to me."

April knelt there in silence, her heart speeding up with every passing moment.

"You see," Vicki said. "You're the type of submissive that resists your nature. The type that fights your desires with every part of your being. You say you want this. In your mind, you want this. Your body gives it away too. And yet, you're still trying to hold onto control instead of letting go."

Vicki shrugged her jacket off her shoulders, placing it on a table to the side. She unclipped the watch around her wrist and placed it next to her jacket.

"So I'm going to start from the beginning," Vicki said. "I'm going to put you in the headspace of a submissive." She leaned down, her lips brushing April's ear. "I'm going to strip away all those layers of yours until all that's left is that primal part of you that craves this."

A frisson went through April's body. Vicki's words, her intense gaze, the raw, feminine power she exuded—it all should have frightened her. Maybe it did in a way. But it thrilled her even more.

April matched Vicki's fiery gaze with her own. "Go ahead and try."

A slight smile spread on Vicki's face. She walked over to a rack on the wall in front of April. It held a variety of whips, canes, and other tools, which could only be used for one thing. Vicki picked out a small leather paddle and returned to stand behind April, trailing her fingertips along April's back as she walked. April resisted the urge to turn and watch her, instead looking straight at the wall ahead. But this left her staring at the rack of whips, which did little to settle the tempest within.

Vicki pushed April's dress up around her waist and caressed April's ass cheeks. She still had her panties on, but they were thin and cut high at the bottom, so they offered little protection. April's skin prickled.

"Remember when I told you that all of this is in the mind?" Vicki asked. "That's true even when it's physical."

April felt a stinging slap on her ass cheek. She sucked in a breath. It barely hurt, but it was a shock to her body and left her skin tingling. She screwed her eyes shut and waited.

"This isn't about punishment or pain," Vicki said. "It's about the experience of having control taken away. It's about the anticipation, the uncertainty, those seconds in between when you know what's coming, but you don't know when, or where, or what form it will take."

This time, Vicki rained down a series of short, sharp smacks on both her ass cheeks. April gasped, each impact rippling along the length of her body.

Vicki continued, punctuating every few words with a slap. "It's about how every strike sets you on edge and overwhelms your senses until you have no choice but to embrace your vulnerability."

April drew a breath in. She could feel the adrenaline pulsing through her, her nerves set alight. Every word Vicki said was right. April wanted this. Her body hungered for this. To throw away her inhibitions and let herself drown in everything she was feeling. With every stroke of the paddle, April felt all the walls inside her crumbling.

She closed her eyes and relaxed her body. She stopped resisting. She stopped fighting.

And it felt good.

A soft moan fell from April's mouth, spurring Vicki on. The other woman continued to rain blows down on April's ass, each stroke like a shock of cold water.

Finally, Vicki gave April one final slap on each cheek, then caressed them gently with the paddle. April purred. The smooth leather felt good on her burning skin.

Vicki rounded the table to stand in front of her. She cupped April's cheek. "Now, that wasn't so bad, was it?"

"No," April said softly, leaning into Vicki's hand.

"Maybe I was wrong about you. Maybe I can mold you into my perfect submissive after all."

Vicki drew April up to sit on the end of the table, then kissed her with surprising tenderness. April murmured with bliss. Her whole body was charged, and everywhere Vicki touched set off a spark. The kiss deepened, and Vicki's hands grew hungrier. Soon, there was a fire flaring inside April.

Vicki's slid a hand down to where April's thighs met and pressed her panties into her slit. "Do you want me to get rid of these?"

"Yes," April said breathlessly.

Vicki pushed April's shoulders down to the table and tugged her panties from her legs. She tossed them aside, then grabbed April's waist and pulled her to the very end of the table.

She parted April's knees and ran her fingers up the insides of April's legs. "A good submissive always gets rewarded," Vicki said.

April quivered, longing to feel Vicki inside her. Vicki had other ideas. She grabbed hold of April's ass cheeks and dove her head between April's thighs.

April let out a gasp. Vicki's mouth felt divine. She sucked on April's nether lips, probed at her entrance with the tip of her tongue, circled April's swollen bud with a butterfly-light touch that drove April wild.

April grabbed onto the sides of the table with both hands. A part of her wanted to drop them to Vicki's head, to pull her in harder and guide her. The rest of her wanted to hand Vicki the reins, to give her body over to the other woman. So she closed her eyes and let Vicki take control.

And Vicki's control was absolute. This time, Vicki didn't try to draw it out. She didn't drive April to climax immediately either, even though she could have. Instead, Vicki ramped up April's pleasure steadily, until the fire inside her became a raging inferno.

"Oh god, Vic-" April jerked and writhed as tremors rocked her body. Vicki continued, her mouth unrelenting, her fingers digging into April's raw ass cheeks, until April fell back down to the table, limp and panting.

Vicki gave her a few moments to recover, then she leaned down and kissed April, stealing the breath from her lungs. She could taste her own arousal on Vicki's lips.

"Now you're going to do something for me," Vicki said.

Vicki guided April off the bench and drew her to the side of the bed. April's legs felt loose, and her ass ached, a satisfying, invigorating ache. Vicki stripped off April's dress and bra, then removed her own clothes piece by piece.

When Vicki was left in nothing but a pair of black panties, she pointed to them and issued April a command. "Take these off for me," she said. "Without using your hands."

April blinked. How was she supposed to do that?

Oh. *Oh.*

Once again, the two parts of April—the part that wanted to resist, and the part that wanted to obey—were warring inside. She fixed her eyes on Vicki's. She would follow Vicki's instructions. But she wouldn't let Vicki know how much this was making her weak.

Slowly and deliberately, April got down on her knees. She leaned in and bit the waistband at the side of Vicki's panties, tugging them downward, then did the same on the other side. She worked them down Vicki's hips painstakingly, ignoring the fact that Vicki's pussy was right in front of her face. Finally, she had the panties past the swell of Vicki's hips, and she drew them down until they fell to the floor.

April stared up at Vicki, taking in her body in all its glory. It was the first time she'd seen Vicki completely naked, and she liked what she saw. Vicki's body was slender and toned, and she could see the faint outlines of her muscles underneath her skin. Her small nipples were barely a shade darker than her pale breasts, and at the apex of her thighs, her lips were covered in pale downy hair which glistened with moisture.

Vicki pushed her panties aside with her foot, then sat down at the very edge of the bed. "I'm going to let you show me how much you want to be my submissive. Show me how much you want me. Show me how much you want to please me," she said. "Once again, without using your hands."

This instruction was much easier for April to understand. She buried herself between Vicki's legs as Vicki had done to her minutes ago, the woman's heady scent enveloping her. She feathered her lips along Vicki's thigh, kissing the silky skin there, until she reached her prize. She slipped her tongue into Vicki's slit, savoring her taste. A satisfied groan emerged from Vicki's lips.

April smiled. Vicki might be the one calling the shots, but right now, April had the power to make her fall apart. And April was determined to exert this little sliver of control. She took her time, swirling her tongue over every inch of Vicki's pink folds before finally settling her lips on Vicki's clit.

Vicki shuddered, her face contorting in ecstasy. She threw her legs over April's shoulders and grabbed the back of April's head, pulling her in. Her rapturous cries only spurred April on. Soon, April felt Vicki's body tense.

"Fuck!" Vicki arched out, her hands leaving April's head to grip the edge of the bed. She bucked against April, her thighs hugging April's face.

Then she let out a breath and toppled backward onto the bed.

---

Afterward, April lay on her stomach in the bed, lost in a daze. Vicki had spent the last few minutes kissing April's raw, red ass cheeks, soothing them with her lips. Murmurs rose from April's chest. It felt heavenly. Was this part of what it meant to be Vicki's submissive? If it was, April could get used to this.

Vicki slid back up the bed to lie next to her. "How was that?" she asked.

"Good," April said.

"Just good? Is that all?"

"Fine, it was incredible."

"You know," Vicki said, "it would be easier for both of us if you would just obey me from the start."

April smiled. "Where's the fun in that?"

Vicki shook her head. "You're impossible."

"Someone has to keep you on your toes."

As the silence stretched out, April came back down to earth, and she began to remember why she had come to see Vicki in the first place. She had to make sure Vicki knew how serious she was about the library.

April propped herself up on her elbows. "So, about the library."

Vicki groaned. "Do we have to talk about that now? Can't it wait until the meeting?"

"We're here anyway so we might as discuss it. It's important to me."

"Okay. What do you want to discuss?"

"I want to talk about how we can keep the library open. The community needs the resources it provides-"

"Yes, I heard your little speech the other night. I'll do what I can, okay? I'll talk to the rest of the management team before the meeting and see what kind of solution we can work out. I don't know why I'm agreeing to this," she grumbled.

"Thank you," April said. Eliza had told her to compromise? This was her compromising.

"It's time to add a new rule," Vicki said.

"A new rule? Does this mean that you want to keep doing this?"

"Don't you?"

April thought for a moment. She should have zero interest in pursuing anything with Vicki. Even before everything with the library, she had her misgivings. But that didn't change the way April felt toward Vicki. That didn't change the fact that April was so inexorably drawn to her and the release that she offered.

Besides, Vicki seemed to be coming around on the issue of the library. So maybe they were on the same side after all.

"Yes," April finally said. "I still want to do this."

"Here's my next rule," Vicki said. "When we're together, no talking about work, or the library, or the development project. No discussion of it, no thinking about it. We leave all that at the door. Pretend that it doesn't even exist."

"Will you be doing that too?" April asked.

"I have no problems leaving business at the door. You're the one who came to me tonight, guns blazing."

"Fine," April said. "No work when we're together."

April could do that. And honestly, it might make things easier. She could just pretend that the Vicki she was pursuing this twisted affair with was a different person from the Vicki who she would have to negotiate the library's fate with.

"Good," Vicki said. "My old rules still stand. I expect your complete obedience when we're doing this. No talking back, no trying to push me. Nothing less than absolute submission. Can you do that?"

April hesitated. Everything Vicki was offering seemed contrary to April's nature. Maybe that was why she wanted it so badly. No matter the reason, there was no denying it—April was hooked.

"Okay," April said. "I can do that."

She would play this game with Vicki. Because that was all it was —a game. It wasn't true submission. April hadn't truly surrendered to Vicki.

And she never would.

# CHAPTER NINE

*T*he week that followed seemed to crawl by. April was so busy at work that she barely had a moment to herself. It didn't help that she spent half her time daydreaming about the night at Lilith's Den with Vicki.

It left her feeling so conflicted. She'd enthusiastically agreed to be Vicki's submissive. She loved the way submission made her feel.

But she hated that it was Vicki making her feel this way. Despite their agreement to work together on the library, April felt like their alliance was tenuous at best. She was still wary of Vicki, and she still found the blonde-haired woman irritatingly cocky. No amount of physical attraction, no matter how intense, could overcome that.

Despite it all, April played along with Vicki's games. And Vicki took her games very seriously. That night, they had discussed the finer details of their arrangement. Limits. Expectations. Even more rules.

One of Vicki's rules was that April had to send her a sexy photo every day. The photos were, in Vicki's words, a daily reminder of their agreement. This was one rule April was happy to follow. Whether it was intentional or not, Vicki hadn't been specific about what counted as 'sexy.' So April decided to be creative. She sent photos of herself to Vicki that were sexy but not revealing, enticing while still leaving a lot to the imagination. If Vicki wanted anything more than that, she would have to wait until they saw each other again.

A few times, Vicki had taken the bait, replying with a salacious message that made April blush. Other times, April's photos had been met with silence, and the only reason April knew that Vicki had seen the photo was because her phone showed the message as read.

April was determined not to let Vicki get inside her head. Nevertheless, she found herself thinking about Vicki constantly. That soft, golden hair that she was always playing with. Those piercing eyes. That enticing smile. Every time April closed her eyes, she was back in that room at Lilith's Den with Vicki, the scene playing out, over and over.

Of course, it wasn't Vicki herself that April was addicted to. It was the erotic game the two of them were playing together.

"April?" Lexi asked.

"Hmm?" April looked up to see Lexi squaring away her desk.

"The meeting? Vicki will be here any minute."

"Right." As Vicki promised, her assistant had called April a week ago to confirm the time and date.

"Hopefully it won't be a complete waste of time," Lexi said.

"It won't be. Vicki promised me she would try to work something out."

"She promised you?" Lexi asked. "I thought you said you talked to her assistant?"

"Yeah, I did. I spoke to Vicki herself too," April said, leaving out the fact that she had spoken to Vicki at a BDSM club.

"How did that conversation go? Did you yell at her some more?"

April crossed her arms. "Why does everyone think I'm some kind of tyrant?"

"Who else said that?"

"Eliza."

Lexi chuckled. "That woman is never wrong."

"I did yell at Vicki a little," April admitted. "But then she

239

genuinely seemed to be interested in finding a solution. Maybe we have her all wrong."

"Seriously? A week ago, you were convinced that she was pure evil. What did she say to you that changed your mind?"

"Nothing. I'm just trying something new. I'm being open to compromise and change."

"Eliza?" Lexi asked.

"That obvious, huh?" April got up from her desk. "Let's go."

They made their way to one of the meeting rooms at the other side of the library. Vicki hadn't arrived yet, but everyone else had. As well as the library staff, a few community leaders who were involved in programs that took place at the library had been invited.

April greeted everyone, then sat down at the head of the table, with Lexi to her right. She looked out through the glass walls of the meeting room, watching for Vicki's arrival. Moments later, Vicki appeared, dressed as stylish as ever in a pantsuit and heels. She looked so different than the last time April had seen her, all dressed in leather. But somehow, Vicki managed to look incredibly sexy no matter what she wore.

Vicki spotted them through the glass and strode purposefully toward the meeting room. The head librarian was a few steps behind, struggling to keep up with the long-legged woman.

The two of them entered the room. Vicki apologized for her lateness, then made her way around the table, introducing herself to the staff one by one. When Vicki reached Lexi, the curly-haired woman gave Vicki a stiff, firm handshake. Vicki returned it in kind.

*What was that about?* Perhaps neither of them liked not being the only lady-killing lesbian in the room. April made a mental note to ask Lexi about it later.

But April forgot all about it when Vicki moved on to her. April stood up and took Vicki's outstretched hand. As soon as their skin touched, April was transported back to the other night. Suddenly, the room felt foggy. Could everyone see how weak-kneed Vicki made her?

As soon as Vicki let go of her hand, April sat down before her legs could collapse underneath her.

Finally, Vicki took a seat at the opposite end of the table, right across from April, and placed a folder down in front of her.

"Shall we get started, April?" Vicki looked at April expectantly. "Sorry, do you prefer Miss Reid?"

It took April a moment to find her voice. "April is fine."

"April it is."

"Uh, yes." April wasn't sure if she imagined the suggestion in Vicki's eyes, but she ignored it. "Let's get started. Vicki, can you tell us about how Oasis is willing to work with us?"

Vicki flipped open her folder. "You'll be pleased to hear that Oasis has agreed to lease a property to the library at the same rate the city was paying for this building."

April frowned. Was it really that easy?

"We've recently acquired a property in Springdale which we've determined is an ideal location for the library."

"Springdale?" April said. It was a couple of suburbs away from West Heights. "Isn't that a bit out of the way?"

"It's not Oakmont Street. But with property in West Heights at a premium, there aren't any alternatives in West Heights itself. I assure you, the site is more than suitable. It's on Earlwood Street."

April knew the area. Not only was it nowhere near central West Heights, it was in one of the most crime-ridden parts of the whole city. Most people would never go there alone. And the library's most vulnerable patrons—the elderly, children—wouldn't dare venture there at all. Even if they wanted to, it was miles from the subway and bus stops. Most people in West Heights didn't own cars.

Not only that, but the funding that the library received from the city was dependent on how many customers used the library. If people stopped coming to the library, it wouldn't receive enough funding to stay open. The library would be as good as dead.

"So," Vicki said. "What are your thoughts?" Vicki looked pointedly at April.

The eyes of everyone at the table followed. They were looking to April for guidance. But her disappointment weighed so heavy on her that she found she couldn't speak. Vicki had promised to come up with a solution. This wasn't a solution.

Lexi swooped in to save her. "It's something," she said. "Do you have any more information about the site?"

Vicki flicked through the folder before her and pulled out some glossy printouts. "I've prepared some material for you to take a look at. Here." Vicki passed them around. "As you'll see, the site isn't as big as this one, but Oasis is willing to help out with some improvements."

April took a printout and flipped through it, trying to maintain her composure. But as she looked at the photo of the tiny, ramshackle building, her disappointment turned to anger. April didn't know much about real estate, but she was certain a property like this in such an undesirable location was useless to Oasis. It was no wonder they were offering to lease it to the city.

Vicki spent the next ten minutes explaining Oasis' offer in detail. After a while, the others began to ask questions. Were they actually on board with this?

"April," Vicki said. "I haven't heard from you yet. Do you have anything to add?"

"No," April said flatly.

"Then we're done here. If you have any questions, don't hesitate to contact me." Vicki's eyes landed on April's. "I'm committed to working with you on this."

April kept her eyes locked with Vicki's but said nothing.

Vicki stood up and straightened her jacket. "If you'll excuse me, I have another meeting-"

"Wait," April said.

"Yes?"

"Before you leave, I'd like to speak with you."

# CHAPTER TEN

Once the room had cleared, Vicki walked over to April's end of the table. "So? What do you think?"

"What do I think?" April stood up and dropped the printout onto the table before Vicki. "What is this, Vicki? You said you'd work with us!"

"I am. I don't understand what the problem is."

"The problem is that your solution isn't a solution at all. Do you really think the library can operate in some rundown shack in Springdale? We might as well just shut our doors now."

Vicki pulled out a chair and sat down. "I don't know what you were expecting. Oasis is being very generous. We don't normally do things like this."

"What, so we should be grateful for your charity?" April asked.

"*My* charity?" Vicki asked. "Is it Oasis that you're angry at? Or me?"

April threw her hands up. "You're leading the project, aren't you? You're the Vice President of the company. As far as I'm concerned, this is all you."

"I'm VP of Project Development. I can only control what happens in my department. I still answer to the CEO and the board.

I couldn't change what's going to happen to the library even if I wanted to. The gears are already in motion. The library's fate was sealed when Oasis bought the building."

"Then why did you tell me you'd see what you could do?" April asked, her voice rising. The room was soundproof, but the walls were glass. Anyone could walk by and see the two of them arguing, but professionalism was the last thing on April's mind. "Why did you tell me you would work with me?"

Vicki stood up, her eyes darkening. "I *am* working with you. Why do you think I came to this meeting personally instead of sending someone else? I don't usually spend my workday traveling halfway across the city to meet with a bunch of librarians."

"A bunch of librarians?" April fumed. "So we're not worth your time? *I'm* not worth your time?"

"That's not- Will you just listen to me? I did what I could. I stuck my neck out for you. If it wasn't for me, Oasis wouldn't have even considered helping out the library. I've worked my ass off on this project. If it goes smoothly, I'm looking at an executive level promotion. And I'm risking it all because of you."

April scoffed. "I'm sorry that I'm standing in the way of you getting a bigger paycheck."

"It's not about a paycheck," Vicki said through gritted teeth. "My job is more than just a job to me. But it's clear there's no point trying to make you understand."

"I'm not the one lacking empathy in this situation. You're the one who's rolling into a neighborhood that's hundreds of years old, displacing its residents and turning it into yet another exclusive playground for the wealthy. But I wouldn't expect someone like you to understand."

Vicki's eyes narrowed to slits. "Someone like me?"

"That's right," April said. "I know all about you, Victoria *Blake*."

Vicki recoiled. Had April hit a nerve?

But a moment later, Vicki regained her composure. "You've obviously made up your mind about me." Vicki picked up her folder. "I'm done trying to reason with you."

April shook her head. "I can't believe I actually thought this meeting would make a difference."

"You really don't get it, do you? This project is happening. In a few months, this building is going to be torn down. You're naive if you think there's anything you can do about it."

April put her hands on her hips. "Don't think I'm going to roll over that easily. I'm going to keep fighting for the library until it's a pile of rubble. And I'm going to keep fighting *you*."

"You can try," Vicki said. "But you're wasting your time."

"Just go," April said. "Get out of my library."

Vicki tucked her chair under the table. "If you come to your senses and decide you want to work with me instead of fighting me, let me know."

"That's not going to happen."

"Suit yourself." Vicki turned and headed for the door. Before she left the room, she gave April a charming smile. "It was lovely to see you again."

---

April closed her eyes and slipped deeper into the bath, letting her head sink under the water. She liked how quiet and peaceful it was, submerged like this, how removed it made her feel from all her problems. The events of the day had left her feeling drained.

Most of all, she was feeling torn about Vicki. On one hand, she was angry. Did Vicki really think Oasis' offer would placate her? Was Vicki so out of touch, so used to everyone deferring to her, that she thought April would roll over without a fight?

But at the same time, April wondered if Vicki was being honest when she said that she didn't have any control over the fate of the library. Maybe Vicki was just like everyone else, answerable to someone above her. Maybe April was being too hard on her.

April watched the bubbles of her breath float to the surface. Why the hell was she trying so hard to find a reason to justify Vicki's actions? Why did April even care about Vicki's motivations?

She emerged from the water and took a breath. The relaxing

music playing on her phone filled her ears and the scent of the rose petal bath bomb hung in the air. But it did nothing to calm her.

Giving up, April decided to try a distraction instead. Maybe a podcast would help take her mind off everything. April reached up to the counter and picked up her phone. She had a message.

It was from Vicki.

Before April could stop herself, she opened the message.

*I haven't received my photo yet today. You have two hours. The clock is ticking.*

Every muscle in April's body tensed. Did Vicki really think April was going to send her a photo after everything that had happened today? She was delusional.

April couldn't help but feel like Vicki was taunting her. Vicki had never sent her a reminder like this, although, admittedly, it was getting late. The day was almost over, and time really was running out.

It didn't matter. April wasn't going to play Vicki's game anymore. And she didn't want to think about Vicki for one more second. From now on, her mind was a Vicki-free zone.

An hour and a podcast later, April slipped out of the tub and dried herself off. It was eleven p.m., so she threw on an old shirt, and got into bed.

April closed her eyes. A minute passed, then two, then five. She rolled over, trying to get comfortable, and caught a glimpse of her alarm clock. 11:15 p.m. She rearranged her pillows and rolled over again. Her mattress felt lumpy, and she kept getting tangled in her sheets. She looked at the clock. It was 11:23 p.m.

April let out a curse. She had been tired the whole day, but now, she was wide awake. There was no point lying in bed staring at the ceiling. Instead, she did what she always did when she couldn't sleep.

She opened up her drawer and pulled out a small, pink vibrator.

Underneath her covers, April slipped out of her panties and turned the vibrator on, settling it at the peak of her slit. She closed her eyes, letting the vibrations ripple through her. April had never really considered this something sexual. It was more of a way to blow off steam and release tension.

But tonight, it wasn't working.

She let out a growl of frustration and turned the vibe up a notch. Her mind began to drift back to the events of the day. Inevitably, her thoughts returned to Vicki. To that smug smile. That conceited way she held herself. That expectation that everyone bow to her. April had done just that, twice now.

And she had loved every moment of it.

A moan rumbled in April's chest. She slid her free hand between her legs, gliding her fingers down her folds. She thought about how good Vicki had made her feel that night at the club, how much every kiss of that leather paddle had made her body come alive, how quickly she had yielded under Vicki's dominating gaze.

April's body began to sizzle. She hated the way Vicki made her feel. Like she was drowning, like she was losing control—losing herself—in Vicki.

April slid her fingers inside her entrance, her mind swirling with fragments of Vicki. Vicki's fingertips grazing her skin. Vicki's lips, smothering the flame between her thighs. Vicki's essence, overloading her senses. Vicki's thighs quaking around her head. April didn't want to think about her right now. But she couldn't stop. And she was so close.

April turned up the little pink toy, giving herself one hard burst of vibrations. Her body overcome, she rose up, Vicki's name on her lips as she came.

She sank back into the bed, breathing hard. Whether April liked it or not, Vicki had wormed her way into April's head and wasn't showing any sign of leaving.

A quick trip to the bathroom later, and April was back in bed, her toy stashed away in her drawer. Without thinking, she glanced at the time. 11:54 p.m. Panic washed through her. She had vowed to stop playing Vicki's game. But April couldn't stop glancing at her phone. And with every passing second, her anxiety grew.

Sighing, April grabbed her phone. She thought for a moment. If she was going to do this, she could at least give Vicki something to think about. April pulled her vibrator out of her drawer, pointed her phone at it and snapped a picture. She sent it off to Vicki with only a minute to spare. Vicki could think whatever she liked about that.

Immediately, her phone buzzed.

*Next time don't make me wait,* Vicki's text said.

As April stared at the message, something dawned on her.

Vicki had been waiting for April's photo.

Vicki was annoyed that she had to wait.

Vicki wanted April just as much as April wanted Vicki.

Vicki needed April's submission just as much as April needed to submit.

April smiled. Vicki might have the upper hand now, but the game wasn't over yet.

# CHAPTER ELEVEN

*A*pril sat in the lobby of Oasis Developments, waiting for Vicki.

After the other night, when April had caved and sent Vicki the photo, their affair continued as it had before. April knew it didn't make sense. Vicki was the last person she should have been doing this with. But she couldn't deny how intoxicating she found Vicki, and how much playing Vicki's game excited her.

It was almost like there were two Vickis. One of them was the stuck-up corporate businesswoman who was determined to bulldoze April's beloved library and filled her with righteous fury. The other was the seductive siren who filled April's every waking moment with dreams of submission.

So April told herself that the woman she'd spent those nights with was a different person than the Vicki she'd fought with in the meeting room that day. After all, wasn't April a different person when she was alone with Vicki? The defiant submissive she pretended to be was different than the person April was day to day. In April's mind, the two worlds they existed in were completely separate.

So, April continued to follow Vicki's rules. But that didn't stop her from mounting her own little rebellion. Every day, she would send Vicki a photo just before midnight. At first, it was because she felt conflicted about her attraction toward the woman. After a few days, it became deliberate. April imagined Vicki sitting at home every night, staring at her phone and waiting for April's photo to come. When it did, April made sure the photo was something provocative.

April relished this little slice of power she had over Vicki. She had the ability to get under Vicki's skin. She had the ability to drive Vicki wild. She still had some control. They were on equal footing after all.

With this in mind, April decided to try to talk to Vicki about the library once more. After she'd had a few days to cool off, she had realized that she hadn't actually explained to Vicki the reason why Oasis Developments' proposed solution wasn't enough. Once again, she'd let her temper run away with her. April wasn't usually quite this hot-headed. Vicki had that effect on her.

April messaged Vicki's personal number to set up a meeting. She felt like she was breaking some unwritten rule, mixing business with pleasure, but Vicki didn't comment on it. She agreed to squeeze April in for a short meeting, but due to her busy schedule, April would have to come to her.

Which was how April found herself in the lobby of Oasis Developments late one afternoon.

She shifted in her seat, glancing idly around the lobby. The lavish office was a glaring reminder that Vicki lived in a completely different world from April, one where even the receptionist wore designer clothes and looked like a model. Could she ever expect Vicki to understand her point of view when it came to the library and West Heights? April suddenly felt like she was deep in enemy territory.

A woman, presumably Vicki's secretary, came out into the lobby and led April to Vicki's spacious office. When April entered the room, Vicki was sitting in a chair behind her desk, having a heated conversation with someone on the phone.

"That application should have been submitted three months

ago," she said. "Someone in your department dropped the ball. You need to fix this." Vicki paused, no doubt listening to some poor pencil-pusher's excuses. "I don't care. If you want to keep your job, you have three days to sort this mess out."

Vicki looked up at April, nodding at her in greeting. She gestured for April to sit down at a small glass coffee table by the window.

April took a seat. There was a strange desk toy on the table before her, a small contraption consisting of tiny chrome balls and moving arms on a wooden base. It seemed out of place in Vicki's modern, minimalistic office. April pushed one of the balls, causing the entire thing to rotate and swing. She watched its hypnotizing movements while she waited.

After a few more minutes, Vicki finished with her phone call.

"April. Thanks for coming," she said.

"No problem," April replied.

The room fell silent. Both of them had cooled off since their heated encounter in April's office. But there was a hint of tension in the air.

"Would you like a drink?" Vicki walked over to a cabinet in the corner behind April and opened the door, revealing a small fridge and an assortment of liquor.

"You have a mini bar in your office?" April asked.

"I'm here a lot. Sometimes I feel like a drink after spending twelve hours at work."

It shouldn't have surprised April that Vicki worked so much. It was clear from her job title that she was high up in the ranks. But Vicki always seemed like she coasted through life effortlessly. The idea of Vicki slaving away behind a desk seemed to clash with April's impression of her.

Of course, the desk Vicki slaved away behind looked like it cost a fortune.

"So, would you like a drink?" Vicki asked.

"Sure," April replied. "Whatever you're having."

Vicki produced two glasses and a cocktail shaker and set about mixing a simple drink. She divided it between the two glasses, and brought them over to the table, handing one to April. April took a sip. It was rum mixed with something. She wondered if Vicki chose the drink because she remembered that April was drinking mojitos the night they met.

Vicki sat down across from April, her lean body stretched out in the chair. The sun was still out, and the sunlight streaming through the window made her hair look like spun gold and made her green eyes sparkle.

"Was there something you wanted to talk about?" Vicki asked. "Or did you just miss me?"

April ignored Vicki's quip. "I've been thinking about other options for the Oakmont Street Library. I'd like to discuss them with you."

"Eager to get down to business, are you?"

"You said we only had half an hour."

"My evening meeting was canceled. We have all the time in the world now." Vicki sat back and crossed her legs. "Why don't we take a step back? Tell me about your history with the library."

"Well, what do you want to know?" April asked.

"How long have you been working there?"

"Almost ten years all up. I worked there in high school as a page, but I stopped when I left for college. I ended up working there again after I came back to West Heights."

"Do you enjoy your job?" Vicki asked.

"Yes," April replied. "It's not like I dreamed of working at a library my whole life, but I was offered a job there after college and I haven't looked back."

Vicki took a sip of her drink, studying April over her glass. "Why is saving the library so important to you? The way you talk about it makes it seem like it's about more than just your job."

"You're right," April said. "The library is special to me. I have my reasons for wanting to save it."

Vicki waited for April to elaborate. But April was reluctant to share something that personal with her.

Vicki's words reminded April of something she had said last time they spoke. "You told me that your job was more than just a job for you too. That your promotion wasn't about a paycheck. What did you mean by that?"

Vicki crossed her legs. "It's a chance to prove myself."

"To who?"

"It's personal."

Considering her own reticence, April couldn't fault Vicki for being tight-lipped. Everything between them felt so tenuous, like a truce that could devolve into conflict at any moment.

As April placed her drink down on the table, her eyes fell to the chrome trinket in front of her. Somehow, it was still spinning. "What is this?"

"I have no idea," Vicki said. "My father gave it to me."

"Your father is the Head of Blake International, right?"

"The one and only." There was a touch of irritation in her voice.

April pressed on. "Isn't Oasis one of their competitors?"

"It's Blake International's biggest competitor in the country," Vicki said. "I didn't know you knew so much about the world of property development."

"I don't," April said. "When I heard that you were leading the Oakmont Street project, I decided to do some research. Your family came up when I searched your name online."

"Of course they did." Vicki sighed almost imperceptibly. "There's no escaping the Blake family name."

"Why would you want to?"

Vicki didn't answer her. Not at first. "All of this," Vicki said, gesturing around the room. "My job, my life. You think my success is because of my family, don't you?"

"Well, I..." April hadn't forgotten how she'd thrown Vicki's family name at her that day they had argued in April's office. Or how Vicki had reacted.

"I'm not successful because of my family." Vicki stilled the spinning chrome ball contraption with her hand. "I'm successful in spite of them."

Silence hung in the air. April sipped her drink. It was strange, that they knew so little about each other, yet they had been so intimate, had shared parts of themselves that others never got to see.

"You know," Vicki said, drumming her fingers on the arm of her chair. "You've been cutting it close with your photos lately."

April flushed. "I thought we were keeping business and pleasure separate."

"Actually, I said that we won't let business get in the way of pleasure, not the other way around."

"I don't see what the problem is," April said. "I've sent you a photo every single day like you asked. I haven't broken any of your rules."

"One of my rules was 'do not test me.'"

"Maybe you should have made your rules more specific."

Vicki leaned across the coffee table, speaking in a low voice. "You're very lucky there's an office full of people outside those doors, otherwise I'd do something about your attitude."

April bit back a smile. "What exactly would you do?"

"I'd bend you over my desk and spank you."

Desire flared inside April's body. Vicki's commanding gaze had April mesmerized. At that moment, April knew that if Vicki ordered her to bend over her desk right now, she would be powerless to refuse.

No, she wouldn't even want to refuse.

Vicki straightened up and brushed her fingers through her hair. "But, like I said, there's an office full of people out there. And we have business to attend to."

April blinked. *Right.* She pulled herself together. How was it that after all this time she was still susceptible to Vicki's charms?

"You want to discuss options for the library?"

"Yes." April recalled Eliza's advice. *Be civil. Be open to compromise.* "The problem is, the solution Oasis is offering is practically a death sentence for the library." She explained that their funding was tied to how many people used the library. "If our patrons can't get to us, we won't be able to keep our doors open."

"Do you have any other ideas?" Vicki asked.

"There are other sites in West Heights that Oasis owns that are sitting there, empty. Why not lease one of those to us instead?"

"Most of those have been earmarked for future development. The ones that aren't are far too valuable to lease to a library."

"Then give us more time to figure something out," April said. "We can try to fundraise enough money for a better location or think of an alternative."

"Look," Vicki said. "Oasis is already behind on the Oakmont Street project. We can't afford to put it off anymore. We can't give you any longer than the 90 days you were already given."

"Then what was the point of this?" April's voice rose. "Why did you agree to meet me if you were just going to tell me the same thing again?"

"Because I thought you were going to suggest something reasonable." Vicki finished her drink in one long sip. "We're not a charity."

April clenched her fists, her fingernails digging into the heels of her palms. "So that's what it comes down to for you? Making money no matter the consequences?"

"It's just business."

April stood up, shaking her head. "Here I was, thinking we could work things out. That you actually had a heart and cared about helping the library. I was so wrong." April had tried to be civil. She had tried not to let her feelings control her. But she couldn't contain herself any longer. "You don't give a damn about anyone or anything other than yourself. I hate you, and Oasis, and everything you stand for."

Vicki looked up at April from her chair, somehow still managing to seem like she was looking down on her. "We both know that's not true."

April fumed. "I'm sick of your presumptions. You don't know how I feel."

"Yes, I do. You don't hate me, not really. You don't hate me because I'm working for Oasis. You don't even hate me because you think I'm selfish." Vicki stood up, facing April. "You hate that I'm the only person who can give you what you crave. And you hate that what you want more than anything is to submit to me."

April's skin began to burn. She was certain her red face betrayed the fact that Vicki had hit a nerve. It didn't matter. Because April had Vicki's measure too.

"Maybe you're right," April said. "But I've figured something out. You want my submission just as much as I want to submit to you." She leaned across the table and spoke into Vicki's ear. "I'm the one who is choosing to give it to you. So which of us is really in control here?" Without giving Vicki a chance to reply, April picked up her purse and strode out of the room.

April left the building more determined than ever. Although the meeting had been a disaster, it hadn't been a waste of time. It had proved something important to April—she couldn't rely on Vicki's help with the library. Moreover, she and Vicki were on opposite sides of this fight.

If April wanted to save her library, she would have to do it herself.

That night, she sent Vicki her photo at exactly 11:59 p.m.

# CHAPTER TWELVE

"Is everything okay with you?" Lexi asked April.

The two of them were sitting at a table in a small Mexican restaurant down the street from the library. It used to serve authentic Mexican food, but it had changed ownership about a year ago. Now, it sold 100% organic fusion dishes that tasted nowhere near as good as the old food. However, April and Lexi still came here after work sometimes to chat over dinner.

But for the past ten minutes, April had been so deep in thought that she barely heard a word Lexi said.

"I have a lot on my mind, that's all," April said. "It's fine."

"Are you sure?" Lexi asked. "You seem distracted lately. I know you're taking everything with the library pretty hard, but is that all that's going on?"

April looked down at her plate, avoiding her friend's eyes. She and Lexi usually told each other everything, but she couldn't possibly tell Lexi about what was going on between her and Vicki. Lexi had made her disdain for Vicki clear. Besides, April didn't even understand what was going on between them herself. Just when she was beginning to make sense of their unusual relationship, Vicki would throw her another curve-ball.

*You don't hate me. You hate that I'm the only person who can give you what you crave.*

"I think I know what's bothering you," Lexi said.

April's heart skipped a beat. "You do?"

"It's about Eliza, isn't it?" Lexi said. "I heard that she's moving away. I know the two of you are close."

"Yeah, you're right."

April hoped that Lexi hadn't seen through her lie. And she really was upset about Eliza leaving too. She felt a twinge of guilt. She hadn't spoken to Eliza since the day she had told April she was leaving. April needed to apologize to her for running off.

She sighed. "Between Eliza leaving, and the library, I feel like all the constants in my life are disappearing."

"Well, there's one thing you can be certain of," Lexi said. "I'm not going anywhere."

April smiled. "Thanks, Lex." It was true. Even though Lexi could be flippant at times, she was always there when April really needed her. "Anyway, I can't do anything about Eliza leaving, but I can do something about the library. I've decided it's time we took matters into our own hands."

"Sounds like you have a plan," Lexi said.

"I don't have one yet, but I'm working on it. My meeting with Vicki made it clear that we're not going to get anywhere with Oasis." April scrunched up her napkin in her fist. "I can't stand that woman."

"I know," Lexi replied. "You've said that ten times today."

"She just drives me crazy! And she thinks she knows everything—"

"Can we *please* stop talking about Vicki fucking Blake? I'm sick of hearing her name."

"Sorry," April said sheepishly. "I have been talking about her a lot."

"*Anyway*," Lexi said. "When you come up with a plan for the library, let me know, and I'll do what I can."

"Sure. I'm going to need all the help I can get."

Lexi pushed her empty plate away. "I should head home. I have to go get ready for my date."

"The girl from The Sapphire Room?" April asked.

"A girl from The Sapphire Room. Not the same one as before."

April shook her head. "Of course not."

They paid the bill and went their separate ways. Instead of going home, April headed to Eliza's. As she enjoyed the cool night air, she made a note to ask Eliza if she had any ideas about how to save the library.

But first, she needed to apologize.

April reached Eliza's house and knocked on the door.

Eliza answered with a smile and invited her in. "I'm about to make some tea, want some?"

"Sure," April said. She sat down at the kitchen table. "I'm sorry about last time I was here. I shouldn't have stormed out like that."

"That's okay," Eliza said. "I know you didn't mean anything by it. You were upset."

"That's still no excuse. It was rude. I'm sorry."

"It's fine, don't worry about it. I'm sure it was a shock to hear that I'm leaving after all this time. It was a shock to me as well."

Eliza brought the tea over to the table and handed a cup to April. April inhaled the faintly floral scent. It was calming.

"I've been thinking about moving in with my sister since my diagnosis," Eliza said. "It makes more sense than my living here by myself. But I'm going to miss this place. And West Heights, and all the people who live here."

"We're going to miss you too," April said.

Eliza continued to fill April in on her plans. The sale of her house had just gone through, and she would be moving in a month or so. To April, a month seemed too short.

"That's enough about me," Eliza said. "I hear you're in talks with the woman from Oasis. How's that going?"

April recounted the events of both her meetings with Vicki. "And in the end, all she had to say was 'it's just business.' That's all she cares about. Money."

"All *she* cares about?" Eliza asked. "Is it Oasis you're mad at, or Vicki?"

April folded her arms on her chest. "As far as I'm concerned, they're one and the same."

"You know that's not true. She doesn't deserve to be the target of your anger. She's just one woman trying to do her job. You're always so quick to see the world as black and white, good and evil. There are shades of gray."

"Maybe you're right." Once again, April was letting her feelings about Vicki cloud her judgment. Was it unrealistic of her to try to keep their two worlds separate?

It didn't matter. Right now, April had a more important problem to deal with.

"It's obvious that Oasis isn't open to negotiation," she said. "I'm trying to come up with some other way to save the library, but I'm out of ideas." April recounted everything they'd already tried, from sending out letters to the library's regular donors, to submitting a signed petition to the mayor.

"Maybe you need to cast a wider net," Eliza said.

"What do you mean?"

"My sister was telling me about how a middle school in Seattle was being shut down and combined with a high school halfway across the city. The students and teachers started a petition online to stop it. It was shared all over the internet, and they got thousands of signatures. And it worked. All the negative publicity meant that the school board was forced to rescind the proposal."

"Huh." April had already started an online fundraising page. Maybe she needed to think bigger.

"Could you do what they did?" Eliza asked. "Mobilize the wider community online, really get the attention of Oasis and everyone involved with the project?"

"That's not a bad idea."

April sipped her tea thoughtfully. Eliza was on the right track. But April was going to do far more than an online petition. She was going to turn the entire city against Oasis Developments.

Vicki wouldn't know what hit her.

# CHAPTER THIRTEEN

The following Monday, April had barely returned from her lunch break when Vicki came storming into the office at the back of the library. She was closely followed by the head librarian, who mouthed April a silent apology before scurrying off.

Vicki marched up to April's desk. "What the hell did you do?"

April suppressed a smile. "What do you mean?"

"You know exactly what I mean," Vicki said.

April turned to Lexi, who was sitting at her desk, making a half-hearted effort to look like she wasn't listening. "Do you mind, Lexi?" April didn't like to kick Lexi out of her own office, but she knew that things were about to get heated.

"No problem, boss. I'll go grab a coffee." Lexi got up and left the room, shooting Vicki a withering look on the way out.

"Well?" Vicki asked.

"Well, what?" April said.

"I don't have time for this. This stunt you pulled? Do you have any idea how much trouble you've caused me?"

The stunt that Vicki was referring to? April had taken Eliza's advice. Not only had she started an online petition to save the library, but she'd started a campaign to make it go viral.

Well, it was mostly Lexi. April didn't know much about social media, but Lexi, who ran a popular blog about the city's music scene, was an expert. They made a short video about the library and the important role it played in the community, complete with heart-wrenching testimonies from community members the shutdown would affect. An eccentric historian who spoke about the building's past. A sweet old grandma who moved to America from rural Chile and had learned to speak English because of the library's free lessons. An adorable third grader whose parents couldn't afford to buy her books, so she came to the library every single day. It felt a little exploitative to April, but she had to do whatever she could to achieve her goal.

It worked. Lexi had shared the video with her huge network of friends. She knew everyone, including other bloggers and social media stars. Within a few days, the video had been viewed and shared thousands of times, and the petition had thousands of signatures. The fundraising page they had started months ago had gotten a surge in donations. It was nowhere near enough to save the library. But it was better than nothing.

And the best part? Half the city seemed to have turned against Oasis Developments. Oasis, and companies like them, had been doing similar things in other parts of the city for years, and people weren't happy about it. April had no doubt that their PR department was in damage control. She hadn't even considered the fact that it would directly affect Vicki's job.

But any sympathy she had for Vicki quickly evaporated.

"Do you have any idea how much this has cost me?" Vicki said. "Because of you, everything I've worked for is in jeopardy!"

"Do you really think you're the victim in all this?" April asked. "Oasis Developments, and companies just like them have been pushing people out and destroying communities for far too long. This backlash? It's what you deserve."

"So this is about revenge to you?"

"Of course not. I'm not that petty. It's about saving the Oakmont Street Library."

"I've seen your little fundraiser," Vicki said. "Do you really think a few thousand dollars is going to make a difference?"

"It's not about the money," April said. "It's about putting pressure on Oasis. And you've made it clear that Oasis is feeling the pressure right now."

"You're delusional. I've said it before, there's nothing you can do to stop this." Vicki shook her head. "Why did I even try to help you?"

"I don't know why you bothered either, considering how inadequate your help has been. Which is why I had to take action."

"You're not going to give this up, are you?"

April crossed her arms. "Nope."

Vicki let out an irritated sigh. "The very moment that we met, I knew you were going to be trouble. I should have listened to my instincts. You've been a thorn in my side since day one."

"Don't you remember what you told me the night that we met?" April asked innocently. "You said that you like a challenge."

Vicki planted her hands on the desk and leaned down until her face was inches from April's. "You can't help yourself, can you? You just keep pushing and pushing. It's like everything you do is designed to infuriate me."

April's breath caught in her chest. Although Vicki hadn't raised her voice, her tone was overpowering. And her eyes smoldered. Not with anger, or annoyance.

With passion.

April held Vicki's gaze. At that moment, she wanted Vicki to push her against the desk and do exactly what she had threatened to do that day in her office.

Instead, Vicki turned on her heel and walked toward the door.

"Wait," April said.

Vicki stopped. "What is it?"

April whipped her phone out and sent a message to Vicki. It was a photo she'd taken that morning.

Vicki's phone pinged in her jacket pocket. She pulled it out, glanced at the screen, then slipped it back into her pocket without looking at the message.

"Saving it for later, are you?" April asked.

Vicki shot April a blazing look. "Oh, the things I want to do to you," she said softly. Then without another word, Vicki left the room.

April blew out a breath. She didn't know what she was thinking, provoking Vicki like that at work. Their pretense of keeping business and pleasure separate had been thrown out the window in Vicki's office the other day. However, that didn't mean it was a good idea to ignore the lines they had wordlessly drawn.

A few minutes later, Lexi returned to the room. "Did you and Vicki have a nice chat?" she asked.

"It went about how you'd expect," April replied.

"I wish you hadn't kicked me out. I would have loved to watch you take her on."

April remembered the glare Lexi gave Vicki on her way out. "You really don't like her, do you? What did she ever do to you?"

"Nothing. I just don't like her or the way she treats people, that's all." Lexi said hurriedly. She sat down at her desk. "I better get to work. I have a bunch of calls to make about the charity ball."

That was one part of April's old event coordinator job that she didn't miss. Every year, the library teamed up with a local literacy charity and a private association made of wealthy old ladies to throw a fundraising ball. And every year, it had gotten more and more extravagant. It was a nightmare to organize. To top it off, the event coordinator had to attend the ball to make sure everything ran smoothly. April was just glad she didn't have to go this year.

Still, April sympathized with her friend. "Let me know if you need any help," she said.

Lexi muttered a thanks. "I'll be glad when it's over. Then I can go back to organizing author visits and poetry nights."

April had just as much to do as Lexi. Although Lexi had done most of the work setting up the library's viral campaign, April had taken it over. And it had blown up to the point where it was becoming unmanageable. The library's social media accounts were abuzz with activity. The library had its own hashtag, and people were sending messages of support. It was encouraging to see the community rallying around the library.

Well, most of the community. Apparently, April's campaign had caused a stir in city hall. According to Lexi, who was on top of all the gossip, the Mayor wasn't too happy about how April's campaign made the Mayor and the rest of the city council look. After all, they supported the Oakmont Street development, and had made no effort to help the library. April had about as much sympathy for them as she did for Oasis.

She spent the rest of the day responding to emails and inquiries about the library. Journalists were calling her for quotes, and she had been asked to write an editorial for an online newspaper. A national news station wanted to interview her for a piece on the corporate takeover of historic neighborhoods all over the country. April hadn't meant for things to blow up this much, but she was glad they had. Maybe it would actually make a difference.

By the time five p.m. rolled around, April was wiped out. She could deal with the rest at home. As she got up to leave, her phone buzzed. She unlocked it and read the message. It was from Vicki.

*Tomorrow night. 9 p.m. My apartment.*

# CHAPTER FOURTEEN

*A*pril knocked on the door to Vicki's apartment. She'd barely had time to go home between finishing work and coming here. Today had been as busy as the day before.

April couldn't help but feel smug. She had finally gotten one up on Vicki. But she may have taken things too far in her office yesterday. That look Vicki had given her before leaving made her wonder if Vicki was finally going to do something about April's misbehavior. April's mind raced with possibilities, each more deliciously twisted than the last.

April knocked again. What was taking Vicki so long? It was just past nine p.m., so April wasn't early. She waited for a few more minutes, then tried the door handle. It was unlocked.

April stepped inside, shutting the door behind her. "Vicki?"

She was met with silence.

April looked around, frowning. A few lights were on, but Vicki was nowhere to be seen. Sebastian sat on his perch on the arm of the couch, nothing more than a silhouette in the dim light.

"Where the hell is she?" April asked. *Great, now I'm talking to a cat.*

In response, Sebastian gave her a disdainful stare before slinking off into another room.

April made her way to Vicki's bedroom and poked her head through the door. "Vicki?"

Vicki wasn't in the bedroom either, but it was clear that this was where April was supposed to be. The room was almost completely dark, but the doors of the large closet were flung open, the built-in lights illuminating Vicki's collection of BDSM equipment and toys. And in the center of the rug in front of the bed was a single chair.

April walked over to the chair. A strip of dark red fabric hung over the back, and there was a piece of paper folded in half on the seat. April picked it up. It was a handwritten note with three instructions.

*Sit down.*
*Put the blindfold on.*
*Wait.*

April's pulse began to race. What was Vicki playing at? She glanced at the door behind her. There was still no sign of Vicki.

April took in a breath and sat down on the chair. Taking one last look at the cupboard full of toys, she wrapped the strip of fabric over her eyes and tied it securely behind her head.

She sat back and waited. Was Vicki in the house somewhere, out of sight? It occurred to April that she should have checked the rest of the house before sitting down and blindfolding herself. That would have been the logical thing to do.

Hell, anything other than this would have been the logical thing to do. April had gone into Vicki's empty apartment and served herself up on a platter. Vicki, a woman she'd royally screwed over the day before. Vicki, who owned a large collection of kinky torture tools. Vicki, whose idea of a good time was spanking someone into obedience.

*Oh, the things I want to do to you...*

Something creaked behind April's chair. A footstep? She listened carefully but couldn't hear anything more. She breathed in and caught a whiff of Vicki's perfume. That didn't mean much. April was in Vicki's bedroom—her scent was on everything.

April waited a few more minutes. At least, it felt like minutes, but she had no way of knowing. Alone and blindfolded, with nothing but silence to keep her company, time seemed to pass excruciatingly slowly.

Suddenly, April felt a gust of air breeze past her. "Vicki?" she called out.

Again, the only answer was silence.

"This is crazy," April muttered. Why was she doing this? She should just get up and walk away, stop playing this silly game, no matter how much it turned her on.

A few more minutes passed, and April decided she'd had enough. She stood up and reached behind her head to untie the blindfold.

"Giving up so soon?" Vicki's voice emerged from the darkness.

April jumped. "How long have you been here?"

Vicki didn't answer.

"Victoria!"

Still, Vicki said nothing.

April sighed. Then she sat back down and dropped her hands to her lap.

"That's better," Vicki said from behind her. "Hands behind your back."

"Are you going to tie them up?" April asked.

"Hands behind your back." Vicki placed her hands on April's shoulders.

As soon as Vicki touched her, April's frustration dissipated, only to be replaced by anxious excitement. She crossed her hands behind the back of the chair. Immediately, Vicki's hands were at her wrists, tying a thick, soft rope around them.

When Vicki was done, April tugged at her bonds experimentally. Her wrists were bound both to each other and the back of the chair itself. And with her hands tied, April couldn't remove the blindfold.

She was at Vicki's mercy. There was nothing she wanted more.

Vicki rounded the chair to stand in front of April. "Are you comfortable?" she asked.

"What do you think?" April said.

Vicki swept her hand down April's cheek, her fingertips whispering across April's skin. "I've had enough of your games. Bending my rules, defying me at every turn, trying to get under my skin. Do you have any idea how much you've been driving me crazy?"

April smiled. "I drive you crazy, do I? Make you lose control?"

Vicki took April's chin and tilted her head up. "What did I say about talking back to me?" Vicki's warm breath tickled April's ear.

"That you like it?"

Vicki spoke in a soft growl. "Be. Quiet."

"Make me," April whispered.

At once, Vicki's lips were on April's, kissing her with a ferocity that stunned her into silence. April dissolved into the chair beneath her, every inch of her ablaze.

Vicki tore herself away. "You're going to sit there quietly while I remind you of who you belong to."

A thrill rippled through April's body. That kiss alone was enough to remind April of who she belonged to. It reminded her of why she had been drawn to Vicki in the first place, why she came back to Vicki time and time again, despite everything. Why she always yielded to Vicki in the end.

Vicki slid her hands down April's chest and grabbed the front of her top. She pulled it down, exposing April's breasts. Her fingers grazed April's nipples, causing them to tighten into tiny peaks. Vicki pinched them in her fingertips.

April moaned. That night at Lilith's Den seemed to have flicked a switch in her brain that made pain and pleasure blend and amplify each other in the most delicious way. Vicki trailed her lips down April's chest and sucked her other nipple between her teeth. April bucked in the chair, a cry escaping her.

"Didn't I tell you to keep quiet?" Vicki said.

April bit her lip. Did Vicki really expect April to stay silent while she ravished her like this? Vicki's demanding hands and mouth roamed all over April's chest, her shoulders, her neck. She was like a woman possessed, so consumed with lust that she couldn't hold herself back. April felt the same way, but with her hands bound and her eyes blindfolded, she couldn't do anything except let Vicki have her way.

Vicki slipped her hand down to where April's thighs met. Even through her jeans, Vicki's touch inflamed her.

Vicki leaned in, her lips grazing April's cheek. "This right here? This is mine. Your body is mine. Your pleasure is mine. You. Are. Mine."

April's skin prickled. At the back of her mind, April felt like she shouldn't want this. To belong to anyone, especially not Vicki. But that part of her was drowned out by her overwhelming desire to relinquish everything to Vicki.

Vicki drew her hands up to April's waist and unbuttoned her jeans. She yanked them down April's legs, taking her now-soaking panties with them.

"Open your legs," Vicki said.

April obeyed, her whole body pulsing with anticipation. Vicki ran her hands down April's sides and grabbed her ass cheeks, her nails digging into them. She dragged April's hips forward so that her ass was balanced at the edge of the chair. Then Vicki's fingers were between April's thighs, probing at her slick folds.

April quivered. Mercifully, Vicki didn't tease her. She simply buried her fingers inside April and began to fuck her right there on the chair.

"Oh god..." April closed her eyes, her head tipping back. Vicki's fingers filled her so completely that it was like the other woman was made for her. Every thrust made her shudder and gasp.

April panted and pulled at her bonds, heat flooding her entire body. Vicki was unrelenting. She had one goal, and one goal only— to demonstrate that her possession of April was so complete that she could make April come undone in seconds.

Seconds was all it took.

A fiery orgasm ripped through April's body, the culmination of all the friction they had been feeling toward each other for so long. As April rode it out, Vicki pressed her lips against April's in an urgent, possessive kiss.

April and Vicki lay in bed, draped lazily across each other. They had spent the last hour working off the tension that lingered between them until both of them were too exhausted to move.

April let out a sigh. It was nice, being wrapped up in Vicki's arms, soaking into Vicki's skin. All the animosity she'd been feeling toward the woman had dissipated. Instead, she felt comfortable and serene. April didn't quite understand why she always felt this way after she and Vicki played their intimate games. Maybe it was a side effect of the vulnerability they shared by exposing the deepest, darkest parts of themselves.

April examined Vicki's face. Up close she could see all the different golden tones in her hair, and each individual hair in Vicki's eyelashes. They were long and fine, and much darker than her hair.

"What is it?" Vicki murmured.

"Nothing," April replied.

Vicki brushed her fingers through her hair, frowning. Her unexpected self-consciousness made April smile. The woman who had tied April to the chair earlier had been replaced by someone a little less imposing.

April reached out to sweep her hand over the mound of Vicki's hip and the valley of her waist. "The other day, in your office, you asked me why I care so much about the library. Why do you want to know?"

"I want to understand you," Vicki said.

"I'll tell you," April said. "But I want to know something in exchange."

Vicki raised an eyebrow. "For a submissive, you're very demanding."

April shrugged. "Those are my terms."

Vicki shook her head. "All right. What do you want to know?"

"I want to know why your job means so much to you," April said. "I want to know who you need to prove yourself to."

For a moment, April thought Vicki was going to clam up. Then she rolled onto her back and looked up at the ceiling.

"That ugly metal thing on the table in my office?" Vicki said. "It was my father's, but he didn't give it to me. He loved that thing, he'd never give it away. I stole it from his study the last time I was home. That was almost ten years ago."

"You haven't been home in ten years?" April asked.

"I haven't wanted to go home. And even if I did, I have no idea if my parents would even allow me to walk through the door. I'm the black sheep of the family."

"Seriously?" To April, Vicki seemed like Little Miss Perfect.

"I was never the daughter they wanted me to be," Vicki said. "They wanted someone like my younger sister. She married the son of one of my father's business partners and has popped out three perfect little grandchildren. Me? I never wanted that life. When I was younger, I naively wanted to work for my family's company, to take it over one day. I was smart enough for it. But because I don't have the right plumbing, that honor will go to my little brother. So, there's that. And there's the fact that I'm a lesbian. On top of liking women, I've never conformed to my parents' ideas of how a woman should present, even when I was a young girl."

Suddenly, April felt guilty for assuming Vicki had it easy all her life. She knew all too well that the world could be a cruel place for kids who were different. April reached out and stroked Vicki's arm. She felt the other woman relax slightly at her touch.

"My parents did everything they could to try to change me," Vicki said. "Shoving me into dresses. Trying to set me up with their friends' sons as soon as I hit my teens. Once, they made me meet with some religious nutter who claimed he was a psychologist and said he could 'cure' me. In the end, I kicked up enough of a fuss that they never tried that again.

"After that, I went to college on the other side of the country," Vicki continued. "When I came back, I decided I'd had enough, and that I needed to find my own path. When I told my father, he cut me off. He told me I was a perverted, ungrateful brat who was never going to amount to anything. He said I was crazy for even trying."

"That's awful," April said.

"There was a silver lining. My father's words motivated me to prove him wrong. I had some money of my own tucked way, an inheritance from my grandparents that my father couldn't touch. It got me through business school, but after that, I needed to find a job. I looked for a position where I could put my degrees to use, only to find that my father had effectively blacklisted me. No one wanted to hire Harold Blake's renegade daughter.

"That was until I reached out to Oasis," Vicki said. "They're one of my father's biggest rivals. They offered me a job that was well below my qualifications, but I was desperate, so I took it. It wouldn't surprise me if they only hired me to annoy my father, but I was determined to show them I was worth more. So, I worked my ass off until management noticed me and gave me a promotion. And then another, and another, and so on, and here I am."

Vicki folded her hands behind her head. "Sure, I had an easy start to life in most respects. I had every possible opportunity available to me. But my career at Oasis? I earned it through my own hard work. The promotion I'm up for is a chief operations officer position at our head office in Boston. When the CEO retires in a few years time, as COO I'll be next in line. And I'll finally be able to say to my father, and my family, and myself that I'm capable of succeeding without them. That's why this job is so important to me."

"Vicki," April said. "Your family... how could they?"

A faint smile played on Vicki's lips. "You're a real bleeding heart, aren't you? Don't feel bad for me. Everything with my family is in the past. It doesn't bother me anymore. Every so often we run into each other, and I'm reminded of how much better off I am without them."

April couldn't help but wonder if it was April that Vicki was trying to convince, or herself.

"Now it's your turn. Why is this library of yours so important?"

"It's hard to explain." April sat up in the bed, tucking her knees under her chin. "The library is my sanctuary. Well, not so much now. But I used to go there a lot as a teenager."

Before April could elaborate, Vicki's phone started ringing on the nightstand. Vicki glanced over at it.

"Shouldn't you get that?" April asked.

"Let me check who it is." Vicki rolled over and grabbed her phone, then groaned. "It's Oasis head office. They never call this late unless it's an emergency. I should take this," she said apologetically.

April nodded. "Go ahead."

Vicki got up from the bed, wrapped a robe around herself, and walked out of the bedroom.

April stretched out her arms and made her way to the bathroom. She could hear Vicki's voice faintly from the living room. As she washed her hands and fixed her tousled hair in the mirror, she thought back to everything Vicki had shared with her. All along, she had seen Vicki as this privileged snob who had everything in life handed to her. She was starting to wonder if she had Vicki all wrong.

When April returned to the bedroom, Vicki was waiting for her, phone in hand. "I need to take care of something," she said. "This might take a while."

"I should head home anyway," April replied. She was hoping to go into the library early in the morning to get a start on all the work she had to do.

With a nod, Vicki disappeared back into the living room. April got dressed and left the bedroom. She found Vicki sitting on the couch, her laptop open on the coffee table, the phone to her ear. One bare leg poked out of her robe.

As April approached the door, Sebastian appeared out of nowhere at April's feet, weaving himself around April's legs.

*Seriously? Now that I'm leaving, you decide to get friendly?* As she reached down to pet him, he darted away and went to curl up on Vicki's lap.

Sighing, April waved goodbye to Vicki and slipped out.

She smiled to herself. Despite everything that was going on, she and Vicki seemed to have come to a tentative understanding. It made her wonder. If it wasn't for everything with the library, would things between them be different?

April pushed the thought out of her mind. It could never work, for so many reasons. Besides, it was a dangerous line of thinking. The reality was that they were still working against each other.

April could never forget that they were at opposite sides of this fight.

# CHAPTER FIFTEEN

*L*exi slammed down the phone and let out a heavy sigh.

"Everything okay, Lex?" April asked.

"It's the caterers for the ball on the weekend," Lexi said. "They can't get ahold of the company that's supplying the ice sculptures. This is ridiculous! Why do we even need ice sculptures?"

"You know how it is," April said. "The more extravagant the event is, the more we can charge for tickets. And the more people will donate."

"I have an idea. Why don't we skip the ball altogether and donate the money from the funds we'd save instead?"

"I don't think the association that's funding the ball would go for that. Those rich old ladies need an excuse to throw a party."

"Then they should organize it themselves," Lexi grumbled. "I wish we could throw one of these parties to raise funds for the library."

"If only we weren't so pressed for time," April said. "These things take all year to organize. Plus, we need the money to fund an event like that in the first place." She sighed. "At least the online fundraiser is going strong."

After April's TV interview, things had picked up. Apparently, she had started a discussion, and people from West Heights and the rest of the city were weighing in with their opinions. And April herself was getting a lot of attention. Friends and strangers had even sent her messages of support.

She opened up her social media page to check on things, and groaned. "Not again."

"What's the matter?" Lexi asked.

"People keep leaving hateful comments. First, it was on the library page, and now it's on my page too. Look at this one. 'You should be grateful that Oasis is cleaning up all the trash that lives in West Heights.' And it just gets worse from there. Who is this person and why do they care so much?"

"Ugh." Lexi screwed up her face. "It must be some online troll. I get them on my blog all the time. They seem to get off on harassing people, all while hiding behind the anonymity of a computer screen."

"That's messed up," April said.

"Welcome to the internet, where people can be assholes without consequences." Lexi came over to April's desk and pointed to a little red button at the corner of her screen. "You can report the comments and block him."

April clicked the button and sent off a report. "This isn't even the worst of it. Just yesterday, someone posted a misogynistic tirade on my page. It barely even had anything to do with the library! I don't understand how people can be so nasty."

Lexi squeezed April's shoulder. "Are you going to be all right? Do you want me to take over the social media stuff for you?"

"It's okay," April said. She was a grown woman. She wasn't going to let some online bullies get to her. "I can handle it."

"Let me know if you change your mind," Lexi said. "In the meantime, I'm going to grab a coffee before the meeting with Vicki."

*Right.* April had been so distracted by the unsettling comments that she'd forgotten all about it. After April's TV interview, Oasis had backpedaled, stating that they were still negotiating with the library representatives. The next day, Vicki's assistant called April to arrange another meeting. She didn't give any details, but April was hopeful.

"I'll see you there," she said to Lexi.

Five minutes later, April got up and headed to the meeting room. It was all the way at the other end of the building, and she got lost in her thoughts as she walked.

"Hi, April."

April jumped, her hand flying up to her chest. "Vicki. You scared me." The blonde-haired woman stood next to her, that irritatingly sexy smile on her face.

"I haven't gotten my photo yet today," Vicki said.

April shushed her and glanced around. They were alone. "You'll get it when I'm ready." She continued toward the meeting room.

Vicki placed her hand at the small of April's back. "You know I don't like to wait."

Heat spread up April's cheeks. "What would happen if I didn't send you a picture?"

"Try it and find out."

One look at Vicki's face told April that she wasn't messing around. It only tempted April more. One of these days, she was going to test whether Vicki would actually follow through on her threats. But not today. She had already taken a photo, she was just waiting for the right moment to send it.

Just before they came into view of the meeting room, Vicki pulled her hand away. April's back tingled where Vicki had touched her.

"After you." Vicki opened the door.

April and Vicki entered the room and took their places at opposite ends of the table. They were the last to arrive. Lexi gave April a strange look. April avoided her gaze.

"Sorry we're late," Vicki said. "April and I were having a very interesting conversation."

April ignored Vicki's comment. "Let's get started." Surreptitiously, she placed her phone in her lap and tapped the screen, sending off a message.

Right on cue, Vicki pulled out her phone and glanced at it under the table. Her gaze flicked up to April, the thirst in her eyes hidden from all but April.

"Vicki?" April said. "You called the meeting, is there something you'd like to share with us?"

"Yes." Vicki shoved her phone in her pocket and cleared her throat. "Given the recent attention that the Oakmont Street Library has been getting in the media, Oasis Developments has decided it's in everyone's best interests to delay the Oakmont Street project until a more suitable location for the library can be found."

April's heart leaped. *It worked. It actually worked.* "That's great," she said. The library wasn't safe just yet, but this was the best outcome they could have hoped for. Now they had enough time to figure out what to do.

"I've been talking to the head of our corporate sponsorship program, and he's going to see if we can spare some funds," Vicki said. "It won't be much, but it should help."

"That would be amazing," April said.

"I understand you've been doing some fundraising," Vicki said.

"Yes. And now that we have more time, we can raise even more. And there are some federal grants we can apply for."

The two of them went back and forth, discussing options, the others around the table chiming in now and then. Vicki took plenty of notes and seemed to be taking their feedback and suggestions seriously.

Almost an hour later, the meeting came to an end. As everyone filed out of the room, April told Lexi she'd catch up with her, and stayed in her seat. April didn't have to ask Vicki to stay. Once the room had emptied, Vicki sat down next to April.

"So, what do you think?" she asked.

"This is amazing!" April said. "Why didn't you tell me about it sooner?"

"It wasn't a done deal until this morning. I had to get approval from the board. They weren't exactly pleased with my proposition, but I convinced them that going forward now would be a PR disaster."

"*You* did this?"

"What can I say? You're a tenacious woman. You wore me down."

"Vicki, thank you!"

April beamed. She was so happy, she wanted to throw her arms around Vicki's neck and kiss her, to run her fingers through those blonde locks, to bury herself in Vicki's skin.

But the room they were in had glass walls and everyone could see them. Already, they were sitting much too close.

"I should get going," April said. "I have so much work to do."

"So do I," Vicki replied. "I've been putting out fires all week because of your little campaign."

"I hope you're not expecting an apology."

"I'm not. Even I have to admit, it was a smart play. I'd be commending you if I wasn't the target of this. You should be working PR at a Fortune 500 company."

"I would never take a job like that in a million years," April said.

"Of course you wouldn't," Vicki said. "You're too busy crusading for the greater good. Your talents are wasted here."

"There's nowhere else I'd rather be."

The two of them gathered their things and left the room.

"I'll see you later." April was uncertain of whether it was a question or a statement.

"Oh, I'll be seeing you," Vicki said. "As soon as everything cools down, you're coming to my apartment, and I'm going to give you a taste of the rest of my collection." She straightened up her blazer. "By the way, that picture you sent me. Did you take it at your desk?"

"I did," April replied.

Vicki shook her head. "You're a bold woman." With that, she turned and headed for the exit.

April made her way back to her office. It was almost five p.m., and it was Friday. All the excitement of the week had been taxing. April wanted nothing more than to go home and have a long soak in the bath. She was looking forward to doing absolutely nothing for the entire weekend.

When April reached her office, Lexi was sitting with her feet up on her desk and her arms crossed.

She gave April a cold look. "Have a nice talk with Vicki, did you?"

"I don't know what you mean," April replied.

"I thought you hated her. Now the two of you are acting like best friends?"

"We're working together. I'm just being friendly. It's nothing more than that." April didn't like lying to her friend, but Lexi had made her feelings about Vicki very clear. "What do you have against her, anyway? Did she try to steal some girl you were chasing?"

"Like I said, I don't like the way she treats women," Lexi replied.

"That has nothing to do with our jobs and the library. You're being unfair."

"You're actually defending her now? Unbelievable." Lexi muttered something else under her breath that April didn't catch.

"I don't understand why you're so angry," April said.

"I'm angry because you're falling for her act." Lexi picked up her bag and grabbed her coat. "Vicki Blake can't be trusted. She's just going to end up screwing us over." Without another word, Lexi stormed out of the office.

# CHAPTER SIXTEEN

*A*pril was woken up on Saturday morning by the ringing of her phone. She rolled over and picked it up. It was Lexi. The two of them hadn't spoken since Lexi stormed out of their office the day before. April wasn't upset with her. The two of them had been friends for years, and they were both hot-tempered. It wasn't the first time they'd had a disagreement.

April answered the phone. "Hi, Lex."

"April," Lexi said. "Look, I'm sorry about yesterday. I was just in a bad mood, and I took it out on you."

"It's all right."

"No, it's not. I was being a jerk."

"Seriously, it's fine. God knows how many times you've had to put up with my bad moods." April frowned. "Is everything else okay? You don't sound too good."

"I don't feel too good," Lexi said. "I think I ate something bad last night. I've been up since four a.m. puking into a bucket."

"Are you all right?"

"I'll live," Lexi replied. "Look, I hate to apologize then ask for a favor, but I don't have any other options."

"Sure, what do you need?" April asked.

"The charity ball is tonight. I can't go like this. Do you think you could go in my place? Please?"

April stifled a groan. The charity ball wasn't her idea of a good time. The giant party was always full of insanely wealthy people who had more money than sense and spent the whole night getting dangerously intoxicated.

But she couldn't say no to Lexi. "Sure," April said. "I'll do it." It wasn't like she had anything better to do with her Saturday night.

"Thank you so much," Lexi said. "I promise you won't have to do much. There shouldn't be any surprises, but you can call me if you need help and I'll do what I can."

"Don't worry about it. I've organized these things before, remember? Just rest up." April walked over to her closet. She would have to find something to wear. Even though she intended to spend most of her time hiding behind the scenes, she would stand out unless she was in formal wear.

"You're the best, April," Lexi said.

"You owe me. Next time we get dinner after work, you're buying."

"Done. By the way, there's a theme this year," Lexi said. "You're going to need a mask."

---

April pulled off her black-and-red eye mask. She had borrowed it from Lexi, and it fit too snugly.

She had to admit, Lexi's idea to make the event a masquerade ball was a good one. The ball was in full swing now, and the guests seemed to be enjoying themselves even more than usual. Sure, the ball was always one big display of hedonistic excess, but this year was different. It was like some kind of magic spell had been cast on the room, like the act of putting on a mask made everyone lose their inhibitions. It didn't make sense. It wasn't like the flimsy masks everyone was wearing provided any anonymity. Perhaps even adults liked to play pretend sometimes.

At the very least, rich, drunk people were extremely generous, especially in front of their peers. Someone had made a sizable anonymous donation. It was encouraging to know that all the money and effort put into throwing the ball was worth it.

Lexi hadn't lied when she said April wouldn't have to do much. She'd organized everything well, from the band right down to the stunning ice sculptures. Save for keeping an eye out for rowdy guests, and dealing with some technical issues during the speeches, April's night had been an easy one. She only had a couple of hours before she would be back home in bed with a book.

April's stomach rumbled. The ball had been going for hours, and she hadn't eaten anything since she arrived. She spotted a waiter disappearing into the crowd, his tray laden with appetizers. Although she wasn't a guest, no one could blame April for grabbing a few.

April slipped her mask back on and made her way through the crowd in search of the waiter. She attracted the odd stare, no doubt because of her dress. She had made the mistake of wearing a simple, vivid red gown, one that stood out in a sea of black and diamonds. But mostly, she passed through almost invisible, beneath the notice of the upper-class guests.

She found the waiter, grabbed some canapes, then made her way toward some chairs in the corner, stuffing the food into her mouth. As the crowd thinned near the side of the hall, April's eyes landed on a familiar figure, a slender blonde woman leaning against the wall with her hands in her pockets

*Vicki.*

April froze. She hadn't expected to see Vicki tonight. She wasn't at all prepared for it. Despite everything, April still had a tendency to lose her mind around Vicki. And right now, April was losing her mind just looking at her. Vicki had a flair for rocking suits while still looking utterly feminine. Tonight, she was wearing a fitted black tuxedo, and heels which accentuated her legs and made her look even slimmer. Her soft blonde hair was swept back, and she had a red flower pinned to her lapel. Her mask was a delicate creation of black lace that covered the area around her eyes.

Vicki's eyes met April's, her gaze pinning April in place. April gulped down the rest of her canape as Vicki approached her.

"April." Vicki flashed her a smile. "Don't you look enchanting?"

April's cheeks grew warm. "Vicki. I didn't know you were coming."

"What can I say, I enjoy a nice ball. It's for a good cause after all."

"Do you even know what charity this ball is raising money for?" April asked.

Vicki shrugged. "Something about sick children?"

"Not even close."

"I have to say, you're the last person I'd expect to see here." Vicki's eyes flicked down April's body and back up again. "Not that I'm complaining, of course."

"I'm here on library business," April said. "I'm filling in for Lexi. I should probably get back to work." April didn't actually have anything to do, but being around Vicki while she was looking as devastatingly sexy as she was right now seemed dangerous.

"Wait," Vicki said. "Come mingle with me."

"Mingle? I'm not a guest. And no offense, but this isn't my kind of crowd."

"They're not all bad. Besides, there's something I want to show you."

"What is it?"

"Come with me and you'll find out."

April's curiosity was piqued, but this seemed like a bad idea. "What if someone sees us together? I don't want anyone to think I'm your date. Because of work, I mean," she added hurriedly.

"Nobody knows who you are here," Vicki said. "And everyone is too drunk and self-absorbed to notice you. Besides, between your mask and that wickedly sexy dress you're wearing, even I barely recognized you. You'll just be another face in the crowd." She drew her fingers through her hair. "Who knows, you might even enjoy yourself."

April fidgeted with her mask. It was tempting. To get lost in the crowd with Vicki, to pretend, just for a moment, that they weren't at opposite sides of the battle over the library.

"So? What do you say?" Vicki held out her hand, her eyes speaking a command April desperately wanted to follow, one she had given April so many times before. *Give in to your desires.*

"Okay," April said. "But only for a little while. Then I'm going back to work."

April took Vicki's hand, and Vicki whisked April away into the crowd. As a waiter passed them, Vicki snatched up a couple of glasses of champagne and handed one to April. "Consider it camouflage."

April sipped the drink, the smooth liquid warming her chest. "This is good." In all the years she'd organized the ball, she'd never actually tried the champagne. She'd never stood in the hall like she was right now, in the midst of all the people, doing nothing but soaking in the glitz and glamor. The grand old hall seemed so alive.

They continued through the crowd, Vicki greeting people here and there. Occasionally, Vicki would stop and chat with some of them about everything from gossip and small talk to business. April couldn't see a pattern to the people Vicki talked to. But they all had too much money and too much power, both of which they threw around thoughtlessly. It only proved to April that these were not her kind of people.

As Vicki had predicted, no one took any notice of April, which was fine with her. She simply stood there silently, sipping champagne, until Vicki dragged her off to talk to someone else.

April was beginning to wonder what the point of all this was when they were approached by a pair of women. One of them, a tall dark-haired woman, looked familiar to her, but her elaborate half mask made it difficult for April to place her.

Vicki greeted them both. "April, this is Mel. You've already met Vanessa."

*Right.* April had briefly met Vanessa that night at Lilith's Den. The other woman, a slight brunette, was looking at Vicki with an expression on her face that could only be described as hostile. Was this the girlfriend of Vanessa's that Vicki had "caused trouble" for?

"We meet again, April," Vanessa said, shooting Vicki a look.

"I'm not with her," April blurted. "I just mean, we're not-"

"We didn't come together," Vicki clarified. "We just happened to run into each other."

"What a coincidence," Vanessa said.

"I'm actually working tonight," April said. "I run the library that's sponsoring the ball."

"The library on Oakmont Street, right?" Mel asked. "I heard that it's getting shut down. It's too bad. I work for a non-profit legal service downtown. A lot of our clients use the library. It has some great resources."

"Yes, it does," April said. She glanced sideways at Vicki. "It's a real pity."

"It's not being shut down," Vicki said. "The project has been put on hold until everything with the library has been sorted out."

"That's right," Vanessa said. "The Oakmont Street Project is yours, isn't it, Vic?" She looked from Vicki to April. "How interesting."

April sighed. Despite April's protestations, it was clear that Vanessa didn't believe that nothing was going on between April and Vicki. It didn't help that she had seen them at Lilith's Den together.

Mel, however, didn't share Vanessa's amusement. Her wariness of Vicki was clear on her face. She turned to address April. "Assuming the library is staying open, we should talk about setting up a partnership between the Legal Services Project and the Oakmont Street Library," Mel said. "We're always looking for ways to make it easier for people who need our services to find us."

"That would be amazing," April said. "We get a lot of people coming in to look up legal reference books because they can't afford lawyers."

"Great," Mel said. "I'll be in touch."

"Why don't we leave these two alone?" Vanessa wrapped her arm around Mel's waist. "It was lovely to see you again, April."

Mel said goodbye to April and gave Vicki another withering look before she and Vanessa walked off.

April turned to Vicki. "No one knows me here, huh?"

"I wasn't planning on running into Vanessa," Vicki said.

"And all those other people we've run into? That was intentional?"

"Yes. I'm proving a point."

"Which is?" April asked.

"You'll have to wait and see," Vicki said.

"All this mingling and this mysterious 'something' you want to show me has yet to materialize." April crossed her arms. "I'm starting to suspect you have an ulterior motive."

"Oh? And what would that be?"

"I don't know, to drag me around this party drinking champagne with you?"

Vicki lifted her glass. "You make it sound like such an awful thing."

"Victoria!"

"I was kidding," Vicki said. "I assure you, there's a point to all this. Trust me."

"Okay then," April said. "By the way, what did you do to get on Mel's bad side?"

Vicki waved her hand dismissively. "I made a few harmless comments to her at a ball just like this one, and apparently she took them the wrong way."

Before April could question her further, Vicki's eyes landed on a group of half a dozen people, standing around with drinks in their hands.

"Come on." Vicki held out her arm for April to take. "Try not to lose your temper, okay?"

"What do you mean?" April asked.

Vicki didn't answer her. Instead, she pulled April over to the group, slipping into a gap in the circle.

"Good to see you, Vicki," the woman next to April said. She had straight brown hair and a warm smile, and she looked to be around forty.

"Camilla. This is April," Vicki said. "April, Camilla."

April and Camilla exchanged a brief greeting. As the conversation continued around them, Vicki quietly spoke in April's ear, telling April who everyone was. There was one woman, an older lady, who Vicki simply referred to as 'the Duchess.' Next to her was Senator Williams, who April recognized from TV, and his wife. Everyone looked like they'd had plenty to drink.

When the conversation died down, Camilla addressed Vicki again. "How are things at Oasis? I hear you've been having some trouble with one of your major projects?"

"Yes, the Oakmont Street development in West Heights. The locals are being difficult." Vicki waved her hands dismissively. "They're up in arms because we're 'destroying the neighborhood.'"

The locals? *Difficult?* April couldn't believe what was coming out of Vicki's mouth.

Senator Williams scoffed. "West Heights is prime real estate now, but it's covered in all those ugly old townhouses. They're a waste of valuable space."

"Well, if the locals don't like it, they can move somewhere else," the Duchess said.

April fumed. Did Vicki really expect April to just stand here and listen to these snobs badmouth West Heights? She opened her mouth to retort when Camilla spoke.

"It's unfortunate," she said. "There are some lovely old buildings in the area. Isn't there a museum that's going to be demolished?"

"It's a library," April said sharply.

"Yes, it is a library." Vicki placed a hand on April's shoulder. "April works there."

"Do you, dear?" The Duchess peered at April over her glasses. "It's very generous of you to give up your time like that."

Did this woman think April was some kind of volunteer? Of course, it made a lot more sense than someone who actually had a job at a library being a guest at a party like this. April did look like a guest right now, considering she was walking around with Vicki holding a glass of champagne.

"Yes, she's a real dear, this one," Vicki said, a mocking edge in her voice that only April seemed to notice. "She's been helping Oasis work out a solution to relocate the library."

"Well, I for one don't see the point," the Duchess said. "Do people even use libraries anymore? Can't they just *buy* books?"

"The library isn't just for books," April said. "Plenty of people use libraries for the other resources they offer, like computers and free wifi."

"Don't they have those at home?"

April resisted the urge to roll her eyes. "Some people can't afford them. That's why places like the Oakmont Street Library are so important."

Without thinking, April launched into an impromptu speech about the importance of the library. When she finished, she realized that everyone in the circle was staring at her.

"I had no idea," the Duchess said. "Did you know about this, Vicki?"

"Not until April told me about it," Vicki said.

"Well it sounds like you've got an important thing going there, April," Camilla said. "I'd love to help out. I'm sure I could find some funds to make a donation to the library."

April beamed. "That would be wonderful."

"Yes, I'll speak with my husband about making a contribution," the Duchess said loudly. "He's the Duke of Immingham, you know. We're very charitable people."

Camilla tilted her head toward April and spoke under her breath. "Good luck getting anything from her. Last I heard, 'the Duke' stopped letting 'the Duchess' touch their money after he caught her naked in their bed with the pool boy. No, that isn't right. It was the maid."

April nearly choked on her champagne. She glanced around. The conversation had moved on, and no one else seemed to have heard Camilla's comment.

"So, you work at the library?" Camilla asked.

"I run it, actually," April replied. "I'm the director."

"And that's how you and Vicki met?"

April glanced at Vicki, who was deep in conversation with Senator Williams. "We're not... We just happened to run into each other tonight," April said for the second time that hour.

"Right."

"Really, I'm supposed to be working right now," she said, looking guiltily at her almost empty glass of champagne. "Vicki just wanted to show me around." April still wasn't sure what Vicki was showing her. After Vicki's comments earlier, she was starting to wonder if this was all a big joke.

"You're not missing out on much," Camilla said. "I'd rather be home in a nice relaxing bath, but, social obligations and all."

April smiled. She was beginning to like this woman.

"Your little pitch was the most interesting thing I've heard all night," Camilla said.

"It wasn't meant to be a pitch. I care a lot about the library, that's all."

"I can tell. Your passion will take you far in life. I'll speak with Vicki about helping out the library." Camilla finished off the last of her drink. "Now, if you'll excuse me, I'm going to go find some more wine. God knows I'll need it to get through the rest of the night." Without another word, Camilla slipped away.

Vicki took the opportunity to pull April to the side. But April was tired of being dragged around. And she hadn't forgotten about Vicki's comments about the library earlier.

She put her hands on her hips. "What the hell was that, Victoria?"

# CHAPTER SEVENTEEN

"*L*et me explain," Vicki said.

"What is there to explain?" April threw her hands up. "You just disparaged West Heights and the people who live there to your rich friends!"

"I had to get you fired up about the library somehow."

"What the hell are you talking about?"

Vicki held her palms out in front of her. "Hear me out."

"Fine," April said. "Talk."

"You were just speaking with Camilla, right?" Vicki said. "Not only is she one of my good friends, but she comes from a very wealthy, influential family. The Robinson's are old money. They have fingers in every pot. Politics, banking, real estate. I wouldn't be surprised if tonight's big anonymous donation came from Camilla."

"What's your point?" April asked.

"This is why I asked you to come mingle. I wanted you to talk to all these people." Vicki gestured around the hall. "This room is filled with the most important people in the city. These are the people who hold all the power. They're who you need to lobby if you want to protect West Heights. We both know that all the changes happening in the city are inevitable. But if you work with those in power instead of against them, you can have a say in how those changes are implemented. Direct where the money goes, make sure that there are policies in place to protect the vulnerable, and so on."

"How am I supposed to do that?" April asked. "I run a library. I don't have all these connections like you do."

"You don't need to," Vicki replied. "At least, not yet. Ever since that town hall meeting, I've been thinking about how good you'd be at politics."

"Me? Politics?"

Vicki nodded. "If you want to make a difference, that's how you can do it. You have a talent for it. You took on Oasis and made us listen to you. You even convinced 'the Duchess' that libraries are a good thing. Obviously, running for office takes time, so it won't help the library's current situation."

"Running for office?" April shook her head. "Why do you of all people want me to do something like this?"

"Because I believe you could do some real good. I'm not the evil villain you think I am. I care about the city too. And West Heights."

"Considering your comments earlier, I find that hard to believe."

"Like I said, I had to get you fired up." Vicki smiled. "You're much more persuasive that way."

"You tricked me," April said.

"It worked, didn't it? I was trying to prove my point." Vicki shot April a smoldering look. "And you should know, I find that fire of yours sexy as hell."

April folded her arms on her chest. "You think you can charm me into forgetting what you just did?"

"I'm being honest."

"You're unbelievable."

But as April stared back at Vicki, at her mesmerizing eyes and her charming smile, she realized she couldn't stay mad at Vicki for long. And Vicki looked so captivating in that suit. April allowed her eyes to wander down Vicki's body, then back up again...

April frowned. "Vicki?"

Vicki's gaze had shifted to something behind April, her face set like stone and eyes filled with fury. April turned to see an older couple, a man and a woman with striking blonde hair. The man was glaring at Vicki with the exact same expression as Vicki.

"Victoria," he said.

Vicki's narrowed her eyes. "Dad. Mom."

*These are Vicki's parents?* The very same parents who had all but disowned her years ago? No wonder Vicki looked so angry.

"What are you doing here?" Vicki asked. "You never come to these things."

"Your mother wanted to attend," her father replied curtly.

For a moment no one spoke. April glanced at Vicki's mother. Her face was vacant, like she was pretending Vicki wasn't even there.

Vicki's father looked his daughter up and down. "Still pretending to be a man? I see you haven't changed."

"No, I haven't changed," Vicki said, her voice filled with venom. "And I'm never going to."

"Of course you're not. You just can't help but do everything you can to humiliate us."

April gaped at him. How could anyone treat their own child with such disdain?

"I see *you* haven't changed either," Vicki said. "You still believe the world revolves around you. How arrogant do you have to be to think that I am who I am just to spite you?"

"Why else would you persist in behaving this way?" her father asked. "It's like everything you do is some selfish ploy to shame the family. Dressing like this. Taking a job with those Oasis bastards. Parading around the city with gold-digging sluts on your arm." He gestured toward April.

Vicki seethed. "Say what you want about me, but don't you dare speak about April that way."

"Why not? Whoever this woman is, she's clearly only after you for your money. Why else would she be with someone like you?" He jabbed his finger in Vicki's direction. "You're a disgrace to the Blake family name."

April's hands curled into fists. She had heard enough. "How can you say that?" she said.

Vicki's father looked at April like he'd just been addressed by the wall. "What did you say?"

"How can you say these things about Vicki? Anyone else would be so proud to have a daughter like her! Look at how successful she's become. She's smart, and hardworking, and thoughtful, and brilliant. I don't know how she turned out this way when she had parents like you!" Blood rushed in April's ears. "It's you who should be ashamed."

Vicki's father's face turned crimson. "I'm not going to stand here and be insulted by some lesbian tart."

"Then walk away," Vicki said.

Her father scoffed. "You don't get to tell me what to do."

"Do you really want me to make a scene in front of all these people?" Vicki asked coldly. "I know how much you care about your reputation. I'm not beneath smearing it even more."

Her father glanced around.

"I'll say it again. Walk away and don't come back. Don't ever speak to me again."

Vicki's father scowled. "Don't come crying to us when you end up in trouble."

"It's been ten years," Vicki said. "Ten years since you cut me out of your lives. And I've been doing just fine. I don't need you. I never have."

Vicki's father opened his mouth to retort, then shut it again. He gave Vicki one last glare then took his wife's arm. "Let's go."

Vicki watched them walk away, her body wound tight as a spring.

"Vicki?" April asked. "Are you okay?"

Vicki snapped out of her trance. "I'm fine. Those two know exactly how to get under my skin, that's all." Her brows furrowed. "Are you all right? I can't believe he said those things about you."

"I'm fine." April's heart had finally slowed down to normal. "It helps that I had you to defend my honor. It was kind of sweet."

"Well, you did the same for me." Vicki smiled, her relaxed demeanor returning. "I had no idea you thought so highly of me."

April flushed. "Don't let it go to your head." She readjusted her mask and glanced around the hall. "I should go check on things."

"All right," Vicki said. "Before you go, I want you to look me in the eyes and admit something."

April's breath caught in her throat. "Admit what?"

"That you enjoyed this."

"You mean cozying up to your snobby friends, then getting in a yelling match with your homophobic father?" April asked.

"Not that part. The rest of it. Drinking champagne, wandering around in this beautiful ballroom together. You had fun, didn't you?"

April looked up at Vicki. Her eyes sparkled under the glittering lights, and her cheeks were faintly flushed with pink. In the tightly packed crowd, the two of them were forced to stand close together, and April could feel the warmth radiating from Vicki's skin.

"Yes," she said. "I enjoyed this."

"See? What did I tell you?"

Vicki reached out and placed a hand on April's arm. Before April knew what she was doing, her hands were on Vicki's shoulders. Then Vicki's hands were at April's waist and their bodies were only inches apart.

April let out a breath. This was stupid. Reckless. The two of them should not be seen together like this. But everyone else was so wrapped up in their own worlds that she and Vicki might as well have been invisible.

And April wanted to pretend.

She slid her hands up and wrapped her arms around Vicki's neck, drawing her down close.

At once, Vicki's lips were on April's, and her hands were at April's hips, holding her so tightly that she wondered how either of them could breathe. April closed her eyes and let her world shrink down until it was just her, and Vicki, alone in the ballroom, melding into each other's skin. April's body begged for so much more than just a kiss.

But she was supposed to be working. And she'd been off with Vicki for much too long.

April broke away. "I really have to go."

"Okay, Cinderella," Vicki said.

April drew back, her hands still clasping Vicki's, not wanting to let go.

"April?"

"Yes?"

"I enjoyed this, too," she said.

Smiling, April released Vicki's hands and walked away.

As she wandered through the crowd, she brought her fingers up to her lips, touching them where Vicki's lips had just been.

# CHAPTER EIGHTEEN

The following Tuesday afternoon, April was sitting alone in her office, lost in her head. The library campaign was starting to slow down now, but donations were still trickling in. Between that, and Oasis' willingness to help the library, April was hopeful that everything could actually work out.

Well, everything with the library at least. April was even more confused than ever about herself and Vicki. The constant push and pull between them left her disoriented. That intense kiss they'd shared at the masquerade ball only made things worse. April kept reliving it over and over in her head in an attempt to understand it.

Or maybe she just wanted to experience it again.

April had also been mulling over what Vicki said to her at the ball. Working with those in power, not against them. Doing something bigger. She had never even considered politics before, but she was starting to come around to the idea.

Her thoughts were interrupted when Lexi marched into their office, an inscrutable expression on her face.

She thrust her phone toward April. "Is that you?"

April stared at the photo on the screen. It was from the

masquerade ball. The photo was of a group of ladies posing for the camera.

And behind them were April and Vicki, arms around each other, lips locked.

April cursed.

"That's you, isn't it?" Lexi said. "You and Vicki Blake?"

"Y-Yes," April said. This wasn't good. At the very least, April and Vicki were just two of several people in the background of the photo, just faces in a crowd. And they were wearing masks.

But it hadn't been enough to fool Lexi. "I can't believe it," she said.

"Look, Lex, it's complicated-"

"How could it possibly be complicated? Were you drunk? Was it just a momentary lapse?"

"It was more like a series of momentary lapses." April paused. It was time to come clean. "Remember that night we went to The Sapphire Room, and I met someone?"

"Wait, that was her? Vicki Blake?"

April nodded.

Lexi looked like April had slapped her. "You kept that from me all this time?"

"I didn't mean to. I didn't know who she was until that town hall meeting, and then I was embarrassed, and angry, and then I was just in denial about everything." April knew how feeble her excuses sounded.

"That's why you were defending her the other day. Have the two of you been fucking this whole time?"

"It's not like that," April said. "Well, it kind of is. At least, it started off that way. But I think... I'm really starting to care about her, Lexi."

Lexi's expression softened. "Seriously?"

"I don't know." April groaned. "I have so many feelings about her, and some of them are good, and some of them are bad, and I'm so confused."

"Wow." Lexi pulled her chair over to April's desk and sat down

299

next to her. "I didn't think that the two of you were actually serious."

"We're not. I mean, we couldn't possibly be with everything that's going on."

Lexi was silent for a moment. "You could have told me, April."

"How could I?" April asked. "You're always going on about how much of a bad person she is."

"I guess you're right. That would have made it hard, huh?"

April studied her friend. Lexi had a guilty expression on her face. "What is it?" April asked.

Lexi sighed. "You were right, the other day. My grudge against Vicki is kind of personal."

"What do you mean? Did she steal some girl from you?"

Lexi shook her head.

"What, then? Did she try to hit on you?" April asked. "Wait, did something happen between the two of you?"

Lexi shrugged. "Kind of? I mean, we didn't actually sleep together. We almost did."

April felt a sinking feeling in the pit of her stomach. "I didn't know. Vicki never said anything." Vicki had never indicated that she'd met Lexi before, let alone anything more.

"I didn't say anything to you about it either. And I didn't exactly want to share the fact that I'd gotten played by a woman, let alone the woman who is about to bulldoze the library."

"What happened?"

"It was a long time ago," Lexi said. "Back when I was barely old enough to get into a bar. I used to go to Sapphire every weekend, trying to flirt with women and failing more often than not." Lexi smiled. "Believe it or not, I wasn't always this suave. Anyway, Vicki would come to Sapphire all the time too, and she'd have women wrapped around her finger with only a few words."

*Yep.* That sounded like Vicki.

"I was so jealous of how easy it was for her. Then one night, she came to talk to me, and I was flattered by her attention. I should have known better, but the things she said made me think she was actually interested in me, and not just trying to get into my pants.

So, when she asked me if I wanted to go back to her place, I said yes.

"When we got back to her apartment, things got all hot and heavy, then-" Lexi paused. "I don't know what happened exactly. We were both a little drunk. But one minute we were making out on her bed, and the next, Vicki shoved my shirt into my arms, called me a cab, and booted me out the door with zero explanation. I guess she changed her mind? I was pretty upset about it at the time. I'm not sure if I was upset at her for blowing me off, or at myself for falling for her act in the first place. To top it off, I saw her back at Sapphire the next weekend, doing the same thing as always."

"Wow. I'm sorry, Lex," April said.

"Don't be," Lexi replied. "It was years ago. It wasn't that big a deal at the time either. I mean, I was back at Sapphire doing my thing the next week too. I guess I still resent her though." Lexi flicked one of her dark curls out of her eyes. "I don't know, maybe it's justified. Plenty of women out there have been screwed around by Vicki Blake. Word gets around, you know how it is."

April said nothing, unsure of whether she even wanted to defend Vicki.

"Look," Lexi said. "We're all adults here. I'm not going to tell you that you can't date someone because of one night when we almost slept together years ago. I just don't want you to get hurt, that's all."

"I won't," April said. "I'm being careful about this." That was a lie.

"Okay. Sorry I've been such a bitch about her."

"It's all right. Sorry I kept this all from you. Are we okay?"

Lexi nodded. "We are."

Relief washed over April. She couldn't bear the thought of being on bad terms with Lexi. But with that problem resolved, she still had a bigger one.

"Where did you find that photo of Vicki and me?" April asked.

"The photos from the ball are up on the city's website. They have a society pages section. I was checking them out because I wanted to see the fruit of all my hard work. I have to admit, those ice sculptures looked pretty good." Lexi noticed April's frown. "Oh, you're worried people will see the photo?"

"Yeah. I mean, I've somehow become some sort of crusader for West Heights. And Vicki is high up in Oasis's hierarchy. I can't imagine it'll look good for either of us to be caught sleeping with the enemy, so to speak."

"Don't worry," Lexi said. "No one looks at the city's website. And the only reason I spotted you in that picture is because I recognized that red dress of yours. I was there when you bought it for Caroline's wedding last year. With the masks on, no one is going to recognize you."

That did little to reassure April.

"If you're really worried, you can try to get the photo taken down, but that might draw more attention to it. People love to gossip after all. Do you really want Anne down at City Hall wondering why we're so eager to have the photo taken down?"

"That's a good point," April said.

She would have to work out some way to deal with the photo. And she should probably warn Vicki. April asked Lexi for a link to the photo, and she sent it to Vicki along with a quick message. A few minutes later, she received a reply.

*Thanks for the warning.*

Another message soon followed.

*Can you come to my apartment after work so we can talk about this?*

*Sure,* April replied. Two heads were better than one, after all.

Still, the photo wasn't what was on April's mind when she returned to her work. April had definitely mentioned to Vicki that she and Lexi were friends. Close friends. And she'd had plenty of opportunities to tell April that something had happened between them.

But Vicki had never said a word to her about it.

---

A few hours later, April stepped through the door of Vicki's apartment. Vicki was dressed casually in a loose white shirt and jeans. Her feet were bare, and her hair was slightly ruffled, but she still managed to look incredibly sexy.

Vicki told April to sit down while she cleared her laptop and a stack of documents from the coffee table.

"Working late?" April asked.

"I was," Vicki replied. "But I'm glad you're here. I can't stand to look at another spreadsheet. Do you want a drink? Coffee? Something stronger?"

"Something stronger is about my speed right now," April said.

"Lucky for you, I have a well-stocked bar. Have a seat."

April sat down while Vicki disappeared into the kitchen. Something black and furry leaped onto the table beside her. Sebastian. He sat there, unmoving, watching her with his usual disdainful expression. April was about to ask him what she'd ever done to deserve his scorn when Vicki returned with two mojitos. She handed one to April and sat down next to her, stretching out her long limbs.

"Looks like we were caught in the act," Vicki said.

"Yeah," April said. "What do we do? Try to get it taken down? Ignore it, and cross our fingers that no one notices it? I mean, it looks pretty bad. Could it get you in trouble with Oasis?"

"I'm not too worried. Men in positions like mine get caught doing far more scandalous things. At the work Christmas party last year, our VP of finance got caught with his hand up his secretary's skirt, and no one batted an eyelid. Except for his wife."

April raised an eyebrow.

"Not that this is the same thing, of course," Vicki said quickly. "You're right, it doesn't look good. But it'll be okay. We'll figure out how to handle it. At the very least, we're barely recognizable unless you look closely."

That was exactly what Lexi had said. *Lexi*. April had to ask Vicki about Lexi, but she wasn't sure if there was an answer Vicki could give her that would satisfy her.

"I looked through the photos already, and I didn't even notice," Vicki said. "You have a better eye than I do."

"It wasn't me who spotted us. It was Lexi." April examined Vicki's face for any sign of recognition.

"We're lucky she found it, then," Vicki said.

"You know Lexi, don't you? My friend who works at the library with me."

"She's the event coordinator, right? She was at the meetings we had at the library."

"You've met before that," April said.

"I have?" Vicki asked. "She did seem familiar."

April frowned. Suddenly, it hit her. Vicki hadn't deliberately kept this from April. "You don't remember her, do you?"

Vicki's forehead creased. "What's this about? You're going to have to help me out here."

April crossed her arms. "You picked Lexi up at Sapphire once."

Realization dawned on Vicki's face. "You're right."

"You actually forgot, didn't you?" April shook her head. "Unbelievable."

"I was drunk," Vicki protested. "And we didn't sleep together. Besides, it was years ago. It would have been back when I..."

"When what?"

"When I was going through some things. I was young, and I went off the rails. It's a period of my life that I prefer to forget."

"That's supposed to justify it?" April wasn't sure exactly what 'it' was. The way Vicki had toyed with Lexi? The fact that Vicki had forgotten about ever taking her home? Everything that said about Vicki? It was all tangled up in one big knot in April's head.

"No, of course not," Vicki said. "I take full responsibility for the way I behaved. I treated Lexi badly, and I'm sorry."

This wasn't the reaction April was expecting. "Aren't you going to try to explain yourself?"

"I'm not going to make excuses for my behavior."

"I don't want excuses. I want to know why." April's voice quavered. "And I want to know that you're not that person anymore."

"That person?" Vicki said. "You mean that spoiled, rich womanizer who leads women on and only cares about herself?"

"I didn't say that."

"I'm aware of what people say about me. The truth is, I earned that reputation. As for whether I'm still that person? I'd like to think

I'm not." Vicki folded her hands in her lap. "Look, to start off with, I want you to know that I didn't keep this from you on purpose. I would never keep something from you that I thought would hurt you."

April felt a twinge in her chest.

"As for why I behaved the way I did that night and so many other nights? It's complicated." Vicki stared intently at her barely touched drink. "You've seen firsthand what my parents are like. Things were tough for me growing up. As an outsider in my own family, I lived a lonely life. It left me with a lot of scars. As an adult, I struggled to form meaningful relationships, so instead, I formed superficial ones. And I'm not proud to say it, but I embraced the advantages my privilege gave me. I played the role of the rich playgirl, drinking, flirting, and throwing around money to win women over. It was an easy way for me to feel a connection with someone, even if it wasn't real."

A heavy ache filled April's stomach. She knew what it was like to be an outsider, to feel that desperate loneliness.

"That night with Lexi was around the time my parents cut me out of their lives. I was in a bad place, so I spent my days and nights indulging in all my favorite vices. I was careless about it, too. And Lexi was one of the victims of my callousness.

"I regret the way I behaved back then," Vicki said. "I'm not proud of the person I was. And I'm sorry for the way I treated your friend." Vicki placed her hand on April's. "I'm not that person anymore. It's taken a long time, but I've changed, and grown, and I'm trying to be better."

April searched Vicki's face, unsure whether she was looking for a reason to believe Vicki, or a reason not to believe her. The truth was, April had been looking for reasons not to trust her since day one, reasons to deny her feelings for Vicki.

But April couldn't ignore them any longer.

"I can't hold your past against you," April finally said. "And you've shed your womanizing ways?"

"Of course," Vicki replied. "You're the only woman I've been with in god knows how long. It took me a while, but I realized how hollow that life was. I kept going to my old haunts, but I always went home alone. The night I met you, I wasn't lying when I said I was hoping someone exceptional would walk through the door. And you did." Vicki smiled. "Of course, as soon as I started talking to you, I went into player mode out of habit. But I never meant for you to be a one-night stand."

"Really?" April asked. "Because I remember you being very eager to get me out of my dress."

"What, a woman can't want both sex *and* a relationship?"

April stared at her. "You wanted a relationship?"

"Well, I wasn't going to ask you to move in after one night," Vicki said. "But I wanted to get to know you and see where things could go between us. And then the town hall meeting happened."

April was silent. There was a question that had been lingering at the back of her mind for a while now.

"Have you ever wondered what would have happened if it wasn't for, well, everything?" April asked. "Do you think that if the circumstances were different, there could have been something between us?"

"I'd like to think so," Vicki said. "Who knows, maybe once everything with the library is resolved, we can start over, give a real relationship a try?"

*A real relationship.* It seemed like such a distant possibility. But right now, April wanted nothing more. "I would like that." April smiled. "That is, as long as that relationship isn't-" What was the word Vicki always used? "—*vanilla.*"

A spark lit up behind Vicki's eyes. "Are you saying you still want to be my submissive?"

"I'm saying, I want you to make good on your promise to give me a taste of all those toys in your closet."

"Oh, April. When are you going to learn? It's not about the toys and tools." Vicki pushed April down onto the couch and leaned over her, speaking into April's ear. "It's about power."

# CHAPTER NINETEEN

*B*efore April knew what was happening, Vicki was on top of her, and Vicki's hands were at her wrists, pinning them to the arm of the couch above April's head. April wriggled underneath her, trying to break free, but Vicki had her trapped with what seemed like no effort at all.

April's whole body lit up. "Kiss me," she said breathlessly.

Instead, Vicki adjusted her grip on April's wrists so that she was holding them with one hand. She dragged her other hand along April's cheek and stared down at her, her jade eyes filled with fire. She dipped down low to draw her lips across the bow of April's neck and down to her chest, sucking and nibbling the swell of her breast that peeked out the top of her dress. Her hand traveled down to grab April's ass cheek.

April groaned. "Kiss me?"

Vicki glided her hand along the back of April's thigh, hoisting April's leg up to wrap around her waist. She shifted her body, grinding her hips between April's thighs, kissing her everywhere but her lips. The seam of Vicki's jeans rubbed against April through her dress, sending jolts deep into her core. She arched her chest up, trying in vain to press her body against Vicki's.

She closed her eyes and spoke the only words that could sway Vicki. "Please," April said. "Kiss me, *please.*"

Finally, Vicki grabbed April's chin and pressed her lips on April's. At once, April came apart. She melted into Vicki's body, her mind emptying. Her need for the other woman was so strong that she felt like she was going to burst. Vicki's suffocating kisses told April that Vicki felt the same.

She released April's hands and tore April's dress over her head. April grasped a fistful of Vicki's shirt, so she could pull Vicki down to her.

But Vicki pushed April's wrist down to the couch. "Don't move." Without another word, she got up and disappeared into her bedroom.

April groaned. Just when things were heating up, Vicki left her throbbing on the couch. Whatever Vicki was getting from her bedroom better be worth it. April's frustration only intensified when she thought about all the toys in Vicki's closet and the chest at the end of her bed.

When Vicki finally emerged, it was immediately clear to April what she had been doing in her room. She had taken off her jeans, and her long shirt was unbuttoned, with nothing underneath. Belted around her hips was a dark red strap-on.

Suddenly, there was a hollowness inside April that only Vicki could satisfy.

Vicki strode up to the couch. "This is what I was looking for in my chest that night I picked you up at the bar," she said. "Before you spoiled everything by being nosy."

April gave her a cheeky smile. "Aren't you glad that I did?"

Vicki's response was to fall on top of April again, assailing her with ravenous lips and hands. Somehow, Vicki managed to tear off April's bra and panties, tossing them across the room. Once again, April found herself helplessly trapped by Vicki's embrace.

April clung to her, craving the feel of Vicki's skin against hers. Vicki was just as hungry as April. She groped at April's curves, clawed at her skin, frantically working her way over April's entire body. April trembled. Vicki's body against hers, Vicki's scent, the taste of her skin, the hard strap-on pressing against her—it all threatened to overwhelm her. April could feel them being swept away in a firestorm of lust.

Vicki pulled back. "Wait."

"Is something wrong?" April asked. Vicki's expression was unreadable.

"No, of course not." Vicki gazed back down at April. "Everything is perfect. Which is why I want to take my time. I want to savor every moment. I don't want this to end," she said softly.

April's heart began to thump. "Okay."

Vicki kissed April again, softly this time. Tentatively, April reached up to push Vicki's shirt from her shoulders and drew Vicki to her. As the kiss stretched out, April allowed her fingertips to explore every part of Vicki's body. Her narrow shoulders. Her slender thighs. Her soft ass.

Vicki's hands mirrored April's, her hands roaming over April's skin. April could feel Vicki's restraint in every kiss and every touch. April yearned to tell Vicki to stop holding back, to devour her like she always did. But then everything would be over too quickly. April didn't want this to end either.

April kissed a line down Vicki's breasts and circled her nipple with her tongue. She brought a hand up to the other nipple, brushing her fingertips over the pebbled bud. A fevered murmur rose from Vicki's chest, her whole body shuddering. April reveled in Vicki's unbridled reactions. Who knew that the tough, dominant woman was so sensitive and responsive?

Vicki's hand found its way between April's legs. She slipped a finger inside, teasing April with a shadow of what was to come. The heel of her palm pressed against April's clit. April pushed against her, desperate and aching.

Just when April couldn't take it any longer, Vicki grabbed the strap-on, drawing it down April's slit, and entered her.

April exhaled sharply. God, Vicki felt so good inside. Vicki began to pump in and out, slowly, making every stroke count. April clutched onto her, rising up to meet her over and over.

This wasn't the Vicki of every other night, the hurricane of a woman fueled only by passion. She was just as possessive, and just as insatiable. But she was soft, and tender, and measured. With every movement, Vicki let out a gasp, a faint echo of April's own unrestrained cries. When April looked into Vicki's green eyes, April could see her own boundless desire reflected in them.

April closed her eyes. Vicki was right. It wasn't about all the toys, and the tools, and the kink. It wasn't even the power games that made April submit to Vicki every single time.

It was her. It had always been her.

"Victoria," April said. "I'm yours."

At once, Vicki shifted her hips, delving into April with urgent thrusts. April cried out as her pleasure rose to a crescendo and flooded her whole being. At the same time, Vicki shivered in April's arms, her climax mirroring April's.

Afterward, they ended up in Vicki's bed. April lay nestled against Vicki's shoulder, the blonde woman's arm slung around her. Did Vicki's hair always smell this heavenly?

"You know," Vicki said. "You never finished telling me why the library is so important to you."

"It's a little childish," April said.

"So what if it's childish? Whatever your reasons, they're important to you, and that means something."

"You're right." April drew back, laying her head on the pillow next to Vicki's. "The library was my refuge during a difficult time in my life. That was when I was a teenager. But even now, it holds an important place in my heart."

"It's your sanctuary," Vicki said.

"Yes." April looked at her in surprise. She hadn't expected Vicki to remember that. "You see, when I was in high school, I got bullied a lot."

"Really? You're the fiercest person I've ever met. I can't imagine anyone picking on you."

"I was different back then. Besides, bullying doesn't happen because of the victim's personality. Bullies target people for all kinds of reasons. In my case, I was just unlucky. There was this clique of mean girls everyone was afraid of. One day, out of nowhere, they set their sights on me. I was a quiet, nerdy kid who liked books and kept to myself. I was an easy target for them because they knew no one would stand up for me. So they picked on me relentlessly."

"That must have been difficult," Vicki said.

"It was, especially at first. As time went on, I went to the library more and more after school. I used books as an escape, to pretend I was someone else, somewhere else. I made friends at the library, kids from other schools who were outsiders like me. And I met Eliza. She was the librarian back then, and only ten years older than me. She took me under her wing, gave me advice, and she didn't treat me like my problems weren't real because I was just a kid. As I got older, we became friends. She gave me my first job as a page at the library when I was still in school and offered me another job when I returned from college. She promoted me to director when she left earlier in the year."

"She's a smart woman," Vicki said.

April smiled. "Anyway, by the time I was a junior, the bullies got bored with me and moved on to other targets. I'm ashamed to admit I was happy about that. I didn't care that they were hurting others as long as it wasn't me. It was selfish."

"That's not selfish," Vicki said. "That's just self-preservation."

"Well, I didn't feel good about it. So, after high school, I told myself that I would never stand by and let anything like that happen again, to myself or anyone else. That I wouldn't let bullies win, and I'd stand up for the people around me."

"And so, you became April, defender of the downtrodden. It all makes sense now."

April shrugged. "I guess so. That's why the library is so important to me. It's been mine for so long. That's why I can't bear the thought of it being destroyed."

"I understand," Vicki said. "And I mean it when I say that I'm committed to helping you find a way to save it. We can't save

Oakmont Street, but I'll do my best to make sure the library survives."

"Thanks, Vicki." April let out a contented sigh. "You know, all this time we've spent together has made me realize something. That person I became after high school—someone who always stands up, who fights back—it's made me forget how to let my guard down."

"That's never easy for anyone," Vicki said.

"Well, for me it's been toxic. It's probably why my relationships always end up falling apart. But when you came along, you were offering me exactly what I wanted. I wanted to be vulnerable but didn't know how to let myself. You were right all along. And your strength made me feel like it was safe for me to do that with you. Does that make sense?"

"It does," Vicki replied.

"I'm glad you gave me a chance to try to be your submissive," April said. "I'm not a very good one."

"That's not true. There's no right or wrong way to be a submissive. There are lots of submissives like you, who like to push back, who need to test their dominants to feel at ease." Vicki propped herself up and looked down at April. "Of course, their dominants usually push back even harder, whereas I've been letting you off easy."

"Letting me off easy?" April scoffed. "Last time I was here, you made me wait for you, blindfolded, for god knows how long. And then you tied me to the chair! How is that letting me off easy?"

"Oh April, you have no idea." Vicki chuckled softly. "If anyone knew about all the things I let you get away with, they'd take away my Domme card."

April frowned. "Do you really have a card?"

"Come here." Vicki wrapped her arms around April. "I'm glad I took a chance with you too. It feels good, to be challenged. All this time, I've been wandering through life, just going through the motions. BDSM was just a way for me to feel intimacy without having to get too close to anyone. Then you came along and actually made me feel something real. You made me want to let go of my grip on control and give in to passion. It's been so long since I've done that. I was beginning to forget what it feels like."

"I guess we both needed to step out of our comfort zones a little." April ran her fingers through Vicki's soft, weightless hair. "Does this mean you want me to push your boundaries even more?"

Vicki gave her a stern look. "Don't even think about it."

April rested her head on Vicki's chest. She couldn't help but wonder how she got here. Most of the upheaval and chaos in April's life right now was because of Vicki. But as she lay there next to Vicki, she began to wonder if maybe her sanctuary could be a person instead of a place.

"April," Vicki said. "Stay the night."

Vicki's voice had that compelling quality to it, the one that made it impossible for April to say no to her. And April didn't want to say no.

"Okay," April said. "I'll stay."

Vicki drew her in for a kiss. April closed her eyes, wishing that she'd never have to pull away.

But at the back of her mind, she was aware that everything was still up in the air. The library. The photo of them at the ball.

This wasn't pretend anymore. The two of them couldn't hide behind passion and power games any longer. Their two worlds were colliding.

April hoped they could survive the impact.

# CHAPTER TWENTY

*A*pril wrapped another plate in newspaper and added it to the box. It was Friday evening, and she was helping Eliza pack. Eliza wasn't leaving for another week, but she had an entire house to box up.

April sighed. Eliza leaving was just one of her myriad worries.

"That's it," Eliza said. "I'm sick of all your sighing. Sit down. What's wrong?"

April sat down on the couch next to her. "I have a lot on my mind at the moment, that's all."

"Like what?" Eliza asked.

"Well, there's everything with the library."

"I thought you were making progress?"

"We are," April replied. "Now that that the development project is on hold, we have enough time to look into long-term funding options."

"That all sounds promising," Eliza said. "So what's really the matter?"

"It's complicated."

"Try me."

"There's someone I have feelings for," April said. "Serious feelings. I don't think I've ever felt this way about anyone." She fidgeted with her fingers in her lap. "I think I'm falling in love with her."

Eliza smiled. "And what's the problem?"

"She's someone I shouldn't have feelings for. Someone I shouldn't be with."

"Why not?"

"Because she's Vicki Blake."

"Oh." Eliza paused. "Does she feel the same way?"

"I don't know," April said. "We've talked about giving a relationship a try once things with the library are sorted out. But that could take months. With everything else that's going on, it just seems impossible that we could ever actually be together."

"Impossible? I'm sure it'll be hard, but it's far from impossible," Eliza said. "The two of you will be able to work things out. Just hang in there and be patient."

"I hope you're right."

"I am." Eliza gave April a reassuring pat on the arm. "Now, I can handle the rest of this. Why don't you go home?"

"Are you sure? I don't mind helping out some more."

"It's okay. It's Friday night. You should go home and put your feet up."

"That does sound nice." With the charity ball last weekend, it had been a while since she'd had any downtime.

April said goodbye to Eliza and headed toward her apartment. Her mind drifted to Vicki. April wondered what it would be like to spend a quiet Friday night in with her, like a normal couple, without all the craziness that came with their present relationship. Of course, even if they were a normal couple, their relationship would probably still be crazy. Two headstrong women like them? Where there were sparks, there was bound to be fire. But April liked fire.

April wasn't even halfway home before her phone rang. It was Lexi.

"April, hi," she said. "How are you?"

"I'm fine," April replied. It was a strange question for Lexi to ask, considering they'd seen each other at work a few hours ago.

"Are you at home right now?"

"I'm on my way back from Eliza's, I'll be home soon. Why?" Something in Lexi's voice had her worried.

"I'm coming over, I'll explain when I get there."

"Don't you have a date?" April was sure that Lexi had mentioned she had plans tonight.

"I did. It's fine."

"Lexi, what's going on?"

"It's nothing. Look, I'll be there in half an hour, okay?" Lexi hung up.

April stared at her phone, frowning. She hoped that Lexi was okay.

She reached her apartment a few minutes later. She had some time to kill before Lexi arrived, so she sat down with her laptop and checked her social media feed. Although most of the discussion surrounding the library had died down, there was some local chatter about the Oakmont Street project in general, as well as other developments going on around West Heights. As April scrolled through her feed idly, a post caught her eye.

Her stomach dropped. It was the photo from the ball, with April and Vicki in the background. And someone had drawn a big red circle around them.

*Shit.* April looked at the name of the person who posted the photo. It was a woman who April didn't know, but they had a handful of mutual friends. April scanned the comments underneath the photo.

*That's Victoria Blake. She's one of the top brass at Oasis. What's April doing with her?*

*What a liar. Acting like she cares about West Heights while she's in league with the developers.*

*She's a lesbian? I always knew there was something weird about her in high school.*

*What a fucking hypocrite.*

April felt a clenching in her chest. The rest of the comments were more of the same. She didn't even know who half the people commenting were. But that didn't make their words hurt any less.

April had been called names before. Ganged up on. Bullied. And all those memories were flooding back.

April took a few deep breaths. Everything was fine. She was fine. And she needed to tell Vicki about this. She picked up the phone and dialed Vicki's number. But the phone kept ringing and ringing until it went to voicemail. She tried again. The same thing happened.

April sent Vicki a message.

*I need to talk to you. Call me.*

April glanced at her laptop screen.

*I can't believe I donated to her stupid fundraiser. This is fraud!*

*Now we know whose side she's really on.*

April shut her laptop. She couldn't look at it anymore. Moments later, she received a reply from Vicki.

*Can't talk. Busy with work.*

April cursed. *It's important. Can you call me when you get a minute?*

Vicki's response was a single word. *Later.*

April set her phone down, her stomach roiling with unease. Sure, she'd called Vicki to warn her that the photo was out. But more than anything, April just wanted to talk to her. Of course, it was silly to expect Vicki to drop everything for her.

For the next half hour, April paced and fretted. When she finally managed to calm herself down, there was a knock on her door. For a moment, she wondered if it was Vicki. Then she realized how unlikely that was. Vicki hadn't even called her back.

April opened the door to find Lexi standing out in the hall. In her flustered state, April had forgotten that Lexi was coming over.

"Shit," Lexi said. "You saw the photo, didn't you?"

April nodded.

"How are you holding up?"

"I've been better," April said. "Come on in."

April sat back down on the couch, her legs tucked under her, as Lexi made them tea. Eliza's tea habit had spread to everyone who worked at the library.

Lexi returned to the living room carrying two mugs. "Here." She handed one to April and sat down next to her. "Sorry for the weird phone call. I was hoping you hadn't seen the post yet."

April wrapped her hands around the warm mug. "When I thought about the photo getting out, I wasn't expecting it to show up on social media like this," April said. "I don't even know the woman who posted it."

"I do," Lexi said. "She's city hall's resident busybody. Works for the mayor. And we both know that the Mayor isn't too happy that you made her look bad."

"What, so one of her employees decided to make me look bad too? That's so petty." April sighed. "I don't even care that people know about Vicki and me. I just don't understand why everyone is being so mean."

Lexi shrugged. "That's the dark side of social media."

"But these people don't even know me! Some of them have nothing to do with the library or West Heights! Why do they even care?"

"Don't let it get to you. They're just sad little people hiding behind their screens who have nothing better to do than badmouth others online.

"It feels like the whole world is against me," April said softly. "It's like high school all over again."

Lexi held out her arms and pulled April into a hug. "I know it feels that way. But no one who matters has seen this or thinks you're a hypocrite. And we can fix this. I'll help you get the photo and all the comments taken down."

"Thanks, Lex."

"That's what friends are for," Lexi replied. "You know what else will help? Takeout and a bad movie. Why don't you order dinner while I take care of this?"

April gave her a half smile. "Okay."

An hour later, the two of them were watching a fluffy rom-com while stuffing themselves with Chinese food. Lexi was right. It had taken April's mind off everything.

Except for Vicki.

April checked her phone again. Nothing. Was Vicki really still working at nine p.m. on a Friday night? April couldn't help but feel like she was being brushed off. Or maybe she was reading too much into Vicki's terse messages.

"Are you okay?" Lexi asked.

"Yeah," April said. "I'm waiting for Vicki to call me back, that's all."

"Does she know what's going on?"

"I'm not sure. She's pretty busy with work."

Lexi gave April a sympathetic look. "I'm sure she'll call you back when she has time."

"Yeah. You're right." April yawned and stretched out her arms, then realized this was the first time Lexi had said anything remotely supportive about Vicki. "Does this mean that you don't disapprove of Vicki anymore?"

"I've been holding a grudge against her for too long," Lexi said. "And I know that you really care about her. If you say she's changed, I believe you."

April should have been happy that Lexi had finally come around on Vicki. Instead, April was the one filled with doubts about her.

The rest of the night passed quickly. By the time Lexi left, it was late. All April wanted to do was go to sleep and forget about the events of the day. But now that she was alone in her apartment, her worries bubbled to the surface.

As she got into bed, she took one last look at her phone. Still nothing from Vicki. She opened up the last message she had sent. It was now labeled 'seen.' Vicki had seen the message. She just hadn't bothered responding, despite April telling her it was important.

April placed her phone on the nightstand. Now, when she needed Vicki the most, she was nowhere to be found. Maybe Lexi had been right all along. April had fallen for Vicki's sweet, empty words.

April never should have trusted her.

319

# CHAPTER TWENTY-ONE

*T*he weekend passed, and April's doubts about Vicki only grew. She'd sent Vicki a couple more messages, only to receive vague responses about a 'work crisis.' April could have simply sent Vicki a message about the photo, but she was too angry at Vicki for brushing her off.

So April spent most of the weekend with Lexi, trying to keep her mind off everything. Thanks to Lexi, the photo disappeared from social media, along with all the comments. Still, April felt awful about everything.

When she woke up on Monday morning, it was ten a.m. April groaned. She had slept through her alarm. She had never been late for work in her life.

April rolled over to check her phone. Half of her hoped to find that Vicki had finally called her, while the other half was too mad at her to want to speak to her.

But there was nothing from Vicki. Instead, April found dozens of calls and panicked texts from Lexi. She opened up one of the messages.

*Where are you? Something is happening at the library. Call me.*

April's stomach sank. She dialed Lexi's number.

Lexi was frantic when she picked up. "April? Are you okay? Where are you?"

"I'm fine, I just overslept," April said. "What's going on with the library?"

"There's a guy here saying that we need to shut it down. *Today*."

April's blood ran cold. This wasn't happening. Vicki had promised. She had said they had time.

"I'm trying to get Vicki or someone from Oasis on the phone, but they're giving me the runaround," Lexi said. "I don't know what else to do."

April pushed her worries about Vicki aside. She had to focus on what was important. She vaulted out of bed and grabbed some clothes. "I'm on my way."

---

When April arrived at the library, Lexi was standing out front, arguing animatedly with a man in a suit. He was brandishing a sheet of paper like a shield.

"Look, I'm just the messenger," he said. "I don't know anything. You'll have to speak to whoever's running the project."

"I've been trying to get someone on the phone for the last twenty minutes!" Lexi said.

"That's not my problem."

April approached them. "What's going on?"

Lexi gestured toward the man. "Oasis has sent some lackey over to tell us the library is being shut down and we need to vacate the building next week."

"That can't be right. The development project is on hold. The library is supposed to stay open until we can find another location."

"Like I told her, I don't know anything about the project. I'm just here to deliver this." The man handed April the paper in his hand. "I'm not getting paid enough to deal with this," he muttered.

April skimmed the page. It was an eviction notice. They had seven days to get out of the building. This was even shorter than the three months they'd originally been given.

"This doesn't make any sense," April said.

She looked at the signature at the bottom. It wasn't Vicki's. Where was she in all this? At worst, this was Vicki's doing. At best, she would have known about it. Why hadn't she said anything to April?

Why hadn't she stopped this?

"April, can you call Vicki?" Lexi asked.

April tried to speak, but there was a lump in her throat.

"Oh, thank god." The man was looking toward the street. "Here's Ms. Blake now. You can talk to her about this."

April turned to follow his gaze. Sure enough, Vicki was hurrying over to them. April clenched her fists, anger boiling up inside her.

She marched over to Vicki, meeting her on the sidewalk. "What the hell, Victoria? This man is saying that we have to shut down the library?"

"April," Vicki began. "I can explain-"

"Just tell me it isn't true."

"It is. I'm sorry."

"No." April's voice quavered. "How could you let this happen?"

"The decision went above my head," Vicki said. "A few of Oasis' major projects fell through, so the board decided that they couldn't put the Oakmont Street development on hold any longer."

"The board?" April asked. "So you had nothing to do with it?"

"I was overruled. I tried everything I could to stop this, April. I spent all weekend trying to stop this."

April furrowed her brows. "This was the crisis you were dealing with at work."

Vicki nodded.

"You've known the library was going to be shut down for *three whole days*?" April's voice rose. "Did it ever occur to you to tell me?"

"It did, but-" Vicki brought her hand to her forehead. "Look, I *know* I shouldn't have kept this from you, but I wanted to try to fix it first. I thought that I could salvage one of our other projects, so there wouldn't be any need to rush the Oakmont Street development. I almost pulled it off too, but everything fell apart this morning."

"Is that your excuse for ignoring me all weekend?" April asked.

"It was stupid. But I know how much the library means to you. I knew you'd be devastated if you found out. I didn't want to tell you if I didn't have to. And I knew that if I spoke to you, I'd have to tell you what was going on. I was trying to spare your feelings-"

"*My feelings?* I'm not some delicate fucking girl. I don't need you to protect me. And if you really cared about my feelings, you wouldn't have ignored me like you did. Do you have any idea what I've been going through for the past few days?"

"What do you mean?" Vicki asked.

"You don't even know, do you?" April said. "Someone found the photo of us and posted it on social media, and everyone is calling me a liar, and a hypocrite, and worse for being in bed with you."

A look of horror crossed Vicki's face. "I had no idea. Are you all right?"

"Of course I'm not all right! I needed you. I needed you and you weren't there."

"I'm so sorry," Vicki said.

April crossed her arms. "It doesn't matter. What matters is that I trusted you. You promised me that you wouldn't let the library get shut down."

"I tried to stop this. I got into an argument with the CEO that almost got me fired!"

"Seriously? I'm supposed to care that you almost got fired from your cushy million-dollar job?"

"That's not what I meant." Vicki let out an exasperated groan. "What I'm trying to say is that I did everything in my power to stop this from happening, but it wasn't enough."

"You promised me," April said quietly.

"I'm sorry. Really, I am. And I messed up by keeping this from you. I'll do whatever I can to help."

April shook her head, her eyes clouding with tears. "It's too late, Victoria. You're too late."

April turned and walked back toward the library. Mercifully, Vicki didn't try to follow her. Lexi was waiting by the front door. The man had left.

"What happened?" Lexi asked.

"It's over. The library is shutting down and there's nothing we can do about it."

Lexi cursed quietly. "You and Vicki?"

April shook her head. "You were right about her. You were right about everything. I should never have trusted her."

"I'm sorry." Lexi wrapped her arm around April's shoulders. "For what it's worth, I really hoped I was wrong about her."

"So did I," April said.

# CHAPTER TWENTY-TWO

Over the course of the next seven days, April, Lexi and the other staff packed up the library. Everything was going into storage. Although the building would be reduced to rubble in a matter of weeks, the sudden nature of the Oakmont Street building's closure meant that the city hadn't officially shut down the library yet, but it was only a matter of time.

The somber mood in the library weighed heavily on April. It didn't help that everyone who worked there had heard about April and Vicki. Although Lexi had gotten the photo and the nasty comments taken down, word had gotten around. Lexi assured April that none of the staff held it against her. They all knew she had fought harder for the library than anyone else. It did little to make April feel better.

April grabbed a handful of books from the shelf and slipped them into the box at her feet. She looked down the almost empty aisle. Once they were finished with these last few shelves, there would be nothing left.

This was the end of Oakmont Street Library.

"Are you all right?" Lexi asked April.

"Yeah. It's just sad to see all this go."

"You never know," Lexi said. "Oasis might pull through with that old building they originally offered to lease us. It'll be better than nothing."

"I'm not holding my breath," April said.

After giving the library the eviction notice, Oasis had gone back to radio silence. April hadn't heard from Vicki about the library or anything else, but she was too mad to speak to her, anyway. Lexi had taken over trying to get in touch with Oasis, but she'd been informed that Vicki was "no longer working on the Oakmont Street project", and she had a hard time getting through to anyone else.

April wondered why Vicki wasn't working on the project anymore. April hadn't heard from her since the day they had fought outside the library. She shouldn't have been disappointed that Vicki had washed her hands of April and the library. She'd shown her true colors in the end, after all. As far as April was concerned, the two of them were done.

Yet, whenever April thought about her, she felt something pulling in her chest. She'd shown Vicki a side of herself that she had never shown to anyone else. If it wasn't for Vicki, April wouldn't even have known that part of her existed. She would never have come to accept that the April who fought fiercely for those around her could coexist with the April who craved the freedom that came with vulnerability.

It didn't matter. Right from the start, the chances that things could have worked out between them had been slim. It had been foolish of April to think otherwise.

April taped up her box of books and scanned the shelves before her. There wasn't much left to pack up. "Mind if I head off?" she asked Lexi. "I want to go see Eliza. She's leaving in the morning."

"Sure," Lexi said. "Say goodbye to her for me."

"Will you be all right with the rest of this?"

"Yeah, it's not much. Once we're done here, I have to clean out my side of the office, and that's it."

*That's it. Goodbye Oakmont Street.* "I should get going," April said.

"I'll see you tomorrow morning to hand the place over."

April hesitated. She reached into her pocket and pulled out her set of keys to the building. "Do you think you could handle it by yourself?"

"Sure." Lexi took the keys from her.

April made her way to Eliza's house, watching the neighborhood go by as she walked. Half of the buildings looked unfamiliar. Lexi had been right all that time ago. What happened to the library was inevitable. April had been naive to think she could take on a corporate giant like Oasis.

By the time April made it to Eliza's house, she was a wreck. She tried to keep it together for Eliza's sake, but Eliza could see through her.

She gave April a hug. "Come on in. I'll make tea."

April sat down at Eliza's kitchen table. The house was almost empty, save for some furniture and essentials. Soon, the two of them were drinking tea out of chipped, mismatched mugs and sharing stories about the library.

"Remember that guy who brought back those overdue books from the 80s?" April asked.

Eliza nodded. "He borrowed them when he was a teenager and forgot about them. They still had the old borrowing cards in the front." She chuckled. "Do you remember when the computer system broke down and we had to use the card catalog for a week?"

"That was a nightmare." April sighed. "I'm really going to miss that place. And I'm going to miss you."

"I'll miss you too."

"I mean it. You've been such a big part of my life for so long, I just can't imagine it without you."

Eliza smiled. "You'll be fine. And you're welcome to come visit any time."

"Thanks, Eliza," April said.

They sipped their tea in comfortable silence. They were already onto their third cup. April was all too aware that this was the last time she'd get to sit at Eliza's kitchen table drinking tea with her.

"Have you spoken to Vicki yet?" Eliza asked.

April stared down into her cup. "No." Eliza had been sympathetic about everything that had happened with Vicki, but April couldn't help but feel like Eliza thought she was being irrational.

"Tell me this," Eliza said. "Are you angry at Vicki because she didn't stop the library being shut down? Or are you upset with her because of how she handled everything?"

"Both," April grumbled. She ran her thumb over the chip on the rim of her mug. "I guess I can't blame her for what happened to the library."

"What about everything else? If it wasn't for everything with the library, would you forgive her for it?"

April crossed her arms. "I don't know."

"Just think about it," Eliza said.

"I will."

April didn't leave Eliza's house until late at night. By then, April just wanted to curl up in bed and cry. Her oldest friend was leaving. She had lost her library. She had lost her sanctuary.

But what hurt more than everything else was that she had lost Vicki.

# CHAPTER TWENTY-THREE

*A*pril spent the next few days feeling lost and listless. With the library shut down, she had nothing to do with her time. At the very least, Lexi was in the same position. They'd met up for lunch earlier in the day and spent the afternoon hanging out.

But now, April was alone in her apartment, with nothing to distract her from her worries. She spent the whole evening reading, but only managed to get through a single chapter. Her mind kept returning to Vicki.

April put her book down with a sigh. As usual, Eliza was right. April was blaming Vicki for everything that had happened with the library. But it wasn't her fault. And this wasn't the first time April had blamed Vicki for things she had no control over. April had been unkind to her from the start when they first found out they were working against each other. And all the while, Vicki had put up with April's misdirected anger with barely a word.

April's phone buzzed on the coffee table. It was a message from Mel, the woman she'd met at the masquerade ball that night with Vicki. They'd exchanged a few texts about Mel's workplace offering legal resources to the library's patrons, but they hadn't gotten around to working out the details. It didn't matter now that the library was closed.

April opened the message.

*I heard the good news about the library. I'm glad everything worked out in the end. We should meet up and discuss getting that partnership up and running.*

Clearly, Mel had gotten her wires crossed somewhere. April typed out a reply.

*I don't know what you've heard, but the library has been shut down.*

*What about the new site? Vanessa said that everything with the King Street building has been finalized.*

King Street? That was definitely a mistake. King Street was right in the middle of West Heights, where properties now cost a fortune. And what did Mel's girlfriend have to do with anything?

*I have no idea what you're talking about. I haven't heard anything about a new site,* April sent back.

Mel took a while to respond. *Aren't you working with Vicki on this?*

Vicki. April's stomach fluttered. She began to type out a reply, then gave up and called Mel instead.

"What's going on, Mel?" April said. "What have you heard about the library?"

"You really don't know?" Mel asked. "I thought you were behind all this."

"Behind what?" April rubbed her temples. "Can you just tell me what you know?"

"Well, a couple of weeks ago, Vicki approached Vanessa about helping fund a new location for the library. Vanessa agreed—with a little prodding from me. Vicki updated her today that everything had been finalized."

That didn't make any sense. Vicki wasn't working on the project anymore. What the hell was she up to?

"Are you there?" Mel asked.

"Yeah. It's just, this is all news to me," April said.

"Seriously? I thought you and Vicki were doing this together. Actually, I thought it was all you since Vicki is, well, Vicki. She isn't exactly the most generous person."

"I haven't spoken to her in a while, actually," April admitted.

"Oh, sorry," Mel said. "I didn't know the two of you broke up."

April didn't bother correcting her. "Did Vicki say anything else about this?"

"That's all I know."

"This doesn't make any sense. Why would Vicki do something like that and not tell me about it?"

"That's way above my pay grade," Mel said. "You'll have to ask Vicki that."

"Thanks, Mel," April said.

"No problem. Good luck with Vicki."

April hung up and stared at her phone. Mel was right. If April wanted to get to the bottom of this, she had to go straight to the source.

April dialed Vicki's number and paced next to the couch, waiting for Vicki to pick up. It seemed to take an eternity. She was about to lose her nerve when Vicki finally answered.

"April?" Vicki said.

April didn't give her a chance to say hello. "Mel told me about King Street. What the hell is going on, Victoria?"

There was silence at the end of the line.

"Let me show you," Vicki finally said. "Meet me at the north end of King Street tomorrow morning."

"I'm not waiting until tomorrow," April said. "I want to know *now*."

"All right. Meet me on King Street in an hour?"

---

By the time April arrived on King Street, the sun had set. She was early, but Vicki was already there, standing under a streetlight waiting for her.

April's heart skipped a beat. That part of her that went weak every time she laid eyes on Vicki was still there, no matter how hard April tried to ignore it.

Spotting April, Vicki flashed her that devastatingly sexy smile. "Hi, April."

A storm of emotions erupted inside April. *"Hi, April?* That's all you have to say? I hear nothing from you in more than a week, and now I'm finding out from Mel that you've found a new site for the library? What did you do?"

"Looks like the secret is out." Vicki cocked her head toward the building next to them. "This is it. The new library."

"What?" April looked at the building before them. The beautiful sandstone construction had to be a hundred years old, but it was in perfect condition. It was huge, at least twice the size of the old Oakmont Street Library. "You're saying that this is the new library?" April asked.

Vicki nodded. "It's all yours."

"But... how? There's no way Oasis would pay for something like this. And you're not even working on the Oakmont Street project anymore."

"I'm not. After everything that happened, I decided I was too close to it all, so I passed the lead to someone else. Oasis doesn't have anything to do with this."

"Then who did this? You?"

"Not just me," Vicki said. "I contributed, but there's no way I could afford this by myself. I had help."

"From who?" April asked.

"My friends. Remember all those 'rich snobs' you met at the ball? I convinced them to donate funds toward a new library. Of course, even with help, I couldn't get enough money to buy a place like this. It's worth millions. Luckily, Camilla owns several properties in the area. I convinced her to sell this one to the library at an outrageously low price."

April gaped at the building. "I can't believe it. It's perfect."

Vicki brandished a key. "Want to take a look inside?"

April turned back to Vicki. She had so many things she wanted to say, so many things she wanted to hear Vicki say. And her heart kept beating faster and faster.

But she just nodded. "Sure."

The two of them climbed the stairs leading up to the front of the building.

"You're going to love it." Vicki struggled with the lock on the ornate wooden doors. "It used to be a museum, but it was shut down in the 80s and the building fell into disrepair. Camilla's family bought it decades ago, but they haven't done anything with it. It's been sitting here, empty, all these years."

Vicki finally managed to unlock the doors. She flung them open.

April's jaw dropped. "Wow."

The grand old building was just as beautiful on the inside as it was on the outside. It had high ceilings covered in mosaic tiles and marble floors. And it was huge. Their footsteps echoed through the vast space as they walked.

"This is amazing," April said.

There was so much space. The entrance hall had countless rooms coming off it, some large, some small, and there was a second floor. They wouldn't have to worry about having to adjust the schedule so that AA meetings and book clubs wouldn't fall at the same time. They could add new activities too, and they could even hold events here. There was so much room for the library to grow. Ideas started forming in April's mind. She couldn't wait to tell Lexi.

"As you can see, it needs renovations," Vicki said. "The money from your fundraiser should cover most of it. I can put you in touch with some contractors who will do the work at a discount."

April turned to Vicki. "Why didn't you tell me about this?"

"Well, the last time we spoke, you weren't exactly happy with me."

*Right.* In her excitement about the library, April had forgotten about everything. "Is this some sort of grand gesture to win me back? Were you planning to show up on my doorstep and announce that you'd swooped in to save the library?"

"No, it's not," Vicki said. "Although, if this does win you back, it's a bonus."

April put her hands on her hips. "Victoria!"

"I'm kidding, of course." Vicki held up her hands. "I started this before we even had that fight. I would have told you about what I was doing, but I didn't want to get your hopes up in case it didn't work out."

"Why?" April asked. "Why did you do this if it wasn't to impress me?"

"I did it because you made an impression on me. You're always talking about the library, and the community, and how much it all means to you. You made me realize how important a place like the library is to the people of West Heights. I knew from the start that I was never going to be able to save the Oakmont Street building, so I did the next best thing. I gave the Oakmont Street Library a new home."

April stared at her. "How long have you been working on this?"

"I started setting things in motion a few days after the ball," Vicki replied. "That night, I told you that the people in that room were the people who have the power to effect change. I was speaking about the long term, but it made me realize that I could make a difference right now."

"All this time, I thought you didn't care."

"I didn't, not until recently. I've been wandering through the world, living for superficial pleasures, not thinking or caring about anyone else. Then you came along and spoiled all that." Vicki gave her a faint smile. "You've changed me. You make me a better person."

"Vicki..."

"I didn't do this to get you back," Vicki said. "But that doesn't mean I don't want you back. And I want you to know that I'm sorry for everything. I'm sorry I didn't tell you that Oasis was planning to restart the development project. I'm sorry I wasn't there for you when you needed me. I'll never do anything like that again. I'll never do anything to hurt you again."

April's heart skittered in her chest. "I need to apologize too," she said. "For as long as we've known each other, I've treated you so badly. I was angry about everything, and I took it out on you, and I'm sorry. It wasn't fair. You never deserved it, but you stuck around anyway."

"Of course I did," Vicki said. She took April's hands. "I love you, April."

"I..." April took a calming breath. "I love you too."

Before she knew what she was doing, April's lips were on Vicki's in an urgent, demanding kiss.

# CHAPTER TWENTY-FOUR

*T*he week that followed passed by in a blur. It would be months before the King Street Library could open its doors, but April had so much to do. Scheduling renovations. Chasing up donations. Organizing a large-scale fundraising campaign so that the library could expand its services. April barely had a chance to see Vicki at all.

Finally, on Friday evening, April paid a visit to Vicki's apartment. As soon as she arrived, Vicki dragged her inside, kissing her fervently. After a few minutes of this, they sat down in the living room with a drink. Sebastian leaped up to perch on the arm of the couch next to April.

Vicki smiled. "I think he likes you."

"About time," April reached out to stroke his fur. He purred and closed his eyes.

"I received some news at work today," Vicki said. "About the promotion."

April's stomach swam. She'd forgotten all about it. The job on offer was at Oasis' head office in Boston.

"I didn't even know I was still being considered for the position,"

Vicki continued. "The board wasn't too impressed with me after I gave up the Oakmont Street project. Not to mention the fact that I'm in a relationship with the woman who's been standing in the way of the project."

"Did you get the promotion?" April asked.

"I did." Vicki leaned back and crossed her legs. "They said despite my recent 'indiscretions,' I'm still the best candidate for the job."

"Oh." April avoided Vicki's gaze. "That's great."

"Hey." Vicki took April's hand. "I said no, of course."

"But you wanted this so badly. Your career is so important to you."

"It is. But you're even more important to me. After everything we've been through, I'd be an idiot to throw this relationship away."

"We could move to Boston together," April said. "I could get a job there."

"No," Vicki said. "I couldn't live with myself if I took you away from West Heights. This place is your home."

Relief washed over April. Vicki was right. April could never leave West Heights, let alone the city. At least, not right now.

"Besides, I don't need a promotion to prove myself. I don't need to prove myself to anyone. I know what I'm capable of, and so does everyone who's important to me." Vicki squeezed April's hand. "I didn't realize it until I ran into my parents at that charity ball, but my obsession with my career only meant that my life was still being dictated by my family's expectations, even if I was going against what they wanted for me. By choosing to follow my heart instead, I feel like I'm finally free of them, in a way."

"As long as you're doing what makes you happy," April said.

"I am. Besides, I've been thinking about finding a new job."

"Really? You've been at Oasis for so long."

"That's why I need a change," Vicki said. "I only took the job at Oasis because no one else would hire me. With all the experience I have now, my options have opened up. I've been putting out feelers, and I already have a few tentative offers."

"That's great," April said.

"What about you? How's the new library shaping up?"

"Everything's finally starting to come together. Once renovations are up and running, I'm going to have so much free time." April stretched out and sank into the couch. "I have no idea what I'm going to do with myself."

"I have a few ideas." Vicki took April's glass from her hand and placed it on the table next to them, then she leaned in and pressed her lips to April's.

April deepened the kiss. Her hands roamed down Vicki's body, feeling the slight swell of her slender hips, her flat stomach, her soft breasts. Vicki grasped at April's curves with double the intensity. April let out a blissful hum. Every time Vicki touched her, it set off fireworks inside.

Vicki broke away. "I want you in the bedroom and out of those clothes."

"Yes, ma'am." April jumped up from the couch.

They made their way to the bedroom where April slipped off her jacket and dress. Vicki kicked off her jeans but left her blouse on.

Vicki gestured toward April's bra and panties. "Take those off too. Then stand by the bed and wait for me."

April stripped off her underwear and sat on the bed. She crossed her legs and leaned back on her elbows, watching Vicki's growing irritation.

Vicki's eyes rolled down the length of April's naked body. "You just can't help but test me, can you?"

April grinned.

Vicki shook her head. "You're on very thin ice." She went to the chest at the end of her bed and sifted through it. Finally, she pulled out the red strap-on.

The ache in April's core flared up, her body remembering the last time Vicki had used that strap-on. She waited eagerly for Vicki to step into it.

Instead, Vicki held it out to her. "Put this on."

April stared at her. "You want me to wear that?"

"Is there a problem?" Vicki asked.

"No." April was experienced enough with both ends of a strap-on. She was simply surprised. "Doesn't this spoil your big, bad Domme act?"

Vicki's lips curled up in a smile. "I assure you, I have every intention of topping you, even with you wearing that." She glanced pointedly at her closet door.

"Oh, really?" April said. "And how are you going to do that?"

"That's the second time you've ignored my instructions." Vicki held out the strap-on again. "Put this on, *now.*"

April scowled at her but took the strap-on from her hands. Once April had it fastened around her hips, Vicki walked over to the closet at the side of the room and pulled the doors open.

Excitement welled up inside April. There were so many things in that closet that Vicki could use on her. Ropes. Whips. Gags. Not to mention all the things April didn't even recognize.

"Since you keep ignoring my instructions, I'm going to make it a little easier for you to follow them." Vicki scanned everything on display, her eyes lingering on some loops of rope and some handcuffs hanging from hooks. Finally, she opened a drawer beneath them and took out four pairs of leather cuffs.

April's eyes widened. *Four pairs?* April had been cuffed to a bed before, but not like this.

Vicki brought the cuffs over to the bed and dropped them next to April. "Lie down and put your arms up." As soon as April obeyed, Vicki began to cuff her wrists to the bedposts.

"You know," April said. "For someone who said she doesn't need tools, you sure use a lot of them."

Vicki spanked April on the side of the ass, hard. April squealed and began to wriggle in her bonds.

"Hold still," Vicki commanded.

April stopped moving. Vicki's heavy stare made one thing clear —she wasn't playing around anymore.

Vicki finished cuffing April's ankles. April tested her restraints. They didn't budge. With her limbs stretched to their limits, she was completely immobilized. And with Vicki still in her blouse and panties, April felt exposed in comparison.

Once again, April was at Vicki's mercy. It was clear from the look on Vicki's face that she was going to take advantage of that fact.

Goosebumps sprouted on April's bare skin. Her heart began to race. Vicki didn't actually scare her. It was all a game. But April's body didn't know that. Her body didn't know she was safe. And her body's primal reaction to physical danger was to set all her senses on high alert. It only heightened her arousal.

"You're going to lie there, perfectly still," Vicki said. "Don't move, don't make a sound, until I give you permission. Understand?"

April nodded. Bound as she was, she could barely move anyway.

Vicki slipped out of her panties and crawled onto the bed. Straddling April's body, Vicki began to toy with her. She traced lines all over April's skin with her fingertips, so lightly that it tickled. She drew her fingers down to April's nipples, then pinched them, then ran her tongue over them. She scratched her nails down the length of April's torso and up the insides of her thighs, leaving red stripes behind on her skin.

April trembled on the bed, overcome by it all. The feel of Vicki's moist, ravenous lips on her skin. The scent of her body, musky and sweet. The touch of Vicki's fingertips in sensitive places. She longed to cry out, to speak Vicki's name like it was something sacred, but she held everything back, remaining silent and still.

Just when April couldn't take anymore, Vicki slid down April's body, positioning herself above the strap-on protruding from the peak of April's thighs.

"Remember," Vicki said. "Don't move."

She wrapped her fist around the strap-on, guiding it between her legs, and lowered herself onto it. She placed a hand on April's stomach to steady herself, her other hand flying up to her own head. Closing her eyes, she began to rock her hips.

April hissed. With every tiny movement Vicki made, the base of the strap-on pressed hard on April's clit, sending jolts of lightning through her. April desperately wanted to match Vicki's slow, deliberate motions. But Vicki had given her a command. So April lay there, bursting with need, using all her strength to keep herself from moving.

"God, this feels good." Vicki began to move faster, bouncing up and down. She slid her hands up to April's breasts, kneading them, and rolling the pads of her thumbs over April's peaked nipples.

April whimpered. The sight of Vicki above her, riding her like there was no tomorrow, made her throb inside. There was a faint sheen of sweat on Vicki's brow, and a wisp of her short hair had fallen across her forehead.

Vicki's head fell back. "Fuck me," she said. "You can yell, and scream, and moan. Go crazy."

That was the signal she'd been waiting for. April began to roll her hips, pushing her bound body to the limits of its motion, penetrating Vicki deeper. They got into a rhythm, rocking against each other in tandem. April pulled at her restraints. She'd never come while on this end of a strap-on before, but the pressure between her thighs was rising.

"I'm so close," Vicki said breathily. Thrusting and grinding feverishly, Vicki leaned down and smothered April's mouth with her own.

Suddenly, Vicki let out a cry, as an orgasm overtook her. As Vicki convulsed on top of her, ecstasy surged deep within April's body, rolling through her in unrelenting waves.

Finally, Vicki stilled on top of her, her breath shuddering. "Fuck. That was…" She rolled onto her side next to April.

"Can you uncuff me now?" April asked.

Vicki ran her eyes along April's stretched out body. "I can," she replied. "Or I can leave you cuffed to the bed and spend the rest of the night playing with that exquisite body of yours."

"What do you plan to do with me?" April asked.

"If I told you, it would spoil the fun," Vicki said. "What do you say? I release you? Or I leave you on that bed and I have my way with you for the next few hours?"

April was torn between wanting to keep going and wanting to be free so she could hold Vicki in her arms and never let her go. The thrill of exploring dark, unknown delights with the woman she loved won out.

"I choose the second option," April said.

Vicki cupped April's cheeks and kissed her gently, then got up from the bed and walked over to the closet. She surveyed its contents.

"Now," Vicki said. "Where should I begin?"

# EPILOGUE

## VICKI

*V*icki stood in the entrance hall of the King Street Library, Camilla and Vanessa by her side, watching April make a speech from up on the landing of the staircase. It was the grand opening of the library, and April and Lexi had organized a huge gala event to raise even more funds.

April had taken Vicki's advice and had spent the last few months lobbying the city's policymakers. The room was packed with politicians and influential people. April had more than proven that she could go toe to toe with them.

"She's really something, isn't she?" Camilla said.

Vicki smiled. "She is."

Vicki had to admit, she'd underestimated April when they met. She'd had an inkling that there was more to April than the feisty temptress she'd taken home from Sapphire that night. What she wasn't expecting was this radiant firecracker of a woman who fought hard for what she believed in and constantly drove Vicki crazy.

Vicki wouldn't have it any other way.

"I never thought I'd live to see this day," Vanessa said. "Victoria Blake, tamed and tied down."

Vicki rolled her eyes. "Like you can talk. You and Mel moved in together after, what, a few months? She has you thoroughly domesticated."

"Melanie was very impressed with what you did for the library. Keep this up, and she might actually start to *like* you."

Camilla gave them both a stern glare. "Will the two of you stop bickering?" She downed the last of her wine. "I swear, every time we get together, I feel like I'm babysitting."

"Relax," Vicki said. "We're just messing around."

Vanessa gave Vicki a faint smile. "I *am* happy for you. Really."

"Oh? Does this mean you've finally dropped this grudge you've been holding against me?"

The truth was, she deserved Vanessa's animosity. Back then, Vicki hadn't known how serious Vanessa was about Mel, and she'd never intended to cause so much trouble. That was no excuse. Screwing up the relationship of one of her oldest friends had been a wake-up call for Vicki, one that had set her life on a less destructive path.

"I haven't decided yet," Vanessa said. "Although I've been enjoying watching you grovel, it's clear that you've changed your ways. I have to say, I'm impressed with what you've done for the library too."

"It wouldn't have been possible without both of you," Vicki said. "Thanks again. You've been very generous."

"I'm just doing my part for the city," Camilla replied. "Besides, April made an impression on me at that ball."

"She has that effect on people."

April's speech ended. The crowd broke out into applause. April stood there for a moment, glowing with pride, before descending the stairs.

"You'll have to bring April to the manor sometime," Camilla said. "It's been a while since you've visited."

"April would love that," Vicki replied.

"You too, Vanessa. Bring Mel along. And, if you come in the next month or so, you'll get to meet my guest."

"Your guest?" Vicki asked. "I'm intrigued."

"I think you'd like her," Camilla said, her eyes sparkling.

Before Vicki could question Camilla further, April approached them.

"We'll leave you two alone," Camilla said. She gave them a warm smile before wandering off with Vanessa.

Vicki wrapped her arms around April's waist. "You were incredible up there."

April grinned. "Thanks."

"Seriously, do you have any idea what an amazing woman you are?"

April wrapped her arms around Vicki's neck. "You may have told me once or twice."

Vicki drew April in for a kiss. She heard the flash of a camera going off.

"Caught in the act again," April said.

"I don't care if you don't," Vicki said.

"We better make sure they get a good picture."

April kissed Vicki, harder this time. Her fiery kisses still set Vicki alight. Right now, she wanted nothing more than to find an empty room and tear off that pretty, delicate dress April was wearing.

Vicki broke off the kiss before she could get too carried away.

April gazed around the room. "I just can't believe we pulled this off."

"It was all you," Vicki said.

"I couldn't have done it without you. And all those friends of yours."

"They only helped get things off the ground. You're the one who brought the new library to life. You're the reason that all these people are here tonight."

"About that," April said. "I've made my decision. I'm going to run for city council."

"That's great," Vicki said. "You're definitely going to win. Everyone in West Heights loves you for everything you've done with the library."

"You think so?"

"I know so. And you're destined for far bigger things. Who knows, maybe in a few years you'll be Mayor."

"Let's not get ahead of ourselves," April said. "I mean, I don't know anything about running for office. I'm going to need all the help I can get."

"I'll do whatever I can to support you," Vicki said. "And when you become a councilwoman, you can help me out with building permits."

Vicki had taken a job as CEO at a smaller property development company, one that was far more scrupulous than Oasis. It was a step up in terms of her career, but she had taken a pay cut. It was worth it.

"I'm pretty sure giving my girlfriend building permits would be an abuse of my position. Although it could be fun to have all that power over you. To have you at my mercy." Her eyes twinkling, April stood on her toes to speak into Vicki's ear. "I could even make you beg."

Vicki narrowed her eyes. "You've been trying to push my buttons all day. And I don't like it."

April gave her a cheeky smile. "What are you going to do about it?"

"Oh, you're going to be in so much trouble when we get home."

With her arms still around April, Vicki couldn't help but notice the tiny shift in the other woman's body at her words, and the hint of scarlet that spread up her cheeks.

"I can't wait." April kissed Vicki gently and took her hand. "Come on. Let's go mingle."

# HERS TO KEEP

# CHAPTER ONE

"*L*indsey," Mr. Grant said. "Can I see you in my office?"

"Sure." Lindsey removed her headset and got up from her desk.

She followed her boss through the call center. It was a honeycomb of identical cubicles, all with the exact same desk, computer, and phone. The walls were painted green, no doubt in an attempt to make everyone forget they were cooped up in a tiny, windowless office for eight hours a day. But the paint had faded to a pale, sickly color, which made it even more depressing.

Lindsey sighed. How had she ended up here? All her life, she'd had such big plans. She was going to be a renowned artist, whose works were displayed in galleries all over the world. She was going to travel to exotic places, and have a string of passionate love affairs before meeting the man of her dreams in some tiny European town. And they'd fall in love and live the rest of their lives in a villa in the countryside.

Then Lindsey had grown up. Well, the world had forced her to grow up.

They reached Mr. Grant's office. Lindsey sat down on the stiff plastic chair in front of his desk.

"I think you know what this is about, Lindsey." Mr. Grant tented his fingers in front of his chest. "Your numbers have been slipping lately."

His voice rang with concern, but just like everything else in this place, it was false. Everyone pretended to give a crap, when really, all they cared about was a paycheck. Lindsey saw through it because she feigned the same enthusiasm around her coworkers and the potential customers she called. She was surprisingly good at this job, at selling lies and convincing unsuspecting retirees to sign up for overpriced insurance. Lindsey didn't like what that said about her.

"Do you want to tell me what's going on?" Mr. Grant asked.

"It's nothing," Lindsey said. "I'm just having an off week."

"It's not just this week, Lindsey. Your performance has been steadily dropping for a while now." He leaned back in his chair. "Do you still want this job?"

"Yes, of course."

Lindsey didn't want it. She needed it. She should have been grateful to have a job at all, let alone one that paid this well. Half her art school classmates were working at Starbucks. Plus, she'd been in a car accident almost a year ago that had left her with a steep medical bill. A few years working at Prime Life Insurance, and she could make a serious dent in her debt.

But the idea of doing this for a few years was soul-crushing.

"You know how it works," her boss said. "We have quotas to meet both individually and as a team. You need to pick things up."

"I know," Lindsey said. "I'll work harder, Mr. Grant."

"Good." He gave her a wide smile that looked more like a grimace. "Why don't you get back to work? I want to see that fresh-faced, energetic employee you were when you started here."

Lindsey left her boss's office and returned to her cubicle. She slid her headset back on and brought up a list of names and phone numbers on her monitor.

As she stared at the screen, all the numbers seemed to blur together. Her dreams seemed more out of reach than ever. She was never going to pay off all this debt, let alone make it to Europe. At age 23, she still hadn't fallen in love. And her sketchbook was at the bottom of a box somewhere, untouched since she finished art school.

Lindsey opened her desk drawer and glanced at the phone inside it. She had a message. The office had a strict 'no cell phones' policy, but she didn't care. Looking behind her to make sure no one was around, Lindsey picked up her phone and read the message. It was from her friend Faith.

*Do you have plans tonight?*

*Just grabbing the last of my stuff from my old apartment, then I'll be right over*, Lindsey sent back.

Lindsey's apartment building had been shut down for the foreseeable future because of a dangerous black mold infestation. For now, she was sleeping on Faith's couch. With the housing market in the city as competitive as it was, Lindsey was struggling to find a place within her budget. She wasn't exactly broke, but money was tight.

Faith's reply came through. *Great! We're going to celebrate the fact that we're roommates again.*

Lindsey grinned. She and Faith had lived together during art school. They'd had plenty of fun together. Not to mention that they'd gotten up to plenty of trouble.

Lindsey looked up from her phone and glanced toward Mr. Grant's office. He was standing by the window, staring straight at her.

*Crap.* Lindsey stashed her phone in her drawer. She'd better get back to work. She dialed the next phone number on her list.

"This is Lindsey from Prime Life Insurance. How are you today?"

---

Lindsey fished the spare key to Faith's apartment out of her handbag and unlocked the front door. She dragged her suitcase inside. "Faith? I'm here."

There was no answer, but Lindsey could hear the shower

running. She walked into the living room, set her suitcase down, and eyed the old, gray couch that was now her bed. Lindsey had crashed on it several times before. At the very least, it wasn't too uncomfortable. And Faith sometimes stayed overnight with the family she worked for as a nanny, so she'd given Lindsey permission to sleep in her bed when she wasn't coming home for the night.

Lindsey opened her suitcase and rummaged through her clothes. She wanted to change out of her stifling work outfit, but she had no idea what Faith's plans for the two of them involved. Lindsey hoped it was nothing too crazy. It had been a long week, and she was feeling drained.

Faith entered the living room, dressed in sweatpants and a tee, her dark curly hair tied back in a messy bun. She flopped down onto the couch. "All moved in?"

"Yep." Lindsey sat down next to her. "Thanks again for letting me stay with you. I promise I'll be out of your hair soon."

"Take your time," Faith said. "It'll be fun to be roommates again. It'll be just like old times."

"I'll try not to cramp your style when you bring guys home. Or girls."

"I've given up on guys. Girls are much more fun."

"It must be nice to have that choice," Lindsey said. Faith's sexuality, according to her, was that she 'liked people' and that was that. She never bothered to put a label on it. Lindsey envied that about Faith. She always seemed so self-assured.

Lindsey looked Faith up and down. "What's with the sweatpants? I thought we had plans tonight?"

"We do," Faith replied. "We're staying in and doing what we used to do on Friday nights when we lived together."

"You're not serious, are you?"

Faith nodded. "There's some fruit and a bottle of vodka on the kitchen counter. I bought the cheapest bottle I could find. We're making punch and staying up all night."

Lindsey didn't know whether to smile or groan. It had been a long time since they'd gotten drunk together, and for a good reason. It usually ended in disaster. But wasn't Lindsey just thinking about how boring her life was? Maybe a little excitement was just what she needed.

"Okay," Lindsey said. "Let's do it. But we're ordering dinner first. We don't want a repeat of the first time we did this." That night, they'd both learned the hard way why drinking on an empty stomach was not a good idea.

"Sure," Faith said. "There's this amazing Thai place a few blocks away. And they deliver. Dinner first, then punch. I'll order food, while you get started in the kitchen."

"Deal."

Lindsey got up and went into the kitchen, tying up her long auburn hair on the way. She began to gather the ingredients for their signature alcoholic punch. She and Faith had come up with the recipe in their freshman year. The two of them had been this wild, inseparable pair in college, and their punch recipe had been responsible for more than one crazy night. Since then, they'd outgrown partying, but Faith still retained some of that free-spiritedness. It was another thing Lindsey envied about her. No matter what life threw at her, she seemed to take it in her stride.

An hour and a half later, they were sprawled out over the couch, the coffee table littered with empty takeout boxes. They had started drinking while waiting for the food to arrive, and Lindsey was starting to feel it.

Faith refilled her glass, then looked at Lindsey's empty one. "Want some more?"

"If I didn't know better, I'd think you're trying to get me drunk," Lindsey said. It was already too late for that.

"I just want to see you have some fun," Faith said, drawing out her words like she always did after a few drinks. "You've been so mopey lately."

"Yeah, well everything sucks right now."

"What's the matter?" Faith asked. "Other than getting kicked out of your moldy apartment, that is."

"It's mostly work. Spending forty hours a week stuck in a cubicle trying to sell people something they don't need? It's so soul-destroying."

"Why don't you find another job?" Faith asked. "Something you actually like?"

"I wish I could. I don't have any real skills."

"You were one of the best artists in our class. I think it's safe to say you've got skills."

"Fine, I don't have any useful skills," Lindsey said. "Art doesn't pay the bills. Not unless you're some combination of brilliant and extremely lucky."

"You could try nannying. It wasn't what I thought I'd be doing after college either, but it's fun. And you can make lots of money once you have some experience."

"I'm not good with kids. I wouldn't know what to do."

Faith pursed her lips in thought. "There are other ways to make money, you know." She lowered her voice. "Ways other than jobs."

Lindsey sat upright. "What do you mean?"

"It's probably easier if I show you." Faith stood up. "I'm going to go grab my laptop. I'll be right back." She headed to her bedroom, swaying as she walked.

Lindsey stared at the pitcher on the table. She'd already had far too much to drink. But she was tired of being a responsible adult. She was tired of constantly worrying about work, and money, and debt. All she wanted was to pretend that she was still the carefree young woman she'd been just a year or two ago.

And most of all, she wanted to forget about the fact that she was now living a life that would have made her younger self so disappointed in her.

Lindsey refilled her glass and started gulping her drink down. Just as she finished it off, Faith returned to the living room and sat down next to her.

"I should warn you," Faith said, typing a web address into her browser. "This is a little unconventional."

"I don't care," Lindsey said. "Show me."

That was where her memory of that night ended.

# CHAPTER TWO

*A*fter a long day at work, Lindsey returned to Faith's apartment. She'd stayed back late for yet another meeting with her boss about her performance. It hadn't improved. Lindsey couldn't help but wonder if she was subconsciously sabotaging herself so that she'd be fired.

She sat down on the couch. She could worry about that tomorrow. Lindsey grabbed her laptop from the coffee table and opened it up. Some mindless TV was just what she needed. Lindsey found a show she was midway through binge-watching and pressed play.

Her phone buzzed. A message from Faith, telling Lindsey that she was at the grocery store and would be home soon. Lindsey flicked through her phone, only half watching the show playing on her laptop screen. Her email inbox was full of unread messages. She scrolled through them, deleting most of the emails without opening them.

A particular email caught her eye. The subject line read:
*Welcome to thesugarbowl.com.*

That had to be spam. But the name of the website jogged something in Lindsey's memory. She opened the email.

*Congratulations. Your application to join The Sugar Bowl has been accepted. Click here to view your profile.*

What was this? Lindsey didn't remember signing up for anything like it. She clicked the link. It took her to a profile page on what looked like a dating website. *Her* profile page, complete with photos.

And underneath her profile picture were the words "Sugar Baby looking for arrangement."

*What the hell?* Suddenly, snippets of Friday night started coming back to her. Lindsey groaned. She'd been right in thinking that getting drunk with Faith could only lead to disaster. Lindsey still didn't remember the details, but maybe her friend did. She dialed Faith's number.

Faith answered in her usual cheery voice. "What's up, Lindsey?"

"Why am I signed up for a sugar baby website?" Lindsey asked.

"Oh yeah, I forgot all about that. Does this mean you got accepted?"

"Apparently. But I don't remember any of this."

"Nothing?" Faith asked. "Wow. Well, you did drink a lot. But you seemed really keen on the idea at the time. All I did was help you set up your profile."

Lindsey shook her head. "This is crazy. I should just delete my profile."

"What? You can't! That website is really hard to get onto, especially if you're a woman. There are just too many women who want to be sugar babies. Plus, they screen everyone really carefully."

"How do you even know all this?" Lindsey asked.

"That friend of mine from freshman year?" Faith said. "I guess you don't remember that conversation either?"

"Nope."

"Look, I have to go, but I'll be home in ten minutes. We can talk about this then. Whatever you do, do *not* delete your profile."

"Fine," Lindsey said.

"I'll see you soon."

Lindsey hung up and placed her phone down. She would humor her friend. She wasn't actually considering becoming a sugar baby.

Although, she only had a basic idea of what being a sugar baby involved. And it couldn't hurt to have a look at the website. To take a peek at this world of money, and glamour, and romance.

Abandoning her TV show, Lindsey opened up the Sugar Bowl website on her laptop and logged into her profile. A few pictures of her from social media were at the top, and all her information, from her age to her height, was listed underneath. She'd written a short biography too. Lindsey had to admit, she and Faith had done a good job. The profile made Lindsey sound much more interesting than she was in real life. And much more alluring.

There was a red envelope symbol at the top of the screen with the number 23 written next to it. Did Lindsey have 23 messages already? She opened up her inbox and went through the messages one by one.

The first was from a man who listed himself as forty, but he was clearly at least sixty. And his message? It was polite and respectful at first, but then he openly admitted to having a wife and said he was looking for someone 'discreet.'

Lindsey shuddered and moved on to the next message. It was much the same, minus the wife. But it was loaded with hints about the man's sexual prowess. *No thanks.*

The rest of the messages were no better. Several of the men were just looking for sex. A few of them seemed genuine, but they were all old enough to be her grandfather.

Finally, she reached the last message. It was from someone named Camilla.

*A woman?* Lindsey tapped the thumbnail to view Camilla's profile. There was only one photo of her. It showed a gorgeous long-haired brunette with an inviting smile, bright hazel eyes, and an air of unwavering confidence that Lindsey could feel through the screen.

Lindsey scanned Camilla's profile. She was 39 years old, and her biography was concise and detailed. She was a businesswoman, who liked wine, architecture, and art. And nothing on her profile suggested she was after sex.

Lindsey frowned. Why was she even getting messages from a

woman? Any good dating site would have the option to choose gender preferences. And Lindsey was as straight as they came.

Lindsey heard the sound of a key in the front door. A moment later, Faith entered the apartment juggling a few bags of groceries.

"Hey, Lindsey." She walked over to the couch and peered over Lindsey's shoulder. "Is that the Sugar Bowl? Did you get any bites yet?"

"I got a few messages," Lindsey replied.

"Oh? Does this mean you're not going to delete your profile?"

"I don't know. I mean, I'm not against the idea, but I don't know about the 'sleeping with someone for money' part."

Lindsey wasn't a prude when it came to sex. In fact, she was pretty adventurous. But even for her, this was a little too far. Maybe if she was actually attracted to the guy, it would be a different story. But judging by the caliber of men on the site, that wasn't going to happen.

"Being a sugar baby isn't about sex." Faith placed the grocery bags on the coffee table and perched on the arm of the couch. "It's about providing a girlfriend experience. Sometimes that involves sex, but sometimes it doesn't."

"And how do you know so much about this again?" Lindsey asked.

"I already told you, that girl I had a few classes with in freshman year. She started sugaring while she was still in art school. She ended up finding some rich guy who has been paying for all her living expenses for years now."

"Huh," Lindsey said. "He pays for everything?"

"Yep."

"And it's really not about sex?"

"Nope," Faith replied. "Apparently, the guy just likes having the company of a hot young woman. Whether there's sex involved or not, what these men are looking for is all the good parts of having a girlfriend without any of the bad parts. In return, they give their sugar baby gifts. They can be fancy dinners, designer clothes, expensive phones, or even just cash. Some of them give their sugar baby a monthly allowance or help them out with bills."

"That sounds like a pretty sweet deal," Lindsey said.

"Yep. I considered it myself after I graduated and couldn't find a job. Then the Yangs hired me full-time, so I didn't need to worry about money anymore."

"Hmm…" Lindsey glanced at her laptop again. Camilla's profile was still open. "We must have made a mistake setting up my account. My profile seems to be set to men and women."

"That wasn't a mistake." Faith grinned. "I talked you into ticking both boxes. It gives you more options."

"And how is that supposed to work?" Lindsey asked. "Last time I checked, I'm not interested in women. Not all of us are as enlightened as you and don't care about the gender of who we date."

"What about all those girls you made out with in college?" Faith teased.

"That doesn't count. I made out with everyone in college." It was true. But she'd never gone further than a kiss with another woman. She'd never felt any attraction to them.

"Wait, have you been getting messages from women?" Faith asked. "It's rare to find women who are looking for sugar babies."

"I got one message from a woman. Here." Lindsey turned her screen toward Faith. "She actually seems interesting."

"Wow," Faith said. "What a babe. And she's only 39. She messaged you?"

Lindsey nodded.

Faith pointed to a number on the screen. "The two of you are a 97% match. You're insanely compatible."

"How do they know that?"

"Remember all those questions we had to answer for the application?"

Lindsey shrugged.

"Right," Faith said. "You were drunk. They ask everyone a bunch of questions and then use algorithms to calculate how compatible two people are based on their answers. 97% is off the charts."

"Unfortunately, there's one problem with that," Lindsey said. "She's a woman. I don't like women. That's pretty important when it comes to compatibility."

"That might not matter in this case. By the looks of her profile, this woman isn't looking for sex. Maybe she just wants the company."

"Maybe." That could be fun. Going on fancy dates with some rich lady and getting paid to do it. "Either way, I'd be pretending to be interested in someone for their money. Isn't that a little predatory?"

"It's not like the other person isn't getting anything out of the deal," Faith said. "They're pretending too. It's not to say that the relationships can't be genuine. But do you really think these 21-year-old girls are attracted to their 60-year-old sugar daddies? Do you think they'd be with them if money wasn't involved? The sugar daddies—the mamas—they all know the score."

"Hmm." Lindsey chewed her lip. "I have to think about all this."

"Let me know if you have any more questions. I can even put you in touch with that friend of mine if you'd like." Faith got up and picked up the grocery bags from the table. "I'm going to put these away and have a shower. I've been chasing kids around all day."

As Faith left the room, Lindsey went over everything Faith had told her in her head. Maybe it wasn't such a crazy idea. The old Lindsey would have jumped at the chance to do something like this. She would have loved to be taken out and spoiled by some rich suitor in exchange for being their pretend girlfriend. The old Lindsey wouldn't have even cared if that suitor was a woman.

But that adventurous, carefree college kid was long gone, replaced by Lindsey the insurance saleswoman.

Maybe Lindsey couldn't afford to be as carefree as she used to be. But this could really help with her money problems. Lindsey turned back to her laptop. It was still open on Camilla's profile. Camilla seemed much more interesting than all the men who had messaged her, and Lindsey hadn't even read Camilla's message yet.

She went back to her inbox and opened the woman's message up. It was surprisingly short. All the other messages she'd been sent were page-long explanations of what the sender wanted from Lindsey. But this one was just a single sentence.

*I'd love to take you out on a date.*

That was it? It seemed presumptuous. Camilla hadn't asked Lindsey if she'd like to go on a date. She'd simply stated what she wanted. But there was something to be said for being direct.

Lindsey returned to the woman's profile. As she scrolled through it, her eyes landed on something at the bottom of Camilla's bio. She had missed it last time. It was a single word, on a line all on its own.

*Dominant.*

Lindsey's heart jumped. Camilla hadn't elaborated, but she didn't have to. Lindsey had already detected some hint of it in the way Camilla held herself in her profile photo. This woman was a Dominant, with a capital D. Lindsey had dabbled enough in BDSM that she knew exactly what that meant.

And Lindsey was intrigued.

She brought up Camilla's message again. Her hands hovered above the keyboard. There was no harm in going on one date with her. If Lindsey had any reservations after meeting her, she could call everything off.

She thought for a moment, then typed out a response.

*I'm free on Saturday night. Does that work for you?*

Lindsey hit send and closed her laptop. It was done. At once, all sorts of doubts came to her. Had she been too forward? Had suggesting a Saturday night been a bad idea? Night meant dinner, drinks, or dancing. Should she have suggested something casual like coffee instead? But coffee barely counted as a date. Could this really be called a date?

It didn't matter. It was already done. Lindsey got up and shoved her laptop in her suitcase. She had to stop obsessing about this.

A few minutes later, her phone buzzed. She picked it up. It was an email from thesugarbowl.com containing a message from Camilla.

*Saturday night is perfect. Let's have drinks at 8 p.m.*

Before Lindsey could stop herself, she sent off a reply.

*It's a date.*

She set down her phone and sank down onto the couch.

What had she done?

# CHAPTER THREE

"*Y*ou look like a nun," Faith said.

Lindsey stared at herself in Faith's bedroom mirror. Her long reddish hair was pulled back, and she'd spent plenty of time getting her makeup right, however, the black, knee-length dress she wore was pretty conservative. "The place we're going to for drinks is really classy. I don't want to look out of place."

"That doesn't mean you can't show a little skin. Don't you have anything sexier?"

Lindsey looked at the suitcase she'd dragged into Faith's room. "Most of my clothes are in storage. I didn't think I'd be going on a fancy date anytime soon."

"I have just the thing." Faith leaped up from the bed and started to go through her closet. "Where did I put it?"

Lindsey pulled off the dress, careful not to smudge her makeup, and added it to the pile of rejected outfits on Faith's bed. She couldn't remember the last time she'd dressed up like this. And she couldn't remember the last time she'd been this excited about anything, let alone a date. Not that it was a real date. But even though it was pretend, a romantic night out at an upscale lounge sounded like the perfect escape from her dreary life.

"Found it!" Faith held up a black and silver patterned dress. "This. This is perfect."

"That's... short." Although Lindsey and Faith were the same size, Faith was much shorter. And the dress didn't even go down to Faith's knees.

"That's why I picked it. One look at you in this dress, and you'll have Camilla giving you whatever you ask for. Money, fancy clothes, a car."

Lindsey rolled her eyes and took the dress from Faith. "I'm not going to ask Camilla for money. I'm just going to meet her." She slipped the dress over her head.

"Well, you have to talk about the financial side of things, at least. You don't want to go on a bunch of dates only to find that your sugar mama isn't going to give you any sugar."

Lindsey looked in the mirror. The dress was exactly as short on her as she expected it to be. But it covered her up everywhere else. And it did look pretty classy.

"See?" Faith said. "It's perfect."

Lindsey turned in the mirror. "I sure hope so."

"You seem nervous."

"Well yeah. I mean I've never done anything like this before."

"Just treat it like any other date," Faith said. "Well, a date with someone you're really trying to impress. Flirt, compliment her, laugh at her jokes. Show an interest in her life."

"I can do that." Lindsey picked up her phone and looked at the time. "I should get going."

"Okay. Don't forget to check in with me when you get there. Just so I know you're okay and that this woman isn't some creep."

"I doubt Camilla is a creep."

"You never know," Faith said. "And if anything happens, and you need rescuing, call me."

"Is there anything else, Mom?" Lindsey asked.

Faith stuck out her tongue. "I'm just looking out for you. I know you weren't sure about this, so if you start to feel uncomfortable, get out of there."

"I will, I promise. And I don't feel weird about this anymore. I'm actually pretty excited." Lindsey took one last look in the mirror and smoothed down her dress. "Wish me luck."

---

Lindsey's ride pulled up to the club where she was meeting Camilla. The Lounge was an exclusive upmarket bar that catered to the city's wealthy. As Lindsey stepped out onto the sidewalk, she wondered if she'd even be able to get inside. Then she spotted Camilla waiting for her out front.

The woman was even more beautiful in person than in her photos. Her chocolate brown hair was dead straight, and she had the kind of curves that would make a fifties pinup model jealous. Her black dress, which was short and tight but had long sleeves, flattered every inch of her. She was shorter than Lindsey, even in heels, but she somehow managed to look like she stood above everyone else around her. Lindsey knew from Camilla's profile that she was 39, but Lindsey would have pegged her for a bit younger. Either way, she certainly looked older than Lindsey.

Suddenly, Lindsey felt like a high schooler.

As Lindsey stood on the sidewalk examining Camilla, the woman turned her way and gave her a warm smile.

Lindsey collected herself. *Here goes nothing.* She strode over to the other woman.

"Camilla," she said. "Hi."

"You must be Lindsey. It's a pleasure to meet you." Camilla's voice was melodious and clear, and she had a refined way of speaking. "Let's go inside."

Lindsey glanced at the line at the entrance of the bar. They were going to be waiting for a while. But Camilla simply walked to the door and gave a brief nod to security, who stepped aside without hesitation.

They entered the club. It was even more luxurious than Lindsey expected. Glittering lights. Gold accents on everything. Plush seating. Despite the line outside, the dimly lit club wasn't full. Men and women lounged about, all dressed in suits and dresses. The music was loud, but not so loud that they'd have to shout to talk. It was the perfect place to take a date if you wanted to impress them.

And Lindsey was impressed.

Camilla led her to a small corner booth. "After you."

Lindsey took a seat. The booth was only big enough for two. Camilla slid in after her and sat down so that they were half facing each other, half next to each other.

Camilla looked around the bar. "I haven't been here for a while. I have to say, it's a lot tackier than I remember." She brushed some invisible dust off the table in front of her.

Lindsey didn't know what Camilla was talking about. This place was classier than anywhere Lindsey had ever been.

A waitress came over to take their orders. Camilla ordered a cocktail, so Lindsey did the same.

"We'll have the truffle fries too," Camilla said. She turned back to Lindsey. "I hope you're hungry. I don't usually eat this kind of food, but the truffle fries are to die for."

*What kind of person doesn't eat fries?* Lindsey looked around. She couldn't help but feel out of her element. And not just because of the fancy bar. Camilla herself looked like she was too good even for a place like this. She was sitting next to Lindsey with perfect posture like she was having dinner with the queen.

"Is everything okay?" Camilla asked.

"Yeah," Lindsey said. "I'm just a bit nervous. I'm still new to this." She meant the sugar baby part, not the 'going on a date with a woman' part.

"I know it can be nerve-wracking at first. It's easiest to think of it as the two of us getting to know each other. No pressure, and no obligations."

"Okay." Lindsey remembered Faith's advice. *Flirt. Show an interest in her.* Lindsey was too nervous to flirt. Instead, she opted for the latter. "So, what do you do for work?" It wasn't a very exciting topic, but it was all she could think of.

"I run my family's company," Camilla said.

"Wow." Not her family's business. Her family's *company*. "That sounds like a lot of work."

"It takes up almost all my time and energy. I mostly work from home for efficiency's sake, which helps. But I enjoy it. It's been in my family for generations and I inherited the company from my parents years ago. I've managed to build on their successes since then."

"What is it that your company does, exactly?" Lindsey asked.

"Oh, a little of everything. You'd find it all dreadfully boring."

The waitress returned with their drinks, along with a large plate of truffle fries

Camilla took a sip of her cocktail. "Well, at least they still make decent drinks. Here." She pushed the plate of fries toward Lindsey. "Try some."

"Thanks." Lindsey grabbed a few and nibbled on them. They were good.

"How about you?" Camilla said. "What do you do?"

"Well, at the moment I work at a call center selling overpriced insurance to people who don't need it."

"That sounds delightful," Camilla said dryly.

"It's pretty depressing," Lindsey said. "But it pays the bills, and I really need the money." *Crap.* Now she sounded like she was begging Camilla for money. "Sorry, I didn't mean to bring money up."

"Oh, it's fine. I'm not the type to delude myself that some beautiful young woman is actually interested in me and not my money." Camilla looked Lindsey up and down. "All my charms aside, I'm old enough to be your mother."

"You'd have been a pretty young mother."

"Trying to flatter me, are you?"

Lindsey shrugged. "It's true."

More small talk followed, and Lindsey began to relax. No doubt, the cocktail helped. Soon, they were onto their second round of drinks.

"So," Camilla asked. "What are you looking for in an arrangement?"

"Uh, I'm not sure," Lindsey said.

"You really are new to this. Most women have a whole speech ready."

"Actually, you're the only person I've met up with."

"I'm flattered," Camilla said. "But a word of advice? Don't be afraid to speak up about your needs, or you'll get taken advantage of."

Lindsey nodded.

"So, what is it you're after? Someone who will take you out to fancy dinners? Help to pay off your student loans?" Camilla took a sip of her cocktail. "Money for a set of double D's?"

Lindsey almost choked on her fries. "You mean a boob job?"

"It wouldn't be the first time."

"No, that's not what I want. I guess I'd like some help paying off my medical debt. I was in a car accident a year ago, and I ended up with a whole heap of bills that weren't covered by insurance. Plus, my apartment building has been shut down because it's a health hazard, so I need a new place to live, but I can't find anything within my budget. I'm sleeping on my best friends couch for now, but I can't stay there forever. So, help with my living expenses would be great too."

"That's a very sensible answer," Camilla said. "What made you decide to try sugaring?"

"Well, Faith—the friend I'm living with—told me about it, and it seemed like it could be a fun solution to my problems," Lindsey said. "Plus, I've been in a bit of a rut lately. I wanted to do something exciting."

"And? Are you finding this exciting so far?"

A smile tugged at Lindsey's lips. "I am." She'd been worried she'd have to fake interest in Camilla. But Lindsey liked her. "Did someone really ask you for money for a boob job?"

Camilla nodded. "A young woman with aspirations of being an actress. Lovely, but a terrible conversationalist. I've had more interesting chats with my ninety-year-old groundskeeper about the lawn."

Lindsey wasn't at all surprised that Camilla had a groundskeeper.

"Most of the women I've met through the Sugar Bowl have been the same," Camilla said. "Nice, but we didn't click. Don't get me wrong, I'm under no illusions about these types of arrangements. Nonetheless, if we're going to be spending time together, we need to be able to connect on some level."

Lindsey nodded. But there was a question at the back of her mind. "Why did you sign up for the Sugar Bowl? It's not like you'd have any trouble finding a real girlfriend."

"You think I don't know that?" Camilla asked.

"I didn't mean-"

"To put it simply, I'm a busy woman. Relationships are hard work. And they're messy. The way I see it is, I can go out on the dating scene and try to find someone who fits my strict ideas about what I'm looking for in a relationship. Or I can find a beautiful young woman who will give me exactly what I need, in exchange for being spoiled rotten."

Lindsey remembered all the men who had sent her messages filled with innuendo. "What is it that you need, exactly?"

Camilla raised an eyebrow. "Darling," she said, drawing out the 'a.' "If I wanted sex, I would have hired an escort. What I want is a companion of sorts. A girlfriend without all the strings and baggage that normally comes with one. A relationship on my terms, that fulfills certain requirements."

Lindsey sipped her drink and glanced up at Camilla. "What kind of requirements?"

"You suddenly have a lot of questions."

"We're supposed to be getting to know each other, aren't we?"

Camilla sat back and crossed her arms. "If you must know, I like to take charge in a relationship. And I don't just mean in bed. I like control. I like things done a certain way. I like my routines. A lot of women have a problem with that. More than one ex-girlfriend of mine has called me a control freak."

"I don't see anything wrong with that," Lindsey said. "And I don't mind being on the other end. Of giving up control. It's nice, sometimes, to be told what to do. To have someone else make decisions for you. It can be freeing, not to have to worry about the little things."

Lindsey paused, suddenly realizing she was revealing her deepest desires to a woman she'd just met. And Camilla was watching her with an interest that made Lindsey's skin prickle.

"It makes everything simple, that's all," Lindsey said. "My exes thought it was weird too. The last guy I dated thought that 'taking charge' meant being a controlling jerk. I've never broken up with someone so fast."

"You date men *and* women, then?" Camilla asked.

Lindsey froze. She'd gotten so comfortable with Camilla that she'd forgotten about the small matter of her lack of interest in women. But she couldn't bring herself to outright lie about it.

"It's not a problem, of course," Camilla said hurriedly. "I'm not one of those people who think bisexual women are just looking for a vacation from men. I just ask because I find it very hard to believe you're still on the market when you have the pick of all the men on the site. There are so many more of them than women. You're spoiled for choice. And I know someone like you has gotten dozens of messages."

That was a close call. "I have gotten a lot of messages," Lindsey said. "But none of the men who sent them appealed to me. Not like you did." That was the truth.

"Oh? And what exactly appealed to you about me?"

"What can I say?" Lindsey leaned in a little closer. She was feeling daring. "You're gorgeous, for starters. And your profile was interesting. It drew me to you. And your message was very direct. I liked that." She paused. She didn't want to seem like she was fawning.

"Oh, don't stop," Camilla said. "I was enjoying hearing all the wonderful things about me."

Lindsey bit her lip. "And I saw that we have something in common."

"Oh?" Camilla tilted her head to the side slightly. "Are you referring to a love of wine?"

Lindsey shook her head.

Camilla paused. "I take it you're not referring to my interest in classic architecture?"

"Nope."

"Then what is it?" The look in Camilla's hazel eyes made it clear that she already knew the answer.

For a second, Lindsey's words caught in her throat. "You're a dominant."

Camilla's expression didn't change. "And you're a submissive."

"Yes," Lindsey replied, even though it wasn't a question.

A cat-like smile spread across Camilla's face. "Well, this just got a lot more interesting."

A waiter came over to ask if they needed anything. Camilla ordered them both another drink. They sat in silence as the waiter cleared away their empty glasses.

As soon as he was gone, Camilla spoke. "All this time, you knew I was a dominant, yet you still made me tell you about what I require from a relationship?" Her voice dropped to a firm, smoky whisper. "That was very naughty of you."

Heat rushed to Lindsey's cheeks.

Camilla chuckled softly. "Is that all it takes to make you squirm? You really are a submissive."

"Well, I haven't had a lot of experience," Lindsey said. "I wish I had more. But the scene, the clubs, the rules—it's all really intimidating."

"I understand. The scene isn't very beginner friendly sometimes."

Camilla reached out and placed a sympathetic hand on Lindsey's. The fleeting touch seemed to linger on her skin even after Camilla pulled away.

"You were right," Camilla said. "We do have a lot in common."

From then on, the conversation flowed much more freely. It was easy with Camilla. She was warm and witty, and made Lindsey feel at ease. And whenever Camilla made a suggestive comment, Lindsey couldn't help but flirt back.

After they reached the end of their second serving of fries and countless drinks, Camilla sat back in her chair and studied Lindsey.

"I like you, Lindsey. You're the first woman I've met on the Sugar Bowl who doesn't seem like you're working from a script. You're refreshingly honest."

"Good company brings that out in me," Lindsey said. Her cheeks felt warm. "The cocktails help."

A large group of drunk men blustered by their table. A couple of them turned their heads to stare at Camilla and Lindsey as they passed.

Camilla gave them a dark glare until they were out of view. "Clearly, this place is being taken over by riff-raff." She looked at her watch. "It's getting late. I live a little outside the city, so I should head home. Let's get going."

"Sure." Lindsey was surprised by how much time had passed.

Camilla paid off their tab, which Lindsey was sure was extravagant, and the two of them headed outside.

"I'll call a car to take you home." Camilla pulled out her phone. "On me, of course."

"You don't have to," Lindsey said.

"But I want to. I have to call one for myself too." Without waiting for a response, she tapped the screen of her phone a few times and tucked it back into her purse. "Done. They should be here in a few minutes."

The two of them walked a short distance down the street, away from the entrance to the bar. The night air was cool on Lindsey's skin.

Lindsey broke the silence. "This was... nice."

"It was," Camilla said. "I've certainly enjoyed this more than all my recent dates. Probably because they were all with women who were so painfully straight that they couldn't keep up the illusion. If this is going to be one big charade, the least everyone could do is be convincing about it."

*Right.* Lindsey couldn't tell Camilla that she was just like all of those other straight women. She was in too deep now.

"What is it?" Camilla asked. "I find it hard to believe you've suddenly gotten shy."

"It's just, I, actually… I've never been with a woman before," Lindsey blurted out. "On a date, I mean." That much was true.

"Oh?"

"But I've kissed one," she added. "Well, more than one."

Camilla's lips curled up. "Would you like to kiss another one?"

Lindsey barely even hesitated. She'd already gone this far. If she was going to do something crazy, she might as well go all the way. "Yes," she said. "I would."

Camilla took Lindsey's chin in her fingers and leaned in close. "Then kiss me."

Lindsey's pulse raced. Camilla's smooth, commanding voice resonated deep into her body, compelling her to do as Camilla told her.

Closing her eyes, Lindsey kissed Camilla. It was a brief touch of the lips, nothing more. But it seemed to go on and on. For a moment, Lindsey forgot herself, as Camilla's lips took over all her awareness.

Camilla pulled back. "Your car is here."

Lindsey opened her eyes. A black car had pulled up beside them.

Camilla opened the door for her. "I'll send you a little something for tonight?"

Did she mean money? "You don't have to," Lindsey said.

"Once again, I want to, so I'm going to. You really haven't done this before, have you?"

"It just feels weird, getting paid for something like this."

"I'm not paying you," Camilla said. "It's a gift. Accept it."

"Okay. Thank you." Lindsey slid into the backseat of the car. "Goodnight."

"Goodnight, Lindsey. I'll talk to you soon."

# CHAPTER FOUR

*L*indsey was in Faith's living room on Sunday afternoon when Faith returned home from work. They hadn't seen each other since before Lindsey left to meet Camilla the night before.

Faith walked over to the couch, lifted Lindsey's legs up and sat down next to her. "Tell me all about your date."

Lindsey stretched her legs across Faith's lap. "I already told you about it last night." Faith had insisted Lindsey check in afterward.

"Yes, but you didn't tell me the details."

Sighing, Lindsey told Faith everything, from the moment she stepped out of the cab, all the way to when she and Camilla left the bar. "And then, we kissed."

"Whoa, hold on," Faith said. "You and Camilla kissed? And you're only telling me this now?"

Lindsey shrugged. "I was feeling kinda weird about it. Not because it was bad or anything. It was… nice."

"Ooh, do I detect a crush?"

"It was just a kiss. No matter how amazing Camilla is, she doesn't have the right equipment."

"This may come as a shock to you, but when it comes to women who are into women, a lack of equipment is rarely a problem."

Lindsey picked up a cushion and threw it at Faith, who batted it away harmlessly.

"Did you talk about money, at least?" Faith asked.

"Not directly. We talked about what we both wanted from an arrangement. And she sent me some money through the Sugar Bowl website after the date. A gift, she called it."

"How much money?"

"Three hundred dollars," Lindsey replied.

"Seriously?"

Lindsey nodded. "I was blown away too. Three hundred dollars just to spend a few hours with someone in a nice bar? Even if Camilla hadn't given me money in the end, I wouldn't have considered it a waste of time. We get along really well."

And Lindsey couldn't help but feel flattered. It wasn't every day Lindsey met a gorgeous dominant who was interested in her.

"See," Faith said. "The website's algorithm was right about the two of you being a good match."

Lindsey crossed her legs in Faith's lap. "We do have a few things in common."

"Like what?"

"Well, she likes art." The two of them had discussed art, but Lindsey hadn't mentioned that she was an artist. It wasn't like she'd ever be a real one. "And, she's a Domme."

Lindsey watched her friend's face for a reaction. She'd told Faith about her unconventional tastes one night when they'd been drinking together. Faith hadn't been fazed, but she didn't seem to understand it either.

"Weren't you just saying you're not into women?" Faith asked. "And now you're excited because Camilla likes kinky sex?"

"BDSM isn't about sex," Lindsey said. "Sure, there's usually a sexual element to it, but it's about so much more than that."

"Right." The skepticism on Faith's face grew.

"I know it doesn't look that way from the outside, but-" How could Lindsey explain the magnetic appeal of a Domme to Faith?

There were certain things that Faith seemed completely naive about, and this was one of them. "A lot of people view it as something like a hobby or a lifestyle. It's an interest we're both passionate about, like hiking or something." It wasn't quite the same, but it was the only comparison she could think of.

"It's definitely more interesting than hiking," Faith said.

"Well, Domme or not, woman or not, I want to see her again," Lindsey said. "There's something about her that... I just can't describe it. She's so captivating."

"It's nice to see you happy about something. Does this mean the two of you are going to go out again?"

"We don't have anything planned, but she said we'd talk soon before we parted ways on Friday night. I haven't heard from her yet, but she seemed interested in going out again." Lindsey had been checking her phone compulsively.

"That's great," Faith said. "Aren't you glad you listened to me and didn't delete your profile?"

"I am," Lindsey admitted.

"When your sugar mama starts buying you fancy clothes, you better let me borrow them."

"It's a deal."

As if on cue, Lindsey's phone rang.

Faith leaned over and peered at her screen. "It's her! Hurry up and answer it."

Lindsey stood up. "I will. In private."

"You're no fun," Faith said.

Lindsey walked into the bathroom and shut the door behind her. "Hi, Camilla."

"Lindsey." Camilla's sweet voice came through the line. "I hope I'm not interrupting anything."

"No, it's fine." Lindsey sat down on the edge of the bathtub. "I'm just hanging out with Faith in her apartment."

"The friend who convinced you to sign up for the Sugar Bowl? I should thank her."

"God, no. Faith would love that. She's been so smug and happy about the fact that I went on a date with someone."

"And how do *you* feel about said date?" Camilla asked.

"I'm pretty happy about it too," Lindsey replied. "I had a great time."

"So did I. I'd love to take you out again."

"I'd like that."

"Next Saturday," Camilla said. "We'll go to dinner."

"Okay. I can't wait." Lindsey hesitated. "And thanks for the gift." She wasn't sure if it was more impolite to mention it or to not thank her for it.

"My pleasure. I do enjoy having someone to spoil. It isn't quite enough money for a boob job, but I hope it'll help with those bills of yours."

Lindsey smiled. "It will. I'll see you on Saturday."

She hung up and let out a breath. She was really doing this. Lindsey got up, opened the bathroom door, and almost walked right into Faith.

"So," Faith said. "What did Camilla say?"

"Were you listening the whole time?" Lindsey asked.

"I was trying to, but I couldn't hear anything through this stupid door." Faith put her hands on her hips. "Well?"

"Well, we're going out again on Saturday. She's taking me to dinner."

"That's great," Faith said. "You're going to need something to wear."

# CHAPTER FIVE

"*J*hope you left room for dessert," Camilla said. "I have a sweet tooth, and this place does an amazing crème brûlée. The servings are enormous, so we'll have to share."

"Sure," Lindsey said.

The night was going well. Just like their last date, Camilla had taken Lindsey somewhere fancier than she'd ever be able to afford herself. And, like their last date, Lindsey had started out a bundle of nerves, but Camilla had made her feel at ease. Dinner had simply flown by.

There had been a minor incident when Camilla had sent back a perfectly good plate of scallops because they 'tasted like something from the bottom of a supermarket freezer.' Lindsey wondered if Camilla had ever eaten anything from a supermarket freezer before. Or if she'd even set foot in a supermarket.

"They also do an amazing tiramisu," Camilla said. "Which do you prefer?"

"I don't mind," Lindsey replied. "Whatever you want."

"Whatever I want? What if I wanted you to kneel by my feet while I fed you dessert?"

ANNA STONE

An image sprung up in Lindsey's mind. Of herself, kneeling on the floor next to Camilla's chair in the middle of the restaurant in front of everyone.

She looked Camilla in the eye. "I would do it."

"You really would, wouldn't you?"

"I would if you told me to."

"That's right. You like being told what to do."

Camilla folded her arms across her chest and leaned back, examining Lindsey silently. Lindsey shifted in her seat.

"Have I told you about where I live?" Camilla asked suddenly. "Robinson Estate?"

"No," Lindsey replied.

"It's an hour outside the city. The grounds are lovely. It's almost like living in the countryside. The estate dates back to the 1700s, but the manor itself has been renovated so many times that it's basically brand new. It spans two floors, and there are over 100 rooms. And it's equipped with every luxury imaginable."

"That sounds incredible." Lindsey waited for Camilla to continue. It looked like she had more to say, but she seemed to be thinking deeply.

Finally, Camilla folded her hands in front of her. "I have a proposal for you. It's unconventional, but it could be a solution to some of your problems."

"What is it?" Lindsey asked.

"Come live with me," Camilla said. "Move into my manor for three months. In exchange, I'll give you enough money to pay off all your medical bills and more."

Lindsey blinked. Had she heard that right? "That's... my medical bills. They're a lot."

"How much?"

Lindsey told her.

"I'll give you triple that," Camilla said.

Lindsey's jaw dropped. "Seriously?"

Camilla nodded. "I'll give you a generous weekly allowance too, just so you don't feel like you're being held hostage."

"No way," Lindsey said. "That's too much."

"Please, I have handbags that cost more than that."

Lindsey didn't know if Camilla was exaggerating about the handbags. What she was offering was enough money to pay off all Lindsey's medical bills, as well as a big chunk of her student loans from her useless fine arts degree. And she wouldn't have to worry about money for a while. She could quit her job at the call center and take her time looking for something better after three months was up.

"On top of that, my manor will be your home for three months," Camilla said. "I'll provide you with everything you could ever want. Luxury beyond your wildest dreams."

Lindsey pictured it all in her head. Would there be even more fancy dinners? Expensive clothes? Parties? Servants? It all seemed too good to be true.

Lindsey took a step back. "What do you want in return?" she asked. "What do you want me to be for you?"

"That's up to you," Camilla said. "I'd be fine with you being nothing more than my companion. It gets boring sometimes, living in that enormous house with no one else around except for the help. I'd appreciate the company, and I think you can agree that we get along well. But there are other options if you're interested."

"Like what?" Lindsey asked.

"You can be my temporary live-in girlfriend." Camilla paused. "Or, you can be my submissive."

*Her submissive?* Lindsey couldn't deny that the idea appealed to her. She'd never been anyone's submissive before. She had only seen glimpses of Camilla's dominant side, and she liked what she saw.

But still, Camilla was a woman. And that wasn't something Lindsey could ignore, could she?

"Is something the matter?" Camilla asked.

"It's just that…" Lindsey hesitated. "Like I said, I've never actually been with a woman before." She felt a twinge of guilt. She was avoiding the whole truth.

"I said from the start that I'm not after sex. Quite frankly, I can take it or leave it. And I would never pressure you in any way. I take consent and boundaries very seriously." Camilla fixed her eyes on Lindsey's. "What I want is something much more intimate than sex, and far more satisfying. A submissive who will be mine 24/7. Who will obey me, and defer to me, and serve me. Who will do as I say without question and thank me for it every single day."

Lindsey's skin flushed. On the surface, Camilla always appeared laid back, if not a bit stuck up. But it was becoming clear that behind her cool demeanor was someone who needed to maintain an iron grip on control.

And the thought excited Lindsey.

"Whatever you decide, this won't be a one-way agreement," Camilla said. "I have certain conditions, but we can negotiate something we're both comfortable with."

"Wow," Lindsey said. "This is just…"

"Crazy? I realize that. I'm not in the habit of asking sugar babies to move into my manor. I've never even had a sugar baby before. But when you mentioned your housing problems, the idea came to me. I think this arrangement could be beneficial to both of us."

*This arrangement.* Because that was all it was, in the end. Camilla knew that it was all pretend. And this offer was too good to pass up.

"If you're not interested, I won't be offended," Camilla said. "I'm open to a more conventional sugar baby arrangement."

"No," Lindsey said. "I'm interested. It's just, it's a lot. Can I think about it?"

"Of course. Take all the time you need."

Lindsey didn't want to take time. She wanted to say yes right now. But leaping into something like this was irresponsible.

A waiter approached their table. "Will you be having dessert?" he asked.

"Yes," Camilla said. "Let's see. The crème brûlée, or the tiramisu? I simply can't decide." She thought for a moment, then smiled.

"We'll have both. Life is too short. Why not live a little?"

By the time Lindsey returned to Faith's apartment, it was late, and Faith was already asleep. Lindsey wished her friend was awake. She wanted someone to talk to about Camilla's proposal.

She sat down at the kitchen table and placed her phone in front of her. She was still reeling from the kiss Camilla had given her when they parted. Lindsey liked kissing Camilla. She liked just being around Camilla. She wanted nothing more than to say yes to her.

But Camilla was practically a stranger. Although, after two dates, Lindsey was beginning to get a sense of what the woman was like. She could be warm and outgoing at times, sharp and cynical at others. And Camilla seemed very conscious of the fact that their arrangement was nothing more than just that.

So why not take Camilla up on her offer? Lindsey could just treat these three months like a job. She was selling her soul at the call center every day, so this would be an improvement. Not to mention that it would be a step up from her current life. Three months of luxury and romance, with a magnetic woman who wanted to spoil Lindsey in exchange for her submission.

It was strange. This past year, Lindsey had been a constant mess of anxiety and indecision, lost and directionless, but too afraid to take the slightest risk.

Right now? She had no doubts about what she wanted to do.

Lindsey picked up her phone and dialed Camilla's number.

Camilla answered after a few rings. "Hello, Lindsey. I wasn't expecting to hear from you so soon."

"Camilla," Lindsey said. "I was thinking. About your proposal."

"And?"

"And my answer is yes."

The other end of the line was silent.

"Which parts of my proposal are you referring to?" Camilla asked.

"All of it," Lindsey said. "Yes, I'll come live with you. Yes, I'll be your companion. Yes, I'll be your submissive. Yes to everything."

"I'm glad you decided to accept my offer. We can discuss the details over the next few days. Once we've come to an agreement, you can move in whenever you like."

"Okay," Lindsey said.

"And Lindsey?" Camilla asked.

"Yes?"

"From now on, you'll call me Mistress."

# CHAPTER SIX

"This is crazy," Faith said from the kitchen. "You know that, right?"

"I know." Lindsey tossed a pair of jeans into her suitcase. "But I'm doing it anyway."

It was 8:30 a.m. Lindsey had a couple of hours before the car Camilla sent was due to pick her up. Fortunately, she'd been living out of a suitcase for the past few weeks, so she didn't have much to pack.

Faith sat down on the couch with a bowl of cereal. "How well do you even know Camilla? What kind of woman invites a stranger to come live with her? She could be a serial killer!"

"Camilla is not a serial killer," Lindsey said. "I trust her. And I feel like we have a connection. I wouldn't be doing this otherwise, no matter how much money was involved."

"Okay," Faith said. "But what I don't get is that a minute ago you were on the fence about even meeting her because she was a woman. And now you're going to be her live-in lover?"

"I'm not going to be her lover." Lindsey pulled her phone charger out of the wall and tossed it into her suitcase. "I'm going to be her submissive."

"Isn't that the same thing? Isn't the whole point of all that kinky stuff to get off?"

"Not really," Lindsey said. "There doesn't have to be sex involved. There doesn't even have to be anything physical involved. Fundamentally, it's about power. Giving it up. Taking it away. The way that makes you feel."

"So, you're going to be her slave?" Faith asked.

"That's not Camilla's style. All she wants is someone who will say 'yes, Mistress,' and will happily do whatever she asks of them."

Over the course of the past week, Lindsey and Camilla had discussed their expectations. Lindsey had quickly learned that Camilla wasn't the type of dominant who used force of any kind to keep her submissive in line. She simply expected her submissive to yield to her control without question.

Lindsey was more than happy to do so. It was what she loved the most about submission. It made everything simple. It freed her from all her worries and problems. And right now, she had a long list of problems. She wanted this more than anything. She needed it.

"I still don't get it," Faith said. "Why would you let someone control you?"

"I'm not letting her control me," Lindsey replied. "I'm *choosing* to give her control. There's a difference. And I'm only giving her control of some things."

Camilla had sent Lindsey a long, detailed questionnaire about all things BDSM to fill out. There were questions about her likes, her dislikes, her limits. And they were comprehensive, covering the obvious activities like bondage, as well as things that were more mundane. How would Lindsey feel about being called a pet name, or wearing her Mistresses collar 24/7? Would she like it if her Mistress chose what she wore every day? What she ate? There were plenty of things that Lindsey had vetoed. But there were even more that she enthusiastically agreed to.

"I'm not going to do anything with her that I'm not comfortable with. And she's made it clear that she's going to respect my boundaries." Lindsey zipped up her suitcase and sat down next to Faith. "Plus, I've been thinking about the sex side of things. It isn't completely off the table. I'm not opposed to sleeping with a woman."

Faith cocked her head to the side. "Could it be that Camilla has turned you to the queer side?"

"I'm just a little curious, that's all." And who better to explore with than Camilla? A thought occurred to Lindsey. "God, I don't know anything about sex with women. How would I even know what to do? What if I'm terrible at it?"

"It's all about communication," Faith said. "Just tell Camilla you've never had sex with a woman before."

"I already told her. I didn't mean to, but it was this whole awkward mess and now she thinks I'm bisexual but inexperienced with women."

"Did you tell her you were bi?"

"No, she kind of came to that conclusion herself. And I didn't correct her." Lindsey pushed her guilt aside. "It doesn't matter. Camilla herself said that this was all a big charade. I just have to keep it up for three months."

"Uh huh," Faith said.

"Don't get all judgmental on me now."

Faith held up her hands. "No judgment here. But I should get to work." She pulled Lindsey in for a hug. "I expect updates from the minute you arrive."

"Sure," Lindsey said.

"And be safe. Call me the moment Camilla shows any sign of wanting to tie you up and lock you in her dungeon." Faith grinned. "Although, by the sound of things, both of you would probably like that."

---

The drive to Robinson Estate was a long one. At least, it felt long to Lindsey. Ever since her car accident, lengthy drives made her nervous. But it was nothing she couldn't handle.

The car stopped in front of a large set of double gates, which opened slowly before them like magic. They had reached Camilla's estate.

Lindsey rolled down the window and stuck her head out, staring at the sprawling grounds. She could only just see the manor itself in the distance, a large white building at the end of a long, winding driveway.

Finally, the car pulled up in front of the manor. The mansion looked even more impressive close-up. Lindsey got out of the car and stood staring at the house as the driver took her bags out of the trunk.

She scratched the back of her head. What was she supposed to do now? Knock on the door?

Moments later, the front door opened, and a short blonde woman came hurrying out. Her hair was pulled back in a bun, and her face wore a neutral expression. She was dressed in a navy-blue maid uniform, complete with a frilly white apron. She looked around Camilla's age or older.

"You must be Lindsey," the woman said.

"Yep, that's me," Lindsey replied. "Hi."

"My name is June. I'm the head housekeeper. Come with me."

Lindsey turned to grab her bags.

"Leave those. They'll be taken to your room."

Lindsey followed June into the manor. It was just as grand on the inside as it was outside. The entrance hall was vast and tall, with a huge chandelier hanging from the ceiling two stories up. Before them was a wide staircase that split into two at the top, branching off into each of the wings of the house.

"Let me take you to one of the guest suites," June said. "Camilla is still preparing your permanent rooms."

*Rooms?* As in, more than one? Lindsey followed June up the stairs and to the right, gaping at every room and hall they passed through. Everything was modern and new, but it had the elegance and sophistication of an old house. There were fireplaces and chandeliers everywhere. And Lindsey had thought Camilla was exaggerating when she said the house had over a hundred rooms, but it seemed like she was telling the truth.

June stopped in front of a door and opened it wide. "This is where you'll be staying for now."

Lindsey walked inside. It was like a five-star hotel room, complete with a massive bed and a spacious adjoining bathroom. And her suitcase and carry bag were right there in the room. How had they gotten there before her?

"If you ever need anything during your stay here, call me. There's an intercom next to every door." June pointed to an intercom, which camouflaged surprisingly well with the house's decor. "I'll do my best to fulfill any requests personally. There are other staff who work here, but I'm the only one who is here 24/7, so you can seek me out at any time."

"Okay," Lindsey said.

"Now, would you like to relax and settle in? I can bring you refreshments? Or, I can give you a tour of the house."

Lindsey glanced at the plush bed. She was just dying to throw herself onto it. But she'd have time for that later. "A tour would be great."

June nodded. "Come with me."

Lindsey followed her out the door. June kept a brisk pace.

"Now, Camilla has said you're to have free run of the house while living here," June said. "That is, except for Camilla's rooms. I'll show you where they are when we get there."

They went back the direction they came. When they reached the entrance, June took Lindsey left and gestured down a hall.

"The east wing is that way," she said. "It's not in use anymore, and it hasn't been renovated like the rest of the house. All you'll find down there are empty rooms and peeling wallpaper."

They returned to the entrance hall and continued through the manor, from the ground floor up. June pointed out various rooms. There was a gym, a home theater, a library, even a lap pool. It was like there was a room for everything.

Finally, they reached a set of white double doors. June stopped before them. "These are Camilla's rooms. You're explicitly forbidden to go beyond this point. Camilla likes her privacy."

Lindsey nodded. "Where is Camilla, by the way?"

"Camilla will be with you when she can," June said.

*What does that mean?* But Lindsey could tell by June's expression that she shouldn't pry.

"Now, let me show you around outside. There are several gardens on the grounds as well as a swimming pool and tennis courts." June turned and started back down the hall. "There are stables too, but we haven't had horses here in years."

Lindsey glanced at the doors to Camilla's rooms one last time, then walked away.

---

It wasn't until later that evening that Lindsey finally got to test out her bed. It was just as comfy as it looked.

She sank into it and closed her eyes. This was the life. She'd spent the day exploring the manor and the grounds, taking in the beautiful scenery. The old Lindsey would have loved to sketch it. A small part of her wanted to. But she didn't have her art supplies anyway. She'd also found an overgrown hedge maze, which she'd quickly gotten lost in. When Lindsey had finally gotten out, she'd found a quiet corner in one of the gardens, among sculpted topiaries and marble statues, and called Faith to reassure her that Camilla hadn't kidnapped her.

Where was Camilla? June hadn't specified whether Camilla was in the house or not. Lindsey found herself wishing Camilla had been the one to show her around the manor.

Her stomach rumbled. June had served Lindsey lunch after the tour. She hadn't eaten since then. She was debating whether to call June and ask, when there was a knock on her door.

*Camilla?* Lindsey leaped up and opened it. But instead of Camilla, she found June.

"Oh," Lindsey said. "Hi, June."

"Would you like to come down for dinner?" June asked. "Or, I can bring something up."

"I'll come down." Lindsey paused. "Is Camilla going to be there?"

"Not tonight."

"Why not? Is everything okay?"

"She's... indisposed," June said.

Lindsey frowned. What did she mean by that?

To Lindsey's surprise, June gave her a reserved, but sympathetic smile. "She'll be with you when she can. Now, let me take you to the dining room. Finding your way in this house can be difficult at first."

"Thanks, June," Lindsey said.

"No need to thank me. Camilla has instructed me to make you feel as at home as possible."

That was nice of her. But what Lindsey really wanted was to see Camilla.

Where was she?

# CHAPTER SEVEN

The next morning, Camilla didn't appear at breakfast. By the afternoon, Lindsey still hadn't seen her, but she'd glimpsed June carrying a tray of food into Camilla's quarters after lunch.

Was this normal? Was this how it was going to be? It seemed unlikely that Camilla would pay Lindsey an outrageous amount of money to come live here if she wasn't going to spend any time with her.

Once again, Lindsey had spent most of the day exploring the grounds and the gardens. As she walked back inside, she almost ran into June.

The housekeeper was carrying a tray laden with tea, coffee, and pastries. "I was just coming to find you, Lindsey. Camilla wants to see you."

*Finally.* Lindsey had been starting to feel rejected.

"She's putting the finishing touches on your rooms. She wants you to meet her there. I'll take you to her."

"Thanks," Lindsey said.

She followed June upstairs and through the maze of a house. They came to an open door. June stopped before it.

"Your rooms are through there," June said. "She's waiting for you."

Lindsey paused at the doorway. She'd been waiting for this moment ever since she arrived, and her anticipation had only grown. She pulled herself together and entered the room.

It wasn't a bedroom like she expected. It looked like a kind of sitting room, with several doors coming off it. Camilla was seated on a lounge in the middle of the room. She looked as elegant and put-together as on their first date, although she was dressed more casually. She certainly didn't look like she'd been 'indisposed.'

"Lindsey." Camilla gestured to the seat across from her. "Come. Sit."

Lindsey sat down. June set the tray of refreshments on the coffee table and began to lay everything out.

"Sorry I wasn't able to come and greet you yesterday," Camilla said.

"It's okay," Lindsey replied. "Is everything all right? June said you were indisposed."

"Did she now?" Camilla gave June a sharp look. "I assure you, I'm fine. I have quite a lot to do, but I wanted to take a moment to show you your rooms and talk about our arrangement." She paused and waited for June to finish setting everything out.

June straightened up and wiped her hands on her apron. "Is there anything else you need?"

"No, that will be all," Camilla said. "Thank you."

With a nod, June disappeared.

Camilla waved a hand toward the table. "Help yourself."

"Thanks." Lindsey picked up a pastry.

"Now, I hate to start on such a serious note, but there's a lot that we need to discuss," Camilla said. "Firstly, house rules. June tells me she's already shown you around. You're free to go wherever you like, except for my rooms. They're off limits unless you're with me, understand?"

Lindsey nodded. Camilla's manner suddenly reminded her of a teacher she'd had in middle school, who could turn from warm and kind to serious and stern at the flick of a switch. And if you did something to disappoint her, she became as cold as ice.

Lindsey had always liked that teacher.

"Everything in the house is at your disposal," Camilla said. "If you need anything at all, ask June. My only request is that you treat her with respect. She's not a servant. She's kept this house running for the last 15 years. And it's far too hard to find good help these days."

"Okay," Lindsey said.

"You're also free to come and go as you like. If you want to go somewhere, ask June to call you a car. I'd prefer it if you let me know if you're leaving."

"I will."

"I ask that you avoid leaving the grounds when we have plans to spend time together." Camilla folded her hands in her lap. "Which brings me to our schedule. Breakfast is at 8 a.m. After breakfast, I'll retire to my study to work, and you'll be free to do whatever you want. Lunch is at midday. After lunch, I like to take an hour or so to relax, during which time you'll join me. In the afternoon, I'll return to my study until dinner. And after dinner, the evenings are for us to spend together."

"Okay." Lindsey was beginning to understand why Camilla's exes had called her a control freak.

"Now, about our arrangement," Camilla said. "If at any point you have a problem with any part of it, tell me. I don't want you to ever feel pressured or uncomfortable. Dominant/submissive relation-ships are complicated enough, even without our unusual circum-stances. Communication is essential."

Lindsey nodded.

"Have you chosen your safeword?"

"Yes. Apple."

"Good," Camilla said. "Use it whenever you feel you need to. Even if you simply want a time out from our day-to-day routine. It's not like I'm going to be leading you around the house on a leash, but being a submissive 24/7 can be hard. If it gets exhausting, let me know."

Lindsey nodded. "I will."

"Otherwise, if you break any of my rules or the rules of this house, a punishment will be in order."

Punishments were one of Camilla's non-negotiable requirements, but she promised she'd never use them without a good reason. Lindsey didn't mind. And mercifully, Camilla had allowed Lindsey to choose her own from a very long list. Lindsey had picked the punishments which seemed the least severe. Cleaning, writing lines, time-outs. But she didn't expect that Camilla would go easy on her. It was clear that Camilla was a harsh Mistress. Yes, Camilla was going to spoil her. But she demanded a lot in return.

"I have this schedule and these rules for a reason. I don't like disruptions to my routine. And I don't like surprises."

Lindsey nodded.

"Do you have any objections?" Camilla asked. "Or, is there anything you'd like to negotiate?"

Lindsey shook her head, then remembered herself. "No, Mistress."

A hint of a smile crossed Camilla's lips. "Good. I'd love to stay and chat, but unfortunately, I have work to do. However, I want to make it up to you for being absent this past day or two. How would you like to have dinner in the courtyard garden tonight? I have a chef on call who makes the most delectable French cuisine."

"I would like that, Mistress."

"Good. Wear something nice. The emerald halter-neck dress is perfect for the occasion."

"What dress?" Lindsey asked.

"I bought you a few things. Have a look inside the closet in your bedroom once I'm gone." Camilla stood up. "I'll see you tonight."

As soon as Camilla left the room, Lindsey got up and located her bedroom. It was just like the guest room she'd been staying in, only larger, and it had its own balcony with a view of the grounds. After admiring the room, Lindsey walked over to the closet and opened the doors.

"Wow."

Inside was what had to be a whole new wardrobe. Formal

dresses, casual wear, and everything in between. She even had workout clothes and swimwear, as well as shoes and all sorts of accessories.

This was more than 'a few things.' It was everything she could possibly need.

Lindsey grinned. She was going to like it here.

Later that evening, Lindsey went out into the courtyard garden to join Camilla for dinner. As instructed, she wore the emerald dress she'd found in her closet. She'd paired it with some silver earrings and a necklace she'd found in a jewelry box on her dressing table.

Camilla was already seated on an outdoor lounge nearby, a bottle of wine and two glasses on the table next to her. Like Lindsey, she was dressed in a cocktail dress, but hers was a vibrant blue. She spotted Lindsey and smiled. "That dress looks just as lovely on you as I imagined. It brings out that striking red hair of yours."

"Thank you, Mistress," Lindsey replied.

Camilla gestured to the seat next to her. "Sit."

Lindsey sat down and looked around. She'd spent some time in this garden yesterday during the daytime. It looked lovelier at night. At the other end of the courtyard, June was setting a table for the two of them.

Camilla picked up the bottle from the table beside her and held it up. "Wine?"

"Yes, please," Lindsey said.

Camilla poured two glasses of wine and handed one to Lindsey. "So, how are you finding the house so far?"

"I love it. It's so beautiful."

"It's been in my family for generations. I inherited it after my parents passed." Camilla turned her gaze toward the manor. "You should have seen it 25 years ago. It was so much livelier. We had horses in the stables, and the orchard was carefully tended. And my parents were always throwing parties. Of course, back then the house had a full-time staff. I downsized when I took over. That's why the east wing is closed. Keeping the entire house running is almost impossible."

"I can imagine," Lindsey said. "This place is so big. I've already gotten lost a few times."

"It can take some getting used to," Camilla said. "Let me know if there's anything you need. This is going to be your home for the next three months after all."

"Thank you, Mistress. You've done enough for me already."

"I take it you found your new things, then?" Camilla said. "It's all yours, by the way. You can take everything with you when you leave."

"Seriously?" Lindsey asked. "Thank you! Not that I'm complaining, but you didn't have to do all that."

"It's no trouble. And I did promise to spoil you. You'll have the best of everything while you're here. Besides, there's something immensely satisfying about lavishing an appreciative woman with gifts."

"I definitely appreciate it," Lindsey said. "Thank you, Mistress."

"You're very welcome," Camilla replied. "Now, we haven't had a chance to properly discuss your answers to that questionnaire. Who knew you had such wicked desires hidden away in that innocent head of yours?"

Lindsey's face began to burn. She wasn't at all shy about her unusual appetites, but Camilla had a way of getting under her skin.

"I have a question for you," Camilla said. "Of all the kinky things you like, what is it that you like the most?"

"Well," Lindsey thought for a moment. "I like being spanked. It's not that I like that it hurts. I just like the way it makes me feel."

"And me bringing up how naughty you are makes you feel the same way, doesn't it?" Camilla lowered her voice. "It hasn't escaped my notice that every time I do, you turn a delicious shade of red."

Lindsey's face grew even hotter, making Camilla chuckle.

"What about you, Mistress?" Lindsey asked. "What do you like the most?"

"Personally, bondage is my tool of choice," Camilla said. "Handcuffs, ropes, even suspension. There's something so intoxicating about having a sweet, willing submissive all bound up for me. And based on your answers to the questionnaire, you would enjoy that too."

"Yes, Mistress." Just thinking about it gave Lindsey a rush.

"But blindfolds are a soft limit for you, correct?"

Lindsey nodded. She had quite a few hard limits, most of which were activities that most people would consider extreme, but blindfolds were her only limit that was negotiable. "I don't know why I'm fine with bondage, but not blindfolds. I guess if someone is going to tie me up and flog me I want to see it coming."

Camilla laughed. "That's fair."

"But it's a soft limit for a reason. I do want to try it sometime. I'd just have to be really comfortable with someone to do it."

"I understand. It requires a lot of trust. So, no blindfolds. Or anything else that you haven't explicitly agreed to."

*Sex.* Camilla had made it clear that she wasn't going to cross that line without the go-ahead from Lindsey. But Lindsey was starting to wonder if she should just give in to her curiosity.

"That still leaves us with a lot of options," Camilla said. "I have a very well stocked playroom."

"Seriously?" Lindsey said. "You have a playroom in your house?"

"Darling, the manor has its own ballroom. The first thing I did when I inherited this place was to convert one of the rooms into a playroom."

"Can I see it?"

"That depends," Camilla said. "I don't let anyone into my playroom who isn't prepared to play."

"I am," Lindsey said. "I want to. Please, Mistress?"

Camilla's hazel eyes searched Lindsey's face.

"All right," she said. "We'll have dessert in the playroom. Would you like that?"

Lindsey smiled. "I would, Mistress."

"Then it's settled." Camilla got up and offered her hand to Lindsey. "But first, dinner."

# CHAPTER EIGHT

*L*indsey followed Camilla down the winding halls of the manor and through the white doors that separated Camilla's rooms from the rest of the house. It was the first time she'd been in this forbidden part of the mansion. It was large enough to make up a house all by itself.

Camilla led Lindsey to a nondescript door and opened it wide. The two of them entered the room. It looked like nothing more than another of the manor's luxurious bedrooms. Unlike the rest of the house, the room was all dark tones, mostly purples and blues, but the lushness of the decor made it feel cozy and warm. There was a huge four-poster bed in the middle, complete with a canopy and curtains made from dark voile. The sheer drapes were tied to the bedposts with velvet ties.

"This is the playroom?" Lindsey asked.

"What were you expecting?" Camilla said. "Some kind of dungeon with chains and shackles?"

"Well, yeah. And where are all the toys?"

"I like to keep everything hidden away so that there are no distractions. I prefer my submissive to be relaxed and focused on me."

Lindsey looked around. There was more storage in the room than a usual bedroom. Cupboards, closets, chests. What secret treasures did they contain?

There was a knock on the playroom door.

"That must be June with dessert." Camilla gestured toward a small table at the side of the room. "Have a seat. I'll be right back."

Lindsey walked over to the table and sat down. Camilla slipped out into the hall, shutting the door behind her. Moments later, she returned, balancing a tray covered with a silver lid in her hands. She placed it in the center of the table.

Lindsey watched her eagerly. It was clear that Camilla planned for them to do more than just eat dessert. Sure enough, Camilla walked over to a cabinet and opened the door. Inside were a variety of restraints. Ropes, leather cuffs lined with fur, heavy-duty handcuffs, belts. Lindsey was sure she spotted a spreader bar too.

Camilla picked up a coil of thick black rope. She ran it through her hands from end to end, straightening out the kinks, and brought the rope over to Lindsey. "Cross your wrists at the back of the chair."

Lindsey obeyed. Camilla crouched behind her and wound the rope around Lindsey's wrists, tying them with a series of knots. When she was done, Lindsey tested her bonds. They were unyielding.

Camilla sat down across from Lindsey and removed the cover from the tray. What was underneath almost made Lindsey drool. It was a spread of sweet treats. Fruit, chocolate fondue, and all kinds of tiny confections.

"Doesn't this look marvelous?" Camilla said.

"Yes, Mistress." Lindsey wanted to try everything.

Then she remembered her hands were tied behind her back.

Camilla picked up a plump blood-red grape and dipped it in chocolate. She slipped it between her lips and closed her eyes, chewing slowly.

"Mm, this tastes wonderful." Camilla selected a bright red strawberry, the same color as her lips, and slid it into her mouth. "This is my one weakness. I love all things sweet." She reached across the table and drew a finger down Lindsey's cheek, leaving behind a streak of chocolate.

Suddenly, Lindsey found herself with a craving that had little to do with dessert.

Camilla took another strawberry and dipped it into the chocolate. She held it up before Lindsey. "Would you like to try one?"

"Yes please," Lindsey said.

Camilla slipped the strawberry into Lindsey's waiting mouth.

Lindsey let out an involuntary moan. "This is incredible."

"The strawberries were picked fresh this morning. The chocolate is made from the finest Ghanaian cocoa beans. Here." Camilla picked up a small square of dark chocolate. "Try some by itself."

Lindsey leaned forward, accepting Camilla's offering. It was bitter and rich in Lindsey's mouth. Camilla went through the tray, sampling everything before feeding a portion to Lindsey. There was something alluring about watching her Mistress eat. Was it the way her lips would purse around each tiny morsel? The blissful sounds she made? The tantalizing looks she gave Lindsey every time she picked out a sweet treat?

Lindsey had never thought that having things fed to her could be so sensual. Now and then, Camilla's fingers would brush against Lindsey's lips, sending a frisson through her.

"That's enough for now," Camilla said. "I don't want you stuffed full for what comes next."

"What comes next?" Lindsey asked.

"Next, I'm going to give you a sampler of all my favorite spanking toys. Would you like that?"

Lindsey's breath quickened. "Yes, Mistress."

Camilla went over to a cabinet, a different one this time, and pulled out a long, black leather roll with a velvet tie around it. Lindsey was reminded of a roll-up case she used to carry her paintbrushes around. But this one was longer than Camilla's arm.

"Go lie on the bed on your stomach," Camilla said.

Lindsey got up from the chair, which was a feat in itself with her hands tied behind her back. As she climbed onto the four-poster bed, she noticed that peeking out from the curtains at the foot of the bed was an X built into the frame, made up from the same dark wood. Camilla said she liked to tie up submissives. Would Camilla one day tie Lindsey to it?

Lindsey lay down on her stomach, her head tilted to one side to watch Camilla. Camilla untied the roll, set it down, and unraveled it along the bed next to Lindsey. The roll had a dozen long, thin pockets. But instead of paint brushes, it contained a variety of whips, crops, and canes. There were also a handful of short paddles and floggers as well as a few implements Lindsey had never seen before.

"First, I'm going to get you all warmed up," Camilla said.

She dragged her fingers up the back of Lindsey's legs, all the way to the top of her thighs. Her hands stayed above Lindsey's dress. Camilla was staying true to her word not to cross any boundaries. But right now, Lindsey was ready to throw those boundaries out the window.

"Move your hands," Camilla said.

Lindsey lifted her bound wrists up to the middle of her back.

Camilla raised a hand and slapped Lindsey on her ass cheeks, over and over. Lindsey cried out, her skin sparking with electricity. It barely hurt. But with every slap came the perverse thrill of being punished, of enjoying something that she knew she shouldn't, the taboo of playing at a game so deliciously twisted. All those feelings blended together made a heady cocktail.

After a minute or so, Camilla stopped. She straightened up and surveyed the roll of spanking tools before her. "Let's go from the mildest to the most intense. I'll start with this."

Camilla grabbed one of the paddles from the roll. It was large, flat, and made of hard leather. She flexed it a few times in her hands.

"Didn't I tell you to lie on your stomach?" Camilla said.

"Sorry, Mistress." Lindsey hadn't even realized she'd rolled onto her side to watch Camilla.

"I know this excites you, but I expect you to follow my instructions."

Camilla spanked Lindsey with the paddle a few times, ramping up the force. Each hit made a loud slap that made Lindsey jump and squirm.

"That's all?" Camilla said. "I was expecting much more of a reaction. I'll have to try something with a little more bite." She tossed the paddle to the side, then pulled out a short whip with dozens of tails. "Like this flogger."

She flicked the flogger across Lindsey's ass cheeks. It hit with a heavy sting that made Lindsey yelp.

Camilla whipped her a few more times. "Better. But I don't think we're there yet." Camilla reached into the roll again. "Let's try a quirt."

The item she produced was a short whip, this time with only two thick tails. Lindsey had never seen one like it before. Camilla struck Lindsey with it. She sucked in a breath, the sharp kiss of the tails penetrating deep. Lindsey wriggled and pulled at the ropes around her wrists as Camilla brought the quirt down over and over.

Camilla stroked her hand down Lindsey's arm. "Still okay there?"

"Yes, Mistress." Lindsey craved more. Of Camilla's touch, of the whip, of everything.

"Just one more." Tossing the quirt aside, Camilla picked out a long thin riding crop and flexed it in her hands. "Actually, I think what you really need is a firmer hand."

Camilla returned the riding crop to its place and reached into the pocket next to it, selecting a thick rattan cane. She swung it through the air a few times. It made a sharp, cutting swoosh.

"The cane can be intense, but I think it's exactly what you need. Some old-school discipline for a very wicked sub."

Camilla's words made Lindsey's whole body pulse. She shut her eyes, waiting for that telltale swoosh.

But it all happened at the same time. Lindsey heard the sound and felt the sting on her cheeks simultaneously. Lindsey gasped. Camilla struck her again, once, twice, three times. Every blow vibrated through her, traveling up her spine, down to her toes, and right between her legs.

Camilla slid her hand down to caress Lindsey's ass cheeks over her dress. "You like that, don't you?"

"Yes, Mistress," Lindsey said.

Camilla swatted her with the cane again, over and over. She writhed on the bed, helpless with her arms restrained, adrenaline and arousal rushing through her veins.

She felt Camilla's hand on the back of her shoulder. "That's enough for tonight."

Lindsey whimpered. Her body was awake now. She didn't want things to be over yet.

"Don't worry, we have three whole months to explore all this. I'm going to untie you now."

Camilla unbound the ropes from Lindsey's wrists, releasing her. Lindsey rolled onto her back and flexed her hands, letting out a contented sigh.

Camilla placed the rope to the side, then slipped onto the bed beside Lindsey. "Did you enjoy that?"

Lindsey nodded. "Thank you, Mistress."

Camilla pecked Lindsey on the lips. "There's water on the night-stand next to you. And we still have all that dessert if you're hungry."

"I'm okay." There was something Lindsey wanted, but it wasn't food.

"Then there's only one thing left to do."

Camilla untied the sheer drapes, letting them fall around the bed. Like magic, the outside world disappeared, and it was just the two of them. Camilla wrapped her arms around Lindsey and drew her in close.

Lindsey purred. She liked the feel of Camilla's body against hers, in more ways than one. She knew Camilla's intentions weren't sexual. All of this was just standard aftercare. Camilla was looking after her submissive's needs, making sure Lindsey was warm, fed, hydrated, and most of all, offered comfort and affection to prevent her from crashing both physically and mentally.

But Lindsey didn't want comfort. She didn't want food or water or anything else.

She wanted Camilla.

Camilla kissed her again. This time, Lindsey kissed her back with double the intensity. Lindsey felt a shift in her Mistress's body, a response to Lindsey's obvious hunger. She parted her lips and let Camilla's tongue dance around hers, desire flaring inside her.

Camilla pulled away. Lindsey whimpered in protest.

"What is it?" Camilla asked.

Lindsey's words caught in her throat. She was feeling so many things that she wasn't expecting to feel, and she found it impossible to articulate them all. Instead, she reached out and pulled Camilla back to her.

"Is there something you want?" Camilla's teasing tone made it clear that she already knew the answer.

Lindsey finally found her voice. "You know what I want, Mistress."

"We haven't discussed this part of our arrangement yet."

Lindsey groaned. "Please?"

"I did tell you that I take consent very seriously. I wouldn't want to cross any boundaries." Camilla traced her thumb down Lindsey's chin. "I'll make an exception, just this once. But you're going to have to tell me exactly what you want."

Lindsey nodded. Her chin tingled where Camilla had touched her.

"Tell me," Camilla said softly. "What do you want your Mistress to do for you?"

"Mistress, please." Lindsey's voice quivered. "Take off my dress."

Camilla reached around behind Lindsey and unzipped the emerald-green dress, her hands brushing down Lindsey's naked back. A shiver spread over her skin. Lindsey sat up, allowing Camilla to pull it off. She wasn't wearing a bra underneath the low-backed dress, and her nipples perked up in the cool air. Lindsey lay back down on her side facing Camilla.

"What else?" Camilla asked. "What else do you want me to do?"

"Mistress, please," Lindsey said. "Touch me."

"Like this?" Camilla drew her hand down the front of Lindsey's body, snaking her fingertips down her shoulders and over her chest.

"Yes, Mistress. Like that."

Camilla's hands wandered all over Lindsey's bare skin gently, as if she were touching something precious. Lindsey murmured with bliss.

"Mistress, please," Lindsey said. "May I touch you?"

"Yes," Camilla replied.

Lindsey reached out and swept her fingers along Camilla's side, from her knee, up her thigh, and over her hip. She let her hand creep up the front of Camilla's chest. Her curves were so smooth and supple. Lindsey wanted to ask if she could take off Camilla's clothes, but the way Camilla's hands were exploring Lindsey's own body left her too distracted to focus on anything but her own pleasure.

"Mistress," Lindsey whispered. "Please kiss me."

"Where do you want me to kiss you?" Camilla asked.

"Everywhere."

Camilla pushed Lindsey's shoulder down to the bed so that she was lying on her back, then dipped low, kissing Lindsey's lips, and up behind her ear, and down the side of her throat. The touch of Camilla's soft lips made Lindsey's skin sprout goosebumps. Camilla painted a swathe of kisses down to Lindsey's breasts, then took a nipple in her mouth, circling it with her tongue.

"Oh god." Lindsey's head fell back, her toes curling to grip the sheet beneath her.

Camilla switched to the other nipple, her hands trailing down Lindsey's sides. Lindsey's chest rose up to meet her. Camilla's hands roamed down Lindsey's hips and thighs as she kissed Lindsey all the way down to her bellybutton.

"Mistress," Lindsey begged. But what did she want? She wanted Camilla to kiss her, to touch her, to fuck her, all at once. "Please-"

"Hush." Camilla looked up at her. "I haven't finished kissing you everywhere yet." Without breaking her gaze, Camilla took the waistband of Lindsey's panties and tugged them down her legs, then she pushed Lindsey's knees apart.

Lindsey trembled. Camilla grazed her lips along the curve of Lindsey's hipbone, down and inward to the apex of Lindsey's thighs. Camilla kissed her way down Lindsey's slit, her mouth skimming over Lindsey's swollen bud.

"Oh!" A dart of pleasure went straight through to Lindsey's core.

Camilla ran her tongue up and down, gliding it over Lindsey's folds. Lindsey moaned. She had never been this wet in her life.

Finally, Camilla settled her lips at Lindsey's clit.

Lindsey seized hold of the pillow above her head, writhing against the sheets. Camilla licked and sucked, harder now, every movement of her tongue bringing Lindsey closer to oblivion. Lindsey's eyes rolled into the back of her head, the pressure inside her mounting.

"Mistress!" Lindsey convulsed on the bed as an orgasm rippled through her. She clutched at the sheets, holding on as if to keep herself from getting washed away. Camilla didn't stop until Lindsey sank back down to the bed, whispering the word Mistress like it was a prayer.

Camilla slid back up beside her and pressed her lips to Lindsey's. Lindsey melted into the kiss.

"Mistress," she said. "Thank you."

Camilla settled next to her. Lindsey rested her head in the crook of her Mistress's neck.

But as her haze of bliss cleared, it was replaced by confusion. She'd just had the most mind-blowing sex of her life. With Camilla. A woman.

Maybe she wasn't as straight as she thought she was.

# CHAPTER NINE

*L*indsey made her way down to the dining room for breakfast. Over a week had passed since she'd arrived, and she had finally learned how to get around the house. And she and Camilla were beginning to get into a routine. Camilla followed her schedule to the letter and spent most of the day working. But they always had meals together and spent long, lazy evenings lounging around before retiring to their separate bedrooms.

Since that night in the playroom, they hadn't returned there, and they hadn't had sex again either. They'd had a long discussion about it. Considering the nature of their relationship, Camilla wanted to make sure that Lindsey was comfortable and didn't feel pressured in any way. Lindsey appreciated Camilla's respect for her boundaries. But she didn't feel pressured. If anything, it was the opposite. She just wanted more.

Camilla had awakened something in Lindsey that night. Her attraction toward Camilla had gone from a vague sense of admiration to something much more real, and Lindsey didn't know what to make of it. Was it just Camilla's dominant side that had the submissive in Lindsey so deeply enthralled? It wasn't real attraction, was it?

When Lindsey reached the dining room, Camilla was already seated at the head of the table, reading a newspaper while she waited for Lindsey. Even though it was 8 a.m., she looked flawlessly put-together, as usual. Perfect hair, light makeup, a stylish blouse and skirt that had to be designer. Despite the fact that she wasn't leaving the manor today, Camilla looked like she was ready to take on the world. Lindsey suspected that Camilla dressed like this every day, even when she was alone in the house.

Lindsey walked over to the table. Several dishes were laid out, and a place was set for Lindsey next to Camilla. June placed a vase of freshly cut flowers in the middle of the table.

"Good morning, Lindsey." Camilla tilted her head for Lindsey to plant a kiss on her cheek.

"Good morning, Mistre-" Lindsey clamped her mouth shut. June was standing right there. Lindsey had never called Camilla "Mistress" in front of anyone else.

"Oh, don't worry about June," Camilla said. "She sees and hears nothing. Isn't that right, June?"

"I'm sorry Ma'am," June said. "I didn't catch that."

"You see? Have a seat, Lindsey."

Lindsey sat down. As June left the room, Lindsey was certain she saw the slightest smirk on the housekeeper's face.

She and Camilla helped themselves to breakfast. It seemed like the spread laid out before them was for Lindsey's benefit. Camilla always ate the same thing—poached eggs on toast with a side of grilled mushrooms and a cup of coffee. Camilla was serious about her coffee. It was one of her many indulgences.

"What do you have planned for the day, Mistress?" Lindsey asked.

"The usual. Work, work, and more work. I'm up to my elbows in paperwork. And I have a video conference with the heads of one of our subsidiaries. There have been some irregularities-" Camilla stopped short. "I'm boring you."

"No, you're not. I like hearing about your job." Lindsey was beginning to enjoy their conversations about even the most mundane things.

"What about you?" Camilla asked. "What's on for the day?"

"I brought a few books with me, so I'm going to start reading them. I never had the time to read when I was working full-time at the call center. And I might go for a swim in the pool later."

"That sounds lovely." Camilla frowned. "Where's June with the coffee?"

As the two of them ate, Lindsey examined Camilla's face. She seemed a little stressed. Lindsey wondered if she should say something, but she wasn't sure if it would help.

After a while, Camilla spoke. "Tonight, after dinner. Why don't we watch a movie together? The theater is very well equipped."

Lindsey swallowed her mouthful of food. "I would like that, Mistress."

Camilla seemed to perk up a bit at that. But it wasn't to last. A moment later, June returned to the dining room with a pot of coffee.

"I'm sorry, Ma'am," she said. "We've run out of the Brazilian coffee beans you like."

"Really, June?" Camilla said. "Again?"

"The suppliers have run out. I found you a Colombian blend that's very similar. Just until we can get more."

"That will have to do." Camilla waved June over.

June poured Camilla a cup of coffee and scurried out of the room. Camilla didn't even give her as much as a thank you. She knew Camilla hated any deviations from her routine, but this seemed like an overreaction.

Camilla pushed away her plate, which she'd barely touched, and stood up. "I'm going to get to work. I'll see you at lunchtime." Without another word, Camilla picked up her cup of coffee and left the dining room.

Midday arrived, but Camilla didn't come down for lunch. Lindsey assumed it was because she was busy with work. But when dinnertime rolled around, and Camilla didn't emerge from her rooms, Lindsey began to wonder whether something was wrong. It was just like the first few days after Lindsey had arrived.

As Lindsey finished off her dinner, June entered the dining room. "Is there anything else you need?"

"I'm good," Lindsey said. "Is everything okay with Camilla?"

"Everything is fine."

"Then why didn't she come down for dinner?"

"Look," June said. "You should probably get used to this. It happens with Camilla sometimes."

"But why?" Lindsey asked. "What's going on?"

"It's not my place to say. And I'd recommend that you don't ask her about it either. Let her tell you if and when she wants to."

"Is she okay, at least?"

"Yes, she's all right. Is there anything else I can do for you?"

Lindsey took the hint. "No. Thanks, June."

June nodded and began clearing the table. Lindsey got up and headed back to her room. It was safe to say that her and Camilla's plan to watch a movie together was canceled.

Lindsey sighed. Things had gone from wonderful to confusing in the space of a few days. She thought about calling Faith to talk. Although they had spoken yesterday, Lindsey hadn't told Faith that she'd had sex with Camilla. She didn't think Faith would understand why Lindsey felt so uneasy about it. Faith's Zen attitude to life never helped when Lindsey was worried about something. And these days, all she did was worry.

Lindsey stopped at the bottom of the stairs. She would have to find some way to entertain herself for the rest of the night. She decided to check out the home theater by herself. A movie night was just what she needed.

All she had to do was find the theater. Lindsey knew it was on the second floor somewhere. She could ask June, but Lindsey didn't like bothering her over small things. She still wasn't used to having 'help,' which was what Camilla called the mostly invisible staff who ran the house.

Lindsey headed upstairs and began to wander, opening doors at random. She found the library, and the gym, but no theater. She was sure it was nearby, but everything looked different at night.

Lindsey continued down the hall. Soon, she found herself facing a set of white double doors.

The doors to Camilla's rooms.

Lindsey stopped before them. Camilla had made it clear that Lindsey wasn't allowed past this point without her express permission. But Lindsey was tired of being kept in the dark. And she was worried. Camilla had seemed off at breakfast in the morning. What if something was wrong?

Tentatively, Lindsey pulled one of the doors open and peeked past them into the hall. It was empty. She glanced over her shoulder. No one else was around. She slipped through the door and closed it behind her.

Lindsey started down the hall. What was she doing in here, anyway? Was she going to knock on Camilla's door and try to talk to her? Spy on her just to make sure she was in one piece? Burst in and demand to know what was going on?

Lindsey rounded a corner. When she reached the door to the playroom, she paused in front of it. All kinds of naughty thoughts about the other night filled her mind. As she stood there silently, she heard voices coming from the end of the hall.

Raised voices.

Before Lindsey knew what she was doing, she was walking toward the voices. As she got closer, they became clearer.

"I pay you to look after the house, not to nag me." Camilla. Her voice was shrill. "I should replace you with someone who actually follows my orders."

*What the hell?* Lindsey stopped at the door to the room the voices were coming from. It was open, just a crack, but Lindsey couldn't see through it. She listened instead.

"We both know you're not going to do that, Camilla." *June?* It was June's voice, but it had a firmer, less deferential tone. And Lindsey had never heard June address Camilla by anything other than 'Ma'am.'

"Will you just leave me alone?" Camilla said.

"Sure, I'll leave you alone. Right after you eat something."

"Do I look like I want to eat anything?"

"There's no better time than now," June said. "Those painkillers should have kicked in."

"Well, they aren't doing shit."

"I'm sorry, Camilla. But you still need to eat. You haven't eaten anything all day."

Camilla let out a groan that made Lindsey's stomach lurch.

Against her better judgment, Lindsey pushed the door open even more, just enough so that she could see inside. The large room was dark, lit by a single lamp next to Camilla's bed at the far side of the room. Lindsey could only just make out Camilla's figure on the bed, curled up in a ball, the sheets twisted around her. Her hair clung to her forehead, and her cheeks were pale.

"Come on, Camilla." June was seated in an armchair by the bed, her arms crossed. A covered silver serving tray sat on the nightstand next to her. "You've been running yourself into the ground lately. You can't afford to not look after yourself. You know that just makes things worse."

Camilla uttered a curse which Lindsey was shocked to hear come out of her mouth. "Fine. If it'll get you off my case."

"Good." June picked up the tray from the nightstand. "And will you be getting out of bed, Ma'am?"

"I'll sit at the table," Camilla said through gritted teeth. "I hope you're happy."

"In a few days, you'll be happy that you got out of bed. The last thing either of us needs is you stomping around the house, angry that you let yourself lie around doing nothing."

"I hate that you're right," Camilla grumbled.

"I'd be pretty bad at my job if I hadn't figured out what you're like after all these years." June got up and turned toward the table at the other side of the room.

The table that was right between the bed and the door.

*Shit.* Before Lindsey could act, June spotted her and froze.

Camilla turned toward where June was looking. "What-" Her eyes locked onto Lindsey's, and her face clouded over.

Lindsey's every instinct told her to shut the door and get out of there as quickly as possible. But Camilla's eyes held her there. And even from this distance, Lindsey could see every emotion boiling within them. Surprise. Disappointment. Anger. Betrayal.

Lindsey's heart sank. She had messed up. She had seen something Camilla didn't want her to see. But Lindsey's concern outweighed her guilt. Camilla could yell and scream at her all she wanted. She just needed to know that Camilla was okay.

But Lindsey didn't get the chance to ask. Her eyes still on Lindsey's, Camilla spoke, her cold voice cutting through the air.

"Close the door, June."

"Yes, Ma'am." The housekeeper walked over to the door and shut it in Lindsey's face.

# CHAPTER TEN

"*W*hy won't you tell me what's going on?" Lindsey asked.

June began clearing dinner from the table, stacking the dishes on the dining cart next to her. "We've been through this. All you need to know is that she's okay."

It had been two days since Lindsey had witnessed the scene in Camilla's room. Two days, and she still hadn't seen Camilla. Lindsey had asked June about her a dozen times, but the housekeeper remained tight-lipped. Even more infuriatingly, June continued to act like nothing had happened at all.

"She didn't look okay." Lindsey's mind went back to that night. She'd gone over it again and again in her head. From what Lindsey had overheard, it sounded like it was something that happened a lot. Was Camilla sick? Was there something seriously wrong with her? Was she dying? Naturally, her mind went to the worst possible explanations. "If she's okay, why is she still locked up in her rooms?"

"She's not locked up," June said. "She has everything she needs."

"Can't you just tell me what's wrong with her?" Lindsey's voice shook. "Please, June."

June stopped what she was doing. "Look, it's not my place to say. Camilla doesn't like to talk about it."

"Camilla can speak for herself."

Lindsey and June turned to the doorway where Camilla stood. She was dressed in a pale pink satin robe, her brown hair hanging loose. She looked a lot better than the other night, but she seemed drained, and her lips were pressed in a thin line.

"Good evening, Ma'am," June said, as if nothing was out of the ordinary. "Would you like some dinner?"

"Later," Camilla replied. "I need to have a word with Lindsey."

*Oh.* Lindsey had been so worried about Camilla that she hadn't given much thought to the fact that she'd gone into Camilla's rooms when Camilla had expressly forbidden it.

And Camilla looked furious.

"I'll get out of your hair." June grabbed the cart of dishes and practically sprinted out of the room.

Camilla strode to the head of the table and sat down. "Lindsey." She clasped her hands in front of her. "We need to talk about the other night."

Lindsey's stomach stirred. Camilla's face was hard and cold. Just how mad was she? Would she throw Lindsey out? End their arrangement? Lindsey didn't care at that point. She just wanted to know that Camilla was all right.

"I'm sorry you had to see me like that," Camilla said.

"What do you mean?" Lindsey asked. "I just want to know what's going on. Are you okay?"

"I'm fine. I have a chronic medical condition called endometriosis."

"What's that?"

"It's what happens when the tissue that lines the uterus starts growing in other places in the body," Camilla said. "Places where it shouldn't grow."

Lindsey frowned. That sounded horrifying.

"It's relatively benign. But it causes some problems with inflammation and pain, as well as a laundry list of other symptoms. If you want the grisly details, you can look it up."

"Is it going to kill you?" Lindsey asked.

"What? No, not at all." Camilla paused. "You were that worried?"

"Of course I was! You just disappeared without a word, for the second time, and then I saw you curled up in bed in too much pain to eat, talking about taking painkillers and yelling at June to leave you alone! What was I supposed to think?"

Camilla's expression softened. "You're right. I'm sorry. I would have spoken to you sooner if I knew you were so concerned. I assure you, I have a long and full life ahead of me, okay?"

Lindsey nodded.

"Now, is there anything else?"

"No." Lindsey had a million other questions, but it was clear that Camilla didn't want to discuss this any further.

"That's not all I wanted to speak to you about," Camilla said. "You came into my rooms without my permission. You invaded my privacy. You broke one of my rules."

"I'm sorry." Lindsey looked down at the table. "I was just worried about you."

"That doesn't change the fact that my rooms are off limits. You agreed to the rules when you came here. And you agreed that if you broke them, you would be punished."

*Crap.* Lindsey had forgotten all about that part of their agreement.

"I want five hundred lines. 'I will not go into my Mistress's rooms without her permission.' Five hundred lines, neat and legible."

"Yes, Mistress," Lindsey replied.

"I'll check on your progress tomorrow night." With that, Camilla got up and marched out of the room.

---

Lindsey put down her pen and flexed her fingers. She'd spent most of the day at the desk in her sitting room, writing "I will not go into my Mistress's rooms without her permission" over and over again, and she had barely made any progress.

She let out a groan of frustration. At this rate, it would take her days! Lindsey had chosen writing lines as a punishment because she thought it would be easier than the other options, but she hadn't anticipated the number of lines Camilla would make her write.

And real punishment was nowhere near as fun as the 'discipline' Camilla had doled out in the playroom that night.

Lindsey began again. *I will not go into my Mistress's rooms...*

She sighed. After she learned that Camilla was not, in fact, dying, she began to feel the weight of what she'd done. Lindsey hadn't just disobeyed Camilla's orders. She'd violated Camilla's privacy in a big way, and she'd seen Camilla at her most vulnerable. It was obvious that Camilla didn't like being vulnerable.

There was a knock on the door to Lindsey's sitting room. Was it Camilla, come to check on her? She got up and opened the door.

"Oh. I mean, hi June."

"I brought you some dinner." June held up a tray. "You didn't come down, so I thought you might be hungry."

"Thanks." Lindsey had been so busy writing lines that she'd lost track of time. Besides, her overwhelming guilt had caused her to lose her appetite.

"I'll set it up for you over there." June headed to the table by the window and set the tray down. She removed the lid and laid everything out. "Do you need anything else?"

"No." Lindsey paused. "Did Camilla go down for dinner?"

"No. She's still not feeling well."

"Oh."

"Are you all right?" June asked.

"I'm fine." But Lindsey couldn't keep her voice from quavering. "Thanks for bringing dinner."

June hovered by the table. "Lindsey, Camilla isn't angry with you."

"She seemed pretty angry to me," Lindsey said.

"Well, yes, she's angry with you. But she's mostly angry that she didn't get to choose how you found out about her illness."

"Did she say that?" Lindsey asked.

"No," June replied. "But I've known her for so long that it isn't hard for me to tell what's going on in her head." She patted Lindsey on the shoulder. "I'll come back for everything in an hour."

As June left the room, Lindsey noted to herself that for a woman who 'sees and hears nothing,' June sure knew a lot about what was going on between Lindsey and Camilla. But Lindsey was grateful. She was beginning to think she'd need an instruction manual to understand Camilla. And after the scene she'd witnessed, it was clear that June and Camilla were closer than they seemed.

As Lindsey ate her dinner, she thought on June's words. Maybe this punishment wasn't just because Lindsey had broken Camilla's rules. But it wasn't because she was mad at Lindsey either. Maybe it was Camilla's way of taking back control the way Lindsey had taken control away from Camilla.

A short while later, June returned to collect Lindsey's tray. When she was done clearing the table, June announced that Camilla wanted to see her.

"She's in her bedroom," June said. "Do you remember the way, or do you want me to take you?"

"I remember." Lindsey hesitated. "She said I should go to her room?"

June's lips curled up at one side. "I see you've learned your lesson. Yes, Camilla gave you her express permission to go to her room. She also said to 'bring your lines.' I'm assuming that means something to you."

Lindsey nodded. So there were things that June didn't know about her and Camilla's relationship after all. Lindsey liked that she and Camilla still had their secrets.

"I recommend you don't keep her waiting," June said.

"Right. Thanks."

Once June had left the room, Lindsey grabbed her notepad and made her way to Camilla's wing. She was nowhere near finished with her lines yet, but at least she could show Camilla her progress.

Lindsey went through the white double doors and continued past the playroom until she reached Camilla's bedroom. She knocked on the door and waited.

"Come in," Camilla said.

Lindsey opened the door. The room looked a lot brighter than last time she'd seen it. Camilla was sitting up in bed, her legs stretched out and crossed at the ankles. She had a book face down on her lap. Although she didn't seem to be back to her normal self, she looked a lot better than the night before. But she still wore that same cold expression.

Camilla pointed to the bed next to her. "Come. Sit."

Lindsey sat down. "I'm sorry. I haven't finished my lines yet."

"It's all right." Camilla took the notepad from Lindsey's hand and placed it on the other side of the bed. "This isn't about the lines. I wanted to talk to you about everything that's happened."

"I'm sorry," Lindsey said again. "I know I shouldn't have gone into your rooms without permission, and I know I shouldn't have spied on you." Her lip quivered. "I'm sorry for forcing you to tell me about something you didn't want me to know about."

"Lindsey, it wasn't that I didn't want to tell you. What I wanted was to tell you on my terms. You found out in the worst way. And you saw me on one of my worst days in a long time. I wasn't ready to tell you. Not yet."

"You could have told me," Lindsey said. "I would have understood."

"It's always hard to know how someone will react. Most people react badly."

"How do you mean?"

"Where do I begin?" Camilla said. "There are the people who dismiss what I go through as 'lady problems,' or don't understand how debilitating it can be. They see me walking around and living life like everyone else, so they don't believe there is anything really wrong, and they think I'm just being lazy when I can't do things because I'm ill. It's the curse of an invisible illness."

"I would never think anything like that," Lindsey said.

"I wasn't afraid you would. Although it's frustrating, I can deal with people like that. What's worse is when people pity me." Camilla's eyes focused on something in the distance. "I don't want pity. I don't want to be told that it's amazing that I'm still able to live my life despite everything. Sure, it's hard sometimes. But that's just how it is for me. We all have to play the hand we've been dealt." Camilla gave Lindsey a half smile. "And I have to say, apart from my illness, I've been dealt a very good one."

Camilla's voice grew fainter. "I don't want you to treat me any differently. I don't want anything to change between us. And most of all, I don't want this to change the way you see me."

"Camilla." Lindsey placed her hand on Camilla's arm. "This isn't going to change the way I see you. There's nothing that could make me see you as anything other than the strong, funny, beautiful woman you are. And I promise you. Nothing is going to change between us."

Camilla leaned over and kissed Lindsey on the forehead. "Consider your punishment over."

"Really? But I'm nowhere near finished."

"I'm feeling generous. No more lines. But there's something else I need you to do."

"Anything, Mistress," Lindsey said.

Camilla patted the spot on the bed next to her. "Stay here and keep me company for a while."

Lindsey climbed onto the enormous bed and sat down next to Camilla. After a moment or so, she placed her head in Camilla's lap. Camilla's hand fell to Lindsey's head. She stroked her fingers through Lindsey's hair.

A feeling of warmth spread through her. She still had plenty of questions she wanted to ask Camilla, but they could wait for another time.

Camilla broke the silence. "Tell me something about yourself. Something I don't know."

"Uh," Lindsey racked her brains. "I have the same birthday as Benjamin Franklin?"

"That's interesting, but not what I meant. Something meaningful."

Lindsey was silent for a moment. "I used to want to be an artist. I went to art school and everything. But I gave up on the idea after I graduated."

"Oh?" Camilla said. "What changed?"

Lindsey shrugged. "I grew up."

Camilla brushed Lindsey's hair out of her face and looked down at her. "Growing up doesn't mean giving up on your dreams."

"It did for me," Lindsey said. "I have too many bills to pay. And even if I didn't, the chances of me being able to make a living from my art aren't great. That's the reality of being an artist."

"What kind of art do you make?"

"I draw and paint. Well, I used to. I haven't for a while."

"You don't even do it for fun?" Camilla asked.

"Nope. I don't really feel like it these days." Lindsey shut her eyes. "It was a childish dream anyway."

# CHAPTER ELEVEN

"I'm so stuffed," Camilla said. "I can barely move."

Lindsey murmured in agreement. The two of them were sprawled out in the lounge just off the dining room, finishing the bottle of wine they'd opened with dinner. Camilla had recovered from her 'flare-up,' which was what she called those periods where her illness got worse, and she was back to her usual self. In fact, she seemed even livelier than before.

"June should have finished drawing my bath by now." Camilla turned to Lindsey. "Would you like to join me?"

Camilla often disappeared to take long baths before bed. This was the first time she had invited Lindsey to join her nightly ritual. The two of them in the bath together? That could only lead to one thing.

Lindsey's entire body sizzled. That night in the playroom seemed like an eternity ago. Since then, Lindsey and Camilla had barely done more than kiss. It only made Lindsey's desire for her grow. Almost every night, Lindsey would lie awake, alternating between thinking about how good it had felt, and wondering why she felt anything at all.

It shouldn't have been a problem for Lindsey. She'd always been open-minded when it came to all things sex and sexuality. She had no reason to resist what she felt toward Camilla. But this was uncharted, unfamiliar territory. Lindsey had never looked at another woman the way she looked at Camilla, never thought about one the way she thought about Camilla every night.

And she certainly had never wanted to get naked in a bathtub with one.

"Where did you go just now, Lindsey?" Camilla asked.

"Uh, nowhere," Lindsey replied.

"Well, if you're not interested, I'll have to take a bath all by myself." Camilla's voice took on a low, sultry timbre. "It's a pity. I was looking forward to having you in there with me, all naked and dripping wet."

Lindsey swallowed. "I'll take a bath with you, Mistress."

The two of them made their way up to Camilla's bathroom. As soon as Lindsey walked through the door, she was hit with the scent of flowers. It was coming from the enormous tub in the corner which was filled to the brim with milky water covered in a layer of petals. Bubbles propelled by underwater jets rose to the surface, and the air above the bath was thick with steam.

Was this what Camilla's nightly baths were like? No wonder she enjoyed them so much.

Camilla shut the door behind her and sat down on the edge of the bathtub. "Undress," Camilla said. "Then undress me."

"Yes, Mistress!" Lindsey pulled her dress up over her head and hung it on a hook by the door, then slipped out of her bra and panties. Camilla's piercing eyes watched her the entire time. It only excited Lindsey more.

Once her clothes were hung up neatly, Lindsey returned to where Camilla sat.

Camilla straightened out her legs. "Start with my shoes."

Lindsey removed her Mistress's heels one by one, then placed them carefully to the side. Camilla stood up and turned around. Slowly, Lindsey unzipped Camilla's dress, exposing the golden skin of her back inch by inch. She pulled it off, then peeled away Camilla's bra.

Camilla turned to face her. The sight of her Mistress's near-naked body made Lindsey swoon. Camilla's flawless skin glowed, and her hips and breasts were luscious and full. Lindsey found herself wanting to kiss them, and bury herself in them, and get lost in them for hours on end.

"As much as I appreciate you admiring me, I'd like to get into this bath before it gets cold," Camilla said.

Lindsey snapped out of her trance. "Sorry, Mistress."

She looked down at Camilla's panties. They were made of cream-colored silk. Camilla seemed to love silk. Silk sheets, silk nighties, silk lingerie. And these tiny silk panties that Lindsey had just been instructed to remove.

Lindsey dropped to her knees and pulled Camilla's panties down her hips and all the way to the ground. She barely caught a glimpse of what was underneath them before Camilla turned and stepped into the bath.

Camilla slid down into the steamy water with a satisfied groan. "Hang my things up and come join me."

Lindsey did as she was instructed, then got into the bath in front of Camilla, sitting between her legs. Camilla draped her arms around Lindsey's shoulders, pulling her in close. The bathtub was big enough that the two of them could fit without even touching. But where was the fun in that?

"I'll be going away next week," Camilla said. "For five days or so."

"Where are you going?" Lindsey asked.

"To Seattle for work. I have an event to attend the night before I leave, so I'll be staying in the city then going straight to the airport in the morning. It's a fundraising gala for a library downtown. These things are always so dull, but considering I practically gave them the building, I should probably make an appearance."

"You gave away a building?"

"I sold it for a fraction of what it was worth, so I might as well have," Camilla said. "Anyway, I'm letting you know in case you don't want to be alone in the manor while I'm gone. Some people get lonely in this big, secluded house. I won't be offended if you want to make other arrangements."

"I don't mind," Lindsey said. "I think I'll stay."

"You can always go into the city for a day or two. I'll even get you a hotel room if you want to stay the night. Or, you can invite a friend to come here for a few days."

"That could be fun." Lindsey waved her hands through the cloudy water in front of her, gathering a handful of petals. "Faith has been dying to see the place."

"Oh?" Camila said. "You've been telling her all about the manor? About us?"

"Only a little." Well, it was more than a little. Lindsey told Faith everything. Except for the fact that she and Camilla had slept together.

"It's fine, I don't mind if you talk to her about us. And she's more than welcome to come visit."

"Thanks. I'll ask her." Lindsey slipped a little deeper into the bath. "Mistress?"

"Yes?"

"You've been living in the manor by yourself for a while, haven't you?"

"Ever since my parents passed 15 years ago," Camilla replied. "I often have guests though. Friends, relatives, the occasional lover."

"Do you ever get lonely out here in this big house?" Lindsey asked.

"No. I've always preferred solitude, ever since I was a child. I think that's why I like this place so much. My sister used to think I was a freak because I spent every summer of my childhood hiding in the hedge maze reading books. Or I'd just go in there to get away from the craziness inside the manor. You'd think in a house this big, it would be easier to find some peace and quiet."

Lindsey turned to look at Camilla. "You have a sister?"

"She's ten years older than me," Camilla said. "We don't speak very often."

"Why not?"

"We don't exactly get along." Camilla drew her hands down the front of Lindsey's shoulders. "But my sister is the last person I want to think about when I have a beautiful naked woman in my bathtub."

Camilla's hands slithered down to Lindsey's chest. Lindsey's breath hitched. She couldn't help but feel like Camilla was trying to distract her from their conversation. But Lindsey wasn't complaining. She'd been turned on since the moment Camilla had commanded her to undress.

"Lie back and let your Mistress take care of you," Camilla said.

Lindsey leaned back against Camilla, sinking into her skin. Camilla's breasts pressed into her back, and the scent of the rose petals mingled with the steam from the bath, making her head spin. Camilla began massaging Lindsey's breasts with her slick, soapy fingers. A flood of heat went through her.

Camilla ran her hands downward, all the way to the insides of Lindsey's thighs. She pulled them apart gently and slipped a finger into Lindsey's slit. Lindsey's mouth fell open in a silent moan.

"Are you wet because we're in the bath?" Camilla asked. "Or are you wet for me?"

"For you, Mistress," Lindsey replied.

"Aren't I lucky?" Camilla glided her finger up and down. "I want you to ask me for permission before you come, okay?"

"Yes, Mistress."

Camilla dragged a finger up to Lindsey's clit, circling it slowly. "I'm having some special items made for you." Camilla's other hand crept back up to Lindsey's breasts. "For both of us. Once they arrive, I'm going to take you into the playroom again. Would you like that?"

"Yes, Mistress," Lindsey whispered.

"I'm looking forward to it. I love toying with this lovely body of yours."

Between Lindsey's legs, Camilla's fingers had gone from slow and light to hard and fast. The soap-filled water made every touch feel even more sensual.

Lindsey exhaled sharply. It hadn't been long, but she was already close. Her head tipped back onto Camilla's shoulder. Camilla responded by kissing and biting Lindsey's bared neck.

Lindsey shuddered. "Mistress, can I come?"

"Not yet," Camilla said. "And if you do, I'll be very disappointed."

Lindsey groaned and let out a curse.

Camilla withdrew her hand. "Watch your language."

*Seriously?* Some of Camilla's demands were ridiculous, but Lindsey wasn't about to argue with the woman who had control over her pleasure. "Sorry, Mistress."

Camilla slid her hand back down to stroke Lindsey between her thighs. Lindsey whimpered. Her eyes screwed shut as she focused all her energy on holding back the storm raging within her and keeping herself from going over the edge. Just when she thought she couldn't take anymore, Camilla spoke.

"You may come now."

At once, an eruption went off inside Lindsey. Her cry echoed through the bathroom as she bucked against Camilla. Her Mistress held her in place, her fingers still strumming away until every drop of pleasure had been drained out of Lindsey.

She let out a breath. "Thank you, Mistress."

Camilla continued to caress Lindsey's body, her fingers wandering over Lindsey's skin. She traced her hand along Lindsey's collarbone, skimming the long scar that ran along it.

"Where did this come from?" Camilla asked.

"It's from the car accident," Lindsey replied. "Well, the surgery that came after it. I broke my collarbone." She brought her hand up to touch it. It had healed well, and most of the time, she forgot that it was even there.

"I'm sorry, I didn't mean to bring up something sensitive."

"It's all right," Lindsey said. "I have another one on my thigh. I broke my leg too, among other things."

Camilla took Lindsey's hand. "Turn around."

Lindsey twisted to face her. Camilla guided Lindsey's hand down her stomach.

"Do you feel that scar?" She ran Lindsey's finger over a little dip in Camilla's skin. "It's from surgery for endometriosis. I have three of them."

Lindsey had noticed the three round dimples on Camilla's

stomach when undressing her earlier, but she hadn't thought anything of it.

"You see?" Camilla said. "You're not the only one with battle scars."

Lindsey smiled softly. It was nice to know they had that in common. But it wasn't those scars that Lindsey cared about. After her accident, she'd realized that the worst scars were the ones no one could see.

# CHAPTER TWELVE

"*H*ave you finished with your breakfast?" Camilla asked. "There's something I need to show you."

Lindsey gulped down the last of her coffee. "All done." She got up and followed Camilla out of the dining room. "Where are we going?"

"You'll see in a moment."

Camilla led Lindsey through the house, walking with purposeful strides. It seemed like whatever she wanted to show Lindsey was of the utmost importance.

Camilla stopped in front of a door. "Here we are. Why don't you have a look inside?"

Lindsey opened the door and entered the room. It was a large, light-filled space, enclosed by glass walls on three sides. The view of the grounds outside was magnificent. The room was set up like an artist studio, and a well-equipped one at that. There were easels, a drawing table, and an assortment of art supplies.

"What is this?" Lindsey asked.

"This is the sunroom," Camilla replied. "At least, it used to be. Now, it's your studio."

Lindsey had visited this room while exploring the day she'd

arrived at the manor. Back then, it had been furnished with a lounge and a couple of armchairs. "Where did all this come from?"

"Most of the furniture was in storage in the east wing. The easels, the drawing table—they belonged to my grandmother." Camilla strolled up to the table by the window and ran her hand over the smooth, dark wood. "As for the art supplies, I had them delivered yesterday. I wasn't sure what you'd need, so I asked a friend of mine who's an artist to recommend some basics."

Basics didn't even begin to describe everything in the room. It held everything an artist could ever need. Canvases of all shapes and sizes. Pencils, sketch pads, different types of paints. And all of it was of the finest quality, from all the best brands. Camilla's friend had advised her well.

"I hope this is adequate," Camilla said.

"This is more than adequate. I would have killed for this stuff in art school." Lindsey peered into a box filled with very expensive oil paints. She felt a twinge of guilt.

"What's wrong?"

Lindsey hesitated. "I don't know if I'm going to use it, that's all."

"That's where you're wrong," Camilla said. "I've decided you have it too easy doing nothing all day when I'm working. So you're going to do some work of your own."

"What do you mean?"

"From now on, you're going to spend an hour in here after breakfast every day working on your art."

Lindsey opened her mouth, then shut it again. Was Camilla seriously going to force her to do this? "But-"

Camilla folded her arms across her chest. "This isn't a request."

Heat bubbled up inside Lindsey's stomach. For the first time in as long as she could remember, she felt angry.

"You can't just tell me what to do!" Lindsey said.

"The last time I checked, I've been telling you what to do for weeks now," Camilla replied.

"This is different. This isn't like everything else!"

"Why not?"

Hot tears gathered at the corners of Lindsey's eyes. Why was she suddenly finding it so hard to express herself?

"Apple," she said.

At once, Camilla took Lindsey's hand and drew her to a window seat beside them. "I'm sorry, darling. Are you all right?"

"Yeah," Lindsey grumbled.

"I was trying to help. I thought you needed a little push. But I pushed you too hard, didn't I?"

Lindsey nodded. Her frustration had reduced to a simmer.

"Do you want to talk about it?" Camilla asked. "When we spoke the other night in my room, it was obvious that you didn't really want to give up on your art. I could hear it in your voice. Is something holding you back?"

"It's just that, it used to be so easy," Lindsey said. "I used to have this constant desire to create. I used to find inspiration everywhere I looked. But now, every time I even think about trying to draw, or paint, or anything else, it's like I'm paralyzed. I just... can't."

"Well, my grandmother used to say that creating art is work like anything else. Sure, you need talent and inspiration. But sometimes, you just need to sit down and do it."

"I don't think I can."

"You'll never know if you don't try," Camilla said.

Lindsey frowned in thought. It was true that she hadn't actually tried. She'd told herself that she was too busy, or that there was no point because she was never going to be able to make a living from her art.

But those reasons alone shouldn't have stopped her from doing what she loved. Were they just excuses? As Lindsey looked around the studio, she realized she was avoiding the truth. She was scared. Scared that she'd fail. Scared that she'd lost that innate part of herself that was capable of creating great things.

Scared that the person she was before the accident no longer existed.

"Do you think you can do that for me?" Camilla asked. "Just try? Maybe not this morning, or even today, or tomorrow. But one day, in the time you have left living here with me, will you try to find the joy that art used to bring you?"

Lindsey blinked away her half-formed tears. "Okay," she said quietly. "I'll try. I'll try now." She knew that if she put it off any longer, she'd lose her resolve.

Camilla kissed her gently. "Are you going to be okay?"

"Yes. I will."

"If you're not, come find me in my office. And remember, this room is yours, and yours alone. I'll never come in here without your permission. If you need more supplies or anything specific that you can't find in here, let me know, and I'll get it for you."

Lindsey nodded.

"I'll leave you to it."

Moments later, Lindsey was alone in the room. She felt so overwhelmed. Where should she even start? She hadn't picked up a pencil or a paintbrush since she'd finished her art degree. Did she still have it in her? That passion that fueled her creativity? That sense of wonder about the world around her, and that need to capture it all on a piece of paper or canvas?

Could she ever get that passion back again?

Lindsey didn't have a choice but to try. Camilla had decreed it. Sure, Lindsey didn't really have to listen to her. But she knew that if she didn't, Camilla would be so disappointed.

She gazed out toward the garden just outside. This particular garden was filled with bright, colorful lilies. The sky was clear and the morning sun cast dappled light through the leaves of the nearby trees. As Lindsey looked on, a tiny bird flew down to perch on the edge of a birdbath in the center of the garden.

*Seriously?* The scene couldn't have been more picturesque. Clearly, it was a sign.

Lindsey glanced over at the desk. On top of it was a sketchpad and an assortment of pencils and boxes of charcoal. She grabbed the sketchpad and a stick of charcoal, pulled a chair over to the window, and sat down.

Taking a deep breath, she put the charcoal to the paper and began to sketch.

Lindsey put her sketchpad down in her lap. It had taken her several attempts, but she'd finally managed to capture the scene before her in a way that she didn't hate. The lighting wasn't right, and the leaves on the trees were nothing more than vague scribbles, but it was a lot better than her first few attempts. The floor around her was littered with crumpled up balls of sketch paper.

Lindsey looked around. She was sure there was a clock in here somewhere. She spotted the old timepiece on the sideboard and gasped. It was 12:30. She'd been in here for hours! And she was late for lunch with Camilla. Lindsey cursed. One of Camilla's rules was to stick to the schedule.

And Lindsey had learned her lesson about breaking Camilla's rules.

She returned her sketchpad to the desk, and dashed out into the hall, heading for the dining room. When she reached it, she almost knocked June over outside the doorway. Lindsey murmured an apology and entered the room.

Camilla was sitting at her place at the table, flicking through a newspaper, her empty plate pushed aside. She looked up at Lindsey. "How nice of you to finally join me."

"I'm sorry, Mistress!" Lindsey said. "I lost track of time. I was working on a sketch."

"In that case, I'll let it slide." Camilla pushed out the chair next to her. "Sit. June will bring you lunch."

Lindsey sat down, her stomach rumbling. She hadn't realized how hungry she was. Almost immediately, June appeared and set down a plate of sandwiches before Lindsey, then disappeared again. Lindsey began to wolf them down.

"I take it you were enjoying yourself?" Camilla asked.

"I don't know if enjoying is the right word," Lindsey said. "It was difficult. And frustrating. It was like I'd forgotten everything I'd ever learned. But after a while, it all came back to me." A smile spread across her face. "God, I'd forgotten what that felt like. To get so lost in something that it's like the rest of the world just fades away. It's a great feeling."

"I'm happy for you," Camilla said. "And I'm proud of you."

A warm flush washed over her. "You were right. I just needed a little push."

After a few more minutes of conversation, Camilla got up and placed her hand on Lindsey's forearm. "I have to go make a few work calls. But once you're done with lunch, come find me in the library and we can spend a bit of time together. Unfortunately, I need to get some work done, but I can do it with you there."

"Okay, Mistress."

Lindsey finished off her lunch, then left the dining room, nearly barreling June over for the second time. She apologized again, then headed to the library. She didn't know why she was in such a hurry. The events of the morning had filled her with nervous energy.

Lindsey knocked on the door.

"Come in," Camilla said.

Lindsey entered the library. It was one of the smaller rooms in the house, consisting of little more than a desk and two armchairs. But every inch of the walls, from the floor to the high ceiling, was covered in shelves packed with books. A tall ladder on wheels leaned against one wall.

Camilla was seated in the armchair flicking through some papers. She looked up at Lindsey. "I hope you didn't have trouble finding this place."

"I've been in here before," Lindsey said. "It's pretty impressive."

"This was my mother's library. I like to come here to work when I feel like a change of scenery. You're welcome to borrow any of the books. My mother's collection is quite large and varied."

"Okay. Thanks, Mistress."

Camilla gestured toward the floor by her feet, where a thick velvet cushion lay. "Come sit with me."

Lindsey walked over to her and sat down on the cushion, her legs out to the side. After a moment, she leaned her head against Camilla's legs.

Camilla's hand dropped down to stroke the top of Lindsey's

head. "You know, I'd love to see your art someday. That is, if you ever feel comfortable showing it to me."

"Sure," Lindsey said. "It might be a while until I have anything worth showing you, though. I'm out of practice."

"That's okay. Whenever you're ready."

They lapsed into silence. For a few minutes, the only sounds were the scratching of Camilla's pen and the occasional murmur from Camilla.

Lindsey looked up at her. "Mistress? Can I ask you some questions?"

"You can ask me whatever you like," Camilla said, her focus still on her work. "I might even answer you."

"Well, when you told me about endometriosis, you said to look it up. And I did, but it was all medical stuff. I guess I was wondering what living with it is like for you?"

"Well, it isn't the most glamorous of illnesses," Camilla said. "It's like having horrendous period cramps while constantly feeling exhausted and awful in general. Most of the time it's manageable, but sometimes, it can floor me for days, or even weeks. You've seen how bad it can get for yourself. Mine is a relatively severe case though."

"But, isn't there anything you can do about it?" Lindsey asked. "Doctors? Medications? Treatments?"

"Trust me, I've seen the finest specialists in the country, and I've had every possible treatment. But the reality is that there's a lot that medical science doesn't know how to fix. Endometriosis is one of those things. There are little things that help, but nothing that is actually going to cure me."

"That sucks." Lindsey couldn't think of anything to say that didn't sound inadequate. "I know you said not to feel sorry for you, but it just seems so unfair."

"It does make things hard." Camilla paused to study something on the page in front of her. "But, as I said, I've been dealt a good hand otherwise. I have this house and a job that allows me to have a lot of flexibility, with me being the boss and all. And I don't even need to work. I could live off my inheritance if I wanted to. But I don't want that. My family's company means a lot to me, so I'd rather work, even if it means sacrificing other things."

"Like... relationships?" Lindsey asked.

"I have a few close friends. They're all I need."

"But, don't you want to find love?" Lindsey's question sounded childish, even to her.

"It's just not a priority for me," Camilla said. "I don't have the time or patience for dating anymore. Besides, I've worked hard to build this life for myself. Adding another person to it complicates things. And I don't like change."

Lindsey wasn't surprised that Camilla considered a relationship a 'complication.' She knew how much her Mistress hated any disruptions to her carefully organized life.

"That's not to say I'm not open to love. If the perfect woman turned up on my doorstep, I wouldn't turn her away." Camilla patted Lindsey's head, then grabbed a pen from the table next to her and began to scribble on the document she was holding.

It was clear that she was done answering questions. But Lindsey still had something she wanted to ask her Mistress. "What about..."

"Yes?" Camilla said.

"What about sex?"

"What about it?"

"Well, I read that for women with endometriosis sex can be... hard."

"Yes, it can be for me under some circumstances. But I can still enjoy it. It just requires a lot of care. That's why I prefer to take the reins, so to speak."

"Is that why you're a Domme?" Lindsey asked.

Camilla thought for a moment. "I suppose it is, in a way. But not in the way you think." She put her pen and paper down in her lap. "My illness can be unpredictable at times. Sure, there are patterns, but I never really know when it's going to flare up. When you're dealing with a condition that has a lot of ups and downs, it's easy to feel like you're not in control of your own body, let alone your own life. It can be liberating to take that control back."

"That makes sense," Lindsey said.

"Of course, there are other reasons why I like being a dominant." Camilla drew the back of her finger up the side of Lindsey's cheek. Her voice dropped low. "There's something addictive about making a submissive squirm."

A flicker of lust ran down Lindsey's spine. Camilla sure knew how to make her squirm.

"Now, as much as I enjoy your presence, I should get back to work. Why don't you go take advantage of this lovely afternoon?"

"Okay, Mistress."

Lindsey stood up and shook out her numb legs. She had pushed Camilla far enough out of her comfort zone for the day.

Before leaving the room, Lindsey paused by the door. "Thank you," she said.

"For what?" Camilla asked.

"For pushing me this morning. I needed that."

Camilla gave her a half smile. "I'll see you at dinner. Try not to be late this time."

# CHAPTER THIRTEEN

"Lindsey?" June appeared in the doorway of the sitting room. "Faith has arrived."

Lindsey thanked June and made her way downstairs.

It was Friday evening. Camilla had left for her trip several days ago, and she was due back tomorrow night. Lindsey had spent most of the week enjoying the solitude of the grounds. But Camilla had been right. Lindsey was starting to feel lonely, so she was looking forward to having Faith around, even if it was just for one night.

By the time Lindsey reached the front door, Faith had hopped out of the car.

She spotted Lindsey and waved. "Wow, you weren't kidding about this place. It's huge."

"Yep," Lindsey pulled Faith in for a hug. She'd actually forgotten how awesome the manor was. After living here for a month, it had become normal. Going back to the real world was going to be a rude shock. "What do you want to do first? I can show you around?"

"Sure," Faith said. "Let's start with your room. I want to see all the stuff Camilla bought you."

A few minutes and a greeting from June later, they were in Lind-

sey's bedroom. Lindsey sat on the bed while Faith flicked through her wardrobe, squealing with excitement every now and then.

"If Camilla wants another sugar baby, I volunteer," Faith said.

"You get to keep all this?"

"Yep," Lindsey replied.

Faith pulled out a long evening gown that Lindsey hadn't even worn yet. "This would fetch a great price online."

Lindsey hadn't even thought about that. She'd barely thought about her money problems since she moved in. As promised, Camilla had deposited a generous allowance into Lindsey's bank account every week since she'd arrived, but it wasn't like she needed it. She had everything she needed here at the manor, and Camilla provided whatever Lindsey asked for. She'd practically forgotten that money was a part of the arrangement.

Faith hung the dress back up and joined Lindsey on the bed. "So, you're getting paid to live in this huge mansion. You're getting all this free stuff. And all you have to do is keep some rich woman company?"

"Pretty much," Lindsey replied. "But Camilla isn't 'some rich woman.' She's Camilla. She's pretty incredible." She glanced sideways at her friend. "Besides, we've been doing more than just keeping each other company."

Faith's eyes widened. "Are you saying you've been sleeping with her?"

"Only a couple of times." Even though that particular box had been opened, their relationship was still more about their routine, day-to-day power games than sex.

"And? Did you like it?"

Lindsey nodded. "A lot, actually. And I like her a lot."

"Wow," Faith said. "It sounds like this arrangement is really working out for you."

"Yeah. It is." Lindsey's phone started to ring. She glanced at the screen. "It's Camilla. I should take this."

"Go ahead," Faith grinned. "I'm sure you don't want to keep her waiting."

Lindsey ignored Faith's comment and picked up the phone. "Hi, Camilla."

"*Camilla?* That's no way to address your Mistress." There was a sultry edge to Camilla's voice. "Do I need to get out the cane?"

Heat rushed to Lindsey's face. Not to mention other places. She got up from the bed as casually as she could and turned away to look out the window so Faith couldn't see her bright red face.

"Well?" Camilla said.

"Um, I'm hanging out with Faith at the moment."

"Oh? And you're too shy to call me Mistress in front of her?"

"Yes," Lindsey said.

"If you ask me nicely, I might let it slide," Camilla said.

*Seriously?* Lindsey peered over her shoulder at Faith, who wasn't even pretending not to eavesdrop. "Please?" she mumbled.

"Well that didn't sound sincere at all. I know what you sound like when you beg for real."

A sharp, faint breath escaped from Lindsey's mouth. She clamped her lips shut and stared even more intently out the window, trying not to think about the images Camilla's words conjured up.

"Nevertheless, I'm a generous Mistress. I'll let it go just this once."

"Thank you," Lindsey said.

"Tell Faith I said hello, and to make herself at home."

"I will." Lindsey looked back at Faith, who was sprawled out on the bed. "I should warn you, she's already five minutes away from moving in."

Faith stuck out her tongue.

"Well, she's welcome to stay for a few days if you'd like," Camilla said. "Speaking of which, I have some bad news. I have a lot more to do here than I expected, so I'm going to have to stay a bit longer. I won't be back until Tuesday."

"Oh," Lindsey said. "That's okay."

"Let me make it up to you. I've booked a reservation at my favorite day spa in the city for you and Faith. I hope you don't already have plans tomorrow?"

"No, we don't. Thank you!"

"It's my pleasure. But you're going to have to do something for me too." Camilla's voice took on that serious tone she always used when she made demands. "There's a credit card in the top drawer of the desk in my study. I want you to take it with you when you go into the city tomorrow and buy something to wear the night that I come back."

"What kind of something?" Lindsey asked.

"A dress, and some other pieces. There are several boutiques downtown that I frequent. I'll send you their details, as well as some suggestions. Just mention my name, and they'll help you pick out something appropriate. We'll be having a dinner date in the garden. And after dinner, we'll see where the night takes us. Maybe we'll have dessert in the playroom again."

Lindsey felt a throb of desire. "Okay," she said. But 'Yes, Mistress' was what she really meant.

"I look forward to seeing what you pick out for me."

Lindsey hung up the phone and turned back around. Faith was still stretched out on the bed, smiling.

"What?" Lindsey asked.

"Nothing," Faith replied. "What did Camilla want?"

"She's staying in Seattle for a few more days. She's booked a spa day for us as an apology." Lindsey fell down onto the bed next to her friend. "And, we're going shopping."

---

Lindsey slipped her jeans back on and pulled her blouse over her head, then flattened down her hair in the dressing room mirror. She and Faith only had ten minutes before their spa appointment. They'd been shopping all morning at Camilla's boutiques of choice. The 'suggestions' Camilla sent Lindsey ended up being a set of specific instructions on what to buy.

It was typical of Camilla. Even when asking Lindsey to pick out something herself, Camilla was still pulling the strings. Lindsey didn't mind. She was doing this for her Mistress, after all.

Besides, Lindsey had decided to get a little something to complete the outfit. Something that would really surprise Camilla.

She opened the curtain and joined Faith outside the dressing room.

"What did you decide on?" Faith asked.

Lindsey held up a baby blue bra and panty set made of silk and lace. It cost a fortune, but Camilla was paying for it. Camilla hadn't actually told Lindsey to buy lingerie. Lindsey hoped that Camilla would be pleased by the gesture rather than angry at Lindsey for acting without her Mistress's express permission.

*Her Mistress.* This wasn't the first time Lindsey had thought of Camilla as 'her Mistress' rather than just 'Camilla.' It was happening more and more lately, and it did little to help with Lindsey's confusion about her feelings. It was ironic, really. Lindsey had gone into this faking attraction to Camilla and even faking her sexuality.

But right now, everything felt very real.

"Earth to Lindsey," Faith said.

"Right," Lindsey pulled herself together. "Let's go pay for this."

"Hold on. Is something the matter?"

"I don't know." Lindsey sighed. "It's just that, this whole sugar baby thing was just supposed to be a way to make some money. And then when I met Camilla, we really clicked, and I thought, maybe this could be fun. But now that we've gotten closer, and we're having mind-blowing sex, I've started having all these feelings about her. What does that mean?"

"It doesn't have to mean anything," Faith said. "So you're into Camilla. It's not like you have to slap a rainbow bumper sticker on your car now."

"It's not that simple. I know it is for you, but it isn't for me. I've never been anything other than straight. And if I do have feelings for Camilla, what does that make me?"

"Does it matter? Attraction isn't always black and white. Everyone's experience is different. Maybe you like women. Maybe you just like sex with women. Maybe you just like sex with Camilla. Or maybe, you just like her, period. You don't have to put a label on whatever it is you feel."

"But I don't even know what it is I feel toward her. For starters, I can't figure out whether I'm attracted to her dominant side, or if it's really her that I'm attracted to."

"Aren't they the same thing?" Faith asked. "Isn't her dominant side just a part of her?"

"I guess." After all, Lindsey's submissive side was a part of her too. "But I don't know if my feelings are because we've been doing all these intimate things together and I'm mistaking that closeness for something else. And I don't know whether my attraction to her is romantic, or if I'm just getting caught up in this lie that we're living together. I've never felt anything like this toward another woman before. How am I supposed to know if it's real or not?"

"I don't know," Faith said. "But maybe it would be easier to figure out the answers to these questions if your feelings for Camilla weren't all wrapped up in your ideas about yourself. It sounds like you're trying to come to terms with the fact that maybe your sexuality isn't what you think it is while trying to work out how you feel toward Camilla at the same time." She squeezed Lindsey's arm. "Stop worrying about what you think you should or shouldn't feel, and just let yourself feel it."

Was it really that easy? Could Lindsey just let go of everything she knew about herself and embrace her feelings for Camilla? That undeniable pull she felt whenever she was in her Mistress's presence? That insatiable need to please her? The electric charge that went through Lindsey's body whenever Camilla touched her?

And was there really any point in doing that when everything between them was pretend?

cabinets. However, there was a small wooden chest sitting in the center of the table.

Camilla spoke into Lindsey's ear. "I'm glad you wanted to skip dessert, because I'm going to do all kinds of dirty things to you on that table."

Lindsey sucked in a breath. Her Mistress knew exactly which buttons to push. She led Lindsey over to the table and gestured for her to sit on top of it. Lindsey glanced down at the chest on the tabletop next to her. It was made of dark wood, and it was held shut by a small gold padlock. Etched into the lid in gold calligraphy were the letters 'C.R.' Camilla's initials.

Camilla ran her fingertips over the lid of the chest. "I have a friend who does incredible work with leather. I asked her to make some items for us." She slid the wooden box to the side, away from Lindsey. "No peeking. It's a surprise."

Camilla unlocked the chest and opened it up, the lid blocking Lindsey's view. She reached inside and pulled out a set of interconnected straps made of dark blue leather. Before Lindsey could try to work out what they were for, Camilla placed them on the table, reached into the box again, and produced a pair of leather cuffs. They were the same midnight blue color, with contrasting gold buckles and O-rings. The cuffs were embossed with an intricate design.

"There's more, but I'll save the rest for another time." Camilla shut the lid. "Hold out your arms."

Lindsey presented her wrists. Camilla buckled a cuff around one wrist, then the other.

"There," Camilla said. "Do you like them?"

"I love them." Lindsey held her hands up in front of her, inspecting the cuffs. "They're beautiful."

"They're a real work of art. Look at them closely."

Lindsey examined the cuffs. The buckles and O-rings looked like they were made of real gold. And hanging from each of the O-rings was a small, round tag engraved with the same letters that were on the lid of the box. Lindsey read them out loud. "C.R."

"My initials," Camilla said. "You're all mine now. You'll wear these whenever we're in here."

Lindsey's stomach fluttered. "Thank you, Mistress."

Camilla drew her close and pressed her lips against Lindsey's. The kiss rippled through Lindsey's body. Her Mistress pushed herself between Lindsey's knees and slid a hand up the front of her thigh. Lindsey's dress bunched up around her hips. She held onto the edge of the table, steadying herself against Camilla's dizzying passion.

"These cuffs aren't just for show," Camilla said. "We're going to test them out. But first, let's get you out of that dress."

Camilla pulled Lindsey off the table and untied the belt around her waist. She turned around for Camilla to unzip it at the back. Why had she chosen such a fiddly dress?

Camilla tugged at the zipper. An irritated growl emerged from her chest.

Lindsey peered over her shoulder. "Is it stuck?"

"Yes," Camilla said. "But it's an easy problem to solve."

Without hesitation, Camilla grabbed the top of the dress with both hands and tore it down the seam next to the zipper. The strapless dress fell down around Lindsey's hips.

Lindsey gasped. Camilla had just destroyed the absurdly expensive dress that Lindsey had spent half of Saturday picking out. But Camilla had paid for it after all. It was hers. Lindsey was hers.

And nothing turned Lindsey on more.

She spun back around to find her Mistress's eyes filled with fire. A thrill went through Lindsey's body. Camilla wanted her. To own her, to possess her, to make Lindsey hers. She tugged Lindsey's dress all the way down to the floor, then tore off her own blouse and slacks. Then she drew Lindsey in and smothered her with her lips. Her hands traveled up the side of Lindsey's chest to cradle her breast through her thin silk bra.

"Wait," Camilla pulled back and looked Lindsey up and down, her eyes lingering on the pale blue bra and panties Lindsey wore. "Where did you get these?"

*The lingerie.* Lindsey had been so caught up in the moment that she'd forgotten all about it. "I bought them for you."

"Did you now?" Camilla scrutinized her silently.

"They're a gift for you, Mistress," Lindsey said. "Do you like them?"

Camilla walked around Lindsey in a circle, inspecting her from every angle. "I do like them. You look good enough to eat." She backed Lindsey against the table slowly. "It's a pity I'm going to have to take it all off."

Camilla unclipped Lindsey's bra and tossed it aside, then drew a hand up Lindsey's bare chest. Her other hand slid down to Lindsey's silk panties, which were already wet. Lindsey shivered.

Camilla slipped a finger into the side of Lindsey's panties, fingering her slit. "Do you want your Mistress to fuck you?"

"God, yes." Lindsey hadn't forgotten that Camilla had forbidden her from cursing, but apparently, the rule didn't apply to Camilla. Lindsey wasn't about to argue. Hearing her prim and proper Mistress talk dirty was hot as hell.

Camilla stepped back. "Bend over the table and raise your arms up to the corners."

Lindsey did as her Mistress instructed. The solid wood of the tabletop felt cold against her breasts. Those puzzling leather straps that matched the cuffs on Lindsey's wrists were still sitting on the table in front of her.

Camilla walked over to a cabinet and pulled out two short coils of rope. One by one, she looped a length of rope through the gold ring on each of Lindsey's cuffs and tied them in place. Then she took the other ends of the ropes and tied them around the legs of the table where they met the tabletop.

Lindsey was left bound to the table, bent at the waist, her ass sticking out. The ropes had some give, but it wasn't enough for her to stand or change position. All she could do was wait patiently for her Mistress to give her what she desperately needed.

Camilla picked up the tangle of leather straps from the table and held them up. "Now is the perfect time to test this out."

Lindsey stared at the straps. They looked like some kind of harness. And there was a large gold ring at the front of it all.

Oh. *Oh.*

Lindsey was pretty experienced when it came to sex. But this was one thing she'd never tried, for obvious reasons.

Camilla headed for a set of drawers by the bed, stripping off her bra and panties as she walked. She opened up a drawer and produced a clear glass dildo. With great care, she threaded it through the gold ring, stepped into the straps, and fastened the whole contraption around her hips, before returning to Lindsey's side.

Lindsey was surprised by how well Camilla wore the strap-on. It seemed natural, like an extension of her body. With every movement she made, it bobbed and swayed with her.

"Are you ready for me?" Camilla asked.

"I'm so ready, Mistress." The other times they'd had sex had been tender and gentle. But after spending a week apart, Lindsey wanted nothing more than for her Mistress to take her and claim her as her own.

Camilla rounded the table behind Lindsey, grabbed the waistband of her panties, and pulled them down to the floor. Lindsey pushed them aside with a foot and spread her feet apart. Camilla slid a hand down Lindsey's slit, stroking her silken folds.

"You really are ready," Camilla said. "Have you been dripping wet this whole time, waiting for me?"

Lindsey's answer was a moan.

Camilla wrapped her fingers around Lindsey's hair, pulling her head up. She leaned down to speak into Lindsey's ear. "That's no way to speak to your Mistress."

"Yes, Mistress," Lindsey said. "I've been waiting for you."

"I'm glad. Because I've been waiting to do this to you too."

Lindsey spread her legs out wider. She ached for Camilla. Again, she felt Camilla probe between her lips. But this time, it was the solid glass head of the strap-on. Lindsey's breath quickened.

Finally, Camilla grabbed onto Lindsey's waist with one hand and entered her. Lindsey's mouth fell open in a silent cry. She clutched the sides of the table, holding on as Camilla thrust in and out, sending surges of pleasure through her.

"Mistress…" *Harder*, Lindsey wanted to say. *Faster.* Instead, she closed her eyes and surrendered to her Mistress's control. Camilla plunged deeper, each stroke nudging that sensitive spot inside. And when Camilla's fingers laced around Lindsey's hair again, she lost the ability to form words altogether.

Moments later, an orgasm hit her hard and fast. Lindsey jerked against her restraints, her body racked with tremors, as Camilla buried herself inside her. Then she slumped down on the table, overcome.

Camilla rounded the table and kissed Lindsey softly. After removing the strap-on, she untied the ropes binding Lindsey to the table but left the cuffs fastened around her wrists. Together, they made their way over to the bed and collapsed onto it.

"Mistress?" Lindsey said breathlessly.

"Yes?"

"I really liked that dress."

Camilla laughed. "I'll buy you another. I'll buy you ten dresses. I'll buy you anything you want." She cupped Lindsey's cheeks and kissed her.

As Lindsey lost herself in Camilla's lips, she realized that it wasn't pretty dresses, or fancy dinners, or expensive gifts that she wanted. What she wanted was Camilla, in every way she could possibly want another person.

She and her Mistress had built this irresistible lie together. And Lindsey was starting to find it hard to separate the lie from the truth.

# CHAPTER FIFTEEN

*L*indsey dove into the pool and swam to the other end in one breath. She surfaced, pushed her wet hair out of her eyes and looked over at the deck. Camilla was lounging on a chair in sunglasses and a wide-brimmed hat. She had a stylish one piece on under her wrap, but it was clear that she had no intention of getting into the pool. Even though it was just after lunch, and Camilla wasn't supposed to be working, she'd spent the last fifteen minutes sending emails on her phone.

Lindsey swam over to the edge of the pool. "Mistress?"

"Yes, Lindsey?" Camilla murmured.

"Want to join me in here?"

Camilla peered over her sunglasses, her eyes rolling down Lindsey's bikini-clad body. The bikini Camilla had bought her, of course. "Why should I get in there, when I have this lovely view from here?"

"Because this pool would be a lot more fun with you in it."

"Believe me, I'm tempted. But we both know what's going to happen if I get in there with you. And I have far too much to do right now to be distracted."

Camilla had seemed busier than usual with work in the past couple of days. And she seemed a little stressed about it.

Maybe Lindsey could do something to help. "Can I come sit with you, Mistress?"

"Sure," Camilla said. "Dry yourself off first. I don't want water on this wrap."

Lindsey swam to the steps and hopped out of the pool. After drying off, she spread her towel out next to Camilla's chair and sat down on it, resting her head against the side of Camilla's thigh. She could have just sat in the chair at the other side of Camilla instead of on the ground. But Lindsey's small gestures of submission always seemed to please her Mistress. Maybe it would help her relax a little.

Camilla's hand dropped down to caress the side of Lindsey's face, while her other hand typed away on her phone. "How would you feel about having some friends of mine come visit?"

"Sure," Lindsey said. What would Camilla's friends be like? And what would Camilla say to them about Lindsey? Would she tell the truth about their unconventional arrangement?

"Maybe I'll throw a dinner party. It's been a while since I hosted one."

"That sounds like fun." Lindsey closed her eyes, letting the warm sun beat down on her skin. This was the life. Luxuriating by the pool next to a mansion, with her beautiful Mistress next to her.

Lindsey never imagined herself in this situation. But what was more unexpected were her feelings toward Camilla. She'd taken Faith's advice and stopped worrying about what those feelings meant. It had made things a little clearer. But that still left her with one problem.

Everything between Lindsey and Camilla was just a lie.

Camilla yawned. "How's your art going? Do you have anything to show me yet?"

"Not yet," Lindsey replied. "Soon, though." She was out of practice, both in terms of her craft and mentally. It was still a daily battle to sit down and force herself to work every morning. She still felt that paralyzing fear. But it was nowhere near as bad as before. And once she got started, creativity would flow from her for hours and hours.

"June said you've been wandering around with your sketchpad of a morning."

"I've been sketching the grounds. There's so much beautiful scenery here. I don't usually draw landscapes, but the grounds are too picturesque not to try to capture."

"My grandmother spent most of her retirement painting the grounds," Camilla said. "She was very talented. Her paintings are stashed away in the east wing somewhere if you'd like to see them. I'll have June dig them out for you."

"That sounds like a lot of trouble," Lindsey said. "I don't want to make more work for June."

"Nonsense. I pay her outrageously so that I can ask her to do whatever I need done. She won't mind."

"Then I'd love to see them. Thank you, Mistress."

Camilla placed her phone down on the table next to her. "All right. Get up here." She held out her hand and pulled Lindsey up onto her lap. "I can't get anything done with you sitting there. You're much too distracting."

Lindsey grinned. "Sorry, Mistress."

"You're not sorry at all, are you?"

Lindsey threw her arms around Camilla's neck. "No, Mistress, I'm not."

Camilla's mouth fell open. "What has gotten into you today? I ought to take you into the hedge maze where no one can find us and punish you."

"Please do, Mistress." Lindsey was pushing it. Camilla had made it clear in the past that she didn't like misbehaving submissives. But her playful tone suggested that the kind of punishment she was referring to didn't involve writing lines.

"Oh, you're being such a brat right now." Camilla grabbed Lindsey's waist and pulled her closer. "Luckily, I know just how to stop you running that mouth of yours."

Camilla covered Lindsey's mouth with her own, kissing her in that soft, slow way that filled Lindsey with need. She shifted on Camilla's lap, pressing herself against the other woman. Camilla's hand slid up the side of Lindsey's hip, all the way to her chest. A faint moan escaped Lindsey's lips. She really hoped Camilla's talk of taking her into the hedge maze wasn't just a threat.

"Who the hell is this?"

Camilla tensed. Lindsey's eyes flew open. She turned to see a short middle-aged woman standing right beside them. Several feet behind her, June was hurrying toward them, an apologetic look on her face.

"Denise?" Camilla said. "What are you doing here?"

"What do you think?" the woman replied. "I'm visiting my baby sister."

This was Camilla's sister? They did look alike. Both women had the same hazel eyes and straight brown hair, although Denise's was cut into a short bob. And Denise's face had none of Camilla's warmth and humor.

Denise narrowed her eyes at Lindsey. "I wasn't aware you had a guest, Millie."

Lindsey remembered she was still sitting in Camilla's lap, her hand hovering dangerously close to Camilla's breast. And she was fairly sure Denise had seen them making out like horny teenagers only moments ago. She jumped to her feet.

The motion seemed to break Camilla out of her shocked state. "Lindsey, this is my sister, Denise. Denise, this is Lindsey. My... girlfriend."

*Girlfriend?* "Uh, hi." Lindsey held her hand out to Denise.

Denise ignored it. Instead, she looked Lindsey up and down, her nose wrinkled in disdain. "She certainly has the 'girl' part down."

Lindsey folded her arms across her chest. Suddenly, she felt very naked in her bikini.

"Lindsey, darling, you'll have to forgive my sister. She isn't normally this rude." Camilla shot Denise a withering look. "Oh, who am I kidding? Yes, she is."

The other woman didn't react. "I didn't know you were seeing someone."

"It's a recent development. Now, I'm sure you're tired after your flight. I'll have June make up one of the guest suites. Why don't you go relax in the drawing room? June can show you the way."

"I grew up in this house. I know where the drawing room is."

"Well, it's been so long since you've been here that I thought you might have forgotten."

"It hasn't been that long." Denise rolled her eyes. "I'm going to go freshen up, then catch up on some work. I'll come down for dinner." She turned to address June. "Seven thirty, in the formal dining room."

"June isn't a servant," Camilla said. "And she doesn't take instructions from you. Dinner will be in the west dining room, as usual. And it will be at seven thirty because it's always at seven thirty."

"Whatever you say, Millie."

"It's *Camilla*. It's been Camilla since I was sixteen."

And if Lindsey hadn't known better, she'd think the pair of them were sixteen. They sure were acting like it.

"I don't have time for this. If you need me, I'll be in my rooms." Denise turned on her heel and stormed back to the house.

As soon as she was out of earshot, Camilla turned to June, a dark look in her eyes. "Why didn't you warn me she was here?"

"I'm sorry, Ma'am," June said. "I was tidying up in the east wing. I didn't hear her arrive."

"Just go make sure she stays away from my rooms. And lock the playroom door for me. You know how she is about that kind of thing."

June nodded, then strode off after Denise.

Camilla turned to Lindsey. "I'm sorry for putting you on the spot like that. Denise would never approve of our arrangement."

"It's okay," Lindsey said.

"Of course, if you're not comfortable with me pretending you're my girlfriend, I can think of something else."

"No, I don't mind." It wouldn't be any different to what they were already doing. Although, Lindsey was going to have to remember not to call Camilla 'Mistress.'

"Thank you." The relief was clear on Camilla's face. "Do you mind sleeping in my room for now? You can keep your own rooms for when you need your own space, of course."

"Sure." All this, just to fool Camilla's sister? Lindsey had never seen Camilla so frazzled. "Are you okay?" Lindsey asked.

"It's just my sister. She's the only family I have left, but we don't see eye to eye." Camilla rubbed the back of her neck. "She's a senator like my father was, and we have completely different views on everything. She's never approved of the life I live. I had to come out to her three times until she took me seriously. Then it took another two years before she stopped referring to my girlfriends as 'friends,' and-" Camilla blinked. "I'm rambling. None of that is important. What matters, is that she never stays long. We'll only have to play these roles for a day or two."

# CHAPTER SIXTEEN

"*I*'m staying for a week," Denise said.

Camilla paused, her fork halfway up to her mouth. "A whole week?"

Lindsey focused intently on the food on her plate. Dinner had just started, but the air was already thick with tension. Denise didn't seem to like the fact that Camilla was sitting at the head of the table, and just minutes ago, the two sisters had gotten into an argument because Denise had ordered June to set the table 'the right way.'

Not to mention that Denise had been giving Lindsey dirty looks the entire time.

"Is that a problem?" Denise asked.

"Well, I was planning on throwing a dinner party, but it can wait," Camilla said.

"Oh, don't let me stop you from throwing one of your little parties."

"It's fine. I wouldn't want to cut into our quality time together." Camilla paused. "As much as I enjoy spending time with my dear sister, I have to ask. Isn't campaign season starting soon? Shouldn't you be out there making false promises to the masses?"

"That's why I've come here," Denise said. "I'll be extremely busy from now on, so it'll be my last chance to visit the house in a while."

"How thoughtful of you to see me one last time before you disappear for several years again."

"Stop being so dramatic, Millie. It hasn't been years."

"You're right," Camilla said. "It hasn't been years. Not this time, anyway."

Denise sighed. "When are you going to let that go?"

"Let it go? Our mother had just died, and you were nowhere to be found!"

"We all grieve in different ways. I came back for her funeral, didn't I? Besides, I was busy. I had a family of my own to raise."

"Let's not pretend you actually raised the twins. We both know that the nanny did all the work before you shipped them off to boarding school."

Lindsey glanced at Denise. Her brows were bunched up and her jaw was set. Camilla had hit a nerve.

"I'm fairly certain your kids talk to me more than they do you," Camilla said. "Did you know that your daughter was chosen as captain of her school debate team?"

Denise frowned. "I'm sure she mentioned it in one of her emails."

"She told me when we spoke on the phone last week."

"Yes, well I'm not surprised she talks to you more than me. You're her fun Aunt Camilla. Of course, you can be as eccentric as you like. It must be nice, not having any responsibilities."

"No responsibilities? Who do you think has been running our family's company for the last 15 years while you're off playing politician? Not to mention taking care of this estate. It's funny how you're out there preaching about family and using the Robinson name to get ahead, but when it comes to your own family, you might as well be a ghost."

Lindsey picked up her glass of water, somehow knocking her fork off the table in the process. It fell to the floor, landing with a loud clatter. Denise and Camilla turned to stare at her.

"Er…"

From nowhere, June swooped in and picked the fork up from

the floor. "I'll get you a new one." She gave Lindsey a sympathetic look. Something told her that June was used to these dinners with Camilla and Denise.

For a while, only silence filled the air.

Then, Denise cleared her throat. "So, Lindsey, how long have you been living in my family's home?"

"Er, a little over a month." Lindsey and Camilla hadn't discussed what they were going to say to Denise, so Lindsey decided to tell as much of the truth as she could.

Denise huffed. "And how long were the two of you together before you moved in?"

"Denise, that's no way to treat my guest." Camilla put her hand on Lindsey's. "As you can see, I got the looks and the brains, and Denise here got the excellent people skills."

Denise shot Camilla a dirty look.

"If you must know, we met around two months ago," Camilla said.

"That's awfully fast, don't you think?" Denise's eyes never left Lindsey's face.

"You know what they say about lesbian relationships. Well, I suppose you wouldn't."

"So, you were together for a couple of weeks before you decided to move in?" Denise held her hand up, palm out, in Camilla's direction. "Don't answer for her. I'm sure she's capable of saying more than a few words."

Lindsey swallowed. "Well, I needed a place to stay, so Camilla invited me. It's just for a few months."

"How generous of you, Millie."

Camilla corrected her again. "It's Camilla."

"What is it that you do, Lindsey?" Denise asked.

"Well, I used to work at a call center selling insurance until recently. It isn't what I wanted to do with my life, but I needed a job after college, so I took it."

Camilla squeezed Lindsey's hand. "She's an artist, actually."

"Oh?" Denise gave Lindsey an icy look. "So you spend your days drawing pictures while leeching off my family's money?"

"For starters, it's my money, and I'll do what I want with it," Camilla said. "And Lindsey isn't leeching off anyone. Even if she was, it wouldn't justify how rude you're being."

"I'm just telling the truth, Millie. Can't you see that-"

"That's enough," Camilla said sharply. "If you say one more nasty thing about Lindsey, you can find somewhere else to stay tonight."

"It's my house too. You can't kick me out."

"Last time I checked, our parents left the house to me. And for a good reason."

Denise scoffed. "Because you're the fucking golden child."

"No, it's because I know the meaning of family," Camilla said. "But that doesn't mean I'm above kicking you out if you continue to disrespect Lindsey. So shut up and eat this lovely dinner that has been prepared for us."

Denise scowled, but she didn't say anything. She simply picked up her fork and continued to eat.

The rest of the meal passed in near silence, but the expression on Denise's face spoke volumes. She didn't like that Lindsey was here.

And she didn't like Lindsey.

After sitting through the whole meal, from appetizers to dessert, Camilla turned to Lindsey and gave her a strained smile.

"Darling, my sister and I have a lot to catch up on," she said. "We'll be in the drawing room if you need me."

"Yes, Mis-" Lindsey flushed. "Sure."

Lindsey kissed Camilla on the cheek and got out of there as fast as she could.

---

Lindsey was lying on the bed in her room with her headphones on, listening to music and messaging Faith, when Denise appeared at the foot of her bed.

Lindsey sat up with a start. "Denise. I didn't hear you come in." She hadn't even knocked, which had to be intentional.

"I just knew Camilla would put you in here." Denise glared around the room. "Typical. This was always the nicest of the guest suites. Only the most important visitors were allowed to stay here. Never our friends or relatives. Certainly not stragglers off the streets."

Lindsey sat up and watched Denise stroll around the room, examining everything. The woman walked over to the closet and opened the door. She pulled out a dress, the emerald one that Lindsey had worn that first night out in the garden.

"I suppose my sister bought all this for you?" Denise asked. "Either that, or selling insurance is more lucrative than I thought."

"Camilla did buy that for me." Lindsey crossed her arms. "So what if she did?"

"I'm not surprised. My sister always had such gaudy tastes."

Lindsey fumed. She'd had it with this woman. "What do you want?"

Denise stuck the dress back into the closet and shut the door. "Do you know what they used to call a woman like you? A woman who lives off the riches of a wealthy lover in exchange for providing certain other... benefits?" She returned to stand at the foot of Lindsey's bed. "A kept woman. It's more polite than 'gold-digger' I suppose. Or something even more unpleasant."

It wasn't hard for Lindsey to figure out what Denise meant. "I'm not after Camilla's money."

Denise scoffed. "Someone young and pretty like you? There's no reason for you to be with Millie otherwise."

"Did it ever occur to you that I like her? That I'm attracted to her? That I want to be with her?"

"Would you still want to be with her if it wasn't for her money?"

"Yes," Lindsey said.

"I don't believe you."

"It's a good thing that your opinion doesn't matter to me or Camilla one bit."

Denise gave a derisive chuckle. "You've got more bite than I expected. Is that how you managed to fool my sister? You manipulated her into thinking you actually like her?"

"I'm not manipulating her," Lindsey said. "Do you really think anyone could manipulate Camilla?"

"Well, you've obviously done something. It's clear that she's fallen hard for you."

"Did you just come in here to make snide remarks about me?"

"No. I came to tell you to stop screwing around with my sister."

Lindsey's brows drew together. Could it be that Denise was actually worried about Camilla, and not the family money? "Look, I'm not screwing around with Camilla. I'm not after her money. Our relationship has only just started, but I'm serious about her. Really."

"All right," Denise said. "Let's pretend for a minute that I believe you. You've known each other for a couple of months. You've been living together, here, for most of that time. Right now, you like her. But what's going to happen when the shine rubs off? You know what she's like, don't you? Temperamental, moody, controlling? You know what living with her is like?"

"Yes, but-"

"And you know about her illness, right? About how she can barely live a normal life?"

"That's not true. Her life is still a normal one. And it's not a problem for me." Sure, Camilla had had a few flare-ups in the time Lindsey had been living with her. But Camilla managed just fine.

"You say that now, but you might not feel that way in a few months' time. She's what, 20 years older than you?"

"I'm 23," Lindsey said. Not that Denise cared about the details.

"You're still so young. What's going to happen when you decide that things are too hard? When you decide that no amount of money is worth being locked away in this manor with an emotionally stunted old woman?"

"That's-"

"Because it will happen. And Millie will be crushed."

"That's not going to happen!"

Denise stared at her, her eyes boring into Lindsey's. She shifted uncomfortably on the bed but didn't look away.

"Christ," Denise said. "You really believe that, don't you?"

"I do," Lindsey replied.

Denise shook her head. "Here I thought you were a gold-digger.

But you're just naive. It's no wonder. You're barely more than a child."

"Maybe you're right. Maybe I am naive. Maybe I'll wake up one day and realize that I don't want this life with Camilla anymore." Lindsey clenched her fists in her lap. "I don't know what's going to happen in the future. But I know what I feel right now. And I care about Camilla more than I even know how to express. I'm not going to leave her. There's nowhere in the world I'd rather be than by her side."

"You're making a mistake," Denise said.

"Why are you trying so hard to turn me against Camilla?"

"I'm just trying to protect her."

"She doesn't need your protection," Lindsey said. "What she needs is your love and support, yet here you are, tearing her down behind her back. Some sister you are."

"You know nothing about this family. Don't talk about us like you do."

"I know enough. And you've shown me exactly who you are just now." Lindsey tried as hard as she could to channel Camilla's commanding manner. "Get out of my room."

To Lindsey's surprise, Denise turned her nose up and walked to the door.

Before Denise left the room, she addressed Lindsey. "Whatever happens, don't you dare hurt my sister." She slammed the door shut behind her.

Lindsey blew out a breath and collapsed onto the bed. As she lay there with her eyes closed, she recalled something Denise had said earlier.

*It's clear that she's fallen hard for you.*

*Camilla? Falling for me?* Lindsey doubted that. It was all just part of the lie.

But as Lindsey lay there, she realized something. Everything she'd said to Denise about her feelings for Camilla?

Not a single word of it had been a lie.

# CHAPTER SEVENTEEN

or the days that followed, Lindsey avoided Denise. She couldn't be in the woman's presence without feeling enraged. Denise probably didn't even notice that Lindsey was avoiding her. On the rare occasion that they crossed paths, Denise appeared determined to ignore Lindsey's existence completely, which Lindsey didn't mind one bit.

She hadn't told Camilla about Denise's visit to her room. Between work and her sister's visit, Camilla was stressed out enough. Nevertheless, she insisted that they all have meals together. These were always awkward affairs.

Breakfast that morning was no exception.

"Denise," Camilla began. "The disaster relief foundation the company supports is holding a charity auction. How about we go through some of mother's jewelry and select a few pieces to donate?"

"Just do it without me," Denise said. "I have too much to do."

"Let me guess. Work?"

That was something Camilla and Denise had in common. Lindsey didn't know why Denise even came to visit considering how much time she spent locked in her room working.

"Well, not all of us can just lie around all day." Denise looked pointedly at Lindsey. "Some of us have jobs."

Lindsey returned Denise's glare.

Camilla put down her knife and fork carefully. "Denise, didn't I tell you to stop being rude to Lindsey?"

"Oh, stop acting like she's some innocent little girl," Denise said. "Lindsey here can dish it out just as well as she can take it."

"What's that supposed to mean?" Camilla's eyes flicked between Denise and Lindsey. "What's going on?"

Lindsey said nothing. After all, she wasn't the one who had started this.

"Denise? You said something to her, didn't you?"

"I don't know what you're talking about," Denise said. "I didn't say anything."

"For a politician, you're not very good at lying."

"Fine. I didn't say anything that wasn't true."

Camilla's eyes clouded over. "You *bitch*. What the hell did you say to her?"

"I'm just looking out for you, Millie."

"Oh, because you've done so much of that in the past, haven't you?"

Lindsey tried as hard as she could to dissolve into her chair. Luckily, June chose that moment to reenter the room, carrying a pot of coffee, which she placed on the table before Camilla. It seemed to remind Camilla that Lindsey was still sitting there.

"Lindsey, darling," Camilla said through gritted teeth. "Do you mind? I need to talk to my sister. Alone."

"Okay." Lindsey got up and followed June out into the hall.

Seconds later, the dining room erupted into shouts.

"I can't believe you said that!" Camilla yelled.

Lindsey stopped just within earshot.

"I'm trying to keep you from getting hurt," Denise replied.

"That's bullshit. You don't get to disappear from my life for months, even years at a time, then come back and stick your nose in my business and pretend to care.

"I'm not pretending, Millie. I do care."

"You have some way of showing it. Calling Lindsey a gold-digger? Trying to drive the person I care about the most away?"

June cleared her throat. "I would have thought you'd learned your lesson about listening at doors."

Lindsey jumped. She hadn't realized that June was still there. "Er, right."

"Trust me. You don't want to get caught up in one of their fights. It's best to just let them talk it out."

"So, they're always like this?" Lindsey asked.

"Their relationship is... complicated." June said. "Now, you didn't get to finish your breakfast. If you'd like, I can bring you something."

"No, it's fine."

"All right." June stood in place, waiting for Lindsey to leave.

"I'll just go then."

June nodded. As Lindsey walked away, she could feel June's eyes on her.

Lindsey spent the morning outside, attempting to sketch the wild, overgrown orchard at the back of the estate. It was no coincidence that it was as far from the manor as possible. The tension between Camilla and Denise seemed to permeate the entire house.

But when Lindsey went back to the manor for lunch, both Camilla and Denise were nowhere to be found. The house felt eerily empty, and there was no one else in the dining room. When Lindsey asked June where Camilla was, the housekeeper informed her that both sisters had requested lunch in their rooms. That was unusual. Camilla never took her meals anywhere but the dining room unless she wasn't feeling well.

Lindsey ate lunch alone, then headed to her room, debating with herself about whether she should go to Camilla, or give her some space. She was so lost in thought that she almost didn't see Denise standing by the entrance to her rooms.

Lindsey stopped in her tracks. "What are you doing here?"

"Can we talk?" Denise asked.

"Sure." When Denise didn't move, Lindsey realized that she was waiting to be invited in. "Come in."

They entered Lindsey's sitting room. Lindsey sat down on the lounge, and Denise took a seat in the Victorian armchair next to the far window. Lindsey crossed her arms and waited. If Denise wanted to insult her again, she wasn't just going to sit there and take it.

"I'm-" Denise cleared her throat. "I'm sorry."

Lindsey said nothing. Denise was going to have to do better than that.

"I'm sorry for all the things I said about you. That you're a gold-digger, and after Camilla's money. It was rude and hurtful, and I apologize."

"Did Camilla tell you to apologize to me?" Lindsey asked.

Denise looked down at her shoes. "Yes. But I really do mean it. I was cruel to you. You deserve an apology."

"What about Camilla?"

"What do you mean?"

"I wasn't the only one you said nasty things about. What about everything you said about her?"

Denise examined Lindsey. "You really do care about her, don't you? Yes, I'm sorry for all the things I said about Millie—I mean, Camilla—too. I didn't mean them. I was just trying to drive you away, to protect her. And I do love her, even though she prefers to think otherwise."

"It sounds like she has good reasons for feeling that way."

"You're right. I know I haven't always been the best sister. Actually, I was a terrible sister from the start. After me, our mother was told she wouldn't be able to have any more children. Ten years later, a happy accident named Camilla was born. Here I was, an only child who was used to having all my parents' attention, and suddenly, this little miracle baby was the center of their world. Our parents spoiled Camilla to pieces. I was jealous of her, so I treated her badly. Naturally, she started to lash out at me too, and we've been trapped in this cycle of resentment ever since.

"Then, after both our parents passed, I found it too painful to be in this house, so I stopped coming to see Camilla, and she's never forgiven me." Denise leaned forward and put her elbows on her knees. "For the past few years, I've been trying to make amends.

"It's okay," Lindsey said. "I think she meant well. She was trying to protect you in her own way."

"The only thing she was trying to protect is the family fortune."

"That's not true. She was worried that I'd break your heart."

"Really?" Camilla looked out the window pensively. "Huh. It looks like we played our roles a little too well."

Lindsey felt a sinking in her stomach. *Right. This is all just pretend.* "Yeah. I guess we did."

# CHAPTER EIGHTEEN

*C*amilla slipped into the bed next to Lindsey and pulled the silk sheets up to cover them both. "Thanks again for agreeing to this charade."

"I don't mind," Lindsey replied. "It's been kind of fun."

Lindsey peered at her Mistress, searching her face. Could Camilla detect the longing in Lindsey's voice? Could she hear the real meaning behind Lindsey's words? Could she tell that for Lindsey, this wasn't a charade at all?

But Camilla's mind was elsewhere. "I'm just glad Denise is leaving in the morning," she said. "She's been getting on my nerves all week. She's so overbearing and controlling. And I'm going to strangle her if she calls me Millie one more time. She knows how much I hate that childish nickname."

After Denise's apology, the tension between Camilla and Denise had settled. But that hadn't stopped the two of them from fighting like teenage sisters. Lindsey bit back a smile. Camilla was such a contradiction of a woman. Sometimes warm, sometimes prickly. Sometimes she seemed older than her years. Other times she was liable to throw tantrums and indulge in sweet things like a spoiled princess.

"Is something funny?" Camilla asked.

"No, Mistress," Lindsey replied. "Not at all."

"Maybe I'm overreacting. It's just that, Denise frustrates me sometimes." Camilla folded her hands behind her head and looked up at the ceiling. "But she's the only family I have left. My parents were older when they had me, and they passed away when I was still in my early twenties, but by that time, Denise was already busy with her own family and her career. She didn't have time for me. I began to resent her for it, and we grew distant. I sometimes wish we were closer, but she doesn't want that."

"Maybe she does, but she's not good at showing it," Lindsey said. "She did come here to visit you, after all. You should give her a chance."

Camilla raised an eyebrow.

"Er, it's just a suggestion, Mistress."

"Perhaps you're right." Camilla paused. "I was thinking of inviting her family to come stay for the holidays, but I changed my mind after all the drama of this week. Maybe I should reconsider."

"I think she'd like that."

Camilla leaned back and stared at Lindsey. "What did the two of you talk about?"

"Nothing much," Lindsey said hurriedly.

"It doesn't matter. Once again, we're talking about my sister when we could be doing more exciting things." Beneath the sheets, Camilla's hand crept up Lindsey's thigh, pushing up the hem of her nightie.

Lindsey gave Camilla her most innocent look. "Like what, Mistress?"

Camilla moved in closer and drew her lips up the side of Lindsey's neck, all the way to her ear. "Like your Mistress finally letting you pleasure her."

"Do you mean-" Lindsey's words died in her chest as Camilla kissed her way down the side of Lindsey's throat.

"Yes," Camilla said. "But you first."

Camilla took hold of the hem of Lindsey's nightie and tugged it up over her head. She wasn't wearing anything underneath. Camilla swept her lips down to Lindsey's nipples. They were already hard from just the suggestion of getting to pleasure her Mistress.

"I'm going to need to get warmed up." Camilla pushed Lindsey's shoulders down onto the bed. "And nothing gets me hotter than wringing one of those delicious orgasms from you."

Lindsey stared shamelessly at Camilla above her. Her silk nightgown was so thin it might as well have been invisible. Just weeks ago, Lindsey had been adamant that she wasn't attracted to Camilla because she had 'the wrong equipment.' Now, every part of Camilla's body made Lindsey throb. Her supple curves. Her soft, insistent lips. The tiny pebbled nipples poking through the fabric of her nightgown.

Camilla slid her free hand down to where Lindsey's thighs met and teased her swelling clit. Lindsey drew in a gasping breath. Camilla leaned down and sucked Lindsey's nipple through her teeth, eliciting a strangled whimper. She tweaked the other nipple with her fingers.

"Oh, Mistress. That feels so good." Lindsey writhed on the bed, twisting the sheets around her. She had never gone from zero to wet and panting so quickly. Her gasps turned to moans as Camilla increased the pace.

"Do you want your Mistress to fuck you?" Camilla asked.

"Yes," Lindsey replied. "Please!"

Camilla glided her fingers down Lindsey's slit and entered her carefully. Lindsey quivered. She had no idea how many fingers were inside her, but they were enough to fill her up. Camilla began to delve in and out, first slowly, then hard and fast.

Lindsey arched up, pushing back into Camilla's hand. She reached up to grab onto Camilla's hip, but all she could grasp was a fistful of silk. She clung onto it tightly. This was so different from when Camilla had fucked her with a strap-on. This way, Camilla had far more control. And with her fingers inside stroking Lindsey's sweet spot, and her thumb grazing Lindsey's bud, she was being flooded with pleasure from all angles.

"Mistress!" She arched up one final time and threw her head

back as waves of ecstasy washed over her. Lindsey held on to Camilla until her tremors subsided and she fell back to the bed.

That earth-shattering orgasm should have left Lindsey spent. Instead, it made her even more eager to please her Mistress.

"Thank you, Mistress," she said. "Can I serve you now?"

"Yes." Camilla's voice rang with passion. "Just remember what I said. I like to hold the reins."

Camilla threw one leg over Lindsey, straddling her, and pulled her silk nightgown up her hips. The lips between her thighs had a wet sheen, like dew on a flower. It wasn't like Lindsey had never seen a pussy before. But she had never seen one that made her want to touch it, and taste it, and explore it. Not until now.

Camilla shuffled up the bed, holding her nightie around her waist, until she was kneeling over Lindsey's head. "Do you want to taste me?"

Lindsey's breath shuddered. "Yes, Mistress." Camilla's intentions were clear. 'Holding the reins' wasn't just a metaphor.

Camilla grabbed onto the headboard. Gently, she lowered herself down onto Lindsey's mouth. Lindsey slipped her tongue into Camilla slit, lapping at her folds. They were like liquid silk, and so hot that they seemed to burn. She slid her tongue down to Camilla's entrance, darting it inside. Her upper lip tickled Camilla's clit.

"God, yes." Camilla shifted her hips, pressing herself against Lindsey's lips.

Lindsey got the message loud and clear. She took Camilla in her mouth, licking and sucking her swollen nub. Camilla gyrated her hips, riding against Lindsey's face. The silk of Camilla's nightie fell down around Lindsey's head, Camilla's dizzying scent enveloping her.

"Faster," Camilla urged.

Lindsey redoubled her efforts, devouring her Mistress. Atop her, Camilla moaned and bucked, nearly smothering Lindsey with her thrusts. The bed rocked and creaked around them.

Finally, a cry erupted from Camilla's chest, and her thighs began to shake. Lindsey licked away gently, until Camilla rose up, climbing off Lindsey and collapsing next to her.

Lindsey rolled onto her side and ran her palm up Camilla's chest. "How did I do, Mistress?"

"I think you know the answer to that." Suddenly, Camilla slapped her hand to her forehead. "Oh, christ."

"What's the matter?"

"I got caught up in the moment. I forgot that you've never done that before."

Lindsey frowned. "Did I do something wrong?"

"Lindsey, if you did something wrong, I wouldn't be lying here completely unable to move."

"What is it, then?"

"It's just that, this was your first experience pleasuring a woman," Camilla said. "And it involved me sitting on your face."

Lindsey burst out laughing. "That's what you're worried about? It's not a bad thing. As far as first experiences go, it's one that I'll never forget."

"Wouldn't you have preferred something more intimate?"

Lindsey shrugged. "That felt intimate to me. Everything we do does. What's more intimate than submission?"

A soft smile formed on Camilla's lips. "I feel the same way. We really get each other, don't we?"

It was true. Lindsey had never been with anyone who understood her desires like Camilla did. But it was so much more than that. More than just Mistress and submissive, more than two people with an arrangement.

There was no denying it. Lindsey had fallen for Camilla so deeply. She hadn't forgotten that this was supposed to be pretend. But it felt more real than anything she'd ever experienced.

Lindsey looked at Camilla. "Mistress?"

"Yes?" Camilla said.

"I'm glad I get to share all these firsts with you."

"So am I." Camilla rolled onto her stomach and gathered her hair over one shoulder. "And I've enjoyed having you sleep next to me these past few days. How do you feel about sleeping in my bedroom from now on?"

"I'd like that," Lindsey said.

"And you can come into my rooms whenever you like. Just don't mess anything up."

"Yes, Mistress."

Camilla lay back down and drew Lindsey's head to rest on her shoulder. "By the way, I was going to reschedule that dinner party for next Saturday, but a friend of mine is having a last-minute engagement party. How would you like to come with me to that instead?"

"Sure," Lindsey murmured. "I'd love to."

"You're going to have a great time. Vanessa really knows how to throw a party."

# CHAPTER NINETEEN

*C*amilla knocked on the door to the penthouse apartment. Lindsey could hear the faint sounds of music and chatter inside. She glanced at Camilla. There was a question Lindsey had wanted to ask her Mistress ever since Camilla invited her to this party. It shouldn't have been a difficult question to ask. Nevertheless, it filled Lindsey's stomach with butterflies.

"Mistress?" Lindsey asked.

"Yes?" Camilla said.

"If people ask about the two of us, what should I tell them?"

"What do you want to tell them?"

"That I'm your girlfriend? It would be simpler after all."

"After a week of playing my girlfriend for Denise, you're not tired of it?"

"Not at all."

Even after Denise left, Lindsey and Camilla had continued with their feigned intimacy. It was almost as though they hoped that if they pretended hard enough, the lie would become real. At least, that was how Lindsey felt. But surely Camilla had noticed that this was no longer an act for Lindsey. Surely Camilla could tell that Lindsey's feelings were real.

Surely Camilla felt it too.

"Okay then. You're my girlfriend." The corners of Camilla's lips curled up. "And once again, I give you permission to not call me Mistress."

Lindsey smiled. It was impossible not to react to Camilla's smile, and her bright eyes, and that stern but playful tone of hers that sent pleasant shivers through Lindsey's entire body.

The door swung open, and a raven-haired woman with pale skin appeared. "Camilla," the woman said. "So glad you could make it." She pulled Camilla into an embrace.

"I wouldn't miss this," Camilla replied. "Congratulations on the engagement."

"Thank you." The woman broke off and turned to Lindsey. "And you must be Lindsey. My name's Vanessa. It's lovely to meet you."

Lindsey stumbled over a greeting. Her stomach swam with both nerves and excitement.

"Here, I brought you a small engagement present." Camilla handed Vanessa a bottle of whiskey with a yellowing label and a bow tied around its neck.

Vanessa took the bottle and held it up to the light. Her mouth dropped open. "Where on earth did you find this? Last I heard, there were only fifty bottles left in the world."

"I convinced an old family friend to part with it as part of a business deal."

"This is incredible, Camilla. Thank you."

Lindsey and Camilla followed Vanessa inside. The enormous, lavishly decorated apartment held a few dozen people, all dressed to the nines. Lindsey now understood why Camilla had bought her a new dress for the occasion.

"I have a gift for Mel too," Camilla said. "I made a donation to the legal aid clinic where she works. I thought she'd like that more than something material."

"Melanie will be thrilled." Vanessa looked around. "She's here somewhere. I'm going to go find her. Make yourselves at home."

Camilla led Lindsey over to a small home bar to the side. They helped themselves to some wine.

Camilla spoke to Lindsey under her breath. "Don't tell anyone this, but Vanessa owns a string of BDSM clubs around the country. There's one right here in the city. Lilith's Den."

"Really?" Lindsey looked over at the woman, who was chatting at the other side of the room. "Is that how you know each other?"

"Yes. I did some business with her when her company was just starting out. It must have been ten years ago. But we didn't really get to know each other until we crossed paths at Lilith's Den a few months later. I'll take you there sometime if you'd like."

"I'd love that, Mistress," Lindsey said. There was no one close enough to overhear them.

"Actually, that's how a lot of us know each other." Camilla looked around the room. "Half the guests here go to that club."

"Really? But everyone seems so proper."

"Unlike the two of us, who look like a pair of sexual deviants?"

"That's a good point."

"You should see this crowd at Lilith's Den." Camilla leaned in and spoke quietly. "Between you and me, it's always the proper ones who are the most perverted. There's nothing quite like sitting through a business meeting with a woman you saw the night before getting spanked on a stage in nothing but a corset and a thong."

Heat crept up Lindsey's face. She wasn't sure if it was embarrassment or arousal.

As the two of them mingled, Lindsey found herself distracted by the idea that some of the people she met were secretly like her and Camilla. She couldn't help but try to pick them out. Of the couples, she thought she saw a few signs. They would give it away with a possessive touch, or a deferential look, or a disguised piece of jewelry that would have been impossible to spot unless she knew what to look for.

Camilla led her over to a group of women lounging nearby. Vanessa was there, perched on the arm of a chair. Below her sat a woman with a serious face who looked around Lindsey's age. She had to be Vanessa's fiancée.

"Camilla," the woman said. "Vanessa told me about your gift. Thanks, that's so thoughtful of you."

"It's my pleasure, Mel," Camilla replied.

She and Lindsey sat down, and Camilla introduced Lindsey to Mel, as well as the others who were sitting across from them. There was a slender woman with short blonde hair and a fitted suit, who had her arm slung casually around the shoulders of a tiny brunette. Everyone seemed to know each other well.

"So, who's going to be your maid of honor, Vanessa?" The blonde woman asked. Vicki was her name. "I can throw you an amazing bachelorette party."

Camilla scoffed. "Sure, if you want strippers and booze, go with Vicki. If you decide you want something more sophisticated, I'll be right here."

Vicki shot Camilla a look. "There are sophisticated strippers. I can put you in touch with some if you like, Camilla. Maybe it'll help with that stick up your-"

"Ladies, please," Vanessa said. "We haven't thought that far ahead yet. Besides, we might not even have bridesmaids. We're thinking of doing something small."

"Vanessa, passing up a chance to make an ostentatious display of love?" Camilla said. "I'll believe it when I see it. Which reminds me, what was the proposal like?"

"If you must know, I took Melanie to a cozy little cabin and proposed to her there." Vanessa's hand fell to Mel's shoulder. "It was all very low key."

"Low key?" Mel said. "The 'cozy little cabin' was two stories high and at the top of a mountain. We had to take a helicopter to get there. And there were fireworks, and-"

"Like I said, low key." Vanessa squeezed Mel's shoulder. "She won't let me spoil her anywhere near as much as I want to."

"That's because you always go overboard." Mel looked at the others. "She wants to have the wedding on a private island. Can you believe it?"

"I'm open to other ideas," Vanessa said. "I recently purchased a lovely villa in the French countryside. It would make the perfect wedding venue."

"What's wrong with having the wedding here in the city?"

"I suppose that would make things easier. And that way, we could invite even more people, and make the whole thing bigger."

Mel twisted the ring around her finger, her face frozen in alarm. Vanessa seemed completely oblivious. Mel looked like she was about to protest when Vanessa spotted someone by the door.

"More guests," she said. "Let's go say hello."

The two women wandered off, leaving Camilla and Lindsey with Vicki and the brunette, April. Camilla had told Lindsey that April and Vicki were a couple, but Lindsey could sense a heavy tension hanging between them.

April nudged Vicki with her elbow. "What was that you were saying about putting Camilla in touch with some strippers?"

"I was kidding," Vicki said. "I don't know any strippers. At least, not anymore."

"Anymore? What does that mean?"

Vicki shrugged. "It's no secret the kind of life I lived before we met. But it's all behind me now." She crossed her legs. "Do you have something against strippers? How narrow-minded of you. Stripping is a legitimate profession like any other."

April folded her arms across her chest. "That's not what I meant, and you know it."

"Honestly, I had no idea you were so judgmental."

"Stop trying to turn this around on me, Victoria."

Camilla tapped Lindsey's arm and spoke into her ear. "Let's leave those two alone."

Camilla and Lindsey wandered off toward a table of canapes. Lindsey was just relieved to get away from the quarreling couple.

"Don't let those two fool you," Camilla said. "They're always arguing about something or other. I think they enjoy it. Give it five minutes, and they'll be making out in a dark closet somewhere."

An hour passed, and another, and Lindsey began to loosen up. The drinks helped. So did talking to the other guests. Although half of them seemed as accustomed to the glitz and glamour around them as Camilla did, the other half seemed just as dazzled by their surroundings as Lindsey was.

And being here, playing Camilla's girlfriend for all the world to see, was making it all the more apparent that Lindsey wanted everything between them to be real. She didn't know what to do with all these feelings. She'd never felt like this about anyone before.

Did Camilla feel it too? She'd brought Lindsey here tonight as her date. But what if this was just Camilla showing Lindsey off to her friends? Didn't most men do this with their sugar babies? Dress them up like dolls and show them off as status symbols?

Camilla placed a hand on Lindsey's arm. "I need to speak with April. I'll be right back."

"Okay." Lindsey's voice came out as a nervous squeak, but Camilla didn't seem to notice.

As Camilla disappeared into the crowd, Lindsey took another sip of her wine. Her eyes were drawn to Vanessa and Mel, who were standing to the side, arms around each other, smiling. Over the course of the night, she'd heard snippets of the story of Mel and Vanessa's relationship. It was the kind of romance that Lindsey used to fantasize about. Being swept off her feet by some mysterious lover. In Lindsey's fantasies, that lover had always been a man. Of course, that had all changed.

Lindsey finished off the last of her wine and went over to the bar. She refilled her glass and drank some more. How was she supposed to continue everything with Camilla as they had before, knowing what she now felt? How was she supposed to go on?

Her thoughts were interrupted when someone sidled up beside her. It was Vicki. The blonde woman poured two glasses of wine, then turned to Lindsey, a knowing look in her eyes.

"So." Vicki picked up one of the glasses and took a long sip, studying Lindsey carefully. "You're this mysterious guest of Camilla's."

Lindsey nodded. "Yep." She wasn't in the mood to elaborate. And she was tired of lying.

"How long have the two of you been together?"

"A couple of months, I guess," Lindsey mumbled.

Vicki put down her glass and held up her hands apologetically. "Sorry, I didn't mean to pry. Sticking my nose in people's business is a bad habit of mine."

"It's okay. It's not you, it's me."

An uncomfortable silence hung in the air.

"Is something the matter between the two of you?" Vicki asked.

Lindsey hesitated. Vicki seemed to think that Camilla and Lindsey's relationship was real. She was one of Camilla's close friends. Didn't she know the truth?

"What has Camilla told you about me?" Lindsey asked.

"She hasn't said much. Just that you've been living with her. I didn't even realize you were a couple until tonight." Vicki grimaced. "There I go again, running my mouth. I didn't mean anything by it. It's just that Camilla doesn't talk about relationships much."

"No, once again, it isn't you." Lindsey didn't know why she was saying this. "We're not really a couple."

"You're not?"

"I'm her sugar baby."

"Oh."

An awkward silence followed.

"And that bothers you?" Vicki asked.

"Yes," Lindsey replied.

"Because you have feelings for her?"

Lindsey nodded.

"Then you should tell her."

"I can't. I have no idea if she feels the same way."

"There's only one way to find out," Vicki said.

Lindsey just sighed.

The conversation lapsed into silence again. Vicki crossed her arms and looked out into the crowd. Lindsey sipped at her wine. Her eyes fell on Camilla, who was at the other end of the room, talking to April.

Suddenly, Vicki spoke. "It's terrifying, isn't it?"

"What?" Lindsey said.

"Love."

Lindsey looked at Vicki. The blonde woman was staring in the same direction Lindsey had been looking. But Vicki was looking at April, her eyes filled with passion.

"It's this incredible, impossible, overwhelming thing that drives you crazy, and upends your whole existence," Vicki said. "It makes you wonder how a single person can cause so much turmoil."

Was that what this feeling was? Love?

"But it's worth it. Even if it means putting your heart on the line and risking everything, it's so worth it." Vicki turned to Lindsey. "Tell her. Before it's too late. You'll regret it otherwise."

Lindsey's pulse quickened. Across the room, Camilla and April were working their way over to where Lindsey and Vicki stood. Lindsey's eyes met Camilla's. Camilla gave her that warm smile that always made her heart melt.

"You're right," Lindsey said softly. "I have to tell her."

Moments later, Camilla and April joined the two of them by the bar. Vicki picked up the two glasses of wine and handed one to April, who thanked her with a kiss. It was clear that there was only love there. Apparently, their argument earlier had meant nothing.

Camilla slipped an arm around Lindsey's waist. "I hope you weren't causing any trouble, Vicki." The tone of her voice suggested she was only half joking.

"Don't worry," Vicki said. "My troublemaking days are over. Now, I only meddle for good reasons." She took her girlfriend's arm and tipped her head toward Lindsey. "I'll see you later."

As the two of them walked away, Vicki mouthed the words "tell her" to Lindsey behind Camilla's back.

"Well, that was odd." Camilla reached out and brushed Lindsey's hair out of her face. "Are you having a nice time?"

"Yeah," Lindsey said. "I am."

Camilla examined Lindsey's face. "Are you all right, darling?"

"Yeah. I drank a little too much, that's all." She'd only had a few glasses of wine, but right now, Lindsey felt like her world had been tipped on its axis.

"Oh?" Camilla took her hand. "Do you need some water? Or do you want to go lie down? There's a spare room just down the hall."

"No, I'm fine."

"Well, it's getting late anyway. Should we head home?"

"Home sounds great," Lindsey replied.

ANNA STONE

As she and Camilla said their goodbyes, Lindsey realized that for the first time, she'd called the manor home.

---

They spent the car ride back to the manor in near silence. Camilla seemed to accept that Lindsey had drunk too much. But that was just another excuse. As the wine wore off, Lindsey was left with a churning in her stomach that had nothing to do with being drunk.

As soon as they pulled up outside the manor, Lindsey practically ran inside. She knew she had to tell Camilla how she felt. Why was this so hard? When did she become so anxious and fearful? The old Lindsey would have shouted her feelings from a mountaintop.

"Lindsey?" Camilla's footsteps echoed across the entrance hall. "Are you all right?"

Lindsey stopped by the stairs, her arms hugging herself in the cold. *I'm fine*, she tried to say. But she couldn't lie anymore. Her feelings toward Camilla were so strong that they hurt.

"Lindsey." Camilla took her hand and guided her to sit on the bottom step of the grand staircase. "What's going on?"

"Why did you take me to that party tonight?" It wasn't what Lindsey really wanted to say. But she needed some hint, some inkling that everything between them wasn't just a lie.

"Because I thought that you'd enjoy it," Camilla replied.

"So it wasn't so you could show your sugar baby off to your friends?"

"Of course not. Do you really think I'd do that?"

"No, I don't. But I wanted to be sure."

"Sure of what?" Camilla searched Lindsey's face. "What's going on?"

Lindsey's voice stuck in her throat. Her heart was pounding so hard, she felt like it would burst. She took a few deep breaths. Because of Camilla, Lindsey had faced her fears once already, that morning in her sunny studio. She could do it again.

"Camilla," Lindsey said. "I don't want this to be pretend anymore."

484

"What do you mean?"

"These past months, they've been some of the best of my life. It's all been like a dream."

Camilla patted Lindsey's hand. "I'm glad you've been enjoying life here at the manor."

"No, I mean… It's not because of this house, or the expensive clothes, or the gifts. It's because of you."

"Because of me?"

"Yes. Is that so hard to believe?" Lindsey stared at Camilla's bewildered face. Could it be that she really had no idea how Lindsey felt? That she was so determined to live her life alone that she couldn't see what was right in front of her?

"What are you saying?" Camilla asked.

"I'm saying that I'm in love with you."

"Oh." Camilla fell silent.

A lump formed in Lindsey's throat. She was wrong. She had read it all wrong. "Forget it. I never should have said anything."

"No, that's not… I'm sorry. I didn't know. I never thought-"

"Of course you didn't." Tears fell from Lindsey's eyes. "I'm just someone you're paying, like June. How could I be so stupi-"

"Lindsey, stop." Camilla reached out and cradled the side of Lindsey's face. "You're not just someone I'm paying. You're so much more to me. You always have been." Camilla brushed a tear from Lindsey's cheek with her thumb. "What I'm trying to say is, I never thought that you'd return my feelings."

Lindsey's heart skittered. "Return your feelings?"

"Oh, Lindsey. These past few months have been like something out of a dream for me too. And all because of you. I feel the same way you do."

"You do?"

"I do," Camilla said. "It's just that, I didn't plan for this to happen. I'm not good at dealing with anything unexpected."

"Really?" Lindsey blinked away the last of her tears. "I haven't noticed."

Smiling, Camilla pulled Lindsey in close. "I want this to be real too. From now on, no more pretending."

"Mistress, I stopped pretending weeks ago."

Camilla cupped Lindsey's face. Her lips met Lindsey's in a soft, steady kiss. Lindsey dissolved into her. Now that their feelings were finally out in the open, the kiss seemed so much sweeter.

But Lindsey was all too aware that not everything was out in the open. She'd told a little white lie the day they had met. And she still hadn't told Camilla the truth.

Lindsey pushed the thought aside. She didn't want to ruin this perfect moment.

# CHAPTER TWENTY

"*L*indsey?" Camilla called from the hall. "Where on earth are you?"

Lindsey cursed. She hadn't finished setting up yet. "I'm in the dining room."

Moments later, Camilla appeared in the doorway. She stared, first at Lindsey, who was standing next to the dining cart, then at the table where breakfast was laid out. "What's going on?"

"I'm serving you breakfast, Mistress," Lindsey replied.

Camilla looked at Lindsey, her eyes narrowed. "What have you done with June? The only thing that could keep her from her duties is being tied up in the basement."

"June's fine. She's in her room relaxing. I told her that I'd take care of breakfast this morning." It had taken a while to convince the housekeeper to let Lindsey take over, but she'd agreed in the end.

Camilla crossed her arms. "June's in on this too?"

Lindsey nodded.

"Really, both of you should know better. I don't like disruptions to my routine."

"I just want to serve you, Mistress." Lindsey bowed her head and peered up at Camilla. But her expression was inscrutable.

Camilla walked over to where Lindsey stood. She grabbed Lindsey's chin and tilted her head up. "You're lucky that I find this very sweet. I'll allow it. This time."

"Thank you, Mistress."

"Continue." Camilla took her seat at the head of the table. Lindsey had left Camilla a newspaper in its usual place beside her plate, but Camilla didn't pick it up. Instead, she sat back and watched Lindsey, her lips curved up slightly.

Lindsey continued setting everything up. "What do you have planned for today, Mistress?" She asked Camilla this question every day, even though her answer was always the same.

"I have some work to do in the morning," Camilla said. "But I'll be finished with everything by lunchtime. After that, I was thinking we could spend the afternoon in the playroom."

"The afternoon? What about your schedule?"

Camilla raised an eyebrow. "Are you questioning your Mistress?"

"No, Mistress," Lindsey said hurriedly. "I can't wait."

"Good. Because I have something special planned."

Lindsey's stomach flipped. She knew what that something special was. They'd talked about it already. And it excited her.

Lindsey placed the pot of coffee on the table in front of her Mistress. "All done. Your breakfast is served."

Camilla surveyed the spread laid out before her. She poured herself a cup of coffee, then helped herself to her usual dishes. Then she picked up her knife and fork and took a bite of her eggs, chewing slowly and deliberately.

Lindsey stood in place next to her Mistress, waiting for her approval. She'd been planning this for days. Even with June's instructions written down, it had taken her several tries to get everything exactly the way Camilla liked it.

Finally, Camilla placed her knife and fork down. "This is very good. But there's something missing." She beckoned Lindsey closer. "Something important."

Lindsey scanned the table before her. "What is it?" She was sure she'd thought of everything.

"You." Camilla grabbed Lindsey's arm and drew her onto her lap, planting a deep, possessive kiss on her lips. "Now put that cart away and join me at the table. Your Mistress commands it."

———

After lunch, Lindsey and Camilla had a long, sensual bath, before heading to the playroom. Both of them were wearing nothing but robes.

As Lindsey entered the room, her eyes were drawn to the foot of the bed. The drapes had been tied back carefully, leaving the X-shaped cross that was built into the frame completely exposed. That had to be deliberate.

Camilla led Lindsey to the table. Once again, the wooden chest with Camilla's initials on the lid sat on top of it. Camilla untied the belt of Lindsey's robe and slipped it from her shoulders, baring her naked body.

Camilla tapped the table next to the box. "Sit up here."

Lindsey took a seat on the edge of the table and watched her Mistress open the box, once again using the lid to hide its contents from view. First, Camilla pulled out the blue and gold wrist cuffs. Then, she took out a second pair of cuffs that were identical, but slightly bigger. They even had the same little gold tag with Camilla's initials on them. Finally, she pulled a blindfold out of the chest and set it down on the table next to the four pairs of cuffs.

Lindsey stared at the blindfold. It was made of the same midnight blue leather as the cuffs on the outside, but the inside was lined with soft black fur. This blindfold was her one soft limit. Her mountain to conquer. But Lindsey had faced her fears with Camilla so many times now. She felt ready.

"You're awfully quiet," Camilla said. "Having second thoughts?"

"No," Lindsey replied. "I want to do this with you."

"I promise I'll take care of you." Camilla slid her own robe from her shoulders. "And I promise I'll make this a pleasurable experience."

She pulled Lindsey close, kissing her with her whole body. The scent of Camilla's freshly washed skin enveloped her. God, everything about her Mistress was mesmerizing. Her long, dark hair, which flowed down her chest, and the way her nipples peeked out from behind it. Her generous curves, which Lindsey just wanted to drown in. Those full, soft lips that made Lindsey weak every time they touched her skin.

Camilla broke away. Silently, she took Lindsey's hand and drew her fingers all the way down Lindsey's arm from her shoulder to her palm. She picked up one of the small cuffs and buckled it around Lindsey's wrist before doing the same with Lindsey's other wrist. Then she took Lindsey's leg and ran her hands down it gently. She straightened out Lindsey's knee, her fingertips tickling the sensitive skin behind it, and buckled a cuff around her ankle carefully. It was like her Mistress was performing some kind of sacred ritual.

Camilla fastened the last cuff around Lindsey's ankle and stood up. "Now for the final touch." She picked up the blindfold and pulled it over Lindsey's head, adjusting it so it sat covering her eyes.

For a moment, Lindsey wanted to panic. The blackness was so complete. But Camilla's presence was enough to ground her. And her anxiousness was far overshadowed by her arousal.

Camilla placed a hand on the front of Lindsey's shoulder. "How does that feel?"

"Good, Mistress," Lindsey said.

"Here." Camilla took Lindsey's hand. "Come with me."

Camilla led Lindsey in the direction of the bed. Lindsey's pulse thrummed in her ears. Was Camilla taking her to the cross? Lindsey's suspicions were confirmed when Camilla nudged her backward, and her shoulder blades hit solid wood.

"Spread your feet apart," Camilla said.

With the same reverence she'd shown earlier, Camilla trailed her hands down each of Lindsey's legs and attached the O-ring of each of the cuffs to the cross. Lindsey couldn't see how she did it, but she heard a metallic click each time. Camilla took Lindsey's wrist and raised her arm up gently, binding it to the cross, then did the same with her other wrist.

Lindsey's breath grew heavy. This was the ultimate surrender. To be bound and helpless, unable to move, and touch, and see. But she wanted this. Lindsey wanted to give herself over to Camilla so completely, to trust her Mistress with every part of herself, to give her all to this woman who made her feel so many incredible things she hadn't even known she was capable of feeling.

Camilla cupped Lindsey's face and kissed her greedily. Lindsey let out a low murmur. The taste of her Mistress's lips was better than fine wine, or chocolate covered strawberries, or any of the other indulgent delights that she'd shared with Camilla.

Camilla drew her fingertips down Lindsey's cheek, down the side of her throat and between her breasts. Her Mistress's feather-light touch made goosebumps form on Lindsey's skin. Soon, Camilla's hands were all over Lindsey's body, painting invisible lines with the pads of her fingers, sculpting Lindsey's curves with her palms.

Right then and there, Lindsey forgot all about the blindfold. All her other senses were overloaded with Camilla. Her touch, her kiss, the scent of her—it flooded every cell in Lindsey's body with need.

"Oh, you like this, don't you?" Camilla traced her thumb over Lindsey's pebbled nipple. "It's not so scary after all, is it?"

"No, Mistress," Lindsey said.

Camilla slid her palm down to Lindsey's mound, skimming her middle finger between Lindsey's outspread lips with an agonizingly light touch. Lindsey pushed her hips out toward Camilla as far as she could.

"Patience." Camilla pressed herself against Lindsey. "I'll give you what you need, but only if you don't rush me, understand?"

"Yes, Mistress," Lindsey whispered.

Camilla broke away. Lindsey waited in silence. Then, she felt a puff of heat on the inside of her thigh. Camilla's breath.

Her Mistress was on her knees.

Lindsey's lips parted, a gust of air escaping them. Camilla had her tied up and at her mercy, yet she offered Lindsey this small act of submission. It paled in comparison to Lindsey's submission. But it filled Lindsey with a desire so insatiable that she felt like she was drowning.

Her Mistress kissed her way up Lindsey's thigh, grabbed onto Lindsey's ass cheeks, and drew her mouth over Lindsey's lower lips.

Lindsey continued, using everything she could to ravish her Mistress like her Mistress had done to her moments ago. It wasn't long before Camilla let out a gasp, her body quaking as an orgasm took her.

Minutes later, the two of them lay side by side on the bed, totally spent. Lindsey closed her eyes, mumbling wordlessly. She was on another plane, one where nothing existed outside her, and Camilla, and this luxurious bed.

"Lindsey?" Camilla's voice cut through the stillness of the room.

"Mm?"

"I love you."

Something fluttered in Lindsey's chest. When she'd said those words to Camilla, she hadn't expected Camilla to say them back. Just knowing Camilla felt something for her was enough. But hearing her Mistress say those three little words made Lindsey happier than she could have ever imagined.

"I wanted to say it back to you the night of the engagement party, but I was scared."

"Why, Mistress?" Lindsey could tell that this was difficult for Camilla. Maybe it would be easier for her to talk about it as 'Lindsey's Mistress' rather than 'Camilla.'

Camilla shifted on the bed beside her. "Over the course of my life, I've become accustomed to being alone. The truth is, it's easier that way. It means that I don't ever have to worry about being a burden on anyone. I don't have to worry that those close to me will start to resent me for all my limitations."

"I would never consider you a burden," Lindsey said. "And it's obvious that you get along just fine by yourself."

"That's because I've learned to adapt every part of my life around my illness. My carefully regimented routine is a necessity, not a choice. I can't afford to stray from it, to be spontaneous and free. It's restrictive. What happens when it all becomes too much for you?"

"It won't." Lindsey reached for Camilla's hand. "Mistress, neither of us knows what the future holds. All I know is that I want to spend it with you, no matter what."

Camilla was silent. Lindsey turned to look at her. Her eyes were